A DANGEROUS PROPOSITION

A NOVEL

Donna Harris Harrison

iUniverse®

A DANGEROUS PROPOSITION
A NOVEL

iUniverse books may be ordered through booksellers or by contacting:

iUniverse
1663 Liberty Drive
Bloomington, IN 47403
www.iuniverse.com
1-800-Authors (1-800-288-4677)

ISBN: 978-1-5320-2472-6 (sc)
ISBN: 978-1-5320-2474-0 (hc)
ISBN: 978-1-5320-2473-3 (e)

Library of Congress Control Number: 2017910150

Print information available on the last page.

iUniverse rev. date: 07/10/2017

For my husband, Dan, and daughter, Valerie, with eternal love, appreciation for your support, and enormous gratitude for our life together

CHAPTER 1

She stopped directly in front of her office door, rolled her eyes, and sighed. And then she smiled. This routine of opening her office door each day had become a peculiar, actually entertaining, personal challenge. Perhaps because it was the only challenge of the day dictated by as simple, basic, and nonthreatening a thing as physical dexterity, she almost welcomed the familiar obstacle. For if Julianne Sloan could manage to wriggle the key, which she had painstakingly maneuvered from her purse and into her hand during the twenty-floor ride up the elevator, into the lock, turn down the handle with her elbow, throw open the door with her hip, and make it to her desk without dropping her bagel, briefcase, three morning newspapers, and extra large container of black coffee—if she could triumph over this simple challenge—then surely she was on her way to having a great day.

And she almost made it. Only two of the newspapers slid out from under her arm as she bolted for the desk, where she succeeded in setting down the coffee before it dribbled from beneath the plastic lid and down the side of the paper cup, onto her ivory linen blazer. No big deal. It was just the newspapers. Oh, the edit notes, now streaked with the golden signature of Starbucks Breakfast Blend. No matter. Given the two and half hours of her "personal time" that had been diverted by preparing the rough-cut notes last night, they would be promptly deposited on the editor's console before he strolled through the door at nine, stained or not. As long as the coffee and bagel were intact and the blazer made it through desk setup unblemished, the day still held a promise of greatness.

The jarring ring of the office phone at seven forty-five in the morning was an unmistakable clue that *frenzied* was soon to replace *great* as the descriptive word of the day. It instantly annoyed her. Seldom would anyone be so presumptuous as to think that the producers would be manning their phones before nine. If she wanted to work all those hours, she would have stayed in the news department. The glorious truth was that leaving news was one of the biggest favors Julianne had done for herself. That's what she told herself most days anyway. She did not miss the beepers, erratic schedules, or early-morning phone calls such as the one that was currently distracting her from savoring the aroma of her thick morning brew and marveling at the chewiness of the jumbo onion bagel from Moishe's Deli around the corner.

"Hello," she barked, refusing to offer a more professional greeting at so unprofessional an hour.

"Is this Tina?" The woman's hushed voice was raw and tentative on the other end of the line, as if the utterance of each syllable was a struggle. Julianne immediately softened her tone.

"Tina's not in yet. I work with her. Can I take a message?"

"If you work with her, then you probably know about the interview she was going to do with me this morning. But I won't be here when she arrives. Tell her he found me. He was waiting for me outside my bank when I went in to cash my paycheck yesterday, and he yanked me into the alley, smacked me, and snatched it right out of my hand. He kicked me hard … right in the gut. Just once, but hard. He'd never hurt me out in public before, and it really scared me. He'd been warning me that if I ever got it in my head to walk out on him, I'd pay, and I figured maybe this was it—maybe I wouldn't walk out of that alley. There was no one to help me. I rolled over and squeezed my eyes shut like I always do, and when I looked up, he was gone. I thought he just ran off 'cause maybe someone started coming by, but now I figure he was out there waiting for me to come out of the alley so he could follow me here. He was out by the corner waiting for me when I tried to go to work this morning, and he grabbed my hair and started pulling me toward the car. I thought he'd tear it right out of my head. And he kept whispering into my ear that I was a dumb little bitch ... that he'd finally teach me what I needed to know. He only left when two of the other girls came out the door to go to work too, and they yelled to the people inside to call the police. I just came back inside to get my stuff. I'm getting out of here. I don't know where to yet. I just have to get the hell away from here and from him. But I wanted to tell Tina. She's been real nice. Will you tell her for me?" Without waiting for a reply, she hung up.

Dumbfounded, Julianne stared at the phone. This was not a typical call for a typical *Chicago Sizzle* story. But then, Tina wasn't exactly a typical producer either, and she was obviously cooking up a piece she hadn't filled her boss in on yet. *Boss.* Julianne never really felt comfortable with that word or that role. But she had a damn good staff and knew that their unruliness was an offshoot of their passion. And that was okay with her. It was just that this woman's call came out of left field and her fragile voice was so unnerving. Not to mention the gist of the message. *Why the hell is Tina always so late?* Julianne thought in an undeniably agitated state as she was lifting the phone to dial her number.

Oh, wait. It wasn't even eight o'clock yet. That's right. Just because Julianne was a borderline workaholic didn't mean that everyone around her was. No point in calling Tina now. Julianne figured she must have left her apartment for the club where she worked out each morning before coming to the office. So she tossed the yellowed edit notes onto the console in the adjoining office suite to await the magical fingers of whichever editor had lucked out for the daytime shift in the edit bay. She then turned her attention back to the bagel and the headlines, though it was nearly impossible to concentrate on the printed pages sprawled before her. There was nothing to do but kill an hour until Tina arrived -- and no better way to do it than with good old-fashioned newspapers.

The adrenaline started pumping, just like in the old days at the assignment desk when hell broke loose upon word of a sniper shooting, a subway collision, or the dreaded word of an airline disaster out at O'Hare. Okay, so she did miss the adrenaline rush. But not enough to devote her life to it. Julianne had abandoned her career in news after three brief years and four swift promotions, all of which indicated that she was on an accelerated course to upper management. Despite the high visibility, hefty paychecks, and security of grasping onto a facet of the television industry that was a notch more steadfast than most, she turned down the job of assistant news director and made a lateral move from news to programming. She had reconciled herself to the fact that there were creative juices simmering inside of her, and those juices fed on conjuring up show ideas, composing feature stories, and designing series—a far cry from sitting behind a desk in a three-ring circus newsroom, determining whether the story of the berserk gunman or accused child molester should lead the six o'clock newscast.

The decision to turn her back on a professional path laden with sure signs of success was no simple feat. But the difficulty stemmed not from issues so obvious as stability, clout, or cold hard cash. Rather, it was Julianne's inner turmoil over whether her efforts should be targeted toward the more noble, socially redeeming arena of news—a public service of sorts—or whether she should actually indulge in making a living off the frivolous entertainment programming that her family and friends regarded as far less worthy of her talents but that she found alluring nonetheless.

The man she had, until several months ago, considered her boyfriend du jour, Terry Shapiro, could hardly have been considered supportive of her career choice either. Every so often, Terry still crept into her mind. He would have been so easy to wrangle into a permanent relationship, to ease down the altar, had that been her agenda. Terry was a high school principal and, as she learned by their second date, a world-class snob. He turned his nose up at her vocation and could hardly understand how Julianne could conceive of devoting her brainpower to the mindless wasteland of television, though he did find it in his heart to concede that TV news had some redeeming and socially significant qualities—not nearly as many as print journalism but far more than any other aspect of show business. Terry was always a short-timer, someone to keep her company during late dinners, occupy an adjacent seat at the movies, and provide the distractions of weekly romps in the sheets. He met the criteria just fine, though it soon became increasingly annoying to overlook his shortcomings, of which there were many.

For one thing, Terry had this knack for tapping into Julianne's feelings of inadequacy regarding her basic intellect. He was a lot like her father, a professor of political science at Northwestern, whose pastime was serving as personal tutor to his only child, whose grades fell far short of his expectations. Herb Sloan was perceived as brilliant within academic circles, and Mrs. Sloan was no slouch either, having returned to the University of Chicago to earn her PhD when Julianne started first grade. Given her parental brain trust, Julianne was stymied over how she got the short end of the stick in the smarts department. She wasn't stupid. Not by a long shot. But everything's relative, and in a family of triumphant overachievers, being ranked merely as above average is somewhat akin to being perceived as below par.

By her senior year in high school, when her application to Northwestern was denied, Herb resigned himself to the fact that his little girl was what she was and, in accordance with his wife's prodding, attempted to bury his disappointment and take pride in the depth and strength of his daughter's character. Even he was astute enough to see that Julianne's heart and spirit more than made up for her academic shortcomings. Unfortunately, he never did share this acknowledgment with Julianne, who unwittingly continued what had become a lifelong struggle to perform up to her parents' expectations.

As a child, adolescent, and now an adult, she was a pleaser, bound and determined to please those around her, be they her parents, friends, teachers, bosses, or lovers. She understood this about herself, and the insight, while not enough to dramatically alter her behavior, allowed her to cut herself some slack when life became borderline overwhelming, which was, quite frankly, more often than not.

Perhaps that's why, once in the business arena, where street smarts outranked book smarts by at least two to one, Julianne ascended the ladder faster than any of her peers. She was driven to succeed, to prove herself, to earn the praises of those to whom she reported. She got that from her dad. But what she got from her mom was the sense to know that success was meaningless without fulfillment, that happiness came not as the payoff to a completed achievement but from enjoyment of the process. All this created an internal conflict that was part of Julianne Sloan's very core. She derived fulfillment from breaking ratings records, from trimming the department's budget, from pirating away star personnel from competing stations. But as mundane as it seemed to her father and many of her friends—oftentimes even to herself—what she wanted to do with her life was create television shows … and have a family.

Logic told her that she should be capable of targeting the right man for herself. She'd dated enough accountants, physicians, stockbrokers and real estate agents to find one person with whom she could break her ten-month record for staying in a relationship. Yet boyfriend after boyfriend, she found herself in situations in which she felt dwarfed by the intellectual prowess of her partner. Finally, through painful and grudging self-analysis, she came to understand that she had actually been seeking out such men … still fighting to prove her worth, her value. And she realized that she was, indeed smart enough to break that pattern—or at least try to, starting with Terry. Maybe, she told herself, he would transition from temporary status to the real deal. Maybe. If she could just get past allowing his elitist attitudes to be a source of intolerable boredom.

The challenge of enduring Terry grew too great, the rewards too insignificant. So one blustery Chicago evening when a post-movie stroll down Michigan Avenue evolved into a psuedointellectual lecture on the merits of gender-segregated education, she instructed Mr. Terence Shapiro that it was time for her residence to become segregated, a goal easily achieved by his taking a permanent hike. The next day, fortified by a bacon cheeseburger and spurred on by two cappuccinos, she drafted a letter of resignation to the news director. She hadn't planned to do any of it. She'd simply had enough of it all. She hadn't a clue as to where her next paycheck would come from or how she would realize her goal of producing entertainment programming. But she knew this much for sure: Whenever it was a case of sink or swim, Julianne Sloan swam. Always. She was a survivor. She had done so by following her heart all her life and there was no reason to doubt herself now.

Following her two-week notice, she swung out the door of Chicago's WQAM TV and through the door of its chief competitor, just a mile away, where she initiated production of a Saturday-morning kids' magazine show. A year after that, she was wooed away by yet another station in town to create a public affairs magazine series. It was the perfect marriage of her news background and creative passion. Now, several years and awards later, the program *Chicago Sizzle* still suited her just fine.

The format was a media mosaic, and there was an art to coming up with just the right mix and order of material for each week's episode. Still, few stories in the production pipeline ignited her day the way that morning's anonymous phone call had. The voice haunted her, echoing in an otherwise still, undisturbed setting that was characteristic of any television station before nine in the morning.

This time of the morning was one of the best parts of the day for Julianne. Her staff never wandered in before nine o'clock, and the phones usually cooperated in giving her this quiet time to linger over the morning newspapers and online headlines, sip her coffee, and plan her strategy for the day. Hers was a job that required strategy. She was in her fourth year of producing *Chicago Sizzle*, and each day revealed a new set of corporate dilemmas, technical snafus, and—if she were lucky—creative decisions to be made.

The corporate matters were what bogged her down the most. It was a big old boys' club at the television station, and she always had to have her mind working at triple time when handling meetings, presentations, and even simple conversations. Managing upward in "macholand," as she referred to the management structure in which she existed as one of only two female executives, was a pain in the neck. But it was what it was, so she tried to master the corporate and political games and compensate for this downside to her job by making the most of the upside.

And the upside was undeniably wonderful. *Chicago Sizzle* was Julianne's personal key to the city. It was her exclusive passport inside the circles of people who made headlines and celebrated life to its fullest, from outrageous social splashes to elegant premieres to political extravaganzas. She had access to a lifestyle that she relished and with which she grew increasingly comfortable since launching the series. Only recently had she begun to grow a touch bored with it all. But since there was nothing or no one vying for her attention, such as a husband, child, or warm body to cling to under the covers at night, focusing on her professional goals didn't seem to be such a bad idea for the time being.

"Jule? Julianne? You in there?" A soft warm voice came wandering down the hallway to her. It was Jake, her cameraman and probably the only person in the world who could get away with stealing some of her precious hour of pre-work time.

"Hey, Jake, if you're heading for this office, you better have a Starbucks Venti for me," she called back. He stepped through the doorway, armed with the steamy treat in one hand and a vase of semi-withered long-stemmed white roses in the other.

"Hi, sweetheart," he said. "These came for you around five last night, but I guess you left early, so I held them for you. White roses. No big mystery who sent 'em, I guess."

She gazed first at the collection of wilted flowers and then shifted her attention to Jake, happy to see one but not the other. Julianne was crazy about Jake Rossi. All she had to do was think about him, and a smile came to her face. Any time she was near him, she found herself wanting to touch him. She'd pinch his cheek, tug on his chin, tap on his arm, all gestures that seemed quite natural for a touch-oriented person, as she called herself. Only it was different with Jake. She just plain loved being near him. And she knew that he was crazy about her too, in a platonic way. Through their years of working together, he'd never given her a tumble. Not once. Not even after the Cinco de Mayo celebration they shot for the show. They had punctuated the location shoot by polishing off a couple of supersize margaritas at the restaurant on Rush Street where they'd been taping and Julianne used the circumstance to turn on the charm, feigning drunkenness as an excuse to assess whether or not Jake could be swayed by temptation. No dice. It became clear that Jake just wasn't going to play the game.

It was, she lectured herself, probably because she outranked him both in title and salary. Or maybe because she wrapped herself in silk blouses and crepe skirts each morning, while he donned denims and flannel. Or perhaps it was because he was married. Oh yeah. That could be it. Jake was married to Little Miss Perfect, as the staff referred to her when Jake was not around. They could not stand Helene Rossi. Spoiled, arrogant, and self-centered was how they described her on a more merciful day. She dined, shopped, and spent Jake's salary all day, then whined about being married to a man who kept awful work hours all night.

Jake shared his relationship stories with the people he was closest with at work, including Julianne. He did so not to complain but rather to solicit a woman's point of view that would help him better understand his wife of five years. They had no kids. Helene said that at twenty-eight, she just wasn't ready. At thirty-five, Jake knew that he was, but still he wasn't all that sure that his marriage was on solid ground, so he let the issue of having kids pass for the time being. Watching him now, with his long, lanky build filling the doorway as he balanced the large vase, Julianne felt a pang of envy for Her Highness, Helene.

Of course, if Jake had ever nipped at Julianne's bait, given her the slightest indication that he felt anything for her other than brotherly affection, she wasn't at all sure what she would do. Run the other way was the most likely choice. Never, never had Julianne even entertained the notion of becoming involved with a married man—except for the Jake daydreams—much less had an affair with one. And in her line of work, she knew that was an oddity.

Hers was a business of schmoozers and shysters, slick men and sharp women who savored the power and grandeur of the media and became intoxicated by the razzle-dazzle world in which they spent the better part of their waking hours. They celebrated their self-perceived greatness by denying themselves nothing, including the passion of forbidden fruit: someone else's husband or wife. That was how the folks in her line of work regarded the sanctity of marriage—men and women, executives and assistants, on-air talent, and behind-the-scenes flunkies. But not Julianne.

She clung to her parochial upbringing by choice, having watched from the sidelines as friends and acquaintances struggled to mend their broken hearts and massage their bruised egos affair after dead-end affair. She wanted marriage someday. That was the long-term plan. The odds of inching toward the goal line by rubbing up to another woman's man did not hold promise. Not that sex wasn't big on her hit parade. Far from it. Sex was the one thing she loved even more than coffee. And it was during the frequent lapses between boyfriends and dry spells when even her closest friends couldn't come up with one man to set her up with that Julianne reflected upon just how much she relished sex and how incredible she imagined it would be with Jake Rossi.

As for the roses, Julianne was not at all happy to see them. Allen must have sent them to pave the way for what was sure to be a plea for empathy and cooperation in sweeping away emotional debris from the fight they had last week. White roses were Allen's trademark. What he didn't know was that ever since he began using them to ease her pain in the aftermath of their escalating arguments, she cringed at the sight of those pure white petals. Allen wasn't a world-class bore like Terry, his predecessor. He was a far greater mistake.

"You know," she nonchalantly quipped, "There's a lot to be said for classic red roses. Actually, pink and yellow aren't so bad either." She took the vase from Jake and walked out to place them out of the way on a file cabinet, where they would be well hidden from everyone except her assistant, Lianne, who would surely enjoy the fragrance if not the deteriorating beauty. "However, white is strictly taboo around here." She stepped back into her office, brushing alongside Jake's arm as she made her way to the desk.

"Is Allen still taboo around here?" he quietly asked.

"Allen, my friend, is history. He hits. And hitting is the surest way I know to book a one-way ticket out of my life." The moment she uttered the word *hit*, that elusive phone call and stranger's quivering voice resonated through her mind once again.

"I wish it wouldn't have taken you five days to tell somebody that he hit you. I'd have kicked his ass right into the Chicago River," Jake added, anger inflaming his voice.

"I kicked him out onto the Chicago sidewalk. And that's what really matters, right?" she said, appreciative of his protective spirit and obvious affection but intent on demonstrating that she was fully prepared to take care of herself. Regretting that talk of Allen Miller was tainting what was an otherwise bright and sunny morning, she diverted the conversation with a teasing inquiry. "Is that my coffee refill you're holding?"

"No such luck. This is all mine. Besides, you don't have time for a refill. That's the other thing I came up here to tell you. Tina called in sick with the flu. Remember how lousy she looked yesterday? Anyway, she called my extension because she knew I was assigned to the early-morning news cut-ins and she didn't expect you to be in the office yet. She asked if you could either cover her story for her today or cancel the shoot. The file is on her desk."

Yes, this might be a great day shaping up, Julianne thought. Of course she was sorry that Tina, one of her three segment producers, was battling the flu. But with Sam, one of the other producers, on vacation and Louise scheduled for a twelve-hour editing session, the only one left to go out with the crew and cover the story was Julianne herself—and she was chomping at the bit.

"This is a conspiracy between all of you to see how rusty the old lady is, huh?" she laughed. Julianne often joked that this job often made her feel like the mom of her staff and much older than someone who had celebrated her thirtieth birthday only a month ago. "I'll be down at the minicam dock in ten minutes. I just have to leave a note for Lianne. Oh, and I guess it wouldn't be a bad idea to read Tina's file. This is the story I assigned her on the opening of that new women's shelter, I think, and one of the women lined up for an interview already called a while ago to cancel. Hey, if I cover the background story today, maybe I can con Tina into letting me cover the black tie fundraiser on Saturday. Five days isn't really enough time for her to get over the flu, is it?"

"Cute, Jule. Cute," Jake muttered as he headed down the hallway. "Ten minutes. That's ten minutes Jake time, not Julianne time," he teased. Jake was always ribbing Julianne about being late for everything. It seemed to be the only thing about Julianne that got on his nerves.

Julianne headed for her office closet, where, like most producers accustomed to the unpredictability of their profession, she kept an emergency overnight case with extra clothing. She fished out her khakis and a sweater, her old cowboy boots, and a bomber jacket. After a swift wardrobe change, she scribbled a note to Lianne and rushed into Tina's office, where she grabbed the folder marked "Horizons" and headed out the door. She met up with Jake with two minutes to spare. He smiled appreciatively.

Stuffed into the folder was a messy stack of scribbled notes providing basic information for the story.

Horizons was a safe house nestled into quiet neighborhood of Rogers Park, just north of Loyola University and south of the Evanston border. A haven that could shelter a handful of desperate women and their children, it was newly opened following funding from a mix of private and corporate contributors. It had taken six years for the team of four socialite girlfriends who sat on the board of the North Shore Cultural Center to get Horizons off the ground after having been inspired by a documentary shown at their center's annual fundraiser. Within their social circle, they were referred to as the Founding Foursome, and a tenacious group of women they were. At the project's infancy, they relied upon favors from their elite friends and their husbands' business contacts to gain access to corporate chieftains with bank accounts hefty enough to fund the cause and outlooks modern enough for them to recognize that helping abused women was not equivalent to betraying the entire male gender.

The Founding Foursome had worked long and hard for this cause and their prayers for a major financial backer were answered when they finally hooked up with the chairman of Family Pharmaceuticals, a national retail chain based in Glenview, a suburb just north of Chicago. The chairman, Walt Mitchell, played golf with the husband of one of the women working on the shelter team. She cornered Walt at a Fourth of July picnic, convinced him that backing this project would be a great way to use social networking to his advantage by harnessing the support of women influencers, adding that with his business savvy and financial connections, he could be a savior to families needing help ... as well as pharmaceuticals.

Walt came through with flying colors, even taking an active role in appointing the house manager for what would be named Horizons, as well as soliciting the voluntary services of his buddies who could lend their professional affiliations to the cause. Jerry Emberg, one of his Thursday night poker buddies, ran a commercial cleaning service and offered to provide housekeeping maintenance at 40 percent the going rate. The last thing Walt Mitchell could bear was the thought of seeing his spanking new safe house turned into a shambles by a lot of women and kids. Despite his good intentions and thorough support of this project, Walt still came from the old school that believed the kinds of folks who would find themselves in such sorry circumstances most likely came from low-class backgrounds, which, to him, translated to sloppy surroundings and poor hygiene habits.

He was thrilled to take Jerry up on his generous offer. He also showed no hesitation at hitting up Ed Haskum, whose estate stood on the lot adjacent to Walt's own, in the sedate and posh suburb of Kenilworth. Ed operated one of Chicago's largest industrial laundry operations, and even though Horizons would, under normal business circumstances, be far too small a client to bother with, he proceeded to take on the task of providing clean linen and toweling for the residents at a mere fraction of what his other clientele, mostly restaurants and commercial Realtors, would be charged.

Shelby Hacker, the daughter of Walt's CFO, had been looking for a career change, and her background as a schoolteacher matched with a college minor in sociology made her an excellent choice to fill one of the few paid positions at the safe house, that of house manager. Shelby was single, had no children, and agreed to reside on-site for the first year to keep a watchful eye on the shelter during its infancy, moving into a makeshift apartment that had been converted from the servants' quarters of the once-stately family residence. She took on the responsibility of training a small staff who would assist her as well as man the fort during her off hours. Part of the challenge in opening the facility was ensuring that its doors would be open and hotline answered around the clock. Wife beating was not a nine-to-five crisis.

Between minimum wage workers and a team of volunteers, Shelby managed to construct a commendable staffing plan. The Founding Foursome was glad to be relieved of the burden of filling the posts. They had so much on their collective agenda that Walt's assistance in procuring a house manager and Shelby's eagerness to create systems and protocol were welcome blessings. Once Horizons became operational, they predicted that they would see their responsibilities happily dwindle to serving on the board of directors alongside the shelter's major benefactors. Their primary goal would be to continually procure funding from private and corporate sources and ultimately acquire state grants to ease the financial strain. And then they could move on, turning their attention to yet another crusade in a city that had more than its fair share of problems.

With Shelby in place as house manager, the Founding Foursome zeroed in on securing a business administrator to take ultimate responsibility for the shelter, handling disbursements for utility payments and salaries for the meagerly paid staff while also keeping track of what would hopefully be a healthy flow of private and corporate contributions. Once again, guardian angel Walt Mitchell was there to lend support. The role seemed custom designed for Clint Andrews, the younger brother of Walt's wife, Arlene, and a CPA who had gone into semiretirement at the ripe old age of thirty-eight after he and Arlene split a $6.5 million estate inherited from their father. Their mother had passed away when they were teenagers, and good old Dad had stashed away a lot of cash courtesy of a career that established him as one of Chicago's most prominent personal injury attorneys. Arlene, who, like her friends, left all matters pertaining to money to the man of the family, had turned her half of the bounty over to her accomplished husband, Walt, who proceeded to invest it in Family Pharmaceuticals on her behalf.

Clint embraced the notion of stepping away from what had clearly become a mundane professional existence. With no marriage or children to anchor him and, at last, no financial stress, he became intensely committed to a devil-may-care lifestyle, which was the fulfillment of his fantasy. First came the white Porsche Carrera for weekends—he'd look for a more practical weekday car, BMW or Volvo, later—then the Lake Shore Drive three-bedroom condo on the thirtieth floor, with an eastern view overlooking Lake Michigan, and then a fine selection of designer suits and sport coats to fill an assortment of sprawling walk-in closets.

Though Clint's level of interaction with his sister and brother-in-law was minimal at best, his newly adopted way of life became an annoyance of mounting proportion to Walt. After lecturing Clint for two months on the merits of contributing something valuable to society, his sanctimonious sermons appeared to penetrate and Clint Andrews agreed to serve as administrative director of Horizons. The title was impressive, he conceded to Walt, something that women might find attractive. His years as a CPA had done little to establish him as a stud, and a stud was something he had desperately aspired to be. Having been a chubby academic nerd in high school and college, he finally gave up food in favor of cigarettes at age twenty two, shedding sixty-five repulsive pounds during a frustrating two-year battle of the bulge. He was on his quest to attain stud status!

Walt and Arlene suspected that beyond the title, the appeal of Horizons for Clint was that it provided a platform for demonstrating that he was not only a compassionate man but also a supporter of the feminist movement. What a way to woo prospective dates. Besides, he'd be able to go and come as he pleased. With no set hours, he could show up evenings, weekends, and whenever a gap in his social schedule presented itself so that he could tend to the mundane tasks of cutting checks and keeping the books.

As luck would have it for Clint, Shelby Hacker's appointment as house manager was frosting on the cake. Her petite and buxom build was enhanced by a personality as mild-mannered and accommodating as one would expect from a former second grade schoolteacher at an affluent private school on Chicago's North Shore. In addition to it being a breeze to take the commanding position in their working relationship, Clint realized he would also face little difficulty in getting Shelby into the sack. And with a facility of bedrooms at his disposal, the erotic fantasy of having sex in each and every bed and shower stall at Horizons was one he couldn't dismiss.

So Clint Andrews came on board as the shelter's administrative director and created for himself a private office area in the back of the housing structure, while Shelby Hacker occupied the front office and took responsibility for the day-to-day operation of Horizons. They were separated enough to stay out of each other's hair to conduct their respective duties, yet close enough to provide each other with some levity in an environment that was inherently heavyhearted.

In the four months that they had been working side by side, she establishing policies and procedures for the safe house and he managing its funds, their relationship had become clearly defined, just as he had predicted. She grew to lean on him as a strong and trustworthy man in a climate that was predominantly female, and he succeeded in bedding her in a mere eight weeks, though not at the shelter, as he had dreamed. She confessed that she thought it would be a tad too unprofessional to test-launch the bedrooms personally, and rather than push the issue, he escorted her up to his thirtieth-floor oasis, where she could partake in enjoying the fabulous view and succulent sex for hours.

As Clint had predicted, neither Shelby Hacker nor the workload proved to be a problem at all. In fact, he made a mental note to thank his socially conscious brother-in-law for coaxing him into the arrangement. And things became even more stimulating for Clint when the doors to Horizons were at last flung open this past weekend and a flurry of tormented wives, distressed mothers, and victimized girlfriends swarmed across its threshold.

Clint was vaguely aware of the show *Chicago Sizzle* from the ads plastered on the sides of the buses that jammed the Magnificent Mile during his strolls to and from work. Though he had never seen the show, he found it hard to imagine that the opening of Horizons would warrant coverage—hardly "sizzling." However, Arlene explained that the corporation that owned the television station where the show originated had made substantial contributions to the cause, seeing it as a good public service promotional vehicle. Plus, there was an elegant gala scheduled for this Saturday to solicit a final flurry of funds for the shelter's launch, and this flashy event, guaranteed to be attended by the cream of Chicago's society crop, was just the kind of thing *Chicago Sizzle* thrived upon. The worthiness of the cause was packaged in the glamour of the event. It was win–win all around and fine with Clint.

When Julianne assigned the Horizons story to Tina, she asked that it be built around the fundraiser as a glittery, gossipy night-on-the-town segment. She also stressed the need to mix in a profile on the shelter itself, along with some compelling human interest stories to grab the heartstrings and throw light on this cause. Her motives were, of course, split between good corporate politics and a genuine interest in helping the project get on its feet, though the political motives were definitely tipping the scale. Julianne knew how to play the game. She didn't always choose to play, but she definitely knew how.

There hadn't been what one would call an abundance of female role models for Julianne as she embarked upon her ascent up the corporate ladder. Out in the workforce, her personality had evolved, unconsciously for the most part, as she emulated the business styles of her male cohorts. She grew increasingly gruff, inflexible, and direct, adept at taking control of a situation and doing what had to be done without hesitation. The personality shift came so easily to her that she barely noticed that her new business demeanor was permeating her personal life as well. The result was a conflict between the sensitive, mushy, blushing heap of emotion outside of work and the cool no-bullshit businesswoman who pushed her sentiments down and her forcefulness up during the day.

Julianne found it was no easy task to manange her double-edged personality. Things became truly complicated when romance entered her private life. After holding the reins at the office all day long, it was difficult to relinquish or even share them at day's end. There was no time to transition from boss to relationship partner. What the men described as aggressive—a word with decidedly negative overtones—she perceived as assertive, a positive trait.

She'd see a cab and flag it down. She'd spot two seats in a crowded movie theater and dash for them. "How many for dinner?" a maître d' would inquire. "Two," she'd reply in a flash, never for a second thinking to acquiesce to her companion for his reply. To her girlfriends, she had merely become moderately pushy, not so overbearing as to be problematic. Men, on the other hand, were intensely put off by her independence and self-assured presence, usually opting to give her boot in favor of some more traditionally feminine partner before Julianne could put her finger on what exactly had gone wrong with the budding romance.

The rules of the personal and professional playing fields were dramatically at odds with one another. Now that her twenties had come and gone and the fourth finger of her left hand remained naked as the day she was born, Julianne was coming to grips with the fact that it might not hurt to master the dating game just as she had the producing game. The latter was quite under control by now. The former was far from it. Plenty of female peers were in the same boat—driven first and foremost by their work. Judging from the volume and content of the manila folder she was weeding her way through en route to Horizons, Tina was among them.

"Wow," Julianne said to Jake, now taking his place behind the wheel. "Tina is really into this stuff. I think I've been sending her to cover too many fashion segments and celebrity interviews. Give her one story with some meat on it and she devours it down to the bone. I'd better sort through these notes so I can bring back some strong interviews or I'll never hear the end of it. So no radio. And don't talk to me. Until later. Okay?"

"Just read, sweetheart," he said out of the side of his mouth, never taking his eyes off the road. She loved it when Jake called her "sweetheart." The first time followed her telling a story to staffers at lunch one day soon after he started working with her. She was talking about how she told off a cab driver who sent her off with a "Thanks a lot, sweetheart" when she skimped on the tip. She proceeded to talk ad nauseam about how she hated the way men call women "sweetheart" and "honey" and "dear" when they hardly know them. It was pure sexism, she ranted and raved, and everyone at the table agreed. A couple of days later, when Julianne stepped down from the stage at a local awards ceremony after receiving the Best TV Magazine award for *Chicago Sizzle*, Jake greeted her back at the table with a big bear hug and intentional "Way to go, sweetheart." She assumed he was testing for dispensation, which was promptly received. Since then, he used the term of endearment every chance he had.

"My God, these stories are pathetic," Julianne commented, partly to herself and partly to Jake. "I can't believe these women let this happen to themselves. How could you let a man hit you like this?"

"Oh, come on, Jule. I know we'd like to think we're on a different planet from the people we meet doing these stories. But let's get real. You let a guy hit you too."

"I didn't let Allen hit me. It just happened. I guess it can happen to anyone once. And then I threw him out."

She shifted self-consciously in her seat. She was only now beginning to come to terms with the fact that indeed she had succumbed to a pattern of abuse that had only recently been halted. It was an experience so monstrous, so humiliating to her, that she'd kept her feelings tucked away, numbing herself to the realities of that one disastrous relationship rather than owning up to it.

She was consistently the first one to gently urge her girlfriends to see a therapist at the first sign of depression, stress overload or decaying self-esteem. But for herself, Julianne Sloan, power producer, successful career woman, loving daughter, compassionate friend, exquisite lover—in other words, role model woman—the notion of turning to therapy was traumatic. She couldn't admit to herself, much less anyone else, even a trained professional, that a woman as stable as she believed herself to be could possibly let a man whittle his way into her inner core and eat away at her strength and sense of self. The very idea seemed absurd. But it had happened.

"Julianne, this is me you're talking to. Forget being so cavalier about it all. And forget trying to make me believe that prick just hit you once." Dead silence. She buried her face in the file, pretending to read, stunned to learn that what she thought was such a closely guarded secret was no secret at all. The incident she'd finally opened up about—the hit—was the lone reference to violence she had ever made to her friends at work. It wasn't the first incident, true, only the first she'd come clean about. So she never assumed anyone suspected that she was in an abusive relationship. That specific occurrence wasn't even the worst of it. Actually, it was mild by comparison. Only it had pushed her over the edge … nearly.

It happened on a Monday night about a month earlier. She and Allen had been having a heated argument about her refusal to take a week off and accompany him to a business conference in New Orleans. She wanted to join him to try on the role of wife, if truth be told. Allen was charming and confident, respected her career and even liked her parents. She suspected that she was in love with him, though the concept was admittedly foreign to her.

Julianne explained that she had promised station management she would avoid taking time off while her boss, the program director, was on maternity leave. But Allen stormed about the kitchen while they were cleaning up after dinner, ranting that he was tired of letting her job rule their lives. They both grew intensely frustrated and when she told him that she was having second thoughts about going to a movie with him, much less New Orleans, he spun around and cracked her right in the face. When he did, a rough prong on the onyx ring he wore on his right pinky finger cut into her cheek, narrowly missing the outside corner of her eye. He grabbed his coat and bolted out the door to cool off over a beer, while she applied a cold compress to her cheek.

A bright scarlet mark about half an inch long was an ugly reminder of the incident that she had to endure for the next week, telling those at work that she'd scratched herself on a sharp corner of the kitchen cabinet. She attributed Allen's abhorrent physical rage to an isolated temper tantrum fueled by pressure at his job. It was a fluke, an accident. He claimed to be sick over what he'd done and begged her to let him make it up to her. It had been stupid for her to antagonize him about the movie, she rationalized, furious with him but equally upset with herself for not keeping a better lid on the situation. He was an exceptionally bright man, a Harvard graduate, and after growing up with the temperamental outbursts of a brilliant father, Julianne had trained herself to accept such behavior as the typical accompaniment to an extraordinary mind.

After making him swear that he'd never lay a finger on her again, she forgave Allen. When his temper started to erupt one night last week and he made a menacing move toward her, that quivering sick feeling of fear that she had begun experiencing all too often paralyzed her. Then, the shove. Her head hit the wall with such force that she checked for blood. But it was her cheek, not the back of her head, that was bloodied by a rough corner of the mantel. She lunged toward the front door, throwing it open and grabbing the jacket and gym bag he'd left by the entranceway when he came home from the club. She hurled his things into the corridor, and when he stormed out to retrieve them, likely thinking Julianne was just being dramatic, she locked the door behind him and never opened it to him again. That night, it dawned on her that she loved herself even more than she loved Allen. She certainly loved the woman she used to be, the one who managed to flourish deep inside despite a judgmental father, pompous string of suitors, and finally one abusive asshole. It was *that* Julianne who triumphed that night and who would not allow herself to reverse her decision, no matter how miserable she was for days afterword.

Following the fight, Allen left a collection of messages on the answering machine at home and with Lianne, who knew what was going on and was under instructions to keep his calls from going through. Julianne boxed up Allen's belongings from the apartment they shared and sent them off to his brother's house, not even knowing or caring if he was staying there or elsewhere. She changed the locks on the door. She was finished with Allen Miller.

"You knew he hit me before?" she asked Jake, never looking up.

"A few of us got the picture, Jule. When you fed us that story about being clumsy and hurting yourself while you were cooking, we saw right through it. You, sweetheart, are far from clumsy. Besides, Julianne Sloan cooking? Herself? No way. Not when there's Chinese takeout right around the corner."

Julianne looked at him, thankful that he'd found a way to add a little levity to a bleak conversation. She allowed herself a moment to settle her nerves, gazing out the windows to marvel at the newly updated two-story brick apartment buildings that lined the streets of one of her favorite Chicago neighborhoods, Rogers Park. She had been raised in this area, but her parents fled to Chicago's Gold Coast when the neighborhood began to lose its luster and crumble as quickly as the family-owned businesses dotting Sheridan Road.

Now, twenty years later, a squadron of enterprising yuppies was committed to revitalizing the neighborhood, armed with MBAs from the University of Chicago and Northwestern and bolstered by a network of Facebook friends and Instagram followers with deep pockets. Julianne could see that they were doing one hell of a job. If the debacle of this once-glorious neighborhood could be reversed—its beauty and strength restored—could not the same be true for people? What did brick, plaster, and stone have over the likes of Julianne, Sheri, Emily, Helen, Jodie, and the slew of others whose stories were stuffed into the folder resting on her lap?

She zapped Jake with a dash of her signature sarcasm. "Since you knew the kind of bastard I was living with, the least you could have done was broken three of his fingers and two of his ugly little toes for me."

"Don't think I wasn't tempted. But I didn't know who I'd infuriate more, him or you, if you found out I butted in." He stopped at a red light and turned to look her straight in the eye. "Besides, Julianne, you're not the type to need some guy to come to your rescue. We both know that damsel in distress stuff is just garbage. You've got what it takes to look after yourself, and we both know it. That's why it really pissed me off when you kept going out with the guy, much less tossed out the welcome mat at home. Even Helene couldn't stand him, and she only met him that one time at Sam's party."

"Oh, great. Now I have Helene's opinions to worry about."

He looked back at the road. "You don't have to worry about Helene or her opinions. In fact, I'm sorry I brought her up. I know she's not on the Julianne Sloan most-popular-people list."

"Don't even get me started on the topic of Helene, buddy," she said out of the corner of her mouth. "Let's just get ready for this shoot. To tell you the truth, I'm afraid that I just might be a little rusty."

They were only a couple of miles from the safe house when Lianne's number popped up on Julianne's cell phone

"We just got a call. The admin guy at the shelter was delayed this morning. He asked if you could push back the shoot a couple of hours. You're thrilled, I'm sure," she added, knowing that Julianne despised last-minute changes in her meticulously planned production schedule—a schedule which, though only contrived an hour or so earlier, had already become etched in her producer's mind.

"It's ridiculous to head back to the station now," Julianne responded. "Maybe I can get my driver to spring for breakfast." It would be good to have a little schmooze time with Jake away from the office. They never had the chance to spend much time together outside of editing suites and control rooms. Only she hoped he'd leave talk of Allen Miller and her lousy judgment with men behind.

Always one to indulge her healthy appetite and leave talk of calories and carbs to women like Helene, Julianne plopped down at the table of the first coffee shop they spotted and ordered herself an oven-baked apple pancake, heavy on the cinnamon. It would take a good thirty minutes to bake, and that would leave them lots of time to talk. Besides, she was now hungry after losing her appetite at the sight of those limp white roses.

With a day of shooting before her and one of her favorite people in the world beside her, she could sit back and enjoy the moment. She started by preparing Jake for the day's schedule, starting with a joint interview with the administrative director, Clint Andrews, and house manager, Shelby Hacker. This would be followed by an interview with the four women who got the project rolling, then lots of shots of the interiors of the shelter itself. Tina also wanted comments from a few of the women staying at the shelter, but she knew she'd have to get most of them on the fly, catching the moment when they had the strength and were in the mood to talk. The one person who had agreed in advance to be interviewed was this morning's caller, now vanished. Julianne advised Jake to bring in the gear used for a silhouette-style shoot, since she felt certain that even if she could convince some of the residents to speak on camera, they would not want to be identified.

The breakfast break proved satisfying in terms of both food and conversation, and about an hour and a half later, they took off for their initial destination. As they pulled up in front of Horizons, Julianne reached up and took off her pearl earrings and choker, wrapping them carefully in tissue and sliding them into the zipper pocket of her purse. She hadn't worked as field producer for a while now, but she still remembered that you don't walk into a situation like this flaunting expensive jewelry. This producers' ritual always served to remind her of just how lucky she was, with her bureau drawer stuffed with nice pieces of silver and gold and an assortment of gemstones. She took a final glance at the file to make sure she had everyone's names memorized and then met up with Jake who was unloading his gear from the van. Together they headed inside.

CHAPTER 2

Elisa Adams made her way down the hallway with a watchful eye. She had a call to make that was not intended to be shared with her roommate daughter. Nor would she be able to explain any street noise were the call to be placed outdoors. She had observed that just before noon was the best time to get a little privacy in the downstairs reading room. Known to be extraordinarily patient by nature, it wasn't the actual search for an empty nook that hit a nerve with Elisa. It was the reminder that even now, at thirty-three years of age, she still had not even reached a point where she had room to breathe. It seemed like such a basic thing. What had gone so wrong with her life that she was gleeful just to locate an empty alcove? Oh, if only her girlfriends could see her now. The BFFs to whom she had bared her innermost soul. Before. Until her secrets grew so dark and churned so deep that she could share them with no one.

Her friends thought she had grown aloof, preferring the company of moms she'd met through Kelly's school. If only she had let her guard down and opened up, maybe they wouldn't have judged her the way she assumed they would. Maybe they wouldn't have thought she was a fool. Maybe they would have fired her up, taken her by the hand, and escorted her to a good attorney. And maybe the fact that she was starting to think this way was a sign that she was regaining her strength and would, in time, reclaim her friends and rebuild her life. As it was, she would accept her blessings as they came, and right now she was just thankful that she could place a call to her mother with nobody nearby to overhear.

"Hi, Mom. The phone rang so many times I was afraid you weren't home," Elisa said, grateful that she could put this daily ritual behind her.

"*My* phone rang so many times? You should try reaching *you*. I must have called your apartment ten times so far this morning. What could you and Kelly be up to?" she asked in that disapproving tone that grated on Elisa's nerves.

"Kelly's fine. She's a big girl now and likes to run around on errands with her mom. Just like me. Remember?" Elisa hadn't even offered a hint that she wasn't staying at her own home.

Her mother relaxed and laughed. "Do I ever. I could barely keep up with you by the time you were ten. Ten ... like Kelly. I guess you're right—like mother like daughter."

As her mother chatted on, Elisa found herself thinking how unlike her own mother she was. Her mother was always the strong one at home. Everyone liked it that way. Her dad knew that his wife had a good head on her shoulders for managing the family budget and schedule. It freed his head up to concentrate on the papers he was always grading at night. Elisa's parents had an easy, comfortable rhythm to their marriage. Theirs would be lifelong union, one based upon love and trust. They raised their only daughter, Elisa Jane, to respect the institution of marriage and the strength of family. Elisa wished she were more like her mother. As it turned out, she took after her dad: passive, quiet, anxious to please rather than be pleased. She hoped that her own daughter would be nothing like her father, Elisa's husband, Peter. For that matter, she didn't want Kelly to take after her either. Poor Kelly really struck out when it came to getting parents. This thought brought Elisa back to the present and the conversation at hand.

After some generic chitchat, she guided their talk to a close. "Okay, Mom. I'll talk to you tomorrow. I'll be running around a lot again, so don't bother calling me. I'll call you when I get in from shopping. Love you. Bye." Elisa hung up the phone and smiled. She cherished the closeness she shared with her mother, in spite of that aggravating judgmental tone. It was the guilt of lying to her that made these daily conversations so painful. Would it have been so terrible to come clean to her parents? So her husband wasn't the prince she'd painted him to be. So her marriage was a sham. Was she really so terrible a person that they would admonish her? Certainly not. They adored her. It was that adoration that was so crippling.

Maybe it was like that for all only children, she pondered. Parents invest so much of their expectations, dreams, and pride in that lone child that it becomes an emotional burden the child is left to tote all through life. Her failures would be seen as their own, and with no other child to validate their worthiness through triumphant endeavors, they would be deflated and disappointed, in themselves more than in their daughter. All because Elisa couldn't hone in on the proper way to please Peter Tate. She craved her parents' affection and approval, and though she knew that ultimately she would have to share the dirty details of her marriage and flight from it, that reality was purposefully pushed aside until she arrived at a stronger, healthier mental state.

Realizing how close it was to noon, Elisa darted up the stairs to make sure her daughter was ready for lunch. Kelly wasn't having much of a summer this year. But thankfully she loved reading and Elisa knew that helped keep Kelly's mind off of how hard the past several days had been. She escorted her daughter from their room to the dining area promptly at noon each day, just as the kitchen opened up for lunch. That way, Kelly's food wouldn't have a picked-over look and the two of them could nestle into a comfortable corner to eat, away from the racket of the other kids at the shelter.

She knocked at the door across the hall from the small room she and Kelly shared. "Ready?" Marsha asked, opening the door and exiting her own tiny room in one quick motion.

"I just want to get Kelly," Elisa answered, thinking how lucky she was to have made a few friends in this foreign place. "We'll meet you down there in a minute."

"Mommy, can't I just stay up here and finish this chapter? I'm not even hungry," Kelly said as her mom entered.

"Come on, honey. You'll be hungry later and I won't have anything for you. Besides, you don't want me to have to eat without you, do you?" Elisa smiled. She tickled Kelly under her arms, the way she had since Kelly was an infant, and the two of them ambled down the stairs together. It had only been five days since they arrived at Horizons on a rainy Friday afternoon, and Elisa was trying to introduce some sort of routine into their lives so that Kelly would feel as grounded as possible. At least she was safe.

The Friday Elisa and Kelly walked through this shelter door was one of the most crucial days of Elisa's life. It marked the point at which she had harnessed her last inkling of courage and made a desperate attempt to save her daughter and save herself from a life of certain torment with Peter. Peter and Elisa had been married just short of twelve years, and for eleven years and eleven months of that time, Peter had taken out his frustrations, disappointments and temper tantrums on his wife. Right after their honeymoon, when their first monthly bills started pouring in, Peter began manhandling her during endless arguments over money and what he called Elisa's "inept" style of managing a household. In the early stage of their courtship, she'd gotten wind of the fact that Peter had an explosive temper, which he struggled to contain in front of her. It sneaked out whenever he recounted stories of confrontations with his employers or when he became irritated with the lousy driving habits of others on the roads. But he never targeted his anger at her or showed any signs of losing control of his temper during their fourteen months together before marriage. Just afterward—once she was his, attached by a ring and a certificate and an upbringing that sanctioned standing by your husband for better or for worse. And things definitely got worse. Quickly.

Elisa worked on improving her system of shopping and balancing the checkbook, even quizzing her girlfriends on how they managed to keep so well organized and maintain peace on the home front. As it turned out, Elisa realized later, she was probably the best organized of the bunch; that was why the others never took her comments too seriously, attributing her anxieties to those of an overzealous newlywed.

"Just tell Peter he'll have to get himself a promotion to keep you in the style to which you'd like to become accustomed," her best friend, Deena, would laugh. It became clear to Elisa that her friends had different kinds of relationships with their husbands than she had with Peter. At the same time, it seemed to her that these women must also be better wives. And though she studied their conversations for clues to their happiness, she never seemed to match their talent for keeping their husbands pleased. She grew increasingly annoyed with herself, especially after Kelly was born and she felt pulled in more directions than ever.

Peter was crazy about his little girl, but not about the fact that Elisa spent so much time catering to Kelly's needs over his own. "My mother handled four kids with less fuss and complaining than you with one baby," he'd shout day after day after day. Their money became as tight as her time when the restaurant Peter managed suddenly took a dip in profits thanks to increased competition and decreased Zagat ratings. He was forced to choose between taking a pay cut or losing his job altogether. The decision to take the pay cut was a tremendous blow to his ego and responsibility for that choice, made for the sake of his wife and baby, was placed squarely on Elisa's shoulders, lasting several years, until a new owner took over the restaurant and gave Peter a raise in pay in exchange for an expanded workday.

Elisa was secretly relieved that Peter was forced to spend less time at home and she worked extra hard to make sure that by the time he arrived at their apartment each evening, the place was straightened up from Kelly's playing and that Kelly was already put to sleep. This would allow her to focus on her husband's needs and ensure that they'd have some peace during their nights together.

As the baby grew older, this plan grew weaker. Kelly wanted to stay up late and see Daddy, and Elisa was constantly juggling Kelly's needs with Peter's, until chaos would eventually erupt, setting off Pete's volatile temper. From shoving, he progressed to slapping, then punching … always Elisa, not his little girl. Though her efforts to be perfect were unwavering, Elisa continually fell short of Peter's expectations, and she grew increasingly angry and disappointed with herself, willingly accepting the blows he doled out and vowing to prove to her husband that she was as good a wife as his mother, her mother, and his friends' wives were. She knew she could do better if she just tried harder. It was a tiring existence but Elisa was grateful to have a husband who held down a reliable job and who was such a good father to Kelly. All this changed over the course of a few unforgettable hours.

A week ago Thursday, Kelly had been pleading for permission to go to her best friend's slumber party the following Wednesday, the night of her friend's birthday. Elisa had told her that they would all discuss it over the weekend, when Daddy wasn't so tired. Kelly was so excited, though, that she couldn't keep her request buried for whole two days. So as soon as Peter cut into his lamb chop, she bombarded him with reasons she should be granted permission to attend the party, despite their no–sleepovers–during–the–week rule. Kelly took his lack of responsiveness as a "no" and began whining for an explanation, until his typically stone-like face grew bright red and distorted and he rose from his chair, shoving the kitchen table with a thunderous force. The food and plates flew into the air and the table slammed into Kelly's chest, toppling over her chair and sending her crashing to the floor. She was too stunned to cry for a minute. Peter seemed equally stunned by his own action.

Then Kelly seemed to melt into a pool of tears on the floor. "Mommy," she whimpered. "Mommy." With that, Elisa scooped up her daughter and carried her to her bedroom, where she cradled her daughter in her arms until, at last, Kelly drifted off to sleep. Then she sneaked into the kitchen to clean up the mess Peter had left behind when he headed to the living room to open his laptop. Once every trace of the incident was swept away, she tiptoed into their bedroom, pretending to be deep asleep when Peter finally entered around midnight.

The next morning, Elisa and Kelly slipped out of the house early in order to avoid confronting Peter. She'd never just walked out of the house that way and knew he'd be furious when he woke to find an empty apartment and cold coffeepot. It was too early to drop Kelly off at the community center to play for the day, as she did each Friday during the summer months, so Elisa first took her to the nearby diner, where she tried to explain why Daddy had been so upset the night before. He'd been tired and his two best girls had not been sensitive to his mood. Kelly would be a wife one day, Elisa explained, so it was important that she learn the role of a good wife.

The night, she admitted to her daughter, had been a horrible one, but the lesson was important and should not go unnoticed. She invented a string of apologies that she told Kelly had come from her daddy. Kelly agreed to accept these pleas for forgiveness and put the stormy night behind her. To make her daughter feel even more secure in her father's love, Elisa lied that Peter had granted permission for her to attend the slumber party. When she returned home after dropping Kelly off at the center, Peter was long gone to work. She barely had enough energy to keep her eyes open and went directly to bed, where she slept for a couple of hours until Peter's phone call jolted her awake.

"What the hell do you think you're doing sneaking out on me? If I can't trust you, then you can just stay put in the house until I say you can go out. It's your own doing, Elisa, for Chrissake. Sometimes I think you don't have a brain in that head of yours. I'm not going to wake up in the morning to no wife and no kid and no breakfast on the table. What the hell am I, a piece of garbage? And I don't need you running 'round and turning my kid against me. I didn't even have a chance to talk to Kelly this morning. You're so goddamn selfish. When I get home tonight, I'll give you a real explanation of how I feel about the glorious way you started my morning." He spewed all this out in one long, ugly stream that grew increasingly vicious, ultimately slamming down the phone without even waiting for her response.

For several minutes, Elisa sat at the edge of the bed, paralyzed. She knew that a "real explanation" had something to do with five fingers and an outstretched palm. Peter had never threatened her before. His fits of rage had always erupted unpredictably. But he had never hurt Kelly before last night either. Things were sure to get ugly that evening. Elisa decided to call the mom of Kelly's best friend, Amy, and ask if Kelly could spend the night. Amy had the flu, she learned, and it would definitely not be a good time for Kelly to visit. And then reality set in: Elisa was afraid for her daughter ... and herself ... to be in their own home. She was not a crappy mother, no matter what Peter said. The only truly crappy thing she could do would be to allow her daughter to live in jeopardy and to become tainted by her exposure to this hellish excuse for a family.

The anguish, the uncertainty, and the ugliness of this situation crystallized in one shocking moment. Right then Elisa headed for her laptop and started to Google search information on local shelters for battered women. It was the first time she had assigned that label to herself and it stung, but not as harshly as Peter's slaps. She reached for her cell phone and dialed the number listed below the photo of a two-story beige brick house with a modest front lawn, a blend-into-the-neighborhood exterior, and a name with promise: Horizons.

Once the ringing stopped and was replaced by a cheery "Hello," she froze. She didn't know what to ask, why she was calling. She didn't know what she wanted, other than some miracle cure for a festering marriage. She certainly wasn't prepared to walk out on her life, to abandon the man she'd been devoted to for more than a decade. She just needed someone to talk to, an expert in such matters, someone who could pinpoint what it was that she couldn't seem to get right. Part of her, she knew, was seeking reinforcement that she didn't have it so damn bad after all, that her circumstances were no different than anyone else's. Was she just incredibly intolerant? Or naive about the actualities of marriage? Had her mother neglected to share the brutal reality of married life with her daughter, leaving her to discover the harsh truth for herself? Was there a secret way past the problems, a magic wand lurking right before her eyes, just waiting to be clutched and waved through the air to miraculously clear the web of obstacles to contentment? Forget joy. Contentment would be just fine.

What Elisa did in fact reach on the other end of the line was a voice belonging to a woman named Shelby. It was a soft, empathetic voice, yet one that carried a tone of conviction and strength. Timidly Elisa poured out her story so rapidly and openly that she surprised herself. Shelby listened, then responded with purpose, clarity and unapologetic advice. "Get out—and get out now. Once you're safe, you can think things through, figure out how to get your life on track. But first get safe. You don't have to endure the hell. Nothing will change unless you make it change."

Those were not the words Elisa expected to hear and they pained her ears as she sat motionless on the edge of her bed—their bed—the telephone cradled on her shoulder. She instantly resented the naïveté of the so-called helper who wasn't helping her at all. It was easy to dole out such counsel, to tell others to go for broke. Try doing it. Try walking out on the only way of life you know. To face the fact that you're such a failure, that you can't even provide a decent home for your little girl. Try exposing your life as one big lie to everyone who knows you, letting your parents and friends and neighbors see that you're not even good enough to earn your husband's love.

She wanted to bang the receiver down, but first to give this Shelby woman a good verbal thrashing. She wanted to, but she couldn't. She could only sit there staring into the adjoining bathroom, fixating on the mirror above the sink, knowing that just hours ahead, that mirror would be reflecting images of bruised cheeks and swollen lips, as it had too many times before. She needed the voice to help her, but the voice kept reminding her that only she had the power to help herself and see to it that her daughter would be okay. Her daughter. Kelly deserved better. Nothing could erase that haunting fact from her mind. Not yet a victim of her own hysteria, Elisa realized that Shelby's gentle urging might actually work--if she could just conquer the fear of taking the first step out the door.

Elisa remained calm as Shelby proceeded to dispense emergency coaching slowly, logically—what to pack, what papers to carry with her, what to bring for Kelly so that her little girl would not feel thrust into the coldness of an unfamiliar world. And she advised her of the need to file a form with the authorities that was specifically designed for women in her situation so that her husband could not claim she had absconded with their daughter.

With the telephone still cradled in the crook of her neck and a barrage of instructions buzzing through her brain, Elisa walked into the bathroom and stared more closely at her reflection, at the creamy skin, the trembling lips, the vacant eyes brimming with tears. She studied herself as if examining a stranger who had infiltrated her most intimate domain, forcing those eyes to see the truth. And then what she knew to be true came into clear focus. If she didn't get out now, she'd never free herself from the prison that had become her life. Forget the hopes, the prayers, the blueprint for reconstructing this broken life. She needed to have the guts to face what was real, to tackle the terror and give it her best shot. Just once.

She prepared to hang up the phone as Shelby dispensed the final notes, stressing the need to write the address and phone number of the safe house on a slip of paper and tuck it inside her purse. The numbers would easily become lost in the whirlwind of her mind as soon as she hung up the phone. Finally, reluctantly, each woman hung up the phone, hearts thundering. For Shelby, there was only waiting. For Elisa, there was much to be done and little time to do it.

She gathered her things in a daze, recounting the instructions she had fought to absorb, doing her best to remember it all—the bank books, the insurance policies, the birth certificates. And Kelly's books, mainly the new one she insisted on reading all through dinner. And her ragged stuffed pink bear. She'd be lost without Pinky. Sweaters, pants, and a couple of dresses. And shoes. Oh, and slippers. For both of them. And barrettes and hair bands. They were the key to Kelly's fifth-grade fashion statement and the cause of immense concentration in front of the bathroom mirror each morning. What else? What was she forgetting? Some things would surely be overlooked, no matter how she tried to cover all the bases.

With that concern swimming amongst all the others that crowded her mind in a plea for attention, Elisa exited her apartment with a determined slam of the door. She thought only of the present, this moment, forcing herself to push any other thoughts aside. She had to act now, before she had time to change her mind. She met Kelly at the center and slowly explained, in a diluted version of the truth, why they were toting their bags to a bus stop and riding toward this new place where they'd be staying for a while. There was no way to eliminate the trauma for this ten-year-old who'd been shielded from family trauma until the night before. The best Elisa could do was to allow Kelly to be upset, to embrace it as natural and to provide comfort by assuring her that her mother would stay at her side and that there was nothing to fear. It was a change, an adjustment they'd make together. And she wasn't losing Daddy. She could call him later. And no, it wasn't because she'd behaved badly at dinner the night before.

They sat at the bus stop and talked, Elisa not wanting to board the bus until Kelly was ready, calm. She knew Kelly was feeling guilty, refusing to believe that she had not instigated this mess. And she was as angry as she was scared. Elisa accepted that she was the villain for now, the target of that anger, the cause for the tears that streamed down Kelly's face and labored her breathing. Elisa was doing this terrible thing to her. Her daughter hated her now. It was normal. It would pass. Elisa could handle Kelly, of that she was confident. Their bond was unbreakable.

When the sobs subsided and the emotions had been spent, they silently boarded the bus, making their way across town to a simple but pleasant home with a quiet presence and welcoming front yard. The address was tucked inside her handbag, as Shelby had coached, and Elisa studied it three times as the bus meandered through the late afternoon traffic. She emerged through the doors of Horizons toting two suitcases, a shopping bag of toys and books, and a little girl with a confused frown on her pale face. Shelby was there waiting to get her settled and to talk—listen, really—after she and Kelly rested for a while.

Now, nearly a week later, Elisa still found it hard to believe that such a simple, sparse setting could in fact be so much more tolerable than the warm, carefully decorated home she'd left behind. She felt relaxed for the first time in a very long time … until she saw the pretty brunette with the charcoal suede shoulder bag and armload of file folders step through the door, followed by a lanky man loaded down with camera gear.

CHAPTER 3

Julianne was immediately riveted to the eyes of the frail, yet lovely, woman at the bottom of the stairs. The two women moved with such opposing energy that it was startling to both. Julianne, anxious to jump into the day's assignment, came booming through the doorway armed with a take charge attitude that was immensely out of place in these serene surroundings. Elisa, still feeling vulnerable in this temporary residence, was trying to remain as inconspicuous as possible as she prepared to enter the dining room a few steps behind her daughter. Yet as different as these two women seemed to be, there was a strange connection, perhaps a fascination, that was undeniable and that was quite mutual.

"Hi. I'm looking for the people who run this place, a Ms. Hacker and Mr. Andrews," Julianne blurted out with a bright smile and seemingly forced cheerfulness.

"I suppose you'd want to start with Mr. Andrews. He's in charge, though I wouldn't exactly say he runs the place," offered a heavyset young woman walking alongside Elisa. The strange edge of anger in her words prompted both Julianne and Elisa to turn toward her, resulting in her face turning an embarrassing shade of red.

She led the way through the dining room and into the kitchen. "That's Clint Andrews," she said, and turned away, realizing that no further indication was necessary, as there was only a single man present among the dozens of women and children.

He stood over one of the large pots, sniffing its contents approvingly. *Great-looking guy,* Julianne thought. This assignment might be more interesting than she had thought. About forty years of age, with a tall, athletic build, wavy reddish blond hair, and a slightly freckled complexion that gave him a charmingly boyish appearance, Clint Andrews had one other attribute that Julianne found instantly appealing: no wedding ring.

Jake looked down at her, smiling as if he'd been reading her mind. "Lucky ladies," he commented facetiously. "A virile man to look after them." Then he laughed. "Of course, you know how many guys would kill for a job being cooped up with so many women?" Julianne shot him a disparaging glance. "Okay, bad joke. I admit it. It's just that I'm not used to you drooling over the people you're about to interview."

Just then, Clint spotted them across the room and headed toward them with a grand smile and extended hand. "Clint Andrews. Welcome to Horizons. And you're just in time for lunch." Introductions were completed as Shelby joined the gathering and assisted Clint in ushering their guests to a quiet corner table in the dining room, where she proceeded to drown them with facts about the merits and potential of the safe house. Julianne had been the first of the group to select a chair, and she opted for the one directly across the room from Elisa, gazing at her every few seconds as Clint gave them a nutshell description of the funding of the shelter and need to create greater awareness in order to secure much-needed contributions. With the spotlight now upon him and a beautiful producer eating up every word, he couldn't resist edging beyond his territory and into Shelby's, detailing their methods of operation and policies for residents. As usual, Shelby was content to sit back and let him exercise his control.

"Just open a week and already all forty beds are full. It's hard for people to understand what a shortage of space there is for families in this situation. It makes you feel good just to see their anxiety levels shrink after being here the first few days. It's as if while they're here, they can finally let their guard down."

"But I know most women usually wind up going back to their husbands or boyfriends. How do you help them follow through with plans made here? It's overwhelming, especially when kids are in the picture. Like that woman over there. She's so pretty and petite. Hard to picture somebody throwing a tiny gal like that around. The more defenseless the woman appears, the more appealing she is to those jerks. No worry about anyone fighting back. It's all about power, and some guys really get off on power." He leaned across the table, his voice growing impassioned with his mission to bring a new ally into the fold.

"Do you think after our interview I could chat with some of the women and see if they'd talk on camera?" Julianne turned to ask Shelby. "After I interview both of you and the committee that started this project, of course. Are they here yet?"

"There are four women: Sharon, Lisa, Jan and Kathleen. They'll be here in about twenty minutes," she answered. "I figured I could show you around first." As they rose to exit the dining room, Clint asked several woman at nearby tables how they enjoyed lunch. Each smiled back at him timidly, and as she trailed behind Clint, Julianne noticed that many of the women avoided making eye contact with him, unresponsive to his warm gestures. She realized that regaining trust in the opposite sex must be one of the toughest parts of the healing process.

Clint explained that the shelter residents had already been informed of the *Chicago Sizzle* story and most of them were familiar with the show. Whether or not they would participate in the coverage was strictly up to them, and Julianne and her crew were expected to respect the residents' wishes. No one would be identifiable without her permission, and no names were to be revealed under any circumstances. Many of these women and their kids were in danger of being tracked down by angry, violent husbands and boyfriends, and their whereabouts were to be concealed at all costs.

"Can I see what the rooms are like?" Julianne asked. "Like the room you've given to that woman I was noticing in the dining room. You know, that pretty young woman with the daughter."

Clint slipped back into the dining room to ask permission to enter Elisa's bedroom. She complied nervously, offering a tentative nod. Julianne was impressed by Clint's protective nature. It made him all the more attractive. Cute, sensitive and single. This might be a story worth developing in greater length.

She asked Jake to set up his gear in the director's office for the interviews, and while Clint showed him the way, Julianne and Shelby made the short trek to Elisa's room, room 208. Shelby was called to the phone just as they reached the top of the stairs, but she welcomed Julianne to look around until she could rejoin her.

There was an unusual sense of quiet on the second floor. Everyone was down having lunch, Julianne supposed, making this the perfect time to explore. Clint had handed her his master key and even though Elisa had given consent, Julianne felt awkward about entering someone's room in her absence. Still, she rationalized, the point was to do a story that would help the women at Horizons and so many others walking in their shoes. As a producer, that meant immersing herself into life at a shelter.

She slowly swung open the door to Elisa's room and was stunned by the setting she discovered. Stunned and moved. What she had expected to be a drab, sterile, anonymous place was instead warm, cozy, and personal. Not in the selection of the furniture or window coverings, which were predictably neutral in color and basic in style, but in the embellishments ... the little touches thoughtfully scattered throughout the space that made this room a home—not just a holding ground. This was a room that was alive with a mother's love, love that converted something plain into something special so that a little girl would feel less scared, less confused, less angry at a world that had dealt her such an unfair hand.

Julianne stepped up to one of the twin beds, the one she could tell belonged to the girl. She sat on the edge, fingering a pink heart-shaped pillow that seemed to have a place of honor nestled between a collection of fluffy stuffed animals. It was obviously a homemade treasure of shiny pink satin with a border of white lace roses. In the middle, written out in hand-stitched letters, it read "Daddy's

Sweetheart." Well, Julianne contemplated, who would have thought she'd have something in common with little Kelly? They'd both been suckered by men they loved who tried to win them over with white roses.

A small bedside lamp in the shape of a kitten with a sunny yellow shade sat between the two beds. Hand-knit coverlets in a rainbow of pastels were placed at the foot of each bed. Crayons, a pair of roller skates and a large pad of drawing paper were stuffed into a small toy chest in the shape of a castle, which stood next to the dresser. Children's book were strewn about. There seemed to be very little in the room that belonged to Elisa. Clearly her priority had been to gather up her daughter's precious items and transport them to their new nest. After taking a final look around, wondering how she could capture the poignance, yet hopefulness, of this image with Jake's camera, she wandered back downstairs to begin the shoot.

This round of interviews was straightforward and brief, formalities to acknowledge the efforts of those in charge. Julianne breezed through them. Once she had seen the faces of the women and kids in the dining room, and once she sat on Kelly's bed, holding her pink satin pillow with the pretty white roses, she knew that the heart of the story could only come from the victims, not the rescuers. She also knew that she was taking on a lot more than a five-minute story built around some flashy black-tie fund-raiser.

The facts of domestic abuse had all been out there before, tragic deaths and shocking statistics. It was almost too familiar. The urgency of the crisis had dissipated, with the public outcry for reform diminished. Consciousness-raising had migrated to newer, sexier flavor-of-the-month crusades. Julianne made a mental note to call Tina as soon as she returned to her office in order to start collaborating on a proposal for a documentary.

Jake began striking the equipment. "What next? Want to try to talk to some of the women first or get some interior shots? Your call," he said.

"You head over to the kitchen and pick up some shots of those giant pots and tower of plates. If you can get any backs of heads in the dining room or living room, go for it. But if anyone looks scared or nervous, move on. I'm going to see if we can come back for the resident interviews later. I can't get the real story from these people until I spend some time with them, get them comfortable with me. If we rush this, we'll just get the typical news stuff everyone gets."

She reached out to grab his arm as he was rolling up his camera cables. "You're the man with that scary camera. They have to open up to you, too, not just me. Will you come back here with me … kind of on your own time … to help me? You know, we'll sit and talk. No cameras or microphones. Just us. Then maybe they'll let their hair down after a while and we'll bring in the gear when they're ready. What do you think? I know it's hard for you to squeeze in a side project with the hours we work and with a wife, but it should just be a matter of a few visits. It's a favor, okay? Okay?"

"Yeah, yeah. Okay. Let me go grab those kitchen shots," Jake answered, giving her a smile that seemed intended to show her he approved of being so affected by a story. She sensed that her friends at work felt she had become too far removed from the creative process and was on her way to becoming one of those corporate suits who ran the business instead of loving the business. As he headed out, he brushed past Julianne, whispering, "I think you just want to come back to flirt with your dashing Mr. Andrews," he chided.

Julianne smiled after him and then approached Shelby and Clint with her request to return with Jake in an effort to cultivate a relationship with the women. While she was not in a position to guarantee a documentary focusing on the shelter, the prospect of such an opportunity was enough to win their cooperation. She promised to call the next day in order to talk in greater detail and thanked them for being such great hosts. Shelby explained that tomorrow she was escorting a frightened new resident to the office of family services and wouldn't be on-site, but Clint assured Julianne that he'd be available to her.

"The nickel tour was my pleasure," he said, escorting her to the door. "Any chance you'd reciprocate? I've always wanted to see what a television station looks like, and it would be interesting to see you on your own turf."

Julianne was pleasantly surprised. She was hoping he'd make a gesture to see her on a more personal basis but feared that he would be too cautious of his position to say anything. "You bet," she quickly responded. "Name the time."

"How about tomorrow? Why don't I come down to your office for a tour—maybe at the end of the day—and we can grab a cup of coffee and talk about your program plan? How does that sound?"

Julianne smiled at him, just a touch flirtatiously. "Perfect. Here's my card with the address and my direct line. Call if there's a problem. Otherwise, I'll see you around five tomorrow."

As she approached the front door, she crossed paths with Elisa and Kelly and reached out to gently touch Elisa's shoulder. "Thank you for letting me peek inside your room. I really appreciate it ... and I hope that maybe next time I'm here we can sit and get to know each other a little."

Elisa managed a faint smile. She noted a look of sincerity in Julianne's eyes that wore down her defenses.

Then Julianne took Kelly's hand. "And I love your pink pillow, the one with the white roses on it. I have this thing about white roses." Kelly smiled back at her.

At that moment, Jake came up behind them, ready to leave. "Thank you, ladies," he said with his winning grin. "You have a great rest of the day--and keep the faith." Julianne grabbed the tripod and scooped up the last of the cables. They headed out the door in a much slower, more reflective manner than they had embodied upon arrival.

They'd be back.

Mr. Perfect is in the lobby," Lianne teased, trying to get a rise out of her boss. "Should I bring him back or do you need time for a makeup overhaul?"

"This is as good as I get," Julianne laughed. "And since he is so perfect, I'm sure he'll love me just the way I am. Why don't you go on out and get him? You'll know which one he is; just look for the halo." As Lianne headed for the guest reception desk, Julianne checked herself out in the mirror behind her door. She was a little more nervous than usual about this meeting. Probably, she realized, because she almost never mixed business with pleasure. But since her twenties were a thing of the past, she figured she'd be wise to loosen up her rules a bit. It was hard enough to meet a halfway decent man. She couldn't rule out every prospect she met through business. After all, that was practically the only way she met anyone these days.

Clint rounded the corner and stepped into her office with a breezy, relaxed stride that immediately put Julianne at ease. "So this is where the famous producer sits all day, huh?" he said with ample charm.

Exiting her office, they strolled down the hallway, Julianne explaining what activities were going on in various departments as they traveled from studios to control room to edit suites. She kept moving as she spoke, anxious to get the mini tour behind them and move on to the more interesting part of the evening.

"Now you can tell all your friends you saw the home of Chicago's top rated six o'clock news," she said, pushing the lobby button in the elevator to exit the building.

"I already told them about you ... and after that, a TV newsroom won't seem so impressive."

"I suppose you think a compliment like that means I'm springing for the coffee."

"Absolutely. Only I'd rather have a scotch on the rocks. How'd you like to visit one of my neighborhood hangouts? It's only about ten minutes from here and I have my car."

"I'm all yours."

About fifteen minutes later, Julianne and Clint entered a cozy little Italian restaurant lined with slightly worn red vinyl booths and a small flickering candle on each table. Instead of scotch, Clint opted for a bottle of Chianti, and they decided to really splurge and have a large sausage and olive pizza with double cheese. Clint lifted his glass for a toast. "To the most fascinating woman ever to walk through the doors of Horizons."

"I know you mean well, but let's face it: those doors have just recently opened and those women have a lot more to worry about than being fascinating."

"I'm warning you: Don't give me hard time, Julianne Sloan. I'll make you pay for it later," he shot back with a boyish smile, taking her hand and loosely caressing her fingers.

Julianne almost regretted the arrival of the pizza, for it meant that she would have to pull her hand away from his. But her stomach won out, and she slowly slipped her fingers out of his hand and under a gooey slice. For the next two hours, they nibbled and shared career stories. He found her work intriguing, and she found his much more meaningful. Not only was she moved by the horror of what the abused women had experienced, she was also equally touched by the warmth with which he conveyed their circumstances and by the passion he had for making a difference. With the likes of Allen Miller occupying the "significant male" role in her life for the past several months, she had nearly given up on the chance of finding a man who could actually be sensitive to women. She was beginning to think the male gender simply had a genetic malfunction. Clint Andrews was proving her wrong. As they finished up and headed out to walk off the pizza, she treaded into the tricky conversation zone of dating.

"I don't know if it's my own lousy luck or if it's just a fact of life that you meet a lot of peculiar characters when you throw yourself into this whole dating thing," she started.

He smiled in agreement. "Like Eden, who texts me constantly even though I called it quits a month ago. She's studying for the bar. DePaul Law School. You'd think she'd have better things to worry about."

"Ah, a lawyer. You could do worse."

"Yeah, a lawyer. So you'd think she'd be opinionated, dynamic. Well, forget it. It was 'Whatever you want to do, Clint. Wherever you want to go, Clint. Whatever you think, Clint.' I couldn't even get her to say whether she liked her steak rare or medium well for Chrissake. I can't stand a woman who has no mind of her own!"

"Oh, she usually has one. She's just afraid to use it. It's generally perceived as an unattractive trait. Passive women are sexy women, to paraphrase an authority on catching a man." He laughed and shook his head in disbelief.

"I'm glad you find that so amusing. But I'm not kidding. Walk through any relationship section of a bookstore and scan the shelves. It's there in black and white, usually couched in subtleties, of course. Passive women are sexy women." Clint was startled by the matter of fact tone with which she delivered this revelation.

"Passive is not sexy—don't let any self-proclaimed expert on the matter convince you otherwise. I'm surprised to hear a woman like you espousing such theories. You made the high-power decision of which toppings to order on our pizza, and you're the one who steered us from the eighteen dollar bottle of Merlot to the twenty dollar bottle of Chianti. Crucial decisions like those babies don't seem the work of a passive woman. And I defy anyone to say that Julianne Sloan is not sexy."

"Yeah, yeah. That all sounds great. But I still don't buy it. You may go along with letting me select olives over onions, but let's raise the stakes. How about deciding where we should live or how many kids we should have or whether or not we should stash our cash in an IRA or play the stock market?" She was building steam in spite of her intentions to gloss over the topic. Julianne had been burned by too many men who proclaimed their liberal, enlightened views on feminism but then ran for the door the instant she went head-to-head with them on discussions of politics, investments, even basketball. Yes, Julianne loved basketball and had held season tickets to the Bulls games for the last four years. But even attempting to critique Jordan versus Pippin as the team's all-time best Bull had resulted in a first date disaster. Nothing Clint Andrews could say would convince her that all men carried, at the very least, a hint of sexism in their souls. Still, she allowed herself to marvel at the idea that there could be one man on the planet who had his head on straight when it came to the battle of the sexes and that just maybe she was out on a date with that very man tonight.

After strolling a few blocks, they headed back to Clint's car and Julianne directed him to her apartment building where she turned to him. "Thanks for the pizza...and the stories." The glint in his eye told her she might on the evening's menu as a succulent dessert. But his words took a different direction.

"There are lots more stories to tell and Horizons could really use the exposure." It was awkward sitting there in front of her doorway, determining how to wrap things up. Julianne respected Clint's desire to bring the conversation back to the comfortable territory of business rather than push the personal aspects of this budding relationship. "I'm sure you could see there's a lot more work to be done to make the shelter first rate, and it takes contributions. Anything you can do, anything you need, just ask."

"Can I come by on Sunday and just hang out for a few hours— with Jake?" Julianne asked. "It will help loosen people up if they get used to seeing our faces around there."

"If you guys are willing to work on a Sunday, no problem. I'll leave word that it's okay, but I probably won't be there. I have tickets for a Cubs game, and I know you wouldn't want me to blow off Wrigley Field."

"I'm sure Jake and I will be fine on our own," she said.

He leaned toward her and softly brushed his lips against hers. "Mixing business with pleasure is bad policy. But I think we have to live dangerously once in a while. How about' you?"

"I'll think about it," she said teasingly as she started walking into her lobby. Then she turned back and looked at him. Her voice became hushed and her eyes softened. "Call me," she added, and walked inside.

The Chicago skyline was at its finest as Clint headed north on Lake Shore Drive for the brief three–mile drive to his apartment. He took pleasure in the way his new black BMW 530i rounded the curve and shimmered in the moonlight. Yes, he'd made the right choice going with this car as his weekday mode of transportation. Though not quite as sexy as the Porsche he had test-driven, it satisfied his needs nicely, stately enough to provide a solid professional image, pricey enough to show that he wasn't in the habit of pinching his pennies, while at the same time not being so extravagant as to flaunt his financial comfort to a sea of money-grubbing women in pursuit of a fat-cat husband. Finally, it was sleek enough to catch the eye of a different category of women: those not nearly so driven to land a man as to have a hell of a time with one. Take Julianne Sloan. To her, the Porsche would have seemed self-indulgent and reckless, not nearly as effective as the BMW. He'd already decided that he'd like to be highly effective with Julianne Sloan.

She didn't present much of a challenge to him. That was the downside. But frankly, it was becoming increasingly difficult to set his sights on women who'd give him a run for his money. This predicament struck him funny, to be sure. For Clint Andrews knew better than anyone that he was hardly God's gift to women. His appearance was fine, above average he supposed. But he'd never take first prize at a Brad Pitt look-alike contest. His wallet was sufficiently fat, though he'd hardly hold his own in a poker game against Trump. He was witty, but not exceedingly. Suave, but not remarkably. But wise? Yes, Clint Andrews believed himself to be inordinately wise.

He was astute enough to recognize that every time he eavesdropped on a gathering of women in line at the movies or sipping coffee at Starbucks, they were passionately bemoaning a shortage of men in the world. Whether in the husband hunt for themselves or scanning the terrain in search of prey for a single sister, girlfriend, or co-worker, there was a desperate quest underway by single women to land single men, and the odds were just the way he liked them. He could have his pick of fine females, string them along until his interest waned, and be rid of them long before they had the slightest notion of what a lecherous scoundrel he really was. It was a wonderful game. Too many years of solitude spent at an assortment of libraries and the harbor of his fourteen-by-seventeen-foot bedroom during his youth had made the adult Clint hungry to get in the game of conquering women. He never tired of it. Nor did he succeed in satisfying the hunger.

He swung onto his exit and wound his way through the clogged traffic on Division Street that was typical of a neighborhood comprised of chic restaurants, over-priced bars and glossy high-rise buildings complete with workout rooms, swimming pools, and vast garages housing a plethora of Mercedes, Jeep Cherokees and, of course, BMWs.

Apartment 30C had only been his home for the past eight months. An accountant by trade, he was cautious in parceling out his inheritance and looked at over twenty condos before he settled on the spanking new skyscraper in the heart of Chicago's Gold Coast. Between the condo and the car, his bank account was not as healthy as he'd like. Still, to service his need to establish himself as a fast lane bachelor, he hired a condo decorator, a move he discovered to be more rewarding than he had imagined.

The selection of his decorator involved an interview process in which he wined and dined and queried his candidates—all of whom had been painstakingly chosen based upon the size of their breasts, length of their legs and fullness of their lips rather than the scope of their résumés. With an economy that made refurbishing one's home a financial indulgence, his eager collection of applicants were willing to give their all to land his account, which he implied would be substantially greater than in fact it was.

After two dinners amounting to six and a half hours of solid flirtation, Lauren Carmichael was awarded the honor of decorating Clint Andrews's three-bedroom condominium. What gave her the edge was not the fact that she was one of the few candidates whose face was as pleasing as her body or that, at twenty-six, she retained a firmness and bounce in her bustline that the over-thirty crowd couldn't match. No, Lauren Carmichael's edge came from the fact that though she was masterful at the art of sexual temptation, she was a champion at holding her client-to-be at bay every time he came excitingly close to reeling her in. He found her level of confidence and coyness both irresistible and titillating. So Lauren was his choice of decorator and once their agreement was executed and he'd invested the better part of two weeks in visiting showrooms and fingering samples with her, all the while weaving his web of seduction, he took her to bed.

As it turned out, the event was a major disappointment. She was not nearly so skillful in the sack as her perfect packaging promised. Her repertoire was limited; the creativity that came across in her work was nonexistent under the covers, and it took forever to make her come. He found himself doing all the work for a payoff that didn't stack up against the effort. After one exhausting night consisting of three mediocre rounds of sex, he'd had his fill of one Lauren Carmichael. But he was, after all, a businessman, and since he'd already signed a letter of agreement with her, he decided to derive maximum benefit from his financial investment by getting the best money could buy for his condo at prices available only to insiders of the design trade.

The result was entirely pleasing to him. He reveled in the richness of the woods and leathers, the crystal and lacquer that adorned his personal palace on the thirtieth floor. His quintessential home base complete, Lauren Carmichael was as done as her assignment.

Lingering relationships were not what Clint Andrews had in mind when it came to courting women. It was different when he was in high school and yearned to win the affection of one of the gorgeous girls he admired from across the cluttered lunchroom and perfectly aligned rows of desks in his classrooms. He couldn't even worm his way into the crowd of cool guys to hang out with, much less nab one of "The Populars." It wasn't that he was disliked. Quite the opposite. Everybody liked Clint Andrews. He was accommodating, gentle and harmless—nothing not to like. He also happened to be severely overweight and dressed like a goody-goody nerd, thanks to a mother who persisted in selecting his wardrobe long after the other moms gave up trying to inflict their old-fashioned tastes on their new-fashioned sons and daughters.

His hair was perfectly trimmed, and just when it would begin to look unkempt enough to be in style, Mom escorted him to the neighborhood barber. Acne plagued him from the time he entered seventh grade until he was in his third year of college. Plus, he stank when it came to sports. Any sports. He was the last to be selected on any team, a situation that was almost as humiliating as the dreaded ritual of exposing his vast nude physique in the showers for phys ed and swimming classes.

After a few years of wallowing in depression, Clint vented his frustrations by throwing himself into his schoolwork. He elevated his meager self-esteem through academic, rather than social, achievements. Thoughts of pretty girls with warm caresses and tasty tongues were left to occasional daydreams and increasingly frequent nighttime fantasies.

When his mother died unexpectedly from a heart attack during his sophomore year in high school, he threw himself into his studies more than ever before. Clint had been unusually close to his mother, physically if not emotionally. She preferred keeping him at home to letting him roam the streets with his few friends and said that, in these times of deteriorating morals and escalating delinquency problems, the Andrews children would be well supervised. Arlene and Clint Andrews loved their mother, despite her smothering and nagging. They just didn't seem to like her very much, and this conflict laid seed to feelings of shame and guilt that both children struggled with long after their mother's death.

With his bedroom and the local library as his chosen places of refuge, Clint had little to focus on other than his books, and he became an honor student in his junior year at Niles North High School, winning a scholarship to Drake University, though his family certainly didn't need the money. It wasn't the most prestigious school he could have selected, but it was just a five-hour ride from his family residence. With his father alone now and his sister in her third year of college downstate, it would be utterly selfish of him to venture farther away than the adjoining state.

Clint's existence at college was not all that different from what he had endured at high school, except for the fact that the nerd population was increased due to the vastness of the student body, enabling Clint to not only stand out less but also to buddy up to fellow nerds more. And it was at Drake that he discovered that geeks came in all shapes and sizes, came from an array of ethnic backgrounds and, most importantly, came in both sexes.

Hannah was the quiet little mouse who sank her hooks into Clint Andrews. He offered little resistance. He was embarrassed by the fact that he was still a virgin and figured Hannah was no worse than the rest of the crop of girl geeks, so he played the part of attentive boyfriend until she sneaked him into her dorm room one Friday night and joined him in the once-in-a-lifetime experience of losing one's virginity.

Hannah knew little about what she was doing under those covers, but it was apparent to both of them that Clint knew even less. The only thing smaller than his sexual prowess was his confidence level and after that night, he avoided crossing paths with Hannah at all costs. Determined to improve his game, he snooped on other guys' conversations of sex and scoring whenever possible, absorbing words of wisdom the campus Casanovas would share as they willingly spilled their guts about their conquests and techniques.

Eventually, he targeted a chubby little blond named Megan who came from Drake's home town of Des Moines. Megan's parents were dead set on getting her to drop those extra fifty pounds of flab they believed were at the root of her nasty disposition, so they had been sending her to a weight loss specialist for the past month and a half. She'd managed to rid herself of six pounds by the time she started dating Clint. Shrewd as he was, he figured it made good sense to take advantage of the diet tips for which his new friend was paying good money. Besides, kicking the food habit was easier with a partner—misery loving company and all—so he committed himself to utilizing the secondhand information Megan shared and while her six-pound loss reversed itself into a nine-pound gain, Clint continued to peel away his poundage.

Over the course of seven months, he shed thirty pounds. Once he got rid of the fat, he got rid of the girl, relishing the thought of making up for lost time by dating like there was no tomorrow and sampling as many sweet young things as his anxious libido could handle. The dieting and compulsive dating stayed with Clint long after he walked away from Drake with his degree in economics, progression to graduate school at the University of Illinois and career as a CPA.

The world of accounting proved far less satisfying than Clint had predicted. It did have a couple of things in its favor. The hours were manageable—Clint could never fathom entering a profession that enslaved a man. Doctors on call at all hours, lawyers clocking in eighty-hour weeks in a struggle to make partner, investment bankers rising at dawn to track the New York stock exchange--not for him.

Once his inheritance came through, he went so far as to forfeit a prestigious position with Chicago's number three accounting firm to venture out on his own, where he could set his own schedule, select his own clientele, and operate at his own pace. He did, after all, have the security of that hefty endowment and fully believed that had the money not been used to buy himself professional freedom in addition to his ample collection of new toys, it would have been of little use overall. His income was more than adequate, and with the loss of thirty-five more pounds over a two-year stretch, Clint was ready to start dressing with style and going after the kind of women who had merely existed in his dreams before. Even though he'd gone girl crazy during the latter years of college, he still had a lot of time to make up for, he rationalized, and what started as a desire to fulfill the fantasies of his youth grew into an obsessive hunger for women, sex and more sex.

He had devoured women of every age, tax bracket, and ethnic heritage, yet his appetite still wasn't quelled. And when he went the rough sex route, timidly at first, then arduously, he found that satisfaction could be derived not only from the physical act but also from the aggressive foreplay leading up to it. It was a dangerous discovery, not for Clint but for the delicate, refined females who became his favorite playthings. Unlike most men, whose sexual heydays were gone by their early thirties, Clint was approaching forty and just hitting his stride. And thanks to his brother-in-law's innocent generosity in ensconcing him at a woman's shelter, life was more stimulating than ever.

CHAPTER 4

If there had been any doubt among the readers of *Vogue* and *Women's Wear Daily* that black and white were the chic colors of the day, one had only to join the pageantry in the grand ballroom of the Ritz Carlton to dispel any such notion. The gathering was a vision in black and white: black tuxedos and white dinner jackets for the men; black lace, white satin and chiffon in spatterings of both hues for the women. The cream of Chicago's social circle had come out to dine and dance, all in the name of a worthy cause. The event must have done wonders for the couture collections that dotted the city's elegant Magnificent Mile shopping district.

Perhaps this simplicity of the crowd's color palate was what enhanced the arrival of the astonishing brunette. Her calf-length gown in a magnificent shade of peacock blue attracted the watchful eyes of the ladies and men milling about the foyer with their martinis and flutes of champagne. Julianne Sloan had mingled with this crowd before. Her stature as one of the city's premiere television producers had brought her within the fold many times. Attending such events proved to be an appreciated departure from the usual Saturday night festivities of catching a movie or basking in the flames of sizzling saganaki in Greektown with girlfriends. Yet the predictability of the dress code and stodgy behavior at these galas had begun grinding on her nerves as of late. So while she was fully aware of the fact that her dynamic attire was not in keeping with her peers, it was a calculated choice.

It was not only the boldness of the shade that garnered an impressive amount of attention, however. It was the cut of the neckline, the shape of the bodice, the snug fit of the design as it hugged the curves of her legs from thigh to ankle. Had the adornments of the fabric and detail of the beading failed to attest to the sophistication of the creation, one would have questioned the propriety of the garment within these somewhat conservative ranks. But yes, the dress was an excellent choice and one that consumed the better part of a week's pay.

Satin, pearls and a three-hour visit to the hair salon provided Julianne with a much-needed boost. The breathtaking result dissolved any remnants of anguish over the extravagance of the purchases and discomfort of having her head prodded, painted, and crimped into place for the hours that afternoon. She'd grown bored with the sandy blond highlights that were strewn about her brunette tresses for nearly a decade. Auburn. That was the move. Deep auburn highlights cast a rosy glow to her skin and brought out the dark green speckles in her hazel eyes. The thick hair, usually left to fall in a disheveled mass just above her shoulders, had been converted into a lush cluster of loose waves that shimmered wildly as she ambled about the crowd. Always attractive, yet in an understated way, Julianne was anything but demure tonight, and while she was not entirely comfortable with her presence, she was not nearly as uncomfortable as she had expected to be.

This was, after all, a business engagement for Julianne. When, as suspected, Tina was in no shape to accompany the crew to the event to capture video of the posh fundraising effort for Horizons, Julianne stepped in, assessing both the value of the shoot for their story and the caliber of the list of attendees.

Since her company was one of the key sponsors of the cause, it had purchased two tables of seating. Ted Marshall, Don McBain, and Pam Avery would be among the senior management members present. They would, she anticipated, offer a collective double take at her appearance. Producers were trained to be inconspicuous, putting as much effort into blending into a crowd as others did into standing out from it. Jake would be surprised as well. But none of them would go so far as to question her professionalism or risk the rudeness of calling attention to her judgment in personal presentation.

The key opinion of the evening would come from the one person whose approval was critical and at the root of every selection, down to the ultra sheer pantyhose. Clint Andrews had been invited to dine at Walt and Arlene Mitchell's table and, due to the five hundred dollar per plate price tag, Julianne suspected that he would be arriving alone. If, however, she had underestimated the Mitchells' generosity and Clint arrived with a beautiful companion in tow, perhaps that Shelby Hacker, then Julianne was not to be outdone.

The plain taupe slacks and subdued sweaters Julianne had donned during her past encounters with the promising Mr. Andrews didn't paint her in the most exotic light, and there was something about this man that bode of a taste for the exotic in women. Maybe it was the way his eyes gravitated, almost unwillingly, to the most striking women on the street during their brief stroll. Whatever it was, Julianne sensed that Clint had an appetite for intriguing companions and this conjecture prompted a jolt of excitement within her.

She spotted the long, lanky stride breaking through the crowd long before Jake had time to peruse the crowd for his producer. She was glad her eyes were upon him when he found her. His reaction dismissed any doubt regarding the choice of hair and wardrobe. It was a good thing too, for his eyes revealed his words did not. He was nearly speechless.

"Nice duds," he offered with a warm smile which conveyed his full appreciation.

"You clean up pretty well," she quipped. He looked wonderful in his herringbone sport coat and tie. This was as dressed up as Jake would be for any job assignment. In fact, the tie was a big give. So rarely did she see him dressed in this fashion that she couldn't take her eyes off of him and her approving gaze made him shuffle for an awkward moment. His camera was at his side, a light already affixed to the top. A heavy strap of batteries was draped over his shoulder like a holster. This cameraman stood ready for action.

In production, this was known as a "cake shoot," strictly routine and requiring no special elements. There were no interviews to procure, actions to grab on cue, schedules to meet. The purpose of the shoot was to gather glamorous video shots that could be edited into a minute-and-a-half story heralding the charitable partygoers. Tina would write the narration when she returned from her sickbed. One quick screening of the video would tell her all she needed to know. There would be no shortage of glitz and glamour.

Julianne's directions to Jake were perfunctory at best. He knew which shots to grab, how to dress up his angles and stylize his images with lighting and filters to capture a radiant glow. While her feet remained planted firmly alongside her professional partner, her eyes raced around the room, scoping out the crowd in anticipation of discovering one particular man. But the only familiar face in the crowd was that of Ted Marshall, whom she caught giving her a head-to-toe once-over while his wife chatted amiably with the woman to her left. Behind them stood Pam and Randy Avery, both of whom nodded warm greetings from across the room.

The image of Pam and Randy together gave her cause to stand back and reflect on the Saturday afternoon last month, just one day after Mollie was born, when she stopped by the hospital to offer congratulations. Randy was perched at the foot of the bed, staring in contented astonishment as his wife nursed his new baby girl. They didn't even notice Julianne's entrance, so engrossed were they in their joy. It was an image she would never forget, one that said more about the treasures of marriage and motherhood than the scores of books and magazines that obliterated her living room coffee table. The thought of marriage had been far from urgent until recently. There was always so much time—time to build the career, time to prove her talent to her parents and herself, time to enjoy the parties and indulge in the vacations, pampering herself completely before her attention would be siphoned off to tend to a husband and children.

The touch to her shoulder was so light, so gentle, that she

acknowledged it by simply stepping a few inches to her right. She assumed that she was being politely informed by one of the crowd that she and her cameraman were blocking the way to the hors d'oeuvre buffet. So she was clearly annoyed when, having already made the adjustment in her stance, the tap was repeated. She swung around to display her irritation and found herself staring straight into the eyes of Clint Andrews.

She was speechless at first, riveted to his deep brown eyes and then the soft curve of his lips. He had beautiful lips, well-defined and full, forming a winning smile that brightened his entire face. That smile broke into a full burst of laughter as he realized that he'd caught her off guard.

"Not too shabby, Ms. Sloan," he said as his eyes took in every inch of her carefully decorated body. "We're going to have to get you out of those work clothes more often."

"Just something I pulled out of the closet. I need to go out on the town every so often to air things out." She figured she'd let him know that she was ready, willing and able to be his playmate-- starting immediately.

He looked striking. His black tux was of a rich fabric with a subtle texture and his sleek white shirt was crisp and bright with tiny black studs adorning the front. The bow tie and cummerbund were smoky silver and the overall effect was entirely striking. By the glint in his eye, the feeling was mutual. Even better than his appearance was the fact that no companion stood at his side.

Jake lowered the camera and raised his eyes to check out the man whose arrival had clearly distracted his associate. Clint extended a hand, and the two men exchanged a brief but silent handshake.

"I'm going to head into the dining room before the doors open to the masses and catch some shots of the tables and decorations. I'll be back in a minute," Jake shared, taking a few steps and then turning back to her, aware of the fact that technically she was his boss and should be regarded as such. "Anything special you want?"

"Just the usual—the crystal, flowers ... and see if you can get some glam shots of those incredible chandeliers they have in there. We can create some kind of fancy dissolve between scenes by changing focus on the chandelier lights."

The minute she said it, she realized there was no need to dispatch instructions. No trained shooter would overlook the opportunity to capture the light fragmentations off those magnificent chandeliers. He'd given her those exact shots dozens of times in the past. But he indulged her directions with a brief "You got it" and left her to devote her attention to the would-be suitor in his polished attire.

"Does dinner come with the gig?" Clint prodded.

"Dinner? At five hundred dollars a plate, the working press is definitely not invited to join in dinner!" she teased.

"I bet you'll be mighty hungry after working your way through the droves of diners, air laden with the aromas of prime beef and onion tart. Desperately hungry, I'd guess."

"Umm. Desperately," she concurred with a sly grin.

"If you're lucky, some kindhearted guy might offer to buy you a burger, seeing as how you're all dolled up and everything."

"Think I might be that lucky?"

"Could be." He lifted her hand to his lips, gracing it with a delicate kiss. "I'm at table four. Swing by when you've completed your duties, Commander, and we'll blow this pop stand." He lowered her hand with a tender caress and also lowered his gaze to once more consume the power of her presence. Without another word, he disappeared into the flock. She caught her breath and weaved her way through the gathering to find the entrance to the ballroom and the cameraman who would be inside.

"Where's my iPhone when I need it?" She laughed, juggling the overstuffed corned beef sandwich in her hands as she fought a losing battle to confine the mountain of meat to the skimpy slices of rye bread intended to hold it in place. "Scarfing down kosher pickles and potato salad at midnight in my best gown is an image that should definitely go viral."

"I told you Jerry's Nosh makes the best corned beef sandwich in town. And after that fancy rack of lamb and baked Alaska, I've never craved a good Jewish deli more. That fancy stuff just isn't for me. I'll take Jerry's any day." His words were barely audible, so involved was he in cramming coleslaw into his mouth.

"I can't believe you can actually manage to down that food after you just consumed a five-course dinner."

"Sissy food. It just makes me hungry for the real thing."

"Well, you can't get much more real than this." She giggled, wiping a dollop of mustard from the corner of her mouth with her pinky finger and relocating the limp but hefty slice of pickle to the outermost corner of her plate.

"No way, lady. Eat that pickle. I'm not going to be the only one at this table reeking of garlic. Garlic, as you probably are aware, is incredibly unsexy unless everyone has indulged equally."

Encouraged by the fact that his comments had overtones of romance, she willingly lifted the long green spear and slid it through her lips in a gesture designed to be comically sensuous.

"Just as I suspected. A pickle-eating pro." The double entendre did not go unnoticed, and she found herself blushing. Julianne had never been much of a tease. In fact, she had often solicited the tutelage of her girlfriends on the fine art of flirting. Having been raised in a fairly conservative household, sexual innuendo and off-color commentary by no means came naturally ... until tonight, though her behavior could hardly be considered brazen by normal standards.

"I think dinner should be on the house. We absolutely add a touch of class to this place. Why, I don't think I spot one other tuxedo in the crowd," Julianne joked.

"Yeah, all the other guys around here are too smart to get locked into one of these things." He licked the mustard off his fingers and reached up to loosen his tie. "I'm dying to get out of these clothes. Let's head out of here."

A few minutes later, she was nestled into the black leather passenger seat of the Porsche, letting John Legend lull her into a state of complacency. They were only a few blocks from Clint's apartment, she knew, and she waited to see if he would head in that direction, unsure of how she would respond. Her anxiety, though slight, proved unnecessary. He swung around onto Lake Shore drive and pointed the car in the direction of her apartment building, where he had dropped her off once before.

They rode in silence, his hand taking advantage of stop lights to drift from the gear stick to her lap for a brief squeeze of her hand. The stars glittered just as her dress and delicate earrings did, and the fresh scent of Lake Michigan wafted through the car, inviting thoughts of deep kisses and lingering hugs. He rounded the corner, scanning the street for parking as he approached. He drove past her building, making it apparent that he had no intention of merely depositing her at the doorway. Instead, he opted for a space on the street about half a block down and used the short jaunt back to her apartment to wrap his arm around her waist, gauging the potential need to melt her defenses.

There was no need for meltdown tactics tonight, however. Julianne was generating more than a fair share of the heat and there was no question that Clint would be calling the shots for the rest of the night and into the morning. Silence prevailed, broken only by soft moans of pleasure as he pulled her toward him in the elevator, burying his lips in her neck and letting his tongue roam across the silken shoulders. Those lips on her neck made it clear that Clint would be staying the night.

She struggled to maintain balance as they drifted the short distance from the elevator to her front door, just as she fought fiercely to maintain control of her senses. This man was an unknown, an outsider. Yet he had his hands on her breasts and his tongue scanned every inch of her face and shoulders as though it had every right to do so. She was giving him that right, a total stranger. It was ludicrous. It was stupid. It was fire. And she loved it. There would be no stopping Clint Andrews. No denying herself. For once, the practical side of Julianne Sloan would succumb to her passions.

They moved into her living room. She didn't even remember

fishing the key out of her purse. He steered her to the front windows, and lowered her onto the carpet, the blackness of night and shimmering stars providing a sensual blanket. She hesitated, trying to ease them toward the sofa just a few feet away. But he held her firmly, and she could see that their experience would not be softened by a lush bed or cozy sofa. His mouth grew demanding and his arms grew rigid as she gently unfastened his shirt and stroked his skin. The tenderness had vanished from his touch, and it was all the more exciting to her. He pressed his body against hers relentlessly, never releasing her lips from his mouth. He turned her onto her side and unzipped the dress, not sensuously but almost violently, and he pressed against her back, shifting his hands under her breasts and kneading them with the full palm of his hand. His tongue was thrust inside her ear as he deepened his hold on her breasts, and a raw desire shot through her body. He wanted her. He dominated her.

No man had ever touched her this way before and it set her wild. It was dangerous, frightening, for she knew that she was completely overpowered by this man, that had she wanted him to stop, had she needed to take control of the situation, it would have been impossible, and this aroused her all the more. She groaned, unashamed as he rolled her onto her back and took her breast in his mouth sucking on her nipples with a building frenzy, and she felt his hand slide up under her gown, teasing her inner thighs at first and then rubbing between her legs ferociously. She responded like an animal being fed after a lifetime of deprivation. It was raw and brutal, but it was new and her desire was irrepressible. She reached down to take hold of his face and raise his eyes to hers, attempting to somehow soften the fury of his conduct just enough to remove her anxiety over this foreign surge of sensations. Yet he challenged her actions, maneuvering her onto her side and wrapping her in his arms with powerful strokes that embraced the full length of her body.

She was exploding with a sexual rage that left her mind defenseless, the willing partner, bending with each motion of his body, meeting his every demand. In one violent thrust, he penetrated her from behind, merging pain and pleasure with an intensity that forced her to release a gasp that erupted from her very core, shattering the silence of the dark and steamy room. Again and again he drove himself inside her and she rode the waves along with him, groaning in ecstasy as low guttural sounds were set free from deep inside him. His hands reached around to massage her between her legs and she grasped the carpet, burying her face in the fibers that burned into her flesh.

Deeper, harder, more. His force seemed boundless, and she could hear the roaring of his heart. He widened the reach of his palm between her legs, probing her with every finger and heightening the electricity within her until a fierce jolt ignited both their bodies, propelling them off the ground for a sweeping instant and then grinding them into each other's hold.

And then there was calm. It was if the world had halted, the fury and the rage spent. She was still on her side with her face away from him, resting against the strength of his body.

She could not move. She struggled to breathe. The emotions washed over her body as they came to settle peacefully in the center of her being. She closed her eyes, at once exhausted and exhilarated. She felt him pull away from her and fought to speak, yet words failed her and the stillness of her mind refused to let her body take motion. It was only a moment before she felt his return, soft footsteps approaching. Never opening her eyes, she felt him peel the dress away from her throbbing body, and the coolness of the air startled her. He lowered the plush quilt over her trembling skin and gently lifted her head to place a pillow beneath it. Then he lay down beside her and she felt the naked touch of his strong frame supporting her.

In what seemed a moment's time, the rhythm of his breathing told her that he had drifted to sleep, and she wished that she could do the same, but her body was still cooling down, her mind still racing with remnants of the thrill. It was like nothing before. It was what she had only read about, fantasized about. It was frightening. Frightening to accept the fact that her mind had been powerless to control the desires of her body. Frightening to accept that the act of sex, devoid of love or emotion or any of the intangibles she had been raised to believe must accompany that act, could stir her so intensely.

His breathing was like a lullaby, and she wrapped her leg around his, needing to feel the closeness. Opening her eyes, she gazed out at the star-studded sky as if it were a painted backdrop to her dreams. She moved her arms just enough to tighten the fold of the quilt around her. One deep escaping sigh signaled that she was ready to rest. Rest. Her mind craved it, and her body demanded it. She closed her eyes.

It was four in the morning according to the screen on the phone she pulled from the purse that had been haphazardly deposited on the coffee table. She was alone on the carpeting, head resting on her supple pillow, warmed by the soft quilt he had retrieved from the bedroom down the hall. Sometime in the night he had disappeared, leaving her to the solitude of her apartment and reflections of the erotic interlude. Had it really happened? It seemed distant somehow, surreal. Had he really been there? Was she the woman writhing so relentlessly? Why had he exited so abruptly?

She felt a twinge of anxiety take hold of her. What a fool. What a total fool. What had come over her? She was at once humiliated by her own unbridled behavior and terrified of the realization that such pent-up passions lurked deep beneath her surface. They were dangerous urges because she apparently could not control them and she had never before been confronted by their existence. The anxiety and fear quickly evolved into anger. Julianne Sloan was furious with herself for so many things. Why had she suppressed her desires and denied her sexual appetite for so long? Had she lived up to a code of conduct thrust upon her by her parents, Sunday school teachings, and goody-goody classmates she called friends? Why did it take some stranger to unleash her hidden passions? How could she allow a stranger get close enough to do that? And finally, what had her behavior done to jeopardize the potential for a meaningful relationship with Clint Andrews? Would he classify her as a cheap whore, an easy lay? Had she destroyed what could have been? Was it over?

These excruciating thoughts would have punished her through the remainder of the night were she not so utterly exhausted. She rose from the carpet, realizing for the first time that her body was aching from its adventure. Gathering up quilt and pillows, she stumbled into the familiar comfort of her room and collapsed into bed. If only she could sleep forever.

The alarm jolted her awake at nine o'clock n Sunday morning and Julianne rolled over in bed wondering what on earth had prompted her to forfeit the only morning of the week she could actually sleep as late as she liked, hover around the apartment as messy as she liked, linger over her steaming pot of coffee for as long as she liked. That was not even taking into consideration the fact that her departure from sanity the night before had left her drained emotionally as well as physically. Maybe a Sunday visit to Horizons wasn't as great an idea as it seemed a few days earlier, but what the hell. It was too late to do anything about it. The recollection that Clint would be off the premises and cheering on the Cubs eased her anxiety considerably. She needed time to rehearse her mode of behavior before seeing him again. It dawned on her that the busy agenda planned for this Sunday—the day after—might just be a blessing in disguise.

She had convinced Jake to give up his Sunday with Helene by offering to take him and his wife to brunch prior to whisking him away. Helene would go off shopping for a couple of hours while Julianne and Jake schmoozed at the shelter. Good plan. No time for second thoughts now.

She dragged herself out of bed, then into the shower and finally pulled on jeans and a Cubs sweatshirt. No makeup. It was Sunday, and that was Julianne's Sunday gift to herself -- no makeup and no washing her hair. She glanced in the mirror and thought about her look. She wanted the women at the shelter to be comfortable with her, but she didn't want them to think she was dressing down for them. Why was everything so complicated, even getting dressed on Sunday morning. She decided that no matter what she selected, she'd still have doubts about her choice, so she gave her hair a quick brushing, pulled on her boots, and dashed off to meet the Rossis.

One look at Helene and Julianne wondered where the hell

her head had been when she got dressed. Sweats, no makeup ... and unwashed hair! She had been thinking so much about how the women at Horizons would react to hear that she completely overlooked the fact that Helene was bound to show up for brunch looking as she'd just jumped off the cover of *Vogue*. Great. Well, she comforted herself, at least this way Helene wouldn't have to be jealous about Jake spending a Sunday afternoon with his producer. Looking like this, she was no great threat.

As the trio nibbled away on crepes and strawberries, the conversation inevitably turned to the shelter and circumstances of the families living there. Finally, Helene sighed. "I'm sorry. I know I should be more sympathetic, but let's face it. These women are living the lives they made for themselves. If they didn't want their husbands to hit them, they shouldn't have let them. We shape our own lives. We can't just accept whatever fate throws at us. I can't stand people who let themselves become victims."

It sounded logical, actually. Yet Julianne knew things just weren't that simple. Maybe it was her own brush with Allen's violent behavior that revealed the complexity of abusive relationships. Maybe it was experiencing the combination of love and fear and self-doubt. Whatever it was, Julianne recognized the added burden these women shouldered: the burden of being judged by others who could never understand what they'd been through, who could not see that vicimization isn't a simple matter of choice.

Julianne decided to just let Helene babble. There was no motivation to try to influence her mind-set. Instead, Julianne sat back and sipped her coffee, comtemplating what a strange couple Helene and Jake were. There must be something great about her to catch a guy like Jake, she thought. Or it could be that fantastic face and body. Julianne and her single girlfriends still spent countless hours pondering why intelligent men stopped looking for anything beyond a great pair of breasts, shapely legs and a big behind. Maybe Jake thought all women were really like Helene, just as Julianne had begun to think that all men were like Allen. Anyway, Julianne told herself, she'd forfeited a chunk of her precious Sunday for this brunch to finesse pulling Jake away for a few hours and now it was time to get moving. When they rose she and Helene exchanged an air kiss, vowing to get together soon for another brunch. Then Helene ran for a cab, promising not to do too much damage on Michigan Avenue, and Jake and Julianne hopped into his car to start out for Horizons.

"Is Mr. Charming going to greet you with doughnuts and a hug?" Jake teased.

"I wish. But I'm no match for the Cubs." *If only Jake knew,* she thought. *He'd never believe it, never in a million years.* Jake understood her practically better than anyone else did. Sixteen-hour editing sessions and agonizing shoots during broiling Chicago summers and bone-chilling Windy City winters was a fast way to forge a friendship. He realized that Julianne Sloan was a far cry from an easy roll in the hay and, if anything, restrained when it came to her sexual exploits.

"Oh, you're a worthy foe to a day at Wrigley Field. He just doesn't know it yet."

She sat back, smiled and enjoyed the ride as giant raindrops began sliding down the windshield. If she could have had one wish come true at the very moment, it would have been to bury her head in Jake's warm, massive chest and solicit a gigantic hug. Not an enticing, provocative gesture. Just a loving expression of closeness and comfort. There was no one in the world she longed to be hugged by more than Jake Rossi at this very moment. It was a confusing yearning, a need for a friend, a brother, a sensual male presence.

It was safe to fantasize about Jake, stimulating and innocent, as if dreaming of the unattainable. At the same time, she wondered why, having just spent the most erotic night of her life with one man, she was fixating on another. It made no sense. But neither had any aspect of her behavior the past twelve hours. Had it only been twelve hours? The notion seemed impossible.

She turned toward Jake, so lost in thought that she was unaware of the fact that she was staring unabashedly at his mouth. "Are you all right?" he asked, obviously puzzled by her demeanor.

"Of course. Just peachy."

CHAPTER 5

Elisa and Kelly had their sewing materials carefully laid out in front of them on Horizons' living room coffee table. Sunday afternoons together were a ritual, though Elisa knew that in a couple of years, Kelly would be running off with her pack of girlfriends on Sundays, just as she did every other day of the week. That was just part of being a young woman, she knew. But for now, Sundays were their time, and this week their project was to hand stitch beads and sequins on Kelly's new sweatshirt. Kelly sat sketching the designs, while Elisa dug through her sewing box to find threads that matched the colors of the rainbow of beads. Observing Kelly totally focused on her drawing, Elisa realized that this was the happiest she'd seen her daughter in days. If Kelly only knew what her mom had gone through to get her hands on that sewing box, Elisa thought, she would not be enjoying this project at all.

Earlier in the week, when Kelly was commenting on how cool her friends' jeans and T-shirts looked once they'd personalized them with their own artistry, Elisa suggested that the two of them sit down to do the same. At the time, it didn't dawn on Elisa that her sewing box was back at the house and that she didn't really have spare cash to replace it. So one afternoon after dropping Kelly and two of her friends at the movies, she drove to the apartment.

She was certain that Peter would be at work, but just the same, she stood and listened through the door to make extra sure it was silent inside. She hadn't spoken to Peter since leaving. She had left him a note, explaining that she and Kelly had to get away from him because they were afraid of him. It was that simple. No dramatic narrative was provided. Perhaps she was just too numb at the time to go into detail. But she knew how distraught he'd have have been to wake in an empty apartment. She and Kelly couldn't just disappear from the face of the earth, after all. So the brief note was left on the kitchen table, suggesting he not bother trying to find them. They wouldn't be staying with anyone he knew and he could save them all some embarrassment if he avoided calling family and friends. At the bottom of the note, she scribbled that she'd call him in about a week so that they could try to talk things out. She hadn't been back to the apartment until now.

A odd feeling consumed her as she walked through the door. This was her home, yet she felt like a criminal invading someone else's space. She had to be quick and quiet so that neighbors would not hear her and comment to Peter that they'd seen his wife. Once inside, she dashed to the broom closet, where her sewing kit was perched on the top shelf. Then she made a quick stop into her bedroom and Kelly's, gathering some extra clothes and more of Kelly's play things, small items that Peter would never notice as missing.

As she approached the front door to leave, she turned and looked around. It was as if the energy was suddenly sucked out of her body. She fell back against the door, gazing at the rooms that held her precious belongings. A wave of panic surged through her. What was she doing? How was she going to support herself? Was she just overreacting to a family fight? How was she going to survive? How would Kelly survive? And then it hit her. Her precious belongings were not in those rooms. The most valuable thing in her life was her daughter and that daughter was not going to live in jeopardy even for a minute. With that thought, she turned and walked out the door, heading back to Horizons. Her stride was bold, ready, and determined, so unlike that recent day when she'd made her initial exit.

As Elisa sat and matched her threads to Kelly's sequins, she took pleasure in the fact that she'd managed to reenter the apartment and take what was rightfully hers. It was a crucial step in the right direction. Peter had robbed her of years of laughter and loving, self-esteem and pride. She knew deep inside that, given the time to heal, she could return to the person she once was. Those feelings, and the warmth of her daughter beside her, made this Sunday afternoon one of the best she'd experienced in months. Things were far from perfect at Horizons, just as they were far from perfect anywhere, she told herself. But she could breathe here.

The rain kept more families inside the shelter than was typical, and the others seemed to be in fairly good spirits as well. An odd assortment of people it was. There were young women who barely looked old enough to vote. There were others in their thirties who seemed weathered beyond their years. Many of the women had kids who acted out, creating commotions over the littlest things merely to get attention or release their anger. There was one older woman, almost sixty, she seemed. She rarely spoke to anyone and seemed to be the most frail of all the residents. *So many years of being beaten down would turn stone into sand,* Elisa thought whenever this woman caught her eye.

They were from such diverse backgrounds, these people. Yet they shared an emotional experience that transcended race, age, social standing or cultural upbringing. For a few, mingling with others in this setting was stressful rather than offering a unifying effect. Forced to see reflections of their own pain in the faces of so many others proved humiliating, forcing them to withdraw into their shells. They were the minority.

Actually, in the short time Elisa had been at the shelter, she felt she had already made new friends born of a common trauma and hankering for support. Ashaed to share their pain with family or friends, they had been hiding their anguish for so long that it was a monumental relief to be able to let the curtain down and expose their lives for what they were. A spirit of unity tied them together much as Elisa's threads connected the red, silver and gold of her daughter's beads. Though the serenity was interrupted every so often by an infant's cry or a youngster's outburst, this was the most peaceful afternoon many of these families had enjoyed in a very long time.

This was envisioned as an interim environment, a safe place to collect one's thoughts, structure one's plans and prepare to move forward in life. Horizons suggested a ten-week limit on each individual's or family's stay, a liberal timetable by most shelters' standards. But the board of Horizons ventured to be as flexible and nurturing as funding would allow, even agreeing to open its doors to repeat visitors.

Julianne and Jake were surprised by the number of people crowding the living room when they arrived. Perhaps because so many women had been out scouting jobs at the time of their previous visit, they expected to find a sparse group. They moved through the house, scanning the faces in an attempt to target the most inviting faces. Jake followed Julianne's lead and producer's instincts. She sat down on the floor next to Kelly and rested her back against the couch, where Elisa sat stitching the beads to the sweatshirt. The activity gave Julianne the perfect opportunity to ignite a conversation.

"A girl in my building is working on a sweater with sequins that create the American flag. The fifty stars are killing her, though. I think it's going to turn into a design of the thirteen colonies," Julianne joked to Kelly.

"I want flowers," Kelly responded. "My mom's really good at flowers."

Looking up at Elisa, Julianne said, "Yes, I can see that. It looks great. You wearing it somewhere special?"

"The new girl at school is having a slumber party so we can hang out and see her house. We all have to wear something we designed ourselves."

"I'd be in trouble," Julianne said. "I'm not so good at designing things."

"You're on TV, right? You're the guys we saw the other day. How come you're back?"

"Well, I'm not *on* TV. I just work on some shows. I'm Julianne, and this is Jake." As Julianne spoke, she directed her introduction to both Kelly and Elisa. "Is it okay if we talk to you while you're working?" she asked.

"We can talk a little. Most things we probably shouldn't talk about now, though," Elisa responded, gesturing toward Kelly with her head.

Julianne appreciated Elisa's concern over dragging her daughter into an interview. She'd started to rise and move to another area of the room when Elisa placed her hand on her shoulder, gently stopping her. "What is this talking all about?" Elisa asked.

"My television station is looking into doing a show about ... families living in places like Horizons, to help generate support. Will you let me ask you a few things? You only have to talk about what you're comfortable with. If you think I'm out of bounds on anything, just tell me and I'll stop. I'm not here to give anybody a hard time. And I promise not to use anybody's name."

"I'm going up to get my book, Mom, and then read to Coco. I'm done with this drawing." Kelly turned to Julianne. "Coco and I take turns reading chapters out of my books. Her books are kind of babyish, but I have some really good ones."

"Okay, Sweetie, but you two come down here so I have an eye on you, please."

"See you later," Kelly called back to her mom, Julianne, and Jake as she raced upstairs to gather her book and her friend.

Elisa looked after Kelly and commented, "Kelly's doing great here, almost too great. I'm afraid she's keeping everything bottled up inside. She's crazy about her dad. She doesn't ask me much about him, though. I think she's afraid I'll get upset and I'm all she's got right now. I know she's only ten, but I swear she's trying to protect me just the way I'm trying to protect her."

The two women talked for several minutes, and Julianne was surprised at how open Elisa was with her story. "You're lucky you started off with a blabbermouth, huh?" Elisa smiled. "It's just that I've spent so many years saying nothing that now it's pouring out like the floodgates opened up. The truth is, I'm not even sure of what it is that I have to say. Sometimes I feel like my mind has turned to mush.

I guess that if I could add my two cents to your reporting, though, it would be to say that nothing comes easy. If you're stuck in the mud, you've got to get yourself out. And then you've got to wash yourself off and get on with it. No white knight is waiting in the corner to come to your rescue. Every person has to take care of herself."

She looked Julianne straight in the eye. "And one other thing. We're not all freaks in here. We let ourselves think we are, at least at first. Freaks and failures. Well, we're not, and maybe if we start believing that, everyone else will too. I don't know you or what kind of show you're trying to make. Judging from what I see on TV, though, you're probably going to create the same kind of freaks and geeks show everyone else puts on. So keep that in mind, you with your cameras and microphones. We're regular people just like you, and we're trying to fix ourselves up. I guess that's what I want to say."

She turned to Jake, who was seated on the floor next to Julianne and offered a faint smile, suddenly embarrassed by her tirade. "You're sure a quiet one. The strong and silent type, I guess. My Peter never has much to say either."

"But I'm a great listener," Jake answered back. "How'd your Peter do in that department?

"The worst," she said. "I kind of got used to him not listening to me. Maybe that's why I'm such an easy mark for you reporters. I finally have somebody who wants to hear what I have to say."

Women slowly started joining their circle of conversation. They seemed to feed off one another. There were definite patterns of behavior, she discovered, behavior likely attributed to interaction with the men in their lives, resulting in survival mentality. Without exception, all of the women at Horizons had found this place in a panic-filled time when they feared for their lives—not their comfort or safety but their lives or their kids' lives. Each made the move to free herself from her private hell before she had time to talk herself out of it.

"When you stop to think," Marsha shared, "you wind up too scared of not knowing what's gonna happen to you to do what you ought to do. So you stay. At least you know what to expect where you are."

With that, Marsha shot a glance at Elisa and then at a buxom blonde woman seated between them. It was a look that only the three of them, it appeared, understood. Yet it was a strong enough moment to clue Julianne in to the fact that there was another layer of their story to tell, a story of the unexpected. It would have to wait for later, as she could tell this was something not open for group discussion. She leaned back and rested her shoulders against Jake's propped-up knees, letting the dialogue run its own course.

Marsha had assumed a leadership role in this crowd and willingly shared the gruesome history of a five-year marriage that had been marked by no fewer than three escapes to one of the city's scarce safe houses. Her candor was a testament to her philosophy that spilling out the hurt was the surest way to rid oneself of it. Many of the newcomers here had not yet learned that lesson and in an effort to make this point by setting an example, Marsha readily let these strangers from a television station—strangers who vowed to exercise discretion in using her story—hear the humiliating truth of how she lived with her son of a bitch husband for months after first suspecting that he'd been abusing their three-year-old twin girls.

She had only suspected, she explained. She hadn't actually caught him in the act, so she talked herself into believing that the way he patted and stroked and coddled his daughters was natural and that there was something sick inside her that made her suspect anything else. Never mind that her happy, mischievous toddlers had evolved into sullen, cranky little girls. Never mind that she seldom heard laughing and giggles when Daddy went to play with them or volunteered to handle bathing chores. It was easier to convince herself that she was the sick one for even having such evil suspicions than to think that her babies had been violated right under their mommy's watchful eye and that her husband was one of the most disgusting and sick men on earth.

Besides, where would she go with fifty bucks in her pocket, a checking account that never grew beyond double digits, and a fat chance of finding a full-time job with the unemployment rate what it was, no college education, and two kids who needed to be looked after. Her part-time job at the neighborhood bank was all she could handle since her mother constantly reminded her that looking after the twins three days a week was more than most grandmas would do and was the most she could possibly offer.

It wasn't until late one Saturday afternoon when she was washing up little Andrea after a typical backyard skirmish in the mud with her sister that Marsha was horrified to discover Andrea was bleeding from her bottom and was bruised along her inner thigh. Marsha found herself paralyzed, then enraged and then panic-stricken, all in a matter of seconds. She pulled on Andrea's clothes, went out the back door to collect her other daughter, Abigail, loaded them into the car and ran back into the house to grab her purse and the emergency fifty-dollar bill she kept hidden in her makeup drawer. When she passed through the living room, she was confronted by her husband, Kent, who'd seen her loading the girls into the car through the windows behind the TV, where he was watching the Sox take on the Angels. The frenzied state in which she strapped them in and rushed back inside didn't sit right with him and he rose from the couch with his ever-present can of beer in hand to block her way as she attempted to make a quick exit.

He persisted in asking her where they were going. The stores were due to close soon and she'd already been to her mother's that morning. All she could do was mutter, "I'm just going for a ride. I'm just going for a ride." But he didn't buy it and headed out to fetch his daughters from the car. She chased after him, knowing there was no way in hell he was going to get his hands on her babies. When he was just a few feet from the car in their driveway she grabbed the rake that was lying against the front porch and slammed the long hard handle across his ribs as hard as she could, hurling him off his feet. Once on the ground, she struck him with the stick twice more, each blow more fierce than the one before it. She locked herself in the car with the girls, turned the key, and drove. And drove. And drove.

She had no idea where she was going, where he wouldn't think to look. With the gas tank nearly full, she headed for I-94 and two hours later arrived at her cousin's apartment on the outskirts of Milwaukee.

She deposited the twins there, staying long enough to make sure they were at ease and comfortable with her cousin Jonathan and his wife, Barbara. She wanted to stay there for the night but couldn't risk showing up late for her part-time job at the bank the next day. So she drove the two hours back into Chicago and thought about a safe house a woman at Gymboree had mentioned one day when she suspected that Marsha and the girls might be in trouble. The woman had written down the phone number and forced it into Marsha's palm. Humiliated, she waited until the woman turned away and then tucked the slip of paper inside her wallet, where, at a rest stop midway between Milwaukee and Chicago, she found it and placed a desperate call. The volunteer who answered confessed that they were not only out of beds but out of couches and chairs as well and suggested that she contact this new shelter that had just opened and might not yet be overrun. Before losing her nerve, she clicked her phone's search engine and searched the name she had been given. Shelby Hacker came to her rescue with directions to Horizons.

Marsha knew that she could have brought Andrea and Abigail with her, but she chose not to, in part because her cousin's place was a more homelike environment for them at the tender age of three. Mostly, however, it was because she couldn't even look her own babies in the eyes without wanting to die from guilt at having let them endure such abuse. She was a rotten mother. She knew it even if they didn't, and she didn't deserve their love. Maybe one day she would earn it back, but for now she was content to take the bus up to Milwaukee every weekend—her 2004 Corolla couldn't handle the miles—and spend time with her daughters, who had already been enrolled in a children's counseling center her cousin had managed to track down.

Shelby was coaxing Marsha to go into therapy, as well, and Marsha was considering it, although she wasn't quite ready. Maybe next week. At least her cousins were willing to keep the girls while she, Kent, and the lawyers fought things out. She was realistic enough to know that there was only so much fighting she could expect her lawyer to do on the meager retainer she was able to pony up. This was of paramount concern, considering the circumstances of her separation and her reluctance to file a police report which would subject the kids to a horrific, invasive investigation. An ugly custody battle was looming down the road. She needed strong legal counsel, which meant that she needed a better job, and the unemployment office wasn't a bundle of opportunity. Therapy for herself didn't seem a priority.

It was the first of many stories Julianne and Jake listened to that evening. As the women unraveled their personal miseries, Julianne noticed how easily they spoke among themselves--no shame among sisters. When the pain of the conversation grew intense or triggered aching memories, many sets of eyes swelled with tears. They felt the others' torment. They shared the others' frustration. Julianne and Jake were immersed in the heartache.

A couple of the kids wandered into their circle in the living room, calling for their moms' overdue attention. As Julianne got to her feet she asked permission to come speak with them again. Each nodded approval, stressing that talking like this was fine but that they would never allow their names or faces to be used on TV. Julianne reassured them.

Just as she was about to leave, Julianne turned and walked back to the edge of the couch, where Marsha and Elisa shared a hushed exchange. "Okay if I call to ask if you'll meet me at that diner on the corner for breakfast one day this week?" she asked softly. The producer in her needed to probe into something shared between the two women that apparently was not easily disclosed. Whatever secret these ladies shared must be devastating, she realized. For if they could handle discussing the cruelty, anguish, and humiliation of their marriages in front of strangers, what terrible thing could have prompted the private look she'd noticed earlier?

"Maybe coffee," Elisa responded. "I don't like to leave Kelly by herself for breakfast. She's still not really used to it here." Then she looked down. "There are lots of things even I can't get used to."

"I'll call you," Julianne said, turning to join Jake at the door. By the time they stepped outside, the rain had turned into a mild mist that fell softly on their faces, washing away the stress as they stepped from one world into another. It was not until they had walked halfway down the block that emotional exhaustion slowed Julianne's stride. She felt as if she'd been bombarded with so much suffering in such a short period of time that she didn't know what had hit her. Her legs felt as heavy as her heart as she ambled toward the car.

"I really gave you a fun-filled Sunday, didn't I?" she said to Jake.

He put his arm around her shoulders, wrapping her up the way her dad used to when she was having a rotten day. It felt warm and safe and loving. "Something tells me," he said, squeezing her arm, "that we've just begun this journey. Don't let it drain you or you'll never get the job done. And this is a hell of a lot more important than that story about celebrity psychics we worked on last week," he said with a smile, trying to raise her spirits. She wrapped her arm around his waist where it remained until they reached the car and he tenderly deposited her in the front seat.

When he dropped her off in front of her apartment building, he kissed her on the cheek and laughed. "Consider yourself lucky. You can go up there, grab a pint of ice cream, and stretch out with an old movie. I have at least two hours of Helene's shopping stories to pretend to listen to, plus a fashion show of everything she bought today. What I wouldn't give for a night of Netflix!"

"Good luck," she said, slamming the door. Then she leaned down and said through the halfway opened window, "You're the best, Jake." With that, she turned and went inside.

CHAPTER 6

A bowl of popcorn in her lap paired with *Pretty Woman* on TV nearly transported Julianne into another place and time, a place where she didn't have to obsess over her own conduct or cast judgment on the lives of others. Had she not been out of Ben & Jerry's, chocolate chip cookie dough would have definitely outranked the Orville Redenbacher bag as the menu item du jour. The past twenty-four hours had been too hard, a merry-go-round ride that left her head spinning. Seclusion and a double dollop of butter were her cure for the blues that set in shortly after Jake took leave.

But the bowl was approaching empty, Richard Gere had swept Julia Roberts off her feet, and closing credits filled the screen. Surely she had indulged in this catatonic state long enough. She deposited the bowl in the kitchen sink and reached for her laptop on the table, opening folders prepared by Tina. There were extensive case histories and stats on domestic violence. There, at the kitchen table, she did her damnedest to focus on her work, an escape route that had enabled her to overlook her personal issues for years. Fortunately, the material was riveting, holding her attention and removing any semblance of self-pity. Her life was heaven compared to what she was absorbing from the research.

The buzzer cut through the silence with a startling presence. Late night interruptions made her uneasy. *Thank goodness for doormen*, she thought pushing the speaker button.

"Yes?"

"You have a guest, Ms. Sloan. Mr. Andrews."

Clint was there. And without calling first. That implied intimacy, all right. She was at once relieved and unnerved. She was a wreck. No makeup, a stretched-out old sweatshirt, and crew socks. She'd have time to yank off the socks, but not much more. No glam image tonight. Welcome to reality. Well, what the hell. She giggled, checking out her reflection in the glass panel of the oven door.

His smooth entry as she cracked open the door was evidence that Clint Andrews was not a man to waste time teasing passion's fire. He grabbed her the second the front door closed behind him and jutted his tongue between her lips before she had time to offer a welcome. In spite of a full day of admonishing herself for her lack of discipline the night before, she melted, barely able to stay on her feet as the spark inside burst into full flame. She caught her breath finally and got hold of her senses long enough to remember to turn off the coffeepot. He trailed her into the kitchen, teasing that he was hungry all right and that he had his own entree in mind. He smelled of beer, undoubtedly from the game and the night out with his buddies which followed. The aggressive stance he displayed upon entering the apartment hinted that he may have downed one drink too many. But his skillful maneuvering quickly dispelled any concern that he had crossed the line into drunkenness.

After spending hours that day convincing herself that his middle of the night exit signaled lack of interest, he was now lusting after her feverishly. She wanted to slow things down, to entice him with her kisses, and gradually, seductively feed his desires and satisfy her own. But this was not to be. The fires burned too ferociously. She was pinned against the kitchen counter, and his hands were grabbing her buttocks as he rubbed the front of his body back and forth against hers. She could feel his arousal and the intensity of his hunger for her was its own brand of aphrodisiac.

"I couldn't stop thinking about you all day. It was as if I could still taste you, feel me inside you." The words were whispered in her ear as his tongue trickled down her neck.

She offered no reply. Her only response came from her body as she reached down to stroke him and release him from the entrapment of his slacks. Her touch set him wild, and he reached under the sweatshirt to bury his fingers inside her panties, then tearing them away and pushing himself inside her with a powerful thrust that raised her onto the cool tile counter. She wrapped her legs around his waist and dug her mouth deep into his neck as he rode her relentlessly. His grip moved up from her torso, and while he pulled her against him with one hand, the other tightened around her neck, gripping her throat so forcefully that she became as fearful as she was excited. As he pounded inside her and strained to enclose her throat in the expanse of his palm, she could barely breathe. She needed oxygen. She needed to climax. She could not catch her breath. More. More. Yes. Yes. There. It was over. They had peaked. He loosened his hold. She was breathing.

The strangest thing was that as he withdrew from her, she could not look at his face. She did not feel alive as she had the night before. She felt self-conscious, awkward, embarrassed. This wasn't raw passion taking hold of their senses as it had one day earlier. This was animal sex. Intercourse. Fucking. Nothing romantic or nurturing about it. Fucking. She hated the sound of that word and uttered it only in moments of consuming anger or frustration.

Clint came unannounced into her apartment to fuck her and she had let him, responding with the urges of a love-starved fool. It was pathetic. She was pathetic. And that was the cause of her unexpected humiliation. At that very moment, she didn't like herself very much. Nor did she like him. Yet she knew that once he was out of her sight, she would do little more than relive this encounter over and over again, desperately attempting to rekindle the ecstasy in her own mind and spin it into romance. He would be the protagonist of her dreams, dominating her waking and sleeping hours. Was it the man or the intoxicating sex? Was she falling in love with him or falling victim to the tantalizing tricks he performed on her deprived body? She didn't even know who he was. She wasn't even sure she knew who she was.

She sighed with relief when he stepped away from the kitchen and wandered into the dimly lit living room. The harsh florescents of the kitchen were cruelly revealing. He stood at the window with his back toward her, making no attempt at conversation. Finally, from the dining area several feet away, it was Julianne who broke the silence. "You must be tired. It's been a long day."

"It's getting late, isn't it? I almost didn't come by. But I could taste you in my mind."

After what they had experienced together, she didn't expect to be embarrassed by his words, but she was, choosing to redirect the dialogue.

"Let's just get some rest. We can talk tomorrow," she softly responded.

Clint turned and faced her for the first time since pinning her against the cabinet. His gaze caused her face to turn a deep shade of crimson, and the heat intensified as he stepped toward her. He lifted her chin and planted a single kiss on the tip of her nose. Then he strode to the front door and let himself out. She was glad for his exit. Still, the next few hours were devoted to bringing their erotic escapades to life over and over again in her mind, as expected.

Why was she so famished for his affection ... or was it a matter of any man's affection? She couldn't answer that gnawing question. The sexual appeasement was a treasure with a hefty price tag, that of her dignity. She was none too pleased with herself for coughing up the ante to a man she'd met only days before. She had to get a grip on herself. No one was there to do it for her.

That message resonated in her mind. Where had she heard that theory? Elisa Tate. Her words floated through the recesses of Julianne's consciousness. Elisa was right. Each person was on her own. There were no white knights, no handsome heroes. This was real life, not the movies or a contrived TV drama. There was only the power of one's own soul to rely upon. And she knew damn well that her soul had a hell of a lot of power. She need only to find it.

A half-empty bottle of Merlot sparkled in the flickering light of the four candles of varying shapes and sizes that burned on the coffee table and rich cherrywood mantel at the Rossi household. The other half bottle had been slowly and lovingly consumed over the course of the past hour and a half as Helene Rossi waited for her husband to come home on this Sunday afternoon ... actually, evening now. The fact that he was running late was no surprise. When it came to his job or the multitude of tasks involving his cohort, Julianne Sloan, Jake was always late. The only surprise today was how annoyingly late he was.

She was proud of the way she took the news that he needed to spend a few hours of his only day off doing research with Julianne— research for free, to make matters worse. Helene had intentionally been a damn good sport about it. Lately she'd been henpecking Jake about his schedule, his need to demand a raise along with better hours. Plus, her pleas to finally take the vacation to the Greek Islands they'd been talking about since before they got married had become highly persistent. She was conscious of the fact that she had evolved into a world-class nag who could barely stand herself these past few weeks, but she couldn't seem to help herself. Jake had been neglecting her, putting all else before their marriage, and this was her way of punishing him for it. Maybe she was punishing herself too. After all, she was the mastermind of this marriage.

Helene Rossi did not like herself as much as she used to. Aware of the arrogance, she admitted to herself that at one time, she was the woman she most admired in all the world. At age nineteen, she'd signed on with Elite Modeling after being spotted at an event, previewing the fall line of America's fashion kingpins. It was Chicago's most prestigious fashion event, held annually at the Apparel Center and attracting the country's leading designers. In order to do justice to the creations they would be flaunting, the extravaganza enlisted cream of the crop models from the Windy City's top agencies.

After only eighteen months of doing mostly runway work, Helene Randall was easily on her way to becoming Chicago's most sought-after model, despite—or maybe because of—the fact that she was far more fully endowed than her peers. It seemed designers were at last in stride with the public's fondness for a voluptuous bustline. The changeover was coming just in time for this nineteen-year-old beauty who stood five feet eleven inches in her stocking feet and was eager to shake up Chicago's modeling scene with her 32DD chest.

She strutted the runway at the event as if she owned it, catching every eye in the room. Two weeks later, she signed with Elite, relocated to Manhattan and moved into a modest loft in SoHo, where she could roam the art galleries, collect earrings from the street vendors, and sip espresso to her heart's delight.

The only thing to dampen the excitement of making it to New York and going big time—all American models knew that New York was the only city that mattered on a résumé—was leaving behind a man who had just recently appeared in her life and showed great potential: Jake Rossi.

Jake had been shooting the spring fashion event for a consortium of designers. It was a moonlighting job he undertook to supplement his income from the TV station. He was grabbing some behind-the-scenes shots when he backed up to do some fancy move that would capture the lights kicking off the silver and gold sequins on a Marc Jacobs creation when he took one step too many and bumped into a pedestal that the design assistants used to hold pins and clamps and Velcro for last-minute adjustments. At this particular moment, however, it was also holding an eight-ounce Styrofoam cup filled to the brim with piping hot coffee.

Jake's one step too many sent the pedestal toppling, with an assortment of pins and tacks following suit, and the cup of scalding coffee splashed onto the featerhlight dressing gown Helene was wearing as she prepared to slip into a white silk cocktail dress and jacket by Ralph Lauren. The boiling brew seeped right through the gown, setting her flesh afire and just missing the dress. The frenzy that followed would have had one believing the sky had come tumbling down, instead of an eight-ounce cup of coffee. As the throng of assistants, seamstresses and accessory staff rushed to the aid of the helpless white silk ensemble, Helene stood ignored and in pain. Scalding coffee hurt.

Slighted by everyone else, Helene allowed Jake to usher her to the closest source of relief, a giant tub-like sink used by the maintenance crew. With cold water running full speed, he soaked a towel he'd grabbed from an accessories table and wrapped it fully around her tiny waist. He was only too happy to escape from the screams of terror and dirty looks prompted by his clumsiness. He was even happier when he managed to engage Helene in a feisty conversation about screwed-up priorities of the rag business. It was a conversation they continued over hefty glasses of Roditys and sizzling plates of saganaki in Greektown later that night.

In the two weeks prior to her departure to New York, they'd gone out six times, and it was not until their fourth date that Jake shared the crushing news that he was due to be married in five months. Nice of him to tell her, she remembered saying. She knew that she should have cut him off cold turkey after that, but by then it was apparent that she'd be leaving town anyway, so what the hell. She indulged in two more dates and on what she knew would be their final time together in Chicago, she invited Jake up her apartment and into her bed. She never regretted it. She just went on her way.

Once in Manhattan, she immersed herself in all the city had to offer. For a first-time New Yorker, there was a lot to see, and she was in no rush to become entangled with a man just yet. It was comfortable having no strings and a pocketful of cash, and Helene was enjoying herself just fine. So when Jake Rossi called after she'd been gone only a month and said that he was coming to New York to shoot interviews for a rock 'n' roll documentary, Helene decided to enjoy herself some more. He'd be going back home to his job and fiancée in a few days, and no one would be the wiser. Besides, if there was one thing Helene Randall loved more than money and clothes, it was sex. Well, she loved it more than clothes, anyway.

Jake was scheduled to work in Manhattan for four days. He shot by day and played by night or played by day and shot at night, depending who he was interviewing and where—music company execs in their posh offices on Avenue of the Americas or legendary artists still letting out steam in out-of-the-way music holes in the East Village. But when he extended his stay to spend the weekend with Helene and they experienced two incomparable days of romance, New York style, she was more than a little reluctant to escort him back to the airport and waiting arms of his bride-to-be.

For the first time in her life, Helene fell prey to the green-eyed monster and jealousy, which overpowered her to the extent that she packed up her life three weeks later and put her career on the back burner in favor of a new pursuit: marriage. Once back in Chicago, it was easy as pie to split up Jake and his fiancée. Helene knew her way around men, and with a figure most women would die for—in addition to masses of thick honey-red curls falling halfway down her back and a set of green eyes peering at the world from behind luxuriously long lashes—she never was one to back away from female competition, engagement ring or not.

She got Jake, the ring, the house in the suburbs, and the his 'n' hers charge accounts. What she didn't get was the chance to find out if she had the right stuff to make it to the top in the modeling world. In a matter of weeks, she had catapulted into the inner circle, been close enough to taste the glory, then packed it all in for a marriage license, a two-car garage, and a man she truly adored when he didn't make it so damn difficult to do so by coming home long after the sun had set on his only day off.

By the time Jake walked through the door, Helene already had rehearsed her repertoire of speeches, all proven to trigger grand apologies, guilt, vows for improvement, and, most recently, a nice hot argument. But when she saw the innocence with which he approached her to plant a warm hello kiss on her forehead, she realized there was little use in instigating a fight. He wasn't a bastard. He wasn't a louse. He was just a nice guy who loved his job more than his wife—maybe because it was the right job and not the right wife. It seemed a waste of time to put them both through another miserable evening that wouldn't change anything.

They split the remaining half bottle of wine, ordered a Gino's pizza, and settled in to watch a movie on Netflix about a couple coping with divorce after twenty-five years of marriage. Great fun. When he'd run out of excuses for the yawns and lack of responsiveness, he threw in the towel and admitted he needed to get some sleep. Helene dove for the magazines, killing a little time until she went into the bedroom to join her husband.

A single shaft of sunlight cut through the narrow slit separating the edge of the vertical blinds from the window frame. Dawn had broken only minutes earlier, and the stark rays of daylight had not yet been allowed to infiltrate the dark confines of the office. There was a stillness that seemed natural for this hour, the serenity of a fresh day waiting to be started.

Only the groaning disrupted the tranquility—deep, savage groans that conveyed rage more than pain or discomfort. A large, worn canvas bag rested against the inside door, a black-and-white checked raincoat draped over the mound. On the taut leather sofa, two bodies could be seen in the faint light that filtered through the cracks uninvited. The shape of a woman, small and slender, was nearly obliterated by that of a man, hunched over her with the his broad physique. She lay silent as he thrust himself inside her, his hand entwined in the long mass of auburn hair that fell below her shoulders. He was starting his day in his most pleasurable way.

With a giant heave, he pulled himself from her and disappeared into the small bathroom adjoining his office. She lay there silently, as if in a trance, afraid to move, afraid to rouse trouble. Her face was bruised in several places. The left side of her lips were swollen to the point of distortion, a bluish ring framed the outer edge of her left eye, and a long deep scratch marred her face from just above her left ear to her chin. Yet she didn't appear to be in pain, only in shock. The physical agony had been inflicted hours before, just after midnight, when her drunken husband returned from an evening of entertaining his old college roommate who was passing through Chicago on the way to a family reunion in Indianapolis. They had quite a time, those two, taking each other on in chugalug challenges, just as they did in the old days, reclaiming their college titles.

Wayne and Joey shared everything when they roomed together at the U of I, including the title of beer pong champions at their frat house. And now, when they stumbled through the door at four in the morning, Wayne was still willing to share everything with his bachelor buddy Joey, including his sofa, the contents of his refrigerator, and, amazingly enough, his wife, Maggie.

He jarred her awake, stripping off the covers and pulling her into the kitchen to make sandwiches. He hadn't even given her time to pull on a robe and she rushed through the job at lightning speed, embarrassed to have Joey eying her in the skimpy teddy. She spun around to return the jars and meat to the fridge and felt Joey rubbing up against her as she juggled the items. Annoyed with his drunken behavior, she called for Wayne, softly at first, until she felt the force of Joey's arms tighten around her waist, then ferociously. Wayne never returned to the kitchen, preferring to flop into bed fully clothed while his buddy enjoyed his unparalleled hospitality.

Her piercing screeches irritated Joey, up for a feisty encounter but not one so noisy as to alarm the neighbors or give Wayne cause to rethink this friendly gesture. So he cracked her a few times in the face, just to quiet her down. She was thrown back against the kitchen sink, breathless with disbelief. He was all over her now, pulling down the straps of her teddy to lick and bite on her breasts. She began reaching wildly, grasping for anything she could get her hands on to defend herself. A single pot sat in the dish drainer, drying from that night's dinner. With a giant swing, she crashed it over Joey's head, sending him hurling backward. He lunged for her, stunned, and the jagged fingernail of his right hand tore into her face as he attempted to grab on to her mane. Now in control, she recoiled and pushed him away. He grumbled as he fell to his knees, curling into a ball on the linoleum, more a result of the alcohol than the blow to his head.

Maggie ran to the bedroom, where she found her husband passed out in bed. She stopped dead in her tracks, paralyzed by bewilderment as she stared at his snoring body. It was horrible enough when *he* hit her. She had learned to endure his fits of rage. But to accept such savage treatment from a stranger—to have her own husband pass her around like she was a twenty-buck whore— that was too much. Finally too much. She took her purse, threw some clothes into her canvas gym bag and rushed to grab a coat from the closet. She ran into the drizzling night air, walking briskly toward the corner and the twenty-four-hour food mart down the block. There she fished out the phone from her purse, though she had no idea who she could call upon at such an outrageous hour.

Her sister, Renee, refused to take her in anymore, since she had returned to Wayne twice in the past following bloody beatings that resulted in fleeing to her sister's home for asylum. She dialed her father's number, but there was no answer. This was probably his week on the road. Tears mingled with the tiny droplets of blood from the scratch on her cheek. Standing on a corner outside a mini-market at four-thirty in the morning was hardly safe, and she seemed to have run out of options. She scrolled through her notes app on her phone, searching for the announcement Renee had forwarded after reading it on Facebook. It announced some shindig being held to fund a new women's shelter. Renee thought the item might inspire her sister to get help since she had lost hope of getting through to Maggie and could no longer tolerate witnessing her sister's demise. Maggie read the name of the shelter in the announcment and proceeded to search for the number of Horizons.

Half an hour later, a single canvas bag in tow, she was met at the doorway of the shelter by the man who had answered her call. He had stopped by the safe house in the early hours of the morning, too stimulated to sleep. With no better activity to occupy his time, he relieved the overnight hotline attendant of her duties so that she could fix herself something to eat in the kitchen and picked up the phone to receive the early-morning call. Maggie's call. So anxious was he to welcome her to this sanctuary that he waited for her on the front porch, ushering her into his office before the doorbell or tumult of her arrival garnered attention from the residents or attendant who had returned to her place at the phone.

He presumed her to be helpless, hurting, with nowhere to turn. A shelter was always the last resort. This he had learned early in the job. Now her mind was surely numb, he assumed. She would do anything to find harbor from the night and the terror of homelessness. Anything. Including allow her savior to prey upon her vulnerability by spreading her legs apart on his fine leather sofa in exchange for a clean, warm room when he was through with her. To him, it seemed a benign act of submission in exchange for a place to anchor herself. It made perfect sense to him.

To Maggie, it was all a daze, happening before she could process the reality of her desperate predicament. No one had prepared her for this possibility. No magazines, websites or interviews with women on the six o'clock news had ever shed light on this unthinkable circumstance. It happened too fast, while she lingered over the edge of sanity. It happened, and then it was over.

He returned from the bathroom, staring at the bold shaft of sunlight that reminded him that the others would soon begin stirring. Never looking at her, he walked to the door and lifted her satchel and coat. She trailed after him quietly until he deposited her in a nine-by-twelve room at the end of the hall. He advised her that he'd see to it she'd be safe and comfortable. He said he would explain her situation to the house manager and morning phone attendant, who would be reporting for work shortly. She'd be better off keeping details of her arrival to a minimum. Her tentative nod indicated that she understood his message.

Maggie sat on the edge of the bed, too stunned to speak. She had avoided the rape of one man, only to fall victim to another. She had gathered up the courage to reach for a helping hand, only to be brutalized by it. She now prayed to fall into the oblivion of sleep.

He sat motionless behind his desk, listening for the changing of the guard at the attendant's desk. He'd underplay the explanation of the newcomer, knowing that the arrival of a weary stranger could pass under the radar with ease. His word was gold. He was, after all, the man known to be as generous with his time as he was open with his heart. He loved his new shelter, his contribution to society.

He swung around in his chair, leaning back and reaching for the cord to the blinds, twisting the chain to invite the clean, bright spears of morning sunlight into the sleepy office. The golden beams cast a radiant glow on the contented face of Clint Andrews.

CHAPTER 7

Each Monday at three in the afternoon, the TV station management team met in the third-floor conference room to discuss revenue performance and pressing matters for the upcoming week. Julianne wasn't sufficiently high in rank to attend these meetings on a regular basis. However, were she to have a specific programming item to present, she would be welcomed for what she called her dog and pony show. Without winning over the sales and promotions departments, it was impossible to get a go-ahead for any programming initiative. She hadn't participated in any of these management gatherings since her immediate supervisor, Pam Avery, went on maternity leave. Pam was the program manager and the woman who'd hired Julianne. They had a warm, trusting relationship. Julianne admired the way Pam held her own as the only female department head at the station. It was a boys' club all right, and with the project Julianne had on her mind, the boys' club mentality could prove fatal.

Earlier in the day, Julianne had called the station's general manager, Ted Marshall, and asked if she could pitch a concept for a prime-time special. He invited her to stop up at the start of the meeting but to make her presentation quick, as the station was experiencing a major drop in ad sales and he didn't want to take too much time away from matters of revenue. It was bad enough that she had to pitch a topic like domestic violence to macho management.

Now, she thought with a sigh, she had to do it at a time when ad sales were crashing and a quick way to a quick buck was all that mattered. Still, at five minutes after three, she entered Boys' Town and presented her proposal for an all-out station campaign devoted to the crisis of family violence.

It would launch with a documentary, she began. She and her staff could handle that around their other duties, with minimal overtime, since hiatus was coming up anyway. The doc would be fortified by a series of public service announcements that would rotate through the on-air schedule. They'd feature the station's family of personalities—news anchors and reporters—along with local celebrities like players from the Bears or Bulls or either of Chicago's baseball teams. The PSAs would convey a variety of messages, some flagging the warning signs of abuse, others reminding that abuse affects both genders, some targeting victims who didn't know where to turn when life at home was a living hell. Each would be punctuated with a hotline number to a family crisis center. In an effort to rally support as well as acquiesce to his rank, Julianne turned to Don McBain, vice president of sales, to suggest that the sales department might perhaps find a community-minded advertiser to sponsor the station's own hotline instead of plugging into the local branch a national network. Either way, she concluded, the hotline tie-in was a must, as was the station's need to latch on to a long overdue community service campaign.

The eight men at the table sat back in their chairs, toying with their shiny pens and perusing the e-mails on their iPhones. As she spoke, she took note of the glances they exchanged. They were clearly enduring her speech, not really listening to it. Then, Don McBain sat up in his grandiose fashion and prepared to pontificate. She recognized the posture immediately, even before he uttered a word. It was the way he carried himself whenever he was about to cut those creative programming people down to size.

Looking her straight in the eye with a glare intended to shut *her* up and the *proposal* down, his sharp tongue was ready. "If you stayed up all night, Julianne, looking for a topic that advertisers wouldn't touch with a ten-foot pole, you couldn't have done a better job. Wife beaters. Yeah. I can see the dollars pouring in. Easy sell! Let's do two specials and then we can go out of business altogether."

"We're not just here for the easy sell. Believe me, I'm not blind to the revenue shortfall. I need my job just like the rest of you. But this is a topic begging for attention. Every other station in town has a pet cause they've embraced, and we've done nothing. We can get great public exposure out of this. And awards. Besides, Don, you're the best sales guy in the business. You are the only person I know who can find a way to sell this."

That last comment was Pam's contribution to the pitch. Julianne had called her at home that morning to ask for advice since she knew what a tough sell this would be. Pam had counseled her to appeal to his inflated male ego. "Make him look like a schmuck if he doesn't back the idea. You know, stroke his ego, tell him how only he could take a show like the one you're proposing and actually make it work—that's how good he is. Without sales in your corner, the show is as good as dead."

She followed Pam's plan almost word for word. As it turned out, it was solid advice. Don came around, partly out of pride and partly because he could see that Ted Marshall really sparked to the idea of introducing a public service campaign, especially one that would target female viewers, a key audience demo for advertisers. Ten minutes later, she returned to her office with a green light to proceed.

Her staff was surprised but thrilled at the news of the special. They were itching for a chance to work on something meaty--steak ratther than *Sizzle*--even if it meant overtime. Jake and Tina were especially pleased. Tina pulled up her contacts and plunged into research. She would be Julianne's senior producer for the show. It was Tina's passion that blazed through the Horizons story file in the first place, igniting Julianne's fire.

After apprising the staff and making sure that everyone's regular assignments for *Chicago Sizzle* were covered, Julianne closed her door and put in a call to Clint to share the good news. He made a fuss over her powers of persuasion and rambled on about what this would mean to so many women. Then came an awkward pause in the conversation. With no more business to discuss, the dialogue was about to transition into one of intimacy and she had no way of gauging his frame of mind. Had he lost interest in her? Respect? The pause grew deadly.

"So," he finally said, "how do you feel about dinner with a man with whom you're doing such important business?" He was being flirtatious and charming. All was not lost.

"Fine. As long as you're buying."

"Better than that," he replied. "I'm cooking. Saturday at eight. I'll text the address."

"I'll bring dessert," she chimed in.

The diner was nearly deserted at eleven in the morning. Just a few neighborhood regulars hung out at the counter, slurping down coffee and dragging on cigarettes as they shot the bull with their server. Julianne was at the corner table, anxiously gazing out the window for a sign of Elisa and Marsha. They had warned her that they might be a little late, depending on what was involved in getting Kelly settled for the day—Elisa wouldn't leave until Kelly's plans were in place. Julianne did her best to wait patiently; patience was not one of her finest traits. As the busboy poured coffee refill number three, she spotted Marsha rounding the corner.

"Well, it's your lucky day. You've got me all to yourself," Marsha said nervously as she slid into the booth across from Julianne. "Elisa's not feeling so good today."

"What's wrong?"

"She finally talked to her husband last night. She said it was okay to tell you or I wouldn't say anything. He put a lot of heat on her to come home. The usual: 'I can't believe I've been so lousy to you and my kid. I just looked at this cruise brochure so we can go away to get back on track. I'm nothing without you, baby.' The typical crap. New to her, though. It got her all mixed up. She doesn't feel so good, like I said."

"She won't go back to him will she? I mean, she knows what he's like," Julianne said.

"That's just it," Marsha smirked. "At least she knows what *he's* like."

"I don't get it," Julianne said, truly baffled.

"Nothing. Forget it."

"What? I heard that same tone of voice the other day when you talked about not knowing what to expect in life. What it is?" Julianne asked.

"It's not worth talking about. Besides it's not my business. But I'll say this: Men are men are men. They may dress differently and drive different cars and work at different jobs, but they're all the same inside. You probably already know that, though."

"Is Elisa involved with another man? Is that what brought this thing with her husband to a head? Is she caught up in a relationship with another man?"

"She's caught all right. But it's not what you're thinking. Anyway, I can't speak for Elisa," Marsha added.

Julianne, in producer mode, would not be put off so easily. "You told me she said it was okay to talk to me. So talk to me. Why doesn't Elisa feel so good? What's she caught in?"

"If I tell you, you can't do anything with it. You can't put it in your story or tell anybody about it. Not until Elisa says it's okay herself. Can you promise me that?"

Julianne nodded. "What's going on?"

"Andrews. He's ... he's, you know, forcing some of the women ..." Marsha's voice trailed off.

Julianne's stomach seemed to roll over, and she felt her face become numb, then distorted with anger. What was the motivation for such an ugly lie? "Forcing?" She paused to let the meaning sink in. "Clint Andrews is ... making women sleep with him?" Julianne asked in total disbelief. Her tone conveyed distrust.

Marsha seemed to recoil. "Listen—thanks for the coffee, but today isn't a good day for me. I've got to run. Let's just make like this talk never happened." She scooted to the edge of the booth and started getting up.

"No, wait. Don't go yet. I'm sorry. It's just that you really took me by surprise. I mean, it's the last thing I would have expected to be going on at a safe house." She was really thinking that it was absolutely the most unlikely thing she'd expect to hear about a man she had invited into her bed and her body. It was a nauseating comment, and if it was true, she had made a horrific mistake.

"Are you sure he's forcing women? I mean, it's got to be a lonely time for everybody, and maybe it's just happening on its own." Julianne regretted the words as soon as they left her lips. It was a stupid, condescending and offensive thing to say. She was annoyed that the thought had even occurred to her. But she would be even more annoyed if the accusation had been fabricated for some inexplicable reason. She had to probe deeper.

Marsha grew livid at Julianne's predictable reaction: assigning responsibility for the situation to the women. So typical. They were always to blame. Their husbands told them so. Their parents told them so. So why should this high-class TV person be any different? "Look, I've got nothing to gain by telling you any of this. It's not like there's a big prize for dishing dirt on Clint Andrews. You asked me what's wrong, and I told you. Now, I've got to go."

"I'm sorry," Julianne blurted out. Marsha turned toward her, and the two of them shared a long, intense stare. "I'm sorry," Julianne repeated. She didn't want her to leave, not before clarifying things. Maybe it was an innocent error. Marsha might have misinterpreted something that was said, something she saw. Julianne's voice imparted a tone of desperation as she reached to touch the accuser's hand.

Marsha settled back down in the booth. "The thing is, when you've just gotten up the nerve to turn your back on your husband and your home and your things and you're trying to get your insides strong enough to put the pieces together, this place is like heaven. I mean, it's supposed to be. It never dawns on you that a whole other kind of trouble looms ahead. It catches you off guard. You're totally desperate. There's no place to turn. You've already been brainwashed into believing that you're worthless. So when this guy says put out or get out, there's not much choice, is there?"

Marsha took pause to gather her thoughts, stirring her coffee nervously. Never looking up, feeling almost guilty, she went on. "I could tell he was starting to put the moves on me, just the way he touched me when he'd pass by in the hall and stuff. Always when Shelby was busy doing something in the front office. Then one morning he was standing in the upstairs hallway real early. His office was in the back on the first floor and he never came upstairs, had no call to, really. It was just women and kids up there, and Shelby was the one who we all talked to if we needed anything. But there he was, standing and making like he was fixing the fuse box at the end of the hallway. It must have been before seven. And you know how it is when it's all women around you, kind of like a dorm. We shared the bathrooms, so we'd go walking down the halls in our nighties and underwear and stuff. Well, there he was getting an eyeful. And he didn't even try to hide it. He just kept fiddling with the circuit breakers and peeking at the girls making their morning visit to the john.

"It really pissed me off. I felt like asking him which gave him a bigger charge, the fuses in the wall or the females in the hall. I can be a real smart ass sometimes. But I thought better of it. The last thing I needed was to stir up trouble. I mentioned to Shelby that he'd been up there, though, and she kind of acted like it was weird. I could tell by the look on her face. I guess she asked him about it, because when I saw her at lunch later, she said that the electricity had somehow kicked off in his office but that he managed to track down the problem and everything was running okay now. Yeah. Electrical problems. At seven in the morning. Someone must have plugged in the toaster and coffeepot at the same time. Right. But I wasn't going to get into it any deeper with Shelby. She has a real thing for this guy. Practically drools over him. Too bad too. She's pretty cool. Works hard. We like Shelby. She could do a lot better than Mr. Slick, your friendly household electrician."

Julianne's head was buzzing, and she struggled to maintain composure as Marsha's words washed over her.

"Anyway, he was not about to get the chance to check my circuits, if you know what I mean. I was damn sure of that, even if I wasn't so sure what I was going to do about it. But as it turned out, I didn't have to do anything. When Elisa came, he had a thing for her right from the start. You could tell she didn't know what he was up to. She's got this innocence about her.

"Anyhow, I filled her in. That's how we got so tight. I sort of felt lucky that she took the heat off me, but bad for her, with her little girl and all. I knew she'd go through with it, being so tired and scared. The thing is, she kind of pushes it out of her mind, like it's no big deal. But then sometimes, like this morning, she gets real moody. I guess dealing with Andrews and her jerk of a husband at the same time could put anybody over the edge."

Marsha spoke so calmly and openly about this that it slowly began to sink into Julianne's head that the words might be true. What would she benefit from spinning tales? Why make it up? Yet Julianne was keenly aware that for herself, accepting this allegation would be hellish. It would mean she'd offered herself up to a monster. Worse, she'd abandoned her inhibitions. He'd seen the raw woman that was her most private self. It was all too unthinkable, too much to process.

There was no hiding from it. She was in too deep. She was working with him and sleeping with him. And dining with him this Saturday night. Dining with him. The very notion made her stomach turn. In a moment of self-doubt, she clung to the slight possibility that it was unreal, an ugly mix-up. She needed to hear it straight from Elisa to be convinced. Double-check your sources, ingrained from news training. If it was true, she had no idea what she would do.

Elisa sat in the center of her bed, a blanket cloaked around her shoulders. Her skin was nearly translucent, her body listless. Wearing jeans and a sweater and without a trace of makeup she looked like a teenager. "Come on in," she responded to the light knock at the door. Marsha entered the room first, followed by Julianne.

"You should talk to her," Marsha said softly and calmly. "It's okay. Nobody saw her come in. We entered through the back. She won't say anything if you tell her not to. She promised. You should talk to her." Then Marsha slipped out the door to her room across the hall.

Elisa sat looking blankly at Julianne. She didn't appear to be upset, just tired. "I'm sorry I don't look nicer. I didn't think I'd see anybody today after I dropped Kelly off at her friend's house. You can sit down on Kelly's bed if you want to."

Julianne sat and leaned against the pillows. Then she picked up the small pink pillow with the white satin roses and fingered the design, trying to decide how to start the conversation. Fortunately, Elisa was the one to get the ball rolling.

"I don't think we should make such a big deal about this. It's just temporary and he doesn't hurt me or anything," she said with little emotion. But the look she gave Julianne was curious. It was as if she'd lost track of what was right and what was wrong ... of what was important and what wasn't ... and was looking to this outsider for a fresh perspective.

"It is a big deal, and he *is* hurting you," Julianne said. "Are you the only one?"

"No, but I'm not going to talk about anyone else. It's their business. Besides, I don't want to talk about this anymore. I thought you were trying to do a show about what it's like to be scared of your husband, to be hit by your husband. I thought that's what you wanted to talk about."

"I'm trying to tell the story of abused women, victimized women, and you sure as hell can't tell me this isn't a part of it." Her voice started to rise from frustration. How could Elisa not see this outrage for what it was? Her demeanor, her refusal to muster any emotion, did more to validate the accusation than any tirade or slander could have. It was obvious. It was true. Julianne would have to shelve her own emotional rage for now and concentrate on Elisa and on the story. The skill of manipulating one's emotions was old hat for her, following years of experience with her parents and lovers. It was finally more of a help than a hindrance.

"I have enough on my plate to deal with right now. Peter wants us to come home. Kelly's growing bored here and I'm afraid to take her around the neighborhood much in case Peter or his friends are watching for us. Hell, the way things are at this place, I don't even want her out of my sight at all. She thinks I'm just a nag. She has no idea there's anyone to be afraid of here. And I want to keep it that way. I don't want my little girl living in fear like I've been doing. But now I don't even know if I can put up with staying here or if I have to run somewhere else. And it would probably be just the same when I got there. To tell you the truth, I just don't have the strength to find a new place. Not yet."

She'd been staring off blankly, addressing her comments more to the quilt cover than to the stranger perched on top of it. "And I sure as hell don't have the strength to take on the man in charge here just because it would be good for your TV show. I know you don't mean to aggravate me, but you are. Most everybody is down in the dining room finishing lunch. Why don't you go talk to them? Or do more of your interview with Mr. Andrews. He's always good for a line or two—believe me."

"Did you eat? You should eat. I'll bring something up to you." She needed to do something for this woman, if only to appease the intense guilt that had intensified inside her.

Elisa shook her head. "No, you don't have to. I know Marsha. She'll bring some stuff up to me." She lay back and shifted the blanket around to cover herself up. "I'm sorry, but I've got to get some sleep. I'll see you around."

Julianne walked to the door and turned to look at the frail woman on the bed once more before she left the room. Yes, this was really happening. And no, she couldn't just leave it alone.

Quietly she made her way down the stairs and entered the dining area with an invigorated stride, as if she had just entered the building from the outside. She didn't want anyone to suspect that she'd already been upstairs. Many of the women she and Jake had spoken to on Sunday afternoon were there, and they greeted her warmly. She joined them for a cup of coffee, making casual small talk. She didn't want them to anticipate that every time they saw her, an intense encounter would follow. She wanted to engage them, not frighten them. Today, she told herself, she'd just say a quick hello and be on her way. Just then, Clint entered the dining room on his way to the kitchen. He was startled to see Julianne at the table.

"What a great surprise," he said, initiating a business handshake that she was certain was for the benefit of the onlookers. "It might be a good idea to check into the office when you stop by so that Shelby can make sure you have everything you need, although it wouldn't have helped you much today. She called in this morning to say that her sister called her from Springfield last night—that's where Shelby's from—and their mother had a stroke. It appears to be a mild one, but they were doing lots of tests and Shelby drove down there to help out. I'm not sure how long she'll be gone. In the meantime, I'm your guy if you need anything at all."

Great, Julianne thought, looking around. *Just great. For all of us.* "Anyway," he continued, "do you have a minute to talk?" he asked, gesturing toward the long hallway that led to his office.

Julianne said her goodbyes to the others and followed Clint into his office. "Maybe you can help me with a major dilemma," he said with fake seriousness. "Would a lady be more impressed with homemade cannelloni or blackened swordfish? I know the swordfish is more trendy, but my mom always taught me that Italian food is the most romantic, and I still believe that Mom really knows best."

As he spoke, she could barely focus on what he was saying. So much effort had to go into acting as if nothing had happened to change her feelings toward him that she could conjure up little to say. One thing was for sure. The stupidest thing she could do would be to confront him with what she had heard from Marsha and Elisa. She'd been a producer long enough to know that she had to check out her story and make sure it was solid and all the pieces were in place before she could expose it. In this disgusting situation, the last thing she wanted to do was clue this guy in to the fact that she knew his secret and that somehow she was going to take him down. The thought of a romantic dinner with him was repulsive. Still, maybe she could maneuver things to her own advantage. "I'd have to agree with Mom. I'm just a sucker for Italian food."

She turned and slowly scanned the room as if she'd never seen his office before. Her eyes scrutinized the surroundings for signs of what kind of man Clint really was, any clue to his hidden personality or key to his soul. She took note of the lack of personal effects—no pictures, no trinkets. It was the physical layout of his office that made an impression, along with his choice of furniture.

For the first time, she noticed how large and overbearing his desk was—disproportionately large for the room. A tall masculine black leather chair loomed behind the desk. In front of the desk stood two spindle-legged wooden chairs with floral cushions. The odd thing, something she had not noticed before, was that these chairs were several inches shorter than the desktop. Whoever sat in one would be forced to look up into the face of the man in the large black chair behind his powerful desk. This would put them in a position of inferiority, of vulnerability. One course of college psychology was enough to know that. In this place that was intended to be a respite from dominance and power plays, why would a man create such a setting? With that thought, the tiny lingering hope that what Elisa and Marsha had told her was nothing more than ridiculous fabrication vanished. She saw Clint with a new clarity.

"I've got to be getting back to work," she said. "I just thought I'd show my face so that everyone would get used to my being around."

"I was hoping you missed me," he teased.

"You'll see on Saturday," she answered, starting for the door. He caught her arm as she brushed by him and squeezed her hand. Saying nothing but offering a coy smile, she passed through the doorway and headed back to work and the agony of her own conscience.

"Kelly, come on. You've got to stop reading and go to sleep. Your book will still be here tomorrow," Elisa told her daughter as the time approached ten o'clock at night.

Still glancing down at the pages, Kelly said, "It feels like a long time that we've been here, Mom. I bet Daddy really misses us by now. Maybe we should call him. It's kind of like we grounded him. He has to stay by himself and we get to be with each other."

This was the first time Kelly had asked to call her father. She rarely even spoke of him. Elisa surmised her daughter felt that mentioning him would be an act of disloyalty to her mother. Only occasionally did Kelly allow herself to express the anger and fear that her mother knew was lurking inside. When she did allow such emotions to surface, they were always targeted at her mother. Other than Peter's fit of rage the night before they left home, Kelly had been spared the brunt of his uneven temperament and bouts with depression. He had so little time to spend with his daughter that when Peter was engaged with Kelly, the two enjoyed carefree jaunts to McDonald's or the mall or hung out watching the Sunday games on TV, Peter with Kelly in one arm and a beer in the other. Daddy was the good guy and Mom the villain for "grounding" him, though never had a villain been loved more than Kelly loved her mom.

The conflict between Mom and Dad was a big one for any child, Elisa pondered, realizing how early in life we learn that love is not black or white, right or wrong. It's layered with emotions, years of learned behavior, expectations, and disappointments that can throw a curve at even the most stable of relationships. It was easier for Kelly to be angry with her mom than her dad. Mom was there beside her, a constant presence that wouldn't be driven away by the anger. Besides, it was Elisa who made the move to walk away, to split up the family, to disrupt the only life Kelly had known or understood. Elisa understood this thought process, mostly because she had tried to educate herself.

She read articles in magazines, probed websites on the computer at Horizons and the local library she and her daughter visited many afternoons, Elisa keeping a watchful eye on Kelly in the children's section as she browsed the adult aisles, scanning the shelves for material on parenting and children of divorce, refusing to make Kelly the victim of her parents' mistakes.

It wasn't just luck that enabled some kids to weather the storm of divorce while others turned hostile and rebellious. Elisa was bright enough to know that and anxious to curtail the anxiety that her daughter would surely experience. Kelly had a dad who loved her and whom she loved. One of the worst things she could do was force a rift between them, Elisa knew. Peter was not to be shunned as a taboo in his daughter's life. This would help no one. Still, it wasn't a piece of cake to play the heavy while Kelly refused to see her father as anything but a white knight who had made a lone mistake. That was the real truth.

"When I talked to your daddy last week, honey, he asked all about you, but I didn't want to wake you up to talk to him. I did say that we'd both call him this Sunday morning, okay? And that's just the day after tomorrow. Now, you go to sleep. I'll leave the night-light on. I'm just going across the hall to lend Marsha my sewing kit." Elisa tucked the blanket in around Kelly and leaned down to give her the nightly kiss on her forehead. "I love you, baby."

As she closed the door behind her, she was startled to hear Clint's voice echoing down the hallway from the top of the stairs. "Elisa, I have a package for you. I forgot to give it to you today."

"A package? No one knows I'm here. Are you sure it's for me?"

He knew she'd be worried about her safety if word got back to her husband that she was hiding out at this shelter. No one had packages or mail sent directly to Horizons. He continued, "It's for you all right. Remind me to get it for you in the morning."

"I know it's late, but could you show me the package now?" she asked anxiously.

"Why don't we both go get it? I'm not coming back up here tonight." He took the back stairway down to his office. This instantly triggered her suspicions. He only took this route when he didn't want the women in the living room to notice his whereabouts. Still, she had to make sure that he was mistaken about the package. No one could know she was staying here.

He opened the door to his dimly lit office and stood in the entranceway, gesturing for her to go inside. His body practically filled the doorway, forcing her to brush against his chest as she entered. He closed the door behind them and she heard the lock click. She knew what was coming. Then he stepped behind his desk and produced a large cellophane-wrapped box that looked as if it came straight from the store. It certainly hadn't been mailed or shipped. It wasn't addressed to her or anyone. Her shoulders slumped with relief. "See, a package for you." He smiled. He didn't know how cruel his little joke was, she thought. Or maybe he did.

"The church on Leland Avenue donated some toys for our kids, and I saved the nicest one for Kelly. I'll give the rest of them out tomorrow." He stood gazing at her with that intense stare that made her skin crawl. "Don't you want it?"

She knew better than to create a commotion, so she met him at the desk and reached for the box. As he handed it to her, he set it down on the desktop and slid his hand over hers. His hands were large and forceful. But they were also pale and doughy, the hands of a strong man but indulged little boy. His palms engulfed her, and the perspiration made her fingers recoil, but there was no place to go.

He slowly ran his fingers up her arm, stopping to caress her neck, then tightening his hold to pull her toward him. He positioned her directly in front of him, caressing her shoulders with his two hands. She closed her eyes. She didn't want to see his face, any part of him. She turned her face down, toward the floor, for there was this odor, this unbearable stench that was uniquely Clint Andrews's and that emerged from his body when he became sexually excited. For the most part, it was sweat—this she knew. But in her mind, it was the rot of his soul that filled her head and that consumed her in nausea. If only she could stop breathing.

Then, as if she were an object, nothing more than his personal plaything, he moved his hands over her sweater and onto her breasts, and with one hand on each breast, he began stroking her and playing with her nipples. He moved one hand and lifted her chin, not willing to cheat himself of the helpless look in her eyes. His eye were cold and blank, those of a heartless animal satisfying his urges and reveling in his power. There was no affection or feigned warmth in his expression, only the ugly glimmer of sexual excitement.

"Don't you want to thank me for the gift?" he sneered in a husky voice. Not waiting for an answer, he slid his hands under her sweater and released her bra. She stood there motionless, accepting his actions with an air of inevitability. She was the passive, feeble toy he had taken for himself, and her only prayer was that this evening's playtime would be short. He then pulled her sweater over her head and began grunting as he took her breast in his mouth, sucking on her flesh while at the same time unzipping her jeans and tugging at her panties.

No more words were spoken. He turned her around and lowered her onto the desk, pushing himself inside her. She offered no response. She just submitted, struggling not with him but with herself ... to eliminate her senses ... to become deafened to his groaning, unfettered by his touch and immune to the stench of evil. When it was over, he moved off of her and turned away, straightening his shirt and fastening his pants. Then, never looking at her, he walked into the adjoining bathroom and closed the door behind him.

Mechanically, she pulled up her pants and pulled on her sweater, silently leaving the office, scurrying up the back stairs and entering the bathroom at the end of the hall. She ripped off her clothes and jumped into the shower, soaping herself ferociously.

The promise of safety, the notion of a haven, had merely been further manifestation of her revolting innocence, she berated herself as she stood with her feet planted firmly in the shower stall, ribbons of steaming hot water washing away the external remnants of the encounter. Elisa had settled her into the nest, and then, when she had allowed herself to release her anxiety and, for a moment, rid herself of the peril that had permeated her life, a vulture had swooped upon her and made her his prey. She despised herself herself for such reckless naïveté.

Her backbone had been chiseled away over the years by her husband. Here, she'd thought upon arrival, it might have a chance to rejuvenate itself. But no, not with the system pushing her down. Damn her ego. Damn her weakness. For had she not been too ashamed to confront her parents with the truth of her battered marriage, had she not been so certain of her inability to hold true to her convictions as they coerced her to give it one more try, she could have sought refuge in their safe, familiar home with none of the hidden surprises and heavy price tag of Horizons.

She was livid with herself now as she had been disgusted with herself for her failure to make her marriage work, make her husband happy. A small, haunting voice in the back of her mind whispered that maybe her anger was misplaced. Why was she not enraged at Clint Andrews and incensed at the man who had vowed to cherish and honor her? They were, of course, to be blamed, admonished. But she could not be responsible for them, only for herself. She didn't have the power to change them or their lives, only her own. Yes, there was enough anger to go around. Plenty. But the energy of that anger could only prove useful by turning it on herself and using it to propel herself forward. As long as she still had it in her to become this outraged, she still had a chance to make things right--and she knew it.

Wrapped in a towel, she slipped back into the room she shared with Kelly. She looked down at her little girl's sweet face and then, instead of going to her own bed, stretched out beside her daughter, pulling Kelly close. This closeness brought her back to the real world ... a world in which it was okay to let herself feel. For in those minutes downstairs, she had closed down her mind, shut down her feelings. It was something that had become easier and easier to do as Peter's verbal and physical assaults forced her to retreat from her pain and as envy for her friends' full lives forced her to negate her own suffering.

As she lay there with Kelly, a new thought raced through her head. Could it be that one day she would shield herself with a coat of armor so strong and shut down her feelings so completely that she would never find them again? This question consumed her mind as she lay awake most of the night, finally easing off into sleep as glints of sunlight peered through the bedroom window.

CHAPTER 8

How to feign interest in this week's rumpled copy of *People* was indeed a dilemma. But since she had convinced herself to stop into the Bistro Upstairs for some dinner on the way home and had nothing else to cling to but the magazine, it would have to do. Eating out alone was right down there with ironing and trips to the dentist when it came to her favorite things to do. If anything could drive a person to leap willingly into a dismal relationship or endure the tension of a disintegrating one, it was the experience of dining solo amidst a crowd of couples chattering busily about their work, families and quality of the entrees set before them.

Still, it had been a hell of a lousy day—week, actually—a gigantic jumble of unshackled behavior, gnawing humiliation, big decisions and even bigger disappointments. The thought of heading home to a dinner of microwave popcorn was even less appealing than that of going to the trouble of concocting one of her gourmet recipes for a sad, lone serving. The Bistro Upstairs was nestled between two chic boutiques across from her apartment building and as she headed home from the bus stop, it beckoned to her.

Convinced that the crowd of patrons huddled around the restaurant's collection of small wooden tables had nothing better to do than observe her solitude, Julianne regretted the choice to dine out from the moment the menu was handed to her and the bread basket placed at the center of the table. Damn that busboy. If he hadn't been so efficient in his duties and arrived so swiftly with the basket, she'd have simply slipped away unnoticed. Now, however, she had been served and could hardly be so rude as to escape. Besides, the clatter of dishes and escalating volume of conversations gave her cause to push aside thoughts of Clint Andrews for the time being. For hours, she'd been admonishing herself for being such a complete ass and him for being such a scumbag. She needed a break from thinking about it all.

Sipping Absolut on the rocks, she set down the magazine, preferring to enjoy the sensation of the vodka racing through her veins. Vodka on the rocks was not a typical cocktail for Julianne Sloan, known to nurse one glass of wine for the better part of an evening. However, her mood dictated a drastic change and, for her, deviating from a glass of chardonnay qualified as drastic—especially since she ordered a second round before finishing her steaming cup of tomato bisque.

The familiar laugh pierced through the room, rising high above the gaiety that contributed to this establishment's reputation for spirited ambiance. It came from behind her, darting directly toward her knowing ears. Allen Miller was somewhere in that room. Her attention drifted from the soup, and a bright stream of orange trickled from her spoon to her mauve linen skirt. She needed to tend to it. No. That would mean rising and crossing the room. He would see her. Better to live with the stain. She needed to pay the check and plan an exit route that would be as inconspicuous as it was swift. She needed to do anything but lay eyes on Allen Miller. She wasn't ready to see him. It was too soon, the emotions too raw.

She reached into her wallet and snatched two twenties, probably too much for the two drinks and soup she'd ordered. But she didn't want to risk leaving too little and being delayed in her retreat. With her back to the source of that unmistakable laughter, Julianne meandered through the spacious dining room, now thankful for the clatter and crowd that would mask her movement. She stopped at the checkroom to retrieve her raincoat and spun around with a burst of energy, her mind already envisioning the doorway that would free her. And there he was, standing right beside that doorway, waiting for her. He likely knew she was there all the time, she realized, probably spied her from across the room. His roving eyes, she remembered, always scoped out his surroundings upon arrival, surveying the pickings before settling down with his companion. How could she have forgotten Allen Miller's standard operating procedure?

At first, she could barely force herself to meet his gaze, embarrassed by having been caught in an obvious escape attempt and equally perturbed by her lack of preparedness for this first encounter. But then she did look up. She looked at those eyes, those shoulders, that winning broad smile. She could not look away, momentarily transfixed by the man who had won and overtaken her heart just as quickly only a year ago. Perhaps there was such a thing as chemistry. Perhaps the piercing blue of his eyes or waves of hair obscured the history she should have been jolted into recalling. Yes, chemistry. What was the point in denying it when the man she had convinced herself to hate, to rid herself of, transformed her into a quivering bowl of Jell-O within seconds? The pragmatic Julianne had customarily stifled her more romantic side, but now the tables were turned. First fantasies of Jake Rossi, then surreal escapades with an animal like Clint Andrews, and now the pitfall of Allen Miller. The last time she had seen this man, a stream of curse words had spewed from her lips. Now she was struck silent.

Allen did the talking. Julianne only nodded, occasionally grunting an acknowledgment to his questions, regretting the downing of that second glass of vodka. He fell into step beside her, obviously intending to escort her to the apartment he had shared and the bed they had enjoyed. Somewhere he had a new place to live, maybe even a car waiting at a nearby curb. But there was no mention of either and she knew that this man she despised and pitied was planning to seduce her in the sanctity of her own bedroom.

She did not protest his company, acutely aware of the strength of his body and ruggedness of his frame. Allen Miller was, on a physical level, what Julianne Sloan found to be quintessentially sexy. It was evident from the first time she laid eyes on him. All the arguments, rage and humiliating episodes that had transpired between them over the course of months did not erase that one pure truth. Yet when he followed her through her building's door, chattering nonchalantly about his plans to go skiing at Jackson Hole over the Christmas holiday, she knew it was time to get her emotions in check, to safeguard her well-being. She was determined. But so was Allen Miller.

She'd invited Clint Andrews into her private domain and look where it got her. She despised herself for being so love-starved that she fell victim to one villain and was on the verge of falling victim to another. Why couldn't she stop herself? Why did she need the validation, the sexual satisfaction, to feel whole? And why, afterward, was she left feeling anything but whole?

She extended her hand to say goodbye, and he lifted it to his lips, placing an erotic kiss in her palm. She felt the tingle, the twinge in her stomach, and she instantly drew her hand away, intending to recoil and dash for the elevator, preserving as much of her integrity as possible. So she was startled to find that the hand she was tearing away from his hold had somehow found its way around the back of his neck, pulling his hungry lips closer to hers. God, how she needed this sensation, the awareness that her body was alive. Her mind was pushing him away, but her arms held him tighter and her lips clung to his. He moved his hands down her back with caressing strokes that drew her closer and closer until she could no longer catch her breath.

She turned her head for a moment and saw that they were in the elevator. She didn't know how they'd gotten there, yet suddenly they were at her front door. The need to fish for her keys offered the only chance to reclaim her sanity. Silently she dug into her purse, her mind whirling with questions of what to do … what was right … what was certain destruction. His hands were on her neck, massaging her and reminding her of the pleasures of passion. She wanted to feel it, to explode with that passion. It didn't matter that it was this man, only that it was a physical being who could evoke such a yearning. She craved the experience. She had to have it.

Maybe it would have been easier, better, if Clint Andrews had never lit those fires inside her. Maybe she would have forgotten how desperately she responded to the touch of a man. But now she needed more. Not the rough acts of sex she had yielded to with Clint but the seductive, sensuous style of lovemaking she had shared with Allen Miller. Julianne Sloan, who in her entire life had been with only a handful of men, was now willfully throwing herself at two, each a particular brand of villain. It was as if she were outside of herself, witnessing someone else's foolish exploits. But the tingling sensations of her skin and the searching mouth that was ravaging his lips told her that this was her own dangerous adventure.

They were inside the apartment, and a dim shaft of light from the streetlamp below captured the glint in his eye. He shifted his weight against her, and she melted into the strong wooden door, surrendering to the flood of emotion. His tongue tasted every part of her mouth, and his fingers wrapped around the waves of her hair. She surrendered to his entry as his mouth offered wet kisses to the nape of her neck and his fingers stroked the curve of her back. More. More. She was so hungry, so utterly famished. It was sex so consuming, so titillating that she abandoned all notions of right and wrong and followed only her physical desires. Her body dictated and her mind was forced to follow. She was lost. It seemed like forever. Lost. Until it was over.

She felt him rise and sit back, resting against the closet door. This man who always had the right words on the tip of his tongue was at a loss for what to say. She had allowed him to take her so feverishly. And now there they were, lying on the floor, satisfied yet ashamed, both of them.

She did not love this man. Nor had she made love to him. She had quelled her desires. Julianne always had a wonderful appetite for sex. They both knew that's all this was. Sex. The awkwardness of the moment thickened until she felt she was suffocating, remaining still, turning only enough to shield her body with its disheveled clothing and to hide her face from his. The thought of his eyes upon her was more than she could stand.

No words were exchanged. There was no touching other than a soft caress of her head and slight kiss on her ear as he moved past her and quietly opened the front door, cracking it open just enough to slip through without allowing the harshness of the corridor lights to penetrate the vestibule where she lay, head spinning, stomach churning.

Allen Miller was gone for the night, but the ugly truth was that he was not gone from her life. He still lived in her mind, in her desires. This she could not ignore or wish away. She rose and made her way to the bathroom, using nothing more revealing than the faint glow of the night-light to inspect her image in the mirror. It was a pitiful sight. Rumpled clothing, streaked makeup, tousled hair. She was pitiful. Clint knew it. Allen knew it. Most importantly, she knew it. But she could make it better. Julianne was the one other people came to when they needed to make things better, whether it was a story for the show or a dispute with one's mother-in-law. Hers was the voice of reason, she the chief adviser. Only now she had to come through for herself.

She ran a hot bath, spilling an ample amount of perfumed oil into the swirls of water, anxious to nurture her flesh, soothe her body. She lowered herself into the tub, and once immersed in the steaming pool, she allowed her thoughts to run free. This is how she remained for over an hour, while the tranquil water gradually cooled, trickling away remorse and self-doubt. The sexual glory had vanished as quickly as the vicious hunger that precipitated it had arrived. She'd been starving, and then she was fed, and once fed, she obtained the wherewithal to assess what on earth had overtaken her. How utterly crushed she was with her behavior, how revolted by her actions.

Never would she have believed that she could have done such an asinine thing, succumbed to a man she knew was poison. At least with Clint, she'd been ignorant of the situation. Impetuous and foolish, but ignorant. As for Allen, she had no excuse. She'd allowed him to get the upper hand, enabling his sexual talents to overshadow the detestable way he'd treated her. She'd undone the beginning of her healing and rebuilding of her self-esteem. She'd been weak, and the one thing Julianne Sloan was intolerant of was weak women.

The remorse turned to fury and with that came a jolt of energy that revived her spirit. She'd been stupid, and now she'd pay the price. The healing would have to begin all over again, and the remembrance of her vulnerability and lack of control would haunt her. That was penance enough. Her spirit would be restored and her strength would prevail. That was Julianne Sloan.

She lifted herself from the water, pulled her soft flannel robe securely around her, and stood before the mirror brushing back her hair. From the abyss of the dimly lit glass, the eyes of Elisa Tate came staring back at her. They were tender, kind and insightful. Julianne accepted the gift of that insight, achieving a new level of understanding about herself, about Elisa, Marsha, and the others— about life and love and the struggle that ensues when one is destructive of the other. It's not so easy to follow your head instead of your heart, Julianne admitted to herself. It seems so damned simple to stand back and evaluate someone else's life, decipher an outsider's mistakes, assess others' character flaws. It's not so easy to scrutinize one's own life. Better to crush the magnifying glass? Easier for sure. Yet now she realized, not better at all.

Surrounded by the warmth of the covers and cushioned by the cool softness of her pillows, Julianne's thoughts drifted to room 208 and the small heart-shaped pillow with the white satin roses. Life wasn't as smooth as satin or as sweet as roses. It certainly wasn't painted in shades of black and white. Motionless on the bed, her mind swirled, confronted by her own arrogance and predisposed belief that the women of Horizons were a different breed than she, a lesser breed. She had entered their world annoyed with them for their weakness, their willingness to tolerate the intolerable, their refusal to utilize their own wisdom and strength of conviction to create their salvation. She had been so dense, so pompous.

Now her eyes, as well as her heart, had been opened. She'd learned the hard way, though her journey was not nearly as perilous as those experienced by the women she'd been judging. She got the picture. They were all starving for love. She was no different underneath, just the product of different circumstances. It was all so complicated. She didn't have the answers and she admitted to herself that, driven though she was to find them, they could very well elude her as they eluded most of the human race.

She was so tired. It was time to breathe calmly, release her mind from anguish and surrender to the peacefulness that remained in the night.

CHAPTER 9

J ust past eight in the evening, Julianne rang Clint Andrews's doorbell, armed with a cheesecake, a pint of mint chocolate chip, and one full-fledged lousy attitude. She was going through with this dinner and with the illusion that it was a relationship being forged here instead of a sting. The past couple of days, she could think of little but nailing this louse. The only good thing about commensing the plan was that it gave her a reprieve from playing the Allen Miller incident over and over again in her mind. Allen was poison; she was weak. There was little she could do about that. Clint Andrews was worse. He was contemptible, conniving, and dangerous. She could, however, do something about that. She would expose him. Only first she had to play the game: win him over, get his guard down, wind her way into his demented mind.

He greeted her with a robust hug and guided her into his large apartment. It was a beautiful space with an expansive view of Lake Michigan. The decor was not unlike his office. A massive forest green leather sofa was flanked by two large mahogany end tables. A tall, broad black lacquer entertainment unit dominated one wall, the other wall arching at the center to reveal the adjoining room in which a sleek glass table top was perched atop a sturdy cast iron base to accommodate as many as twelve diners. Wall adornments were sparse and unmemorable, though clearly expensive, indicating safe selections by a decorator who knew little about soul or style of her client.

Clint brought Julianne a glass of Prosecco as she sat nestled into the corner of the sofa. Classic Sinatra was playing and the aroma of fresh basil filled the air. It would have been her ideal evening a week ago, even three days ago. Today it was a farce.

"So," she said, "I half expected you to call and cancel what with Shelby out of town and the extra hours you must be giving to Horizons. You must be sort of overwhelmed, dealing with all those women and such intimate problems. It must be a real change for you, not quite typical for the role of administrative director." It was noticeably odd to delve directly into a business conversation after the incidents of the past week. But she was hardly prepared to feign interest in discussing more intimate issues. Work was her comfort zone so she went right to it. Fortunately, he went along.

"I'll tell you a secret. I'm so committed to Horizons that I draw no lines when it comes to personal involvement. I get these women and what they're going through. You know, it's easy to get numb when it comes to how bad things can really be for people. That heavy stuff is just something we drone on about at dinner parties and read about in magazines at the dentist's office. Now, getting away from my ledgers and getting closer to our residents, well, it helps me understand how people think. Especially women. How they adapt to new circumstances and survive."

"You don't think only another woman could understand what it means to be overpowered and abused by a man?"

"Well, well, madam, I do believe your sexism is showing," he teased.

"Maybe it's sexist, but there are so many things a woman goes through that only other women can really connect with. The glass ceiling, the good old boys' club, all that garbage that's evolved into a bunch of clichés, started with common experience. Men who use physical strength to overpower others, sometimes men but often women. Emotional bullying based on centuries of male entitlement and cultural mores. I just don't know if a man can understand how really horrible and destructive to a woman all that can be." She looked him straight in the eye as she spoke, wondering if he would display any signs of discomfort. He did not.

"It's a good thing you weren't on the committee to get me on board, even as a glorified bookkeeper. Men around that place would have been an endangered species...or gender, I should say," he quipped.

"Did you have to go through any screenings before you became involved? By the founding committee? I'm just curious about how it works."

"When you ask established professionals to work beneath their customary salary range to support a the greater good, you don't dare ask them to go through a screening process. Who'd have the inclination to go through all of that when you're basically doing a favor in the first place? Don't forget that we're talking about a private organization here, not a place run by the state. There wasn't a lot of red tape involved. I had the interest; money wasn't my motivation. I was doing something socially relevant, something I could feel good about. I'm okay financially, so why not? And lucky for you too. Otherwise, I don't know if I could have splurged on the finest ingredients for this dinner. No more shop talk from me. Your days are far more interesting than mine, I'm sure."

Over dinner, they chatted about how Julianne got her first break in broadcasting and how she still lusted after provocative stories and hard-to-crack subjects, along with the "fluff stuff," as she referred to shows like *Chicago Sizzle*. It was strange to be exploring such introductory personal history after the sexual encounter they had already shared, a reminder to Julianne that their relationship would have been developing backward had it the potential to develop at all. She had never found herself in such circumstances before, jumping into the physical before cultivating the emotional. She realized that it wasn't her style, that even if Clint Andrews had turned out to be Prince Charming instead of the Prince of Darkness, she still would have made a mess of the entire affair. She was learning about her hungers, her weaknesses, her motivations. That was the least she could take away from the whole rotten ordeal.

After her second glass of wine, Julianne had to work harder to stay focused and remember her true incentive for being in Clint's apartment and going through the motions of this romantic escapade. His charm and warmth were deceptive, and she could feel herself starting to relax a little too much.

Once the table was cleared and she eased her back toward the living room and the green leather couch, she snapped out of it. Eliminating the possibility of sex was priority one and there was no way she would allow her mind to stray off track. There was only so far she would go for the sake of a story. She was keenly aware of Clint's expectations and the depth of passion that had erupted between them before. She was equally aware of her own vulnerabilities under the influence of a sensual man and a bottle of wine. She was not about to put herself in the position of coping with another psychological disaster. She fought to remember that this man was not the suave dinner companion the evening made him out to be. He seemed so wonderful. That was his weapon.

"I think it's time to walk off that pasta," she said, standing in front of the windows and gazing out at the curvy stretch of Lake Shore Drive that trimmed the lake. "It looks beautiful out there."

"Outside—when it's so comfortable in here?" he asked with a comical pout, not taking the suggestion seriously. It was obvious that he anticipated a night of erotic sex here in his den of power.

"Come on, or we'll be five pounds heavier in the morning," she persisted, reaching for her jacket and purse, knowing she had no intention of returning to his apartment after their walk. "Want to grab a coat?"

"No, I'm fine. Besides, if it gets too chilly, you'll keep me warm, right?"

"Give me a break," she shot back at him. "You're not the type for a corny line like that." They both laughed as she ushered him out the door.

They took a long, casual walk along the lakefront, and after a few minutes, Clint reached over and clasped her hand, holding it gently for the rest of the stroll. *Life can be so unfair,* she thought. It was as if the guy were sent to her from central casting. He could have been the One. What a rotten deal. Maybe the coo-some twosome routine was not in the cards for her. Maybe she should just stop trying so hard, stop thinking about it. The married ones, the cruel ones, the unconscionable ones. Maybe God was trying to tell her something. As she reveled in her pity party, Elisa again flashed through her mind, disrupting her thoughts of elusive romance. Elisa had the rotten deal, Julianne reminded herself. As for herself, she was just having a rotten evening.

They headed back toward his apartment building. Out of the corner of her eye, Julianne spotted a taxi that was about a block down and heading their way. She eased her hand out of Clint's, pretending to pull her jacket closed as the wind sharpened. Then, with no warning, she stepped to the curb and hailed the passing taxi.

"Hey." Clint halted. "What's this?"

"I'm so tired. And a taxi being right here right now—it's kind of an omen. We need to take things slowly, especially since we're going to be working together for a while."

"Okay. But I can get my car and take you home. We just have to run up for the key. I don't want you taking a cab."

"It's done. I don't want this poor man to have stopped for nothing." She opened the taxi door and turned back to Clint to give him a light kiss on the cheek. Apparently startled by her sudden retreat, he accepted the gesture and as she pulled away, he turned her toward him, slid his hand around to the back of her neck, and slowly drew her face toward his. Looking deeply into her eyes for a moment, he then moved still closer and kissed her forehead, then the tip of her nose, softly gliding his lips to her mouth, where he held nothing back in offering a sensuous lingering kiss. She felt herself responding to him, savoring the sensation. She ached for the passion, engulfed by waves of energy that raced through her body, washing away the roadblocks in her mind.

At that moment, Julianne realized just how torn apart she was from this whole ugly mess. Who was telling the truth? Was, she convinced that he was guilty of those filthy accusations? Had she assessed the situation fairly? If she truly believed this man to be a monster, what was she doing in his arms? She was so flustered that words escaped her. As she felt her face turn a deep shade of scarlet, she turned away, into the wind, and never looking Clint in the eye, stepped into the anonymous domain of the taxi driver who was instructed to drive her home.

It wasn't until several hours later, sipping a glass of orange juice and leafing through *Marie Claire*, that her confusion turned to mounting anger. The seed was first planted when Marsha and Elisa confronted her with what was transpiring in the back office of Horizons. She grasped what a treacherous a man Clint Andrews was. He'd put her under his spell, even though she'd been wary. He wielded his power wisely, calculatingly. It made her furious and at the same time relieved that she'd emerged from the experience with conviction of what side of the war she was on. It wasn't often a person was given the chance to get her hands on something that was terribly wrong and through her own initiative and skill make it right. This was her chance. It was an issue of humanity and decency, not money or ratings or constructing a story for some television show to be viewed one night and forgotten the next. This was about people. She'd become so removed from it all, so shielded in her world of affluent friends and posh surroundings. Yet she wasn't so naive as to think she'd remain this sensitive to the realities of life forever. This fit of social consciousness was undoubtedly prompted by the day-to-day production of the documentary. But once completed, the program would air and she would be off on her next mission, just as the Founding Foursome had progressed to their next crusade following the launch of their shelter. It was inevitable. She was no saint, and she knew it. Still, while positioned to do so, she could at least do something to ease the pain of a few women who were in trouble and unprepared to help themselves.

Tomorrow she would return to her job assignments—covering movie openings, bizarre fashion trends, and celebrity scandals—the diet of television junk that producers feed their audiences day after day. Tonight she'd map out her plan for a documentary on abused women. And she'd accelerate her plan for bringing down Clint Andrews.

Julianne could hear the guys laughing all the way down the corridor as she approached Ted Marshall's office. Crowded with sales, promotion and accounting managers, she couldn't help but feel like an intruder. The laughter became subdued upon spotting her entry. Clearly, she was was intruding upon the boys' club fun.

"Come on in and shoot some hoops," Ted said, referring to the toy basketball hoop and foam ball one of his buddies had given him for his birthday, now a staple in the corner.

"Forget it; I'm a lousy shot. But don't let me break up your game. This is what it takes for you guys to act like a team," she said, proud that she'd got in a verbal shot of her own.

"Cute, Sloan. Cute," Don McBain smirked, giving her a patronizing pat on the back as he headed for the door. "Back to work, I guess." The others followed suit, leaving her alone with Ted.

"Thanks for squeezing me in. I really need to talk something through with you. It's kind of a touchy subject so brace yourself. It's about Horizons. I dug up some dirt on that place, quite by accident. Deep dirt."

"Wait a minute. You're not spending your time doing an investigative piece on the shelter we're using as the cornerstone of our public service campaign, are you? You were the one singing its praises and convincing the rest of us to give you support. Don't go laying a bunch of crap in my lap now." His corporate antennae rose from his brain. Ted was next in line to be plucked from local station management and elevated to national headquarters. The last thing he needed was anything—or anyone—rocking the boat.

Still, Julianne was started by his response. Because Pam was usually the one to deal with Ted, Julianne had never seen him get so defensive or nasty before.

"First of all, Ted, it's not a bunch of crap. I thought we all agreed that family abuse is an extremely important issue for us to get behind. I'm not talking about the cause; I'm talking about this one particular shelter, Horizons. There's foul play inside there."

"Julianne, you know that our parent company was one of the backers of that shelter. They coughed up a heap of cash to help get it going and the station went on record as being a big supporter. Don't go stirring a lot of things up just because you're bored." His tone was unbearably condescending. Pam must be a saint, she thought, to put up with this guy fifty-two weeks a year.

"I'm not bored. What I am is diligent, ethical, and good at my job. You might agree if you would at least let me tell you what I'm talking about before you dismiss what I have to say. There's a man at the shelter, the administrative director, in charge of keeping track of outgoing expenses and incoming contributions and that sort of thing. He's not really running the day-to-day operation. There's a woman in that role—house manager they call her. House managers are always women. But others—like the administrative director or public relations adviser—well, they can be men or women. There are no sensitivity issues involved. Theoretically."

She stopped briefly to catch her breath and slow down. "Anyway, this administrative director at Horizons, he's … forcing women to have sex with him, threatening to turn them out if they don't go along with it. He's a man, and these are women used to having men wield power over them. So he puts his cards on the table: put out or get out. These women have nowhere else to go. Hell, they don't even have the strength to think about it. It's easier to just sleep with the guy."

Ted interrupted her. "First of all, do you know for a fact that any of that is true? Who are your sources? I can't believe the other person running things, this house manager person, would let this go on, much less talk to the media about it. Therefore, it must have been the residents. Could it be that you were taken in by a lot of gals who are mad at their husbands and probably taking it out on the only man they can? Man-haters?"

She sat speechlessly as he began massaging his temples, which she took as a clue that he was struggling to remain calm. "You do tend to get rather carried away with your emotions, Julianne. That's not a criticism. It's the way a lot of producers are."

Female producers, Julianne thought.

He continued. "But stop and think about it. Even if a man does put the moves on a woman—and I did say 'if'—that woman doesn't have to stay there and have sex if she doesn't want to. She can leave. No one's putting a gun to her head so she'll stay, right? Just because he makes advances toward them—if he does—doesn't mean he's forcing them. They've got urges of their own, I'm sure. Who knows? You can't let that ruin a man's reputation." He stepped back, his orange foam ball in hand, and took careful aim at the hoop propped up against the wall next to the couch where she was sitting. Finally, he released it to score a basket and stood smiling at his triumph.

She struggled desperately to keep her temper under control. She couldn't decide which was worse, the fact that his remarks were incredibly sexist and cavalier or the fact that he was playing with his little boy toys while she was addressing such a travesty. Not losing sight of the fact that this man was her boss, like it or not, she sat silently for a moment, gaining control over her rage and collecting her thoughts. Instead of taking issue with his notions of man-hating and what a woman would or would not do when propositioned, she decided to try a different strategy. She'd appeal to his business sense.

"Listen, Ted—this story has fantastic promotional value. It has all the angles we need to grab viewers: sex, power, secrets, deception. Every station looks for a story like this for its ratings period. In the last sweeps period alone, our news department aired a three-part story on penile implants, two stories on incest, a two–parter on thriving prostitution rings, a rehashing of breast implants gone bad. All the old favorites. And wife beating has always been an audience grabber. It crops up on every daytime talk show out there and the ratings skyrocket. Now I've got an exclusive take on the topic, a way to add drama, and I'm laying it at your feet." She couldn't believe she got the words out, acutely aware of the truth to her shallow rationale.

This was how programming and news decisions were made every day, like it or not. Push the public's hot buttons. Get the ratings. She'd avoided stooping to such levels but only because she'd been insulated by bosses who stood in the line of corporate fire. How long would she last before she became one of *them*? Would she even know it when she did?

"I know it's a good story. But it's also the precise shelter our owners helped build and my station supports in the press. Find the same angle at a place that's not so close to home. This can't be the only guy trying to have a good time in a house full of hard-up women."

"That's the problem!" she shouted. Now she was exasperated and couldn't help raising her voice. "I'm sure there are guys like this doing what he's doing all over town ... all over the country. That's the story. That's why it's such a big deal. No one regulates these people. There are no controls over them or standards they have to meet or accountability. Just because it's not funded by the government, it's a free-for-all. It's especially true with volunteers, but it's got to spill over to paid personnel at some of these places. And who knows if the shelters that are funded by the government are any different. This is a great exposé. I'm sure we can trigger some sort of legislation. The station can be heroic. We can actually do some good for a change."

"Don't be so dramatic, Julianne," Ted said, again in that condescending voice. "This is your place of business, not your living room. And you should be proud of the good you do here every day. People love your show. The ratings are up eight percent over last year. *Chicago Sizzle* is very important to us, and you know how much I appreciate how hard you work. You don't need to create a heavier load for yourself with all of this exposé stuff."

This was not a man who was innately sensitive to women's issues. Far from it. Talking further with him would be as useful as banging her head against the wall. She needed to approach this a whole new way. After all, she already had the go-ahead to do a documentary on battered women. As executive producer, what was included in that documentary was up to her.

"Yes, I know it's a place of business. I'm going to head back downstairs, Ted." As she walked out the door, she turned and with ample sarcasm added, "Great shot, by the way."

When Julianne arrived back at her office, Jake was stretched out in her chair and Tina was propped up against the desk, staring out the window at the Chicago River.

That morning, they had all gone to the coffee shop to be free of interruptions and eavesdroppers so that Julianne could tell them the Clint Andrews story. They had all agreed that she had no choice but to tell Ted Marshall since the station and its parent company would be held accountable were the story to be exposed. Ted, they hoped, would help them figure out how to get rid of Clint Andrews and would give them approval pursuing the TV angle, perhaps even coercing the news department to collaborate with the programming department to give the topic full coverage.

Now, following the meeting with her boss, Jake and Tina were on pins and needles to hear details of her talk with the top brass. As she gave them the unexpected play-by-play, Jake stared at her, dumbfounded. Tina grew increasingly fidgety and tugged angrily at a rubber band that had been lying in her lap.

"Big shock, I guess," Tina said sarcastically. "I was so sure Mr. Macho would be objective about this." She stood there smirking and staring into space. "He wouldn't be siding with the administrator just because he happens to be a guy? No. Not Mr. Equal Rights. This male-bonding stuff makes me crazy." She turned toward Jake and took aim with the rubber band. "Present company excluded, of course," she added, lowering the rubber band and managing a cockeyed smile.

"I've done my duty. I've informed my boss that the station is connected with a filthy mess. I'm going to type a memo recapping the discussion and send it to Ted. Nothing to tick him off. Just a note of appreciation saying how glad I am that he was willing to share his insights on the Clint Andrews issue. Just enough to document the fact that I did inform him, but nothing that will stir up a hornet's nest. This whole thing could hit the fan, and I'm not going to let myself be the one left holding the bag. We'll simply move forward with producing our special, including a new segment: A look at the topic from inside those protective walls.

"For the record, I never told either of you that Ted forbade us to get involved. As far as you're concerned, you're just following your producer's script. If this mess blows up, there's no reason for us all to take the heat. Besides," she said with a newly invigorated voice, "we wouldn't want Jake to be out of work with all those charge card bills. Helene would have his hide." She smiled at Jake coyly. He responded by settling even deeper into the chair and rested his feet on her desk. He knew exactly how to get a rise out of her. Only this time she sat down on the file cabinet and just let him be.

Looking at him, she wondered how he'd react if she had the guts to come clean about her own encounters with Clint Andrews. Tina would never believe it. Jake probably would, but he'd be stunned. The very notion of either of them discovering the truth made her cringe.

"As long as we're going for it, let's really go for it," Tina said. "You're willing to put yourself on the line with Marshall, huh? How about if I put myself on the line with Andrews? I may not be Jewish, but I have just as much chutzpah as you!" Tina smiled lovingly. "I want to go inside the shelter. No one there knows me. All of my research was done by phone, and then you took over. I can really give us an insider's perspective. I'll be inside. We can say I'm on vacation, that I'm taking some time off to gear up for the documentary. You're my boss. Pam's on leave. So there's no one to question my schedule. I'll take two weeks to start with; then we'll see. What do you think?"

"Really dangerous. There's no house manager around right now. The last time I spoke with Clint, he mentioned that Shelby's mother took a turn for the worse and she's staying down in Springfield for a while. Since it's just a temporary leave, there's no plan to bring in someone else to fill her spot. Clint volunteered to fill the gap, of course. I thought of calling Shelby and confronting her with this mess. I even called Marsha to ask her what she thought of that idea. Shelby seems so smart and nice and all. But Marsha said Shelby is very tight with Clint. Very tight, if you know what I mean. She said Shelby would only rush to his defense and become furious with the women inside for being malicious and disloyal; there's no way any of them would fess up to Shelby anyway. So that idea seems pointless.

"And your idea seems dangerous, no matter how tempting. With no buffer between you and Clint ... I mean, this man forces himself on women. Plus, we can't deceive the women who live there. The ends don't always justify the means," Julianne concluded.

"I think that in this case, the ends do justify the means. We're doing this to help. We're not using anyone's real name. If we don't do it, who will? I'm not as vulnerable as the others. I'll be able to take care of myself. I'll prepare myself. I'll use a lipstick camera that I can hide in my purse to back up my phone cam, in case he's suspicious of the phone. I'll have a can of mace too!"

Jake, who hadn't said one world since Julianne returned to her office, slowly lowered his feet off the desk and stood up, looking from Tina to Julianne. "Want to know what I think? I think you're both nuts. One of you could get fired. The other could get roughed up—or worse. You're not even news producers. You work on a show called *Chicago Sizzle*, for God's sake. Have you completely lost your minds?"

"What I've lost," Julianne said, "is my willingness to sit back and be a passive spectator when I know something needs fixing. No one will take this on without concrete evidence. There needs to be regulation, some sort of protection, so that these women aren't turned into victims over and over again. We won't be able to convince people that it's an actual problem without a case to point to. But Tina doesn't need to be the crusader."

With predictable sarcasm, Tina added, "What can I say? I'm a sucker for a cause. And I'm not about to let my boss outshine me in the ballsy broad department." She blew Julianne a fake Hollywood kiss.

Jake sat back down and buried his face in his hands. "I can see I'm not going to get much sleep till this production's over."

Elisa tapped End Call and leaned back against the wall, motionless. Her Sunday-evening talks with Peter drained her of energy. Keeping up a pleasant veneer while she was on the phone with him was important for the sake of Kelly, who was standing at her side. She never doubted that Peter loved Kelly—even if he couldn't love her enough to diffuse his anger. She wondered if the same sentiments applied to her. Did he love her? She didn't even know if she still loved him.

She couldn't stand hearing Peter, always so strong and reserved, now whining, spewing out empty promises, and attempting to lure her back with what he called "tokens of his commitment to change." That is what rubbed her the wrong way most of all, acting as if *things* compensated for the anguish. Things. He just didn't get it, and until—unless—he did, she could not live with him. If nothing else, living at Horizons was evidence of the fact that abuse would not magically disappear. It could not be willed away. She had heard enough horror stories and met enough women who were on their third and fourth attempts to make a clean break from a bad marriage to realize that returning to Peter would only take her, and her little girl, down an ugly path.

It reminded her of when she quit smoking. She mulled it over as her girlfriends talked about it endlessly—hashing over their failed attempts to quit, then compromising on cutting back instead. The day Elisa decided to quit was the day she found Kelly playing with a lit cigarette left in an ashtray by the bathroom sink as she was getting her daughter's bath ready. She never did figure out how a two-year-old managed to reach up there to snatch the cigarette or how she managed to toy with the mysterious smoking plaything without getting burned. All Elisa knew was that she was damned lucky nothing had happened to Kelly. She flushed the cigarette down the toilet and never lit one again. Once she had decided to give them up, it was a done deal. She had that same feeling about Peter.

God, how things had changed from the beginning! She had loved him so. And she knew that there was a time when Peter Tate adored her more than anything. It was written all over his face when she opened the door to greet him for a date. It was in the way he held her head to his chest when they hugged, the way he pulled the sheet up around her to protect her from the cold after they made love. The way he tickled the backs of her knees as she stood at the kitchen sink tackling the dinner dishes. Watching the effect she had on Peter made her feel like the most feminine, sensual woman in the world.

If she banished those remembrances, she'd have lost conviction in the value of love and its ability to make us shine from the inside out. That would be a loss far greater than her home or even her marriage. The fact that it didn't last forever didn't mean that it had never existed at all. For so long, she had been determined to pinpoint when the relationship fell apart. Surely one of them was to blame. Or there was a clear catalyst to the deterioration. Things could not disintegrate so thoroughly without an inciting factor. Ultimately she accepted that there were no immediate answers and that the search to unravel the clues was a fool's game. The marriage had disintegrated. Dreams had evolved into nightmares. It had all been spoiled. The most revealing answers in the world could not reverse what had been done, so what was the point in expending so much energy to procure them? It was time to move away from what was and attack the present with the gusto that had been key to her personality.

She realized that her current anxieties were over money more than anything else and that realization opened her eyes to the futility of keeping her marriage alive. It was not the man she missed; it was the bank account. She had been living off their joint checking account. Peter hadn't done anything sneaky with that account after she left because he was certain his family would be returning to him and he didn't want to escalate conflict unnecessarily. She sought the advice of a women's rights counselor, who advised her to have their joint savings account frozen until she had the situation under control, just in case. It turned out that Peter had been given the same advice, so there were no hard feelings about freezing the money, except that it did panic Peter to discover that his wife was thinking rationally rather than emotionally. He was anxious to end this whole episode before she got comfortable being on her own.

Money was the overriding obstacle to getting on with her life. She actually grew thankful that it was her greatest hurdle. At least she didn't have to live in fear that her husband would track her down and attack her, take Kelly or badger her with death threats. So many of her new friends trembled at the mere mention of their husbands' or lovers' names. Peter wasn't like that. It was more like his temper consumed him, claimed his mind. But he wasn't an evil man. She was lucky for that. Now she just needed a job.

She needed to plan her move from Horizons quickly, before Clint Andrews turned this shelter into a house of horror. She'd been able to push him out of her mind—to tuck his existence into a slice of reality she could keep locked away—until yesterday.

It was midmorning, and Elisa had just dropped Kelly off at the Leland Avenue church, where she'd enrolled her in a weekly arts program. She headed for the Horizons community room to log on to a computer and search employment sites, stopping in her room to grab a notepad and pen. There, resting comfortably on Kelly's bed with a can of Coke in his hand, she found Clint. This stunning display of boldness was infuriating. Now he had invaded her space as well as her body. This was the sanctuary where her baby slept, played, read her books, and snuggled with her mom.

He never explained being there. He simply saw it as his prerogative, she assumed. This time his touch, his physical being, was impossible to tolerate or dismiss. He was there on Kelly's bed, and his fingers burned into her flesh as he pulled her against him. She pulled away and the can he was grasping in one hand toppled onto the bad, the sticky brown liquid streaming onto Kelly's pink satin pillow with the shiny white roses. Kelly's prize gift from her dad lay soiled and tainted by the animal who pushed her down on her stomach and smashed her face hard into the mattress. He took her from behind, so violently and so quickly that the room spun around her. And then he left her lying there like a piece of trash, dirty, disheveled and worthless. She had never felt that ugly before, and it was a feeling no amount of bath water, lotions, or perfumes could wash away. This time he had penetrated her emotional fortress. It was time to move on—and fast.

Last week's job search didn't hold much promise for Elisa. She had been on three interviews, two through Internet job sites and one through an employment agency. She had a few years of college under her belt, but she hadn't worked since she was five months pregnant with Kelly, so she had no proven skills to fall back on. Two of the jobs were receptionist positions, one in a doctor's office, the other in a hair salon. She didn't think she could live on the salary she'd earn in either spot. Still, she couldn't be fussy, so she put on her brightest smile and sat through the routine interrogations, neither of which left her feeling particularly optimistic about being selected. She was a bit more hopeful about the third prospect.

She had called in response to an ad soliciting an office manager for a company that owned several high-rise apartment buildings along the city's lakefront. She made an appointment for the interview, and when she arrived for her meeting, it was like she had stepped into a circus. The four people in the office were running in and out of one another's offices, exchanging files and looking extremely overwhelmed. *Hardly an opportune time*, she thought. What she didn't know was that the chaos was sparked by the fact that the manager of their Oak Street building had called in sick that day, adding that her husband was being transferred to Boston and that she was hereby giving her two weeks' notice.

After standing unnoticed for several minutes, a sophisticated-looking woman in her later thirties glanced at Elisa, an island of calm amid clamor, watching the curious collection of maniacs with an air of quiet respect. The woman crept to Elisa's side and looked at the associates with an outsider's eye. A slow smile came to her face, and her eyes grew warm and approachable. "Not your classic image of real estate moguls, huh?" she chuckled. "But a nice group of crazies just the same. Are you here to see someone?"

"I'm here to interview for the office manager position. Actually, I think it might be better if I call back later, when everyone's not so rushed."

"If you wait for that, you'll be interviewing in the next millennium. Tell you what--I'm queen of the crazies, Adrienne Phelps. We're all sharing the interview load, and we certainly could use some help right away, so why don't you just sit right here for now. I'll bring you some forms to fill out, and then we can talk for a few minutes." She turned to leave and then looked back at Elisa. "Anyway, it's good that you see the place as it really is." She walked behind the vacant reception desk to retrieve the paperwork and handed it to Elisa. "By the way, if the phone rings, feel free to pick it up," she said as she headed for her office, following it up almost immediately with, "Only kidding!"

About fifteen minutes later, Adrienne returned to escort Elisa back to her office for the interview. They chatted about the beautifully decorated office, the rush hour traffic Elisa had maneuvered in order to arrive on time, the magic of Chicago ... everything but the job. Finally, she said, "I bet you're wondering if I'll ever get down to the reason you're here. Well, first I'm getting a sense of your people skills, how you communicate, your comfort level with mindless chatter ... your schmooze style. Half this job is schmooze. More than half, really."

"I expected it to be mostly e-mails and phone messages," Elisa commented, genuinely surprised. "But I really enjoy talking to people. Uh, that sounds like the stupidest thing I could have said. Okay, let's get real. I don't enjoy talking to everybody. But the thing is that even if I don't enjoy it, I make sure they don't know it. I know how to calm people down." She thought about all the times she managed to get Peter to cool down just when he was on the brink of exploding.

"And I try to speak well, use proper English. It's a thing I do to try to get my little girl in the habit of speaking correctly. Even television today uses terrible English, 'ain't this' and 'ain't that.'" She hesitated for a moment, deciding what to say next. "And I really need a job." She looked down at the floor and then realized that she'd never sell herself unless she sat up straight, adopted an air of confidence, and looked this woman right in the eye. "I haven't worked in many years, so I don't have any job references, but I have all sorts of character references. I prepared a list of names and phone numbers to leave with my application."

After a few more minutes of routine questions about schedule, overtime flexibility, computer skills, and punctuality, Adrienne said that the job paid $950 a week and that she would call Elisa within a few days to let her know where things stood. She walked Elisa to the door, introducing her to the other executives as they passed the conference room on the way out. This time they were sitting back in their chairs, laughing and gobbling up popcorn from a paper coffee maker filter that was serving as a bowl for the time being.

"If you bring me on board," Elisa said, leaving the group, "I promise to get you a giant popcorn bowl and to keep two flavors of Garrett's popcorn on the shelf. I'll bet no one else made you that offer."

"I'll bet you're right," the tall, husky man at the head of the table shot back at her.

"We'll be back in touch with you real soon."

After her latest talk with Peter and latest encounter with Clint, Elisa realized how truly desperate she was to land the job with the real estate company. Up until now, she had maintained the same hidden fantasy: She would hear Peter's voice and realize how much she adored him. She would hear the agony in his pleas for a second chance and find a depth of sincerity in the words. Tonight, however, like all the other nights on which she called Peter, she hung up the phone feeling empty and more certain that she needed to redirect her life. She ended the call by suggesting a meeting to put any lingering doubts about their future together to rest. She would somehow manage to find work and provide for herself and her daughter.

She had been hampered with the notion, instilled in her and generations before her, that a woman was nothing without a man. It was a lie perpetuated by society's enduring male hierarchy, too monumental to be challenged by the beaten-down female gender that had grown weary from fighting for equality and recognition. It was easier to succumb to the notion and believe that any female worth her salt had a man at her side. How many women jumped from lover to lover or endured despicable treatment just to avoid judgement from a world that assessed their value based upon the quality of man they could land.

She went into the living room and took a seat behind Kelly, who was lying on the floor watching TV. She pulled Kelly back toward her so that her head rested against her mother's legs, and the two of them sat quietly until Elisa heard her cell phone ringing. The number on the screen was unfamiliar, and Elisa had a hunch it was about the job. Or was it her mom calling from the landline at her office, which never showed up as familiar on the phone? She had finally broken down and confessed her circumstances to her mother a few days earlier, after tapping out on excuses for never being reachable at home. It was a nightmare conversation, but Elisa survived the questioning from her mom, who practically ordered her to come stay with her parents. In the end, Elisa could not be persuaded, having grown in self-reliance. She knew that once her parents had her in their midst, they'd start brainwashing her to forgive Peter and keep the family together. It would be unusual for her parents to call on a Sunday night, though. They always spoke in the morning.

"Hello." Elisa was hiding anxiety beneath a facade of cheerfulness.

"Hi, Elisa. It's Adrienne Phelps. I know it's strange to be calling on a Sunday night, but you know how our office gets in the morning and I had this feeling the whole day tomorrow would fly by before I had a chance to call you." She paused briefly. "We'd like to groom you for a building manager spot. We went ahead and filled that position that put us in such a tizzy on Friday. But that whole fiasco made us realize that we really need more backups. We figured you could come on and work with us to learn how to run the apartment buildings and we'd move you into a spot when someone else moved on. Until then, you'd assist the four of us and even help with Marty's load when he starts going crazy. We'll pay you nine and a quarter a week until you get your own building, and then it will go up, depending on the size of the building you get. What do you say?"

She stopped for a quick moment and then kept right on talking as if, it seemed to Elisa, she was sure that if she could get all the facts out at once, she could conclude this ordeal quickly and get on with her Sunday night. "You'll have to learn how to run the rental office and run credit checks on apartment applicants and handle delinquent rent checks and all that sort of thing. But you seem like a quick study and you scored an A for your schmooze skills the other day."

Elisa was flabbergasted. "Can I start tomorrow?"

"See you at nine," Adrienne answered, sounding genuinely happy about the situation. Her pleased tone gave Elisa an extra shot of confidence. "Welcome to the insane asylum."

Elisa started back into the living room to share the news with Kelly and Marsha and a few of her other new friends. She felt better than she'd felt in a long time—excited, proud, and just the right amount of scared. Then she stopped to think. Where on earth could she buy a popcorn bowl before nine in the morning?

CHAPTER 10

This Monday morning marked the first time Julianne had entered her office before daylight in a long time. When she was a young producer—anyone over thirty was considered a veteran and nearly over the hill—she did her share of overnight editing sessions. Now, though, her rise up the ranks brought with it the small perk of shorter workdays—just ten to twelve hours instead of the customary fourteen-hour schedule. But today she wanted to get an early start. She was finding it difficult to focus on *Chicago Sizzle* while concentrating on the documentary. Things would get better in a few days, when she completed the last *Sizzle* episode before a four-week hiatus. This was the first time a hiatus had been added in the middle of the season. The station's revenues were down due to tough economic times. Ad revenue was on the decline, and Ted Marshall decided that a hiatus would help compensate for the shortfall. *Chicago Sizzle* would just go into repeats for a while.

It was a blessing in disguise, she felt. This way the staff could fully focus on the family violence documentary. With the Clint Andrews twist, the show would require more attention than originally planned. Investigative work demanded triple-checking facts and extreme legal caution in writing and production. The threat of a lawsuit was looming out there, and station management was unquestionably risk adverse.

Today was definitely going to be a killer, she thought as she nibbled on her bagel and sipped coffee. First she was scheduled to hook up with Jake, who was doing double duty as a cameraman and editor and was scheduled to work with her on new promo spots for the special. Then she was scheduled to meet with Tina to compare research notes. However, it was the prospect of lunch itself that weighed on Julianne's mind. Just before she left the office on Friday, Ted Marshall's secretary had called to say that he'd like Julianne to join him for lunch on Monday. Pam Avery was stopping by to get a handle on what was going on at the station during her maternity leave, and the three of them could grab a bite to eat.

Her first reaction to the call was that she was in big trouble. Ted had never invited her out to lunch before and she knew that Pam hadn't planned on coming by the office. When the two women had spoken a few days earlier, Pam was reveling in her freedom from management crises and ratings pressures and was remarking about how sad it was that this freedom was only to last a few more weeks.

Julianne's first inclination was to get Ted on the phone to try to pry out what was on his mind. She fought the urge, however, as he surely would have interpreted the gesture as that of a paranoid female. Instead, she decided to maintain a cool facade and let herself stew over the situation in solitude over the weekend. Since this scenario resulted in a frustrating night of sleeplessness, she figured she might as well just come into the office and get a head start on the day's activities.

There was so much research to be done. Tina was carrying the brunt of the load, but Julianne needed to focus on the facts too. Private funding versus public funding. Accountability versus good faith policies. Statistics on women returning to their abusers, often with fatal results. Patterns of behavior passed on from generation to generation—men learning to abuse and women learning to endure. There was a great deal to digest, and the voluminous stack of articles and interview notes provided a blessed refuge from personal dilemmas and soul-searching.

She gazed out the window as the sun broke through the heavy

sky and skipped across the choppy Chicago river. The soft but surprising touch of a hand on her shoulder startled her, and she jumped, splashing the hot coffee all over her desk and onto the large plastic blotter pad on her desk that protected a haphazard collection of personal photographs. She spun around to find Jake looming over her with a broad smile on his face. The fact that he'd caught her completely off guard obviously delighted him. Her heart was thumping from the surprise interruption. Maybe, she realized, it was also thumping because there was something special in his smile. His eyes seemed to penetrate her soul in a way no other man ever had. His face and the slow motion of his lanky body stirred up feelings in her that she had fought desperately to suppress for the longest time.

"Another fine mess," Jake said with a smile, offering a laughably weak impersonation of Oliver Hardy as he grabbed a couple of napkins from the dry edge of her desk and began sopping up the coffee spill. When his hand landed over a photo of bikini-clad Julianne sharing a beach with Allen Miller, he lifted the blotter, removed the picture, and began studying it.

"That's okay," Julianne commented. "We can throw the rest of the coffee on that one. No great loss."

"The picture or the guy?" he asked.

"Both," was her matter of fact reply.

"I was sure he'd worm his way back into your heart," Jake muttered thoughtfully, as if talking to himself. Then he looked her in the eye. "Interesting that you haven't gotten rid of his picture."

"I haven't even gotten rid of him" was the response the longed to share, but what was the point? Allen was a dead end, and she didn't want Jake to suspect she didn't comprehend that.

"It was buried under so much stuff that I didn't even realize it was still under here," she answered in total honesty. "You can be sure I'll get rid of it now," she said, snatching it from his hand and tossing it in the trash.

Jake reached down to retrieve it. "Not so fast," he teased. "I like the part with you in your swimsuit. I think I'll hang onto it so I have something to blackmail you with one day."

"Be my guest. Just lose the face of Mr. Self-Absorbed. I can't believe that guy had me dancing to his tune for so long. You're a pal. Why didn't you try to straighten me out?" She didn't even know why she had uttered the words. It was so typical to seek out someone to blame besides oneself. She knew better, but the words poured out nonetheless.

He stared at her with a depth of affection she had never seen before. "You wouldn't believe how many speeches I rehearsed on the subject of you and Allen Miller. But I knew you'd never listen. In case no one ever told you, sweetheart, you have a tendency to be exceptionally pigheaded. Besides," Jake continued, "I wasn't a hundred percent sure I could be objective about the guy."

This was the first time Jake had even eluded to having feelings beyond mere friendship for her. Every part of her practical mind told her to just let the remark pass as if it carried no underlying message. Instead, she stood up and, with a radiant beam of morning sunlight sweeping across his face, placed a hand on each of his shoulders and lifted up on her toes to kiss him. It was an urge that came upon her so quickly she didn't think twice. The kiss was warm and gentle, a timid exploration of a pair of lips she had denied herself for so long. That exploration intensified as she felt his yearning, a hunger that seemed to erupt from the deepest part of him and that rendered her breathless. He enfolded her in his arms and this single kiss that had started in such gentleness transformed into a burst of passion that seemed endless. Finally, their lips parted. She stood awestruck, her eyes fixated on the smooth, soft hollow of his neck. Neither of them said a word. Neither of them stepped away.

Never meeting his eyes, she said, "I've wanted to do that for the longest time. And I'm not sorry." She turned back to her desk, trying to think of how to salvage her dignity and make sure that she hadn't damaged their friendship. She struggled for a way to navigate through the silence, ultimately sitting down, reaching for her cup, and above all avoiding his stare. "Why are you at work so early anyway?"

"I got a call last night that two cameramen on the early crew called in sick and they needed me to fill in. I'll be wrapped up in time for our graphics session." His voice was flat, as if he were masking emotions that threatened to expose his thoughts.

"Just let me know when you are ready for that," she said with a tone of fake coolness. "Now let me just go get some paper towels and clean up the rest of this mess." She stepped around him and succeeded in escaping her office without ever looking into his eyes.

Two hours later, when they sat side by side in the graphics room, a tension built of fear, embarrassment, and a nearly uncontrollable lust separated them. It was as if they had made a silent pact to pretend that the day was only now beginning and that the fiery encounter that transpired only hours earlier had never happened. She decided to turn her thoughts to the safer subject of Ted Marshall and their pending lunch date. Only she wasn't sure that lunch date was safe at all.

The graphics designer explained that she needed to take a short break to set up the equipment for the next phase of their session. In an attempt to divert the conversation from reference to the kiss, Julianne said, "I don't have a good feeling about this meeting with Ted. It just doesn't sit right. Do you think maybe he's going to cancel *Chicago Sizzle*? I mean, I keep hearing about cutbacks. And Pam's coming in for the meeting. I can already picture the ax being sharpened. Local programming is always the first sacrifice. It's a good thing the news team loves you so much. You don't have a thing to worry about."

"What's not to love?" he softly replied. It was more than a witty remark. It was a bridge between two intermingling conversations— one spoken, one buried but burning. She ignored the question. The designer returned to her post, and they resumed the session.

The graphics looked great, and for once no technical glitches delayed their schedule. They wrapped up right on time and she collected her notes and purse, preparing a response for what she was certain would be Ted's announcement that he and Pam had decided to cancel her series. As she turned to leave the room, Jake reached for her elbow and, giving it a friendly squeeze as he often did, whispered, "Good luck at lunch. Call me later and let me know how it goes."

Promising that she would, she made the short trek to Ted's office.

There was an uncomfortable stillness at the table. Part of it came with the natural ambiance of this room. Even though Ted had never invited her to join him before today, everyone knew that the station executives frequented one particular restaurant: The River Club. It was as stiff and dull as most of the executives themselves and was unmistakable male turf—the kind of place she was certain had originated years ago as a men's club and only relinquished its single gender membership status under duress. As she glanced about the room, she noticed very few female patrons, and those she did spot in the crowd sat quietly in their neat, nondescript suits, simple strands of pearls perfectly in place and two-inch-heeled pumps parked beneath their tightly crossed legs. This was not at all the kind of place she felt at ease.

For the first time in the many years Julianne had known Pam Avery, she found it impossible to read her face. She had always been grateful for the wonderful working relationship they shared, one based upon professional respect and personal loyalty. The emotional distance Pam now inserted between them was Julianne's confirmation that trouble was brewing and that she was not going to enjoy this meal.

With the perfunctory amount of small talk and ordering of entrees out of the way, Pam smiled and took a breath as if to brace herself. "Ted was filling me in on the plans for your documentary on family violence. It's a great idea, Julianne. I always thought we should do something along those lines—something that would tackle the stress faced by couples today and focus on keeping families together. I've never seen a show aimed at trying to keep couples together. Not sensational enough for most stations, I guess. But it's definitely the way to go for our image campaign. I think it's a great idea—doing something positive for married people in trouble instead of just dwelling on the negatives of the situation. It was very smart of you. I give you credit." She stopped to pick at her salad, confident that her point had been made.

Julianne gave her credit, actually. She must have put a lot of time into coming up with a diplomatic way to comply with Ted's instructions to make sure this special was risk-free and far removed from any controversy or negative commentary regarding Horizons, while at the same time avoiding alienating her key producer by allowing her to take credit for the mandated direction of the show.

Julianne set down her fork and looked at Pam, attempting to puncture her detached facade while being politically correct. "Pam, I can't tell you how wonderful it was to see all of the managers get behind the topic of domestic violence. We all know what a horror it is, with the statistics escalating year after year. It's to Ted's credit that we're going ahead with this. And I'm really glad that you're going to be back at work in time to help me with the show. You've always had such a talent for digging to the core of personal drama in the way you unfold a story. I can't wait to collaborate on the script with you."

"So," Ted chimed in, "I'm glad we're in agreement that the point of the show is to advise the poor women on how to patch up their marriages—counseling, communication and commitment. That's the message. Nothing's worse than seeing families torn apart."

Julianne understood. She was not being consulted. She was not being asked what she wanted to do. She was being ordered. Smart soldiers accepted their orders with unquestioned obedience and, if they played their cards right, rose through the ranks. At that moment, Julianne realized for the first time in nearly a decade in the business that she had no interest in being a good soldier.

"You're absolutely right, Ted. It's tragic to see family units dissolve. It's so much sadder, though, to meet the women who stay with their husbands, or even boyfriends, through years and years of abuse—horrible violence—because they have absolutely no place to turn. Wait until you see video on these women and hear their stories. I'm sure the show will make some waves with the legislators and shake a lot of people into reality. And I think we'll pick up some awards for you, too."

"It's not about awards, Julianne," he countered. Her stomach turned. She knew that to Ted Marshall, the business of television was about two things: ad sales and the ratings that drove ad sales. She continued looking him straight in the eye, determined that she would not waver in her approach. "The point is to make a difference by using the show to help people."

"Of course." Pam nodded in agreement. "We understand the direction you want for the show, Ted." Then, with a deliberately emphatic, upbeat tone that Julianne realized was entirely for her benefit, Pam continued. "As always, I know Julianne and her people will deliver a program that will make us all proud."

Realizing that this was a matter best handled later, when she had Pam to herself, Julianne decided to play the game and get through this damned lunch of bland salad, weak iced tea, and even weaker leadership. She offered a winning but artificial smile and concluded the conversation with a simple, "Yes. We've only just begun, but I can guarantee this show will be a source of pride." To herself, she added silently, *You'll undoubtedly be infuriated by it, and we may all get fired for it, but it will definitely be a production worthy of pride.* She swallowed her salad with greater ease than she could swallow the bologna conversation, going silent as Ted transitioned to complimenting Pam on how lovely she looked since dropping the baby weight.

"Born to breed, Pam. Anyone can see that," he said, confident that this was the highest praise he could offer a woman—even a strong working professional with ten times his ability. Julianne detected Pam's subtle cringe and empathized. It was a comment any smart woman would find offensive. Pam responded with a polite, "Thank you."

A few minutes later, Ted signed for the bill and they returned to the station. The good news, Julianne realized, was that *Chicago Sizzle* had not been canceled and she still had a steady job. The bad news was that with her plans for the documentary unchanged, despite her bosses' far from sublte message, she probably wouldn't have that job for long.

Juggling a tote bag, three blouses from the cleaners, a pair of newly heeled pumps from the shoe repair, and the world's most overstuffed purse was a sweet feat, but attempting to retrieve the day's mail without setting any of the items down was a lesson in futility. The purse went tumbling, its fall softened by landing on the pile of blouses scattered on the tile floor. With a sigh, she leaned down to collect the items. That's when her eyes caught sight of the oxblood suede loafers heading her way. She'd seen those shoes before and was grateful that they prepared her for the surprise arrival of Clint Andrews at her doorstep. At least she had a few seconds to muster a nonchalant demeanor.

"Having one of those days, huh?" He chuckled at her perplexed state of affairs. "Your doorman took the risk of letting me pass into the mail area when I spotted you back here, although I feel his watchful eyes piercing my back right now. You came in the back way, I guess. I've been waiting in the lobby for about ten minutes." He delivered this entire greeting with an air of cool confidence, as if he had every right to be stalking her at her apartment building. And he was right: the doorman was checking things out to make sure she had no problem with this unannounced guest. The fact was, she had a hell of a problem with him, but it was nothing the doorman could handle.

Forcing a smile, she offered a confused stare. "Did we have plans for tonight that I've forgotten? I'm so sorry." She was fully aware of the fact that she had made no future plans to spend time alone with Clint. "It's a mess too because I have a cousin from Madison staying with me for a few days and I have to meet her downtown for dinner. I just have time to drop these things off and make a quick change." It wasn't the most imaginative lie, but the out-of-town guest line was intended to send the message that a visit upstairs was out of the question, at least for the rest of the week. The truth was that Tina was due to swing through the revolving door at any moment. She and Julianne intended to spend the evening munching on Thai food and structuring the segments for the documentary. The last thing in the world Julianne needed was for Tina to walk smack dab into Clint in the lobby of her building. She had to hustle him out of there. She gathered all her belongings and shifted in the direction of the elevator. There was no way in hell he was going to accompany her upstairs.

"It's okay. We didn't actually have plans. I just called your office and Lianne said you'd left for the day, so I thought I'd take a stab at catching you here before you made other plans. Guess I should have thought of grabbing you earlier." He moved closer and placed his hand on her backside. "I have to admit I've been thinking of grabbing you quite a lot lately." The slick smile was supposed to be a turn-on. It was anything but.

A wave a nausea engulfed her, but she fought valiantly to disguise it, inching toward the asylum of the elevator. "I wish I could invite you up for a glass of wine, but I've really got to change."

"Need some help?" His persistence was as revolting as his reputation.

Again the pat smile. "Not tonight. But thanks for the offer." She turned to make her escape. "I'll call you in the morning."

A minute and a half later, she was safely inside her door, and no sooner had she set down the mail than the doorman buzzed to announce Tina's arrival. It was a close call.

Elisa was more at ease in front of the camera than Julianne had ever imagined. She was concerned at first that her face would not be sufficiently camouflaged since the lens was pointed directly at her and was only a few feet away. But Jake had worked for what seemed an eternity on lighting the room so that she would appear as an anonymous silhouette. The stark beams of the bright lights bounced onto the bare gray wall behind her, leaving her in a safe pool of darkness haloed by light. The innocuous outline of a delicately boned face remained the only visible trace of the woman whose electronically filtered voice would disclose stories of fear, humiliation, and determination.

She had agreed to participate in the production as a personal quest to inspire others who shared her predicament and to educate those who assumed they were immune to such distress. However, secrecy of her identity was critical, she repeated as the crew prepped for the shoot. She even made Julianne, who was seated alongside the camera, take her place in the interview chair so that she could personally inspect the visual effect on Jake's small camera monitor. She was instantly satisfied with what she saw and even joked that Julianne looked so comfortable in the seat that *she* should just stay there and Elisa would interview her.

Elisa assessed the crew members before slipping back into the darkness. In a minute, she would be sharing the intimate, carefully hidden details of her marriage with these strangers and she realized that if, at the very least, she made eye contact with the faces behind the equipment, she would feel slightly less vulnerable. Julianne began making small talk as the audio man clipped the small microphone to Elisa's blouse. Like any seasoned producer, she knew that the secret to a truly good interview was to lead your prey into the conversation easily, to avoid awareness of the moment when the camera began recording. As Elisa settled into the chair and Julianne asked what her daughter was doing while her mom was occupied with her TV debut, Julianne simply slipped her hand behind the cameraman's knee and tapped him emphatically—her signal that he should begin rolling.

An hour later, they turned off the equipment and clicked on a soft light in the corner of the room. The interview had been draining on everyone, as emotionally demanding to hear as it was to tell. Elisa had opened her heart to these people, losing herself in thought and reaching out to connect with the faceless women she knew would be sitting in their living rooms one day soon, listening to her story as if it were their own.

It was the comfort of the shadows and the kindness of the crew, she explained later, that melted her inhibitions and allowed her memories to emerge in excruciating clarity. She spoke of mortifying words her husband had hurled at her during sporadic fits of rage. She spoke of disintegrating self-esteem that threatened to turn her into a robot, of the choice to forfeit her dearest friendships rather than admit to those she loved that her life had become a degrading hell. She spoke of the paralyzing moment when her husband's temper erupted so violently that he struck a blow to her that was far less stinging to her flesh than to her soul.

It came on a Thursday night, when Kelly was a couple of houses down, working on her science fair project with one of her classmates. It was the first evening she'd had to herself in some time. Peter was scheduled to be at work until nine, and Kelly wouldn't be back until that same approximate time. With three precious hours to herself, Elisa decided to indulge in a long, hot bath and escape from the hideous mess that awaited her in the kitchen. Before Kelly's exit, she and her mom had devoted the better part of the afternoon to the first phase of the science project, and remnants of their endeavor were scattered all about the kitchen. Pots, sticks, and rags soaked with assorted dyes filled the kitchen sink and counters. All water soluble, it was temporary disarray, but the explosion of colors was enough to make anyone think the kitchen was a war zone. Paper shavings and bits of Styrofoam were everywhere. What would culminate in being a detailed rendition of the solar system was, at this juncture, a collection of toothpicks and textures, little more than a jumble of components.

A calming bath would definitely help prepare Elisa for the tedious cleanup job that awaited her, and she needed cleanup complete by eight o'clock so she could get Peter's dinner started. Taking a cue from the *Cosmo* she had scanned that afternoon, she carried a pair of candlesticks in from the living room and set them on the vanity adjacent to the tub. Bath oils and candlelight. It had been quite a while since she had pampered herself that way. She immersed herself in the water and lost herself in her dreams.

Perhaps that was why she did not hear the sound of the back door announce her husband's early arrival. The carpeting muffled his march down the corridor so that by the time he blasted into the bathroom in search of his wife, she practically flew into the air in shock. His entrance came with the unmistakable thunder of violence. Something was desperately wrong. She was afraid to ask. Afraid to move. He did the moving for her, reaching down to grab her arm and yank her from the water. For a moment, she thought her shoulder would be pulled from its socket. She stood naked, dripping as he shook her by the shoulders.

"What the hell's going on here? You're taking a luxurious little bath, my darling wife, while this house is a fucking pigsty! What cyclone tore through that kitchen, for Chrissake? What the hell's wrong with you?"

His breath stunk of liquor. Not beer, but hard liquor. He rarely drank the hard stuff and she feared both the reason behind his tantrum and the manifestations of it. Whoever or whatever caused him to go over the edge, she was the one who was going to pay the price.

She knew that she had to remain calm and focus on calming Peter. He was out of control, and it was up to her to rein him in. "It's messy, I know, but it's nothing, really. I'll have it all back to normal in fifteen minutes. I was just taking a little break first. And then I'm going to start your supper. I have a beautiful rib eye steak and those scalloped potatoes that you like. Just give me a few minutes."

The grip on her arm only tightened, and he pulled her through the hallway, not even allowing her to cover herself with the robe that dangled from the bathroom door.

He threw her into the kitchen and pushed her against the stove, where the pots from the dye she had boiled to color the planets sat, still half-full. "Don't tell me this is nothing. It's a fucking junk house. Look at this floor!" His speech was slurred, and beads of sweat merged to form narrow streams that trickled down his forehead. He bent down to run his hand across the shavings and scraps of paper that were strewn everywhere. From his crouched position, he seized her

157

arm and pulled her down beside him. She pulled back, struggling to release herself from his grip. This only fueled his anger, and with one violent tug, he stretched her body face-down on the floor, pinning her into place with his knees pressed into the small of her back.

She lay there motionless. She was paralyzed mentally as well as physically. Her naked body had been flung to the ground as if it were a pile of garbage, her moist flesh a magnet for the scraps and crumbs that littered the floor. He pushed down hard on her face, forcing her cheek into a pile of tinted cellophane she and Kelly had been using to decorate the base of the presentation. It clung to her skin, and she could barely breathe. She didn't want to breathe.

"I can't eat in here!" he exclaimed.

She lay there in naked humiliation and he was worried about his dinner. She thought she'd pass out. To this day, she didn't know for certain if she did or did not. All she remembered after that comment was that Peter flew out the door in search of a more palatable environment to partake of his meal and that sometime later, luckily before Kelly arrived home, she had found the strength to pull herself up from the floor and peel away the filth in a steaming hot shower. She didn't recall cleaning up the kitchen but knew that she somehow must have done so.

She managed to put Kelly to bed, acting as if nothing had transpired. Her primary goal was to spare her daughter anxiety, shield her from awareness of her parents' nightmare marriage. Then she fell into bed herself, for the first time in her life praying that the spot beside her on the sheet would remain vacant. She wasn't that lucky.

When she awoke the next morning, Peter's hungover body was beside her and a dozen yellow roses lay wilting on the dresser. No words were ever exchanged about the incident. It was easier for her to attribute the occurrence to the disastrous results of his uncharacteristic drinking. As for him, it appeared easier to express his regret with a half-dead bouquet of flowers than with the spoken word.

She had buried that horrendous evening in the deepest crevasse of her mind, sharing the story with no one, not a soul, until the quiet hum of the TV gear and unflinching eye of the camera coaxed it to the surface, where, just maybe, it could do some good for someone. Following that painful discourse, Elisa lapsed into silence. The interview was over.

It was a moving, debilitating experience for each person in the room. The soft glow of the lamp that stood in the corner formed an arc that bridged the intimacy of the interview with the reality of the shoot.

Jake stepped to the door, cracking it open just enough to signal that the taping had stopped. Everyone at Horizons was aware of the production and had cooperated in keeping as quiet as possible while the crew was secluded. Jake glanced through the narrow opening to see Clint Andrews leaning against the wall like an expectant father outside the delivery room. He was hungry for the publicity a television show would bring him and could not suppress the excitement he felt at having a production take place right within his kingdom.

Their eyes met for a brief moment. A tall dark-haired woman crossed between them as she and her little boy made their way into the family room and Jake watched as Clint turned his head to follow her footsteps, eying her from head to toe as she moved timidly past his stare. Then, looking back at Jake, he shot a knowing smile and coy wink, happy to be able to share this moment of appreciation for a fine female physique with another man. Jake turned away, disgusted to think Andrews would see them as brothers in an ill-conceived fraternity. But as he glanced at Julianne and Elisa chatting quietly across the room, he couldn't avoid admitting to himself that he and his buddies had probably shared hundreds of those knowing smiles and man-to-man winks over the years. It left him with an uncomfortable feeling and the need to approach the two women he greatly respected as they gathered their things and wandered into the corridor where Clint lingered anxiously.

"Everything moving ahead, okay?" he asked as the trio made their way downstairs. Julianne paid special attention to Clint's demeanor.

She expected that he would be slightly unraveled by Elisa's private interview, uncertain of her ability to hide their little secret. Instead, he was all smiles, the proud father of this heroic refuge. This irritated Julianne immensely. How demented and arrogant could a man be that he would not even doubt the vulnerability of his victim? As always, she camouflaged her emotions, knowing she mustn't rock the boat. Not yet.

"Everything went well. This promises to be quite a program."

As the group prepared to leave, Clint took Julianne's elbow and eased her gently toward him. Jake, who was just ahead of her, slowed his pace and hesitated, as though he needed to take inventory of the video cables he had tucked under his arm. "You don't have to rush back so soon, do you? How about heading out for a glass of wine?" Clint whispered to Julianne.

Jake nonchalantly spun around to catch her eye. "Come on," he prodded. "You know we have an edit session in an hour. Let's hustle."

"Yes," Julianne quickly responded. "I'm coming." To Clint, she smiled innocently, adding, "Duty calls."

Once outside and in Jake's car, she squeezed his hand as it rested on the wheel. "You make a great big brother. Thanks."

"Oh. great. Big brother. Not exactly what I had in mind."

Ignoring the comment, she released his hand and settled into the seat. "It's too late to bother stopping at the office. Why don't you just drop me off at my place?"

The ride back to Julianne's apartment was silent, a good kind of silent. The radio was tuned to soft jazz, and Julianne felt a happy serenity flow through her. This was how she always felt when a new production was under way. It was one of the things she most enjoyed about her job. Even though she had no children, she equated it with a maternal feeling, a feeling of creating something new and wonderful, molding something whose possibilities were endless and developing it into something that bore one's own signature. It was an invigorating feeling despite the heavy emotions entangled with the interview and topic of the documentary.

Jake had worked with Julianne long enough to understand her moods so he left her to her private thoughts as he drove, glancing at her, unnoticed, every few minutes to witness how beautiful she looked with the day's last rays of sunshine lighting her face.

As they turned the corner onto her street, she prepared to jump out at the curb. But instead of slowing down, Jake continued down the block and pulled into a parking space that had miraculously opened up. "I'm on my own this week while Helene visits her folks back East. How about saving me from another night of Colonel Sanders?" he asked, as if her answer were irrelevant. He had already turned the key and popped open his door.

"I didn't plan on going out tonight," she said, obviously flustered. "I already have something in the fridge for dinner."

"Great. I'm sure with your creative juices flowing, you'll come up with a scrumptious way to stretch it for two. What's on the menu for tonight?"

She bowed her head mischievously and offered a coy smile. "Leftover Colonel Sanders."

CHAPTER 11

A soft stream of piano music drifted through the leather-lined alcove of the Coq D'Or lounge on the main level of the Drake Hotel. Elisa had selected the meeting place, and Peter was startled by her choice. He didn't think his wife even stepped foot inside the luxurious hotels of downtown Chicago other than to join him in attending one of the few flamboyant social events his various employers had hosted over the years.

His wife's familiarity with the shadowy, intimate decor of the Coq D'Or was puzzling and left him feeling a nagging twinge of jealousy. Since Elisa had called to suggest a face-to-face discussion, however, he supposed she was finally eager to reconnect with him. So he attempted to put jealously aside and focus on redemption. Each time he and Elisa had spoken on the phone since her departure, he had all but begged for the chance to talk things through in person. The sooner he could look into her eyes and talk some sense into her, he figured, the sooner they could put this whole ridiculous episode behind them. But up until now, she'd held firm despite his prodding.

Her steadfast attitude was something he had not witnessed in his wife, and frankly, he could do without it. An attitude brought on by too many hours spent in front of the tube watching Dr. Phil, he rationalized. Plus, her troublemaker friend Deena Garlinski had probably filled her head with a bunch of feminist crap too. Never mind that Deena had been happily married for nine and a half years. Peter insisted that Deena, his wife's closest friend since high school, was a dike—a word whose very sound made Elisa's skin crawl—and Peter hated dikes. As a court reporter, Deena was the one in her marriage to bring home a steady paycheck. Her husband, Rick, partnered in a house painting business with his brother, but neither of the men was much of a hustler, so their jobs came few and far between. Yet with no kids and a simple lifestyle, they made out just fine. Peter consistently harped on the Garlinskis' financial arrangement—role reversal, as he labeled it.

The Garlinskis were, he perceived, content with their lifestyle. They seemed to enjoy each other's company, splurged on Sunday afternoon cookouts in the tiny backyard of their small Evanston home and managed the bimonthly bowling club comprised of the three couples with whom they were closest. It was a group that, until recently, included him and his wife.

The couples met every other Tuesday for two games of bowling, separated by a couple of beers and a platter of greasy burgers delivered to the lanes from the bar. This arrangement worked out just fine for the Tates since Mondays and Tuesdays were Peter's days off from the restaurant. For Peter, this regularly scheduled gathering amounted to a concession to Elisa rather than a social activity he genuinely enjoyed. He didn't see much in his wife's choice of friends. He was bothered by the fact that the men did not have the brains for, or interest in, the business world. They were all in dissimilar lines of work and saw little sense in boring each other with recounts of their workday, cheating Peter of the chance to impress an audience that was undoubtedy beneath his stature. Other than sports, they talked a lot about their kids and family stuff and occasionally shared a couple of dirty jokes that Peter could take back to the guys at the restaurant. And the women were much too assertive for his taste. Elisa was so much more ladylike, he marveled, that it was surprising she'd remained so close with the other three girls for so many years.

Without a doubt, he saw Deena as the worst of the pack. She spoke her mind on everything from her job to the mayoral race to the deterioration of the city's school system to equal pay for equal work.

She was definitely a ballbuster, and her milquetoast husband just sat back and listened with an attentive ear whenever his wife dominated the conversation, which was all the time, in Peter's opinion.

Peter spent a couple of months mulling over how to gradually extract himself and his wife from this couples foursome without blatantly putting his foot down. The bowling club had been the one social gathering Elisa insisted upon attending. He thought it wise to exercise some diplomacy in tearing her from it, though the fact that he would ultimately do so was clear.

His plans to slowly ease away, were brought to an unexpected halt on a Tuesday evening in early November when, during the beer and burger break, table talk turned to everyone's plans for Thanksgiving. Elisa was explaining how she and Kelly were going to enjoy the holiday with her parents since Peter had to work at the restaurant, and she went on to joke about the fact that she'd probably be in her nineties before she had the chance to cook a holiday turkey in her own kitchen, saying that by then she would be too old and weak to lift the hefty bird from the oven. Peter didn't think it was such a funny joke. He interrupted her, stating that he was sick of her whining about his work schedule and reminding her that he did not appreciate being put down in front of friends. He made it so clear that Deena, he immediately became aware, couldn't stand it.

The jovial mood of the group turned heavy. Peter's face grew beet red, and the hostile, reprimanding tone of voice used as he chewed out his wife evidently appalled and embarrassed everyone present. He sat steeped in anger as Deena looked him straight in the eye. "Hey, Prince Charming, keep sweet talking your wife that way and you're liable to make us other girls jealous." She spewed this at him with more than her typical dose of sarcasm.

"Fuck off," was his swift response. It was not appreciated by Rick. Nor was it appreciated by Deena, who, true to form, did not wait for her willing and able husband to step in.

"No, why don't you fuck off? You know, Peter, we're willing to put up with a lot because we love Elisa, but there is a limit, and I think we've reached it. I know I have. I can't sit here and listen to the way you talk to her." Dismissing him, she turned to Elisa, who stared at her with a flabbergasted expression. She thought her friends were used to Peter's quirky personality by now and were forgiving of it. Until now, Elisa had assured Peter that her friends were nuts about him, as was she. Now he and his wife jointly discovered she was wrong and that Deena was about to deliver a message that had obviously been stifled for quite some time.

"You've got to be crazy to put up with his shit, Elisa. Crazy. If any of the men at this table talked to any of us with that cocky mouth or bullied us the way he does you, he'd be out the door so fast his head would spin. I just don't get it. But I can't stand to see it anymore." She stood up and reached under the seats for her purse, preparing to leave. There was an anger in her voice that Peter saw baffled his wife, and he could sense that Elisa was in a quandry over why Deena would be angry with *her*. With awkward goodbyes, the friends dispersed, and when they gathered together again two weeks later, it was without the Tates. Elisa reluctantly admitted to him that she was relieved when Deena called a few days later to say hello, apparently choosing to ignore what had happened in order to salvage the friendship.

So one way or another, Peter had succeeded in pulling Elisa away from the group of friends that challenged his power over her. He had no idea that she still managed to attend a girls–only lunch date once a month. Elisa, he later discovered, made the wise choice to keep such activities to herself. However, before long, it was a moot issue anyway. Elisa told him she was confused by the polarized experiences in life and love between her and her three friends, leading her to voluntarily withdraw from their little circle.

The name Deena Garlinski was seldom uttered at the Tate residence in the months preceeding Elisa's retreat from the household. Though Deena was a topic that had sparked more than one memorable fight between the Tates over the years, Peter grew bored with attempting to light Elisa's fuse by attacking her best friend, only to have her respond in her predictable manner: silence.

Now he sat on the red leather banquette in the bar at the Drake, waiting for the wife he hoped was no longer discontented, gauging how far he would have to go in the way of promises and niceties to lure her home. He was puzzled by missing her as he did and reasoned that he had never been one to embrace change. On top of that, tending to his personal needs while maintaining his job performance was a royal pain. Maybe it was because she had snatched his daughter away and his daughter was the best thing that ever happened to him. He was haunted by that explosive evening when he sent the kitchen table and chair hurling—and Kelly along with it. He admitted only to himself that he was astounded by his own behavior. She was just a little girl. His little girl.

Peter assuaged his guilt by reminding himself that Kelly was not so little that she couldn't understand what he meant when he explained that he was tired and they'd talk later. She understood English, for God's sake. She shouldn't have provoked him. And if she did find it necessary to test his patience, Elisa should have nipped it in the bud. He'd lost his temper, but it was understandable. And no one was hurt, for Chrissake. The whole thing had blown way out of proportion. Elisa must have been waiting for an excuse to make him crawl and get some attention for herself. Well, okay. She had his attention, and he was about to crawl. Such were the thoughts scrambling through the mind of Peter Tate as he awaited the arrival of his wife this Friday evening.

The first thing that struck Elisa when she saw her husband sitting there after such an agonizing absence was that he was wonderful to look at. She didn't remember his hair being quite that wavy or quite that long. She didn't remember the sharp angles of his cheekbones that lent a hint of the exotic to his dark brown eyes. She didn't remember how broad and strong his shoulders were. All she remembered these past weeks were the outbursts of violence, the curt conversations, and mechanical sex. Those days just before she left, she would look into those deep-set eyes and see only a reflection of herself. And she didn't like what she saw.

But she did like what she saw staring back at her from the small rectangular mirror above the chest of drawers in her room at Horizons, where she'd prepared for tonight's encounter. She had thought long and hard to determine appearance and demeanor for this meeting. The matter of appearace was the more manageable of the two. For her hair, the special conditioning treatment that was generally too time consuming. She went to the trouble of using electric rollers after her blow-dry, something she rarely did. It was either blow-dryer or rollers. There were not enough hours in a normal day to do both. She slid into the maroon jersey dress Peter always criticized for being too clingy and wore the dangling garnet drop earrings her parents had given her for her twenty-first birthday, the age at which, in their collective opinion, she was truly all grown-up and therefore in a position to wear dangling earrings. She recalled the laughs they all shared over that old-fashioned sentiment as she fastened the earrings tonight, feeling that wearing them would lend the hidden support of her parents' unconditional love.

Since fleeing to Horizons, she'd been less active that she was accustomed to—her emotional exhaustion had evolved into physical exhaustion as well. Fatigue was worsened by eating the starchy, more economical, meals the shelter could provide. She had put on a few pounds, to be sure. Looking at herself in the mirror, in that dress, she realized that they were much-needed pounds. She had a tendency to forget to eat when she was upset, and those last months at home, she was upset more often than not. Yes, she understood as she gazed at her reflection before leaving to meet her husband, there was indeed such a thing as *too thin*, and she was it.

She marched confidently toward the alcove at the back of Coq D'Or. Her eyes locked with Peter's. She had rehearsed this entry over and over again in her mind. She would be strong, self-assured, and vibrant. He would eat his heart out when he saw what he was about to lose. She would be in control even if it killed her, which, she felt at this moment, it might.

He stood as she approached and eased into her chair. As he reached to take her hand, she subtly curtailed that action, faking some need to adjust the small clutch bag, which she rested on the edge of the table. Then, as rehearsed in her mind, she placed her hands safely in her lap.

"It seems like I haven't seen you in years," were the first cautious words from his lips. "You look wonderful."

She thought of responding with a heartfelt, caustic comment like, "That's because you haven't bothered looking beyond your own sweet self." But she decided to proceed with forced pleasantries a while longer and make this evening as civil and productive as possible. "You too. Longer hair. It looks nice."

The waiter approached to take their drink order. "I'll have a Dewar's and water, easy on the rocks. And a Manhattan straight up for the lady. Two cherries." He smiled across the table and she knew he was waiting for her to acknowledge the thought they were sharing. The two cherry thing was a carryover from their very first date, when she explained that the only reason she ordered a Manhattan was to get the cherry garnish. From that time on, Peter made sure that bartenders treated her well by provided an extra cherry with her cocktail. She was less affected by treatment from bartenders than from her husband. From his weak smile, as he looked at her now, she could see that Peter never got that—and still didn't get it.

She knew he was proud of himself for remembering the extra cherry, and it annoyed her to think that he surmised such a trivial gesture would warm her heart. Fat chance. Plus, this afforded her the perfect opportunity to establish that she was taking care of herself tonight, tomorrow, and from then on. His days of *protecting* her were over. It took a while, but she finally got it through that thick skull of hers that for Peter, protection equaled control.

She interrupted the waiter as he was about to exit. "Actually, I think I'll just have a tall glass of sparkling soda with a splash of bitters and a twist. Lots of rocks." She ignored Peter's puzzled expression at this departure from habit and decided to keep her momentum going and plow ahead.

"I thought I should tell you in person that I'm not coming home, Peter. Neither is Kelly. I've been advised that you may want to challenge me on custody and I'm fully prepared for that. I have no doubt that custody will be awarded to me. But I'll be flexible when it comes to visitation rights. Kelly loves you very much, and she needs you. I know you love her too. I don't hate you. But I cannot live with you. And I don't want this to be any uglier than it already is. That's really the point I came here to make. I don't want things to get ugly, because I don't want us to scar our daughter any more than we have already." She had made it through the speech perfectly. She had nothing left to say and regretted that the only thing she had neglected to rehearse was a clean conclusion to that concise discourse.

Peter had been prepared for some theatrics, some grand expression of independence, and so he remained calm. The sentiments were colder than expected. He thought she'd explain how she needed more time away, time to heal, time to get over the pain, lots of heavy stuff meant to make him squirm. He didn't think she'd even utter the word *custody*. It was so premature after all. Okay, so he'd squirm a little more than planned. He'd give her the best damn squirming she could want. Then he'd roll out the surprise, the clincher: the promotion.

An awkward silence engulfed the table. Peter prepared to wow his wife with a first-class demonstration of humility. The drinks were set down in front of them, breaking the tension.

"Look, Elisa, let's not jump the gun. I know you've been wanting to get that off your chest. But things are different now. I know how preoccupied I got these past six months or so, and I know I wasn't the easiest guy to live with. I admit it. I'm not denying any of it. But you can't deny that you love me too. Or that we've built a life together. And I've been working to make that life even better. Maybe too hard. Maybe I let it get to me. But I've been breaking my back all year to show the new owner what I can offer, how I can do more if I get the chance. Well, he's opening up this new spot on Ontario Street, just off Michigan Avenue. He told me today he wants me to manage it. It's his baby, and he wants it handled right. He's willing to cough up some major bucks to make sure his baby gets enough tender loving care. It's better money than I ever made, honey. Better than I ever brought home to you. Enough to look for the house you've always wanted in Highland Park. We made it. So now let's enjoy it."

She froze, dumbstruck. She had prepared rebuttals, denials, and protests to his excuses. She didn't think that he'd come armed with a promotion and promise of the house they'd dreamed of for a decade. Her mind started whirling, and her heart started racing. She didn't want to blow it, act in haste, maybe make a mistake that couldn't be reversed. She didn't want to be a sucker either. She didn't know what she wanted. She didn't know what was right. The only thing she knew for sure was that if she stayed there any longer, she'd turn into the spineless jellyfish that was her old self and that she'd learned to despise since leaving her husband. Her decorum was already melting away. She had to make a run for it before he had a chance to break her down.

"I have to go, Pete. I don't know what to think right now, and it would be stupid for me to say anything." She spoke without ever meeting his eyes. She was headed to the door before she had completed the last sentence, and he wasn't fast enough to stop her. She raced to the corner of Michigan Avenue and Oak Street and jumped on a bus, where she stared blankly out the window.

It had been over a year since Jake had been in Julianne's apartment. Julianne had invited Helene and him for a drink before heading out to last year's local Emmy Awards ceremony. He later told her how surprised he was at the style of her apartment. The warm, feminine cocoon was not at all what he had envisioned for the woman he had only seen in nondescript business environments. Away from the steel and electronics of the television station, she had enveloped herself with plush mauve satin draperies, an old-fashioned velveteen couch and love seat, and thick pile carpeting that seemed to whisk the shoes right off one's feet. He was amazed, he confessed to her.

Now, following the Horizons shoot, with Jake at her side, Julianne breezed into the living room, tossing her papers and purse on the corner desk, switching on a small lamp and lighting three candles—two on the mantel and one on the end table. Her friends knew she had a penchant for candlelight; she said it transported her thoughts away from the harsh lights and mechanics of her work. It was important to her that her home feel separate and distinct from her place of business, mostly because she knew that her love of production could easily consume her and a cozy nest to return to at the end of the day would help keep her life in balance.

Jake stood back in the doorway, and she felt approval in his gaze. She felt he was the only man in her life who did not perceive her as a woman with two distinct personalities, each struggling to overtake the other, but as a full woman whose layers of complexity were mystifying and perhaps even intoxicating. Only when they were away from work and alone like this, did she allow herself the freedom to stand back and let that sink in.

She lifted a bottle of Chardonnay from the refrigerator door and handed it to him with the warm, easy glance shared between two people so familiar with one another that words were unnecessary. He uncorked the bottle as she began setting the table. Then, as she reached up into the cabinet for a tray, he walked up behind her, his chest slowly pressing against her back. He reached to the outstretched underside of her arms—arms that were like silk extending from her loose T-shirt. She didn't move but stood motionless in that position, feeling his strong fingertips stroking her skin, not wanting to ruin the moment, not wanting it to end. She leaned back and rested her head against his chest.

For one brief second, she removed herself from the rapture to contemplate its harsh reality. Now, this instant, she would either pull away gradually, salvaging the relationship and silently, emphatically signaling that it would not take a new course. Or she would rebel against her practical, controlled nature and follow a path that was as senseless as it was dangerous. One step to the left and the safety of the plates and glasses awaiting their place on the table and it would be over. But no. Her mind was made up as she sunk back into him seductively. He was warm and sensuous and wanted to make love to her—not have sex, make love. She was unable to control her desire, unable to let her mind rule her heart. It was as if her will were not her own.

Jake's arms enfolded her, his hands gliding across her body to caress her gently. Still standing behind her, their eyes never met. They did not need to see each other's faces as they communicated by touch, admitting to one another that it was time to take this inevitable journey, that the wait had been punishing but necessary. She knew it wasn't a simple matter of physical attraction or a brief episode that would lead to regret the next day. It was the realization of a predestined course. And after the years of denying their feelings, they would relish each second of this event. They would not hesitate. They would not be coy. They would not resist their desires any longer. They would enjoy each sensation, each touch and each movement without apprehension, without guilt.

His fingers aroused her. She turned her head and nestled her face against his neck, nuzzling into the niche of his body like a kitten curling up into the fold of one's arm. She took a long slow breath, as if she were absorbing him into her body—his scent, his warmth. She brushed her face across his smooth skin and lifted her lips to place a soft whisper of a kiss beneath the jutting curve of his jaw, a kiss so light it would barely be felt. She felt him shudder. A soft moan caught in his throat at the ecstasy. The revelation that she could elicit so deep a response from so slight an offering as that kiss sparked a fire within her, a wild urge to give this man every pleasure, to push him to the point where he could stand no more, to own his body and his soul and thereby fulfill her own buried fantasy. There was no turning back.

Jake had met a worthy partner for his lovemaking, she thought. He may have kindled the fire, let loose the spark; but now it was she whose hunger and drive equaled his own, who guided the intensity of this encounter, setting him aflame, then easing back just enough to allow them to smolder in each other's grasp before igniting the fire once again. She let him lead her, then took control again, guiding him back to the bedroom, where they would linger until daylight returned.

Twice in the night Julianne awoke and, propped up on one elbow, watched Jake sleep in peace. He was so strong, so beautiful. After only a few of minutes of gazing at him, she felt her desires overtake her and gently stroked him to stir him from his sleep. She took joy in knowing that he could not resist her overtures, despite his exhaustion. He was hers. They made love each time anew. What began as an act of desperate hunger and physical desire now evolved into an erotic game between two willing partners.

Finally, it was Julianne who grew exhausted, and when she awoke, it was to find herself cradled in Jake's arms, her back against his strong chest, his lips brushed against her hair, and his knee solidly fit into the bend of her own. She kept her eyes closed, consciously storing each essence of this sensation, as she knew she would want to recall it later. As the glint of sunlight crept through the slit of her curtains, she turned and their eyes met. He had been lying there awake, holding her contentedly. No words were exchanged.

She reached down beside the bed and retrieved her T-shirt, slipping it on from underneath the sheets. Then slowly, as if this were a fragile departure, she slid out of bed and into the kitchen, where she started a pot of coffee. As it brewed and the rich aroma flowed through the apartment, she showered and peeked back into the bedroom. The first words of the day were spoken: "Coffee's on." She returned to the kitchen while Jake showered. He met her at the counter, where he nabbed a bagel and munched as a happy serenity filled the room. No trace of uncertainty existed—no explanations and definitely no remorse. The morning was as it should be. As every morning should be. They both knew it.

"Let's take a walk after breakfast," he said casually. "Right now I'm starving."

She searched the refrigerator for food and was relieved to discover cream cheese, a wedge of brie, and two perfectly ripened pears to complement the sack of bagels she routinely kept in her small pantry.

"This should tide us over." Then she offered a playful smile. "Of course, we did work up quite an appetite."

Elisa clutched Kelly's hand as they walked up the short stairway to the buzzers. She knew that Kelly felt far too grown-up to have her hand held, but the gesture was more for herself than her daughter. Kelly seemed to sense that and gave her mother's hand a gentle squeeze that communicated both confidence and determination. Together the two of them rang the manager's bell and minutes later entered the doorway of a simple one-bedroom apartment two floors above the neighborhood deli. Elisa had noticed the *For Rent* sticker on the building's doorway several days ago, when she stopped at the deli to pick up a few things. It was the day after her meeting with Peter, and from the instant she saw it, she couldn't get that sticker out of her thoughts.

The meeting with Peter had been disturbing for reasons quite different from those she had anticipated. She'd gone in prepared for a fierce argument, ugly exchange of insults, or perhaps a saccharine sweet portrayal of his intentions to change his ways. She could have effectively countered any of those options by pulling from a repertoire of scenarios she had played out in her own head over and over again in the solitude of her Horizons room. Mental role-playing was her trick for survival in the midst of this emotionally tumultuous period. If she couldn't scream at her husband, or walk into the bank and suck every dime out of their scant savings account, or throw herself into a daring love affair with an exotic stranger in reality, then she would do it in her dreams. And those dreams played out so vividly and precisely that her imaginary dialogues with Peter seemed almost real. The words were on standby, on the tip of her tongue, the evening she finally faced him across the table at The Drake. Only he confronted her with a totally unexpected bit of news and she was thrown into a tizzy. That was the bad news. The good news was that the tizzy lasted a paltry twelve hours.

Elisa's bus ride home and ritual of getting Kelly settled for the night were a blur. Kelly had no idea that her mom and dad had been talking. Elisa felt that telling her would needlessly raise her daughter's hopes of a reconciliation. So she asked Marsha to keep an eye on her daughter and made sure to be home in time to tuck Kelly into bed, explaining her fancy attire by saying that she was out dining and schmoozing with Deena. She wasn't comfortable lying to her daughter, but it seemed the better option.

She barely got an hour of sleep that night, tossing and turning and replaying Peter's words over and over in her head. If this bold move out of the house did in fact shake him into turning over a new leaf, would it not be unfair to deny him the chance to redeem himself? A normal family life would certainly be in Kelly's best interest. This emotional game of ping-pong went on for hours.

Just before dawn, Peter had the slight advantage; she was weakening. She had just about convinced herself that miracles could happen. Then she turned to check the time. It was nearly eight in the morning, twelve hours since she fled from the confrontation with her husband. As her eyes drifted from the clock on the nightstand, they fell upon that pink satin pillow with the soft white roses. "To Daddy's Sweetheart," it read. How Kelly cherished that gift from her father. She had no idea he had absolutely nothing to do with it. Elisa had stitched and hand embroidered it so that Peter could give his little girl a token of his love on her fifth birthday, when he worked instead of attending her birthday party. Peter had forgotten all about Kelly's birthday that year, not because he didn't love her but because it just wasn't a priority at the time. The pillow softened the blow of his absence for Kelly, just as Elisa knew it would. Staring at it now, she realized that they would never have the family life she longed for, that living happily ever after would be nothing other than an elusive dream unless she personally made it so. Peter was what he was, and even if he could change with some professional help, he had no interest in seeking that help. He thought therapy was for suckers and those who doled it out were con artists.

Who was she trying to kid? She'd just be taking on the burden of rebuilding their lives as she'd taken on the burden of building it in the first place. It dawned on her that more often than not, it was the woman who shouldered the burdens in a relationship and did so willingly, embracing every obstacle as if it were her own predestined challenge. Where was it written that the wife mended the problems while the husband sat in judgment? Who dictated that Mommy donated time to school committees and bake sales while Daddy sat behind his desk or played golf? Why was it that personal counseling or family therapy was always an option to be endorsed by the lady of the house, while the man of the house determined whether or not he was inclined to go along with the suggestion?

It would be a mistake to return to him—a mistake that most of the others nestled within those Horizons walls had made time and time again. It was a mistake she was newly committed to avoiding. She had to stay brave.

So today Elisa managed to muster up the courage to stop in to check out the place described on that white For Rent sticker. She told herself she could do it, finally face the fact that she was ready to move into a place of her own, admit to herself that her marriage was over, and that she indeed had the ability to fend for herself and her daughter. That was the hardest leap to make. After so many years of feeling ineffective and allowing herself to be convinced by Peter that she was incapable of surviving without him, she was ready to stand on her own two feet. Creating her own home through her own means meant she was taking control of her life.

The simplicity of the apartment turned out to be a blessing. A fancier, more elaborate setting might have overwhelmed her. Yet this quiet collection of small rooms was not at all threatening. It was already furnished with the bare essentials, plain but clean. Kelly could have the bedroom, and Elisa would manage with the sofa bed. It was important that Kelly come first. She needed a space that she could make her own. The rent could be managed on her new salary, and the job was off to a promising start. Everyone seemed supportive of her progress, and she handled business details with a self-assurance she'd never displayed in her personal life. A fear tugged at her now, though, as she realized she was about to make a commitment to this place.

Then she looked at Kelly in the center of the bedroom. It was such a departure from the carefully composed room Elisa had created for her daughter at home. Still, when Kelly spun around to look at her mom, Elisa saw a glow on her face that she feared had disappeared forever. This might have been a meager replacement for the room in which she grew up, but it was a place where she would feel safety, comfort, love. The look on Kelly's face was enough to bolster Elisa's courage to sign the month-to-month lease. They would move in the first of September, in time for Kelly to start the year at a new school and make new friends.

That night, in the dining room of Horizons, the new woman came and sat across from her. "I'm Tina," she said as she lowered her tray to the table. "I know we haven't met yet, but Kelly and I are old buddies, right, Kell?"

Kelly turned to her mom. "Tina showed me that magazine I was telling you about, Mom. The one with all our horoscopes in it. Tina, didn't it say this was going to be a really cool month for me? A month of adventure or something like that. Or was that for next month?"

"Actually, next month. But look at it this way--that's only a few weeks away and you have something to look forward to." The three of them sat chatting. Elisa noticed how calm, even cheerful, Tina was. It was remarkable to be that cheerful in this setting. She seemed strangely out of place. Yet if there was one thing Elisa had learned at Horizons, it was that all kinds of women walked through the doorway. It didn't matter if they had money or fancy educations. They were often too ashamed or just plain beaten down to deal with handling their crises. They were running for their lives, and only when they crossed this threshold could they allow themselves the luxury of sitting down and thinking through what to do next.

Yet Tina didn't look ashamed, or beaten down, or even contemplative. After a couple minutes of benign chatting, she left to send a text, and Elisa asked Marsha if she knew anything about Tina.

As it turned out, neither Marsha nor anyone else had any insights to share other than knowing that Tina had turned up at the shelter yesterday with one small suitcase and a story of a brutal, threatening boyfriend with whom she shared an apartment. It was admirable to see how well she had pulled herself together in one day.

Clint Andrews entered the dining room with an iced tea in one hand and a plate of cookies in the other. He set the plate down between Marsha and Elisa and sat down to join them, though they were hardly beckoning him to do so.

Shelby had sent a note to Horizons, stating that she was thinking of her friends there and was anxious to retun to them. Her mother was in a rehabilitation center undergoing extensive physical therapy and Shelby was working with her throughout the day. She expected to return to Chicago soon.

The note was posted on a bulletin board in the dining room. Clint kept it there as a reminder that there were no plans to replace Shelby since good house managers did not grow on trees and Shelby's return was imminent. Meanwhile, Clint was barely tolerable. Even those he didn't pounce on physically grew annoyed with his constant attempts at chumminess and self-righteous concern. Suddenly, he had the opportunity to play therapist and seemed to relished doing so. He thought himself rather good at it, they could tell, so he felt free to spew his words of wisdom to his captive prey. For the most part, the women were deft at letting it flow in one ear and out the other. But it was growing increasingly difficult to ignore him.

Clint, Elisa and Marsha were the only three people lingering in the dining room. The others had transitioned to the family room to scan employment sites and practice interview skills with role-playing peers. The evening would invariably end in frustration for those not yet strong enough to tackle the anxiety of a job search and in anger for others who had finally reached the point of getting good and mad about their circumstances. Anger was the turning point, it appeared, for rebuilding lives. It replaced the fear that had turned them into victims—fear of violence, fear of being alone, fear of being penniless and unable to feed the kids, fear of being undeserving of anything better. Fear was the enemy, anger a welcome friend.

"Something sweet for two especially sweet ladies," Clint proclaimed with a nauseating gesture of fake gallantry.

"We shouldn't, what with our diets and all. But thanks anyway," Marsha said, preparing to make her exit. "Elisa and I have to go up and help Kelly with the puzzle she's doing. She's waiting."

Clint looked straight into Elisa's eyes. "Elisa will be up in a minute. She's been trying to speak with me all day, and this is the first minute I've had to break free." Elisa stared down at her cup. Waiting to see him. Sure. If only he knew how much time she spent each day working out ways to avoid crossing paths with him. "I know it's late, but why don't we stop back at my office, where you can tell me what's on your mind?" he said. Marsha stood at the doorway, not wishing to leave Elisa alone with him but not knowing what else to do.

"Marsha, will you keep an eye on Kelly?" Elisa asked. "I won't be long." Marsha didn't move. "It's okay," she added, rising from the table to follow Clint Andrews to his office. Clint closed the door behind them and turned the lock.

"What did you mean, 'It's okay'? You weren't stupid enough to say anything to her? You weren't stupid enough to leave your kid without a bed to sleep in tonight?"

For the first time, Elisa saw how nervous this nasty man could be. She enjoyed the sight of it but couldn't risk angering him, especially with only a short time to go before she walked out of this place for good. "I just meant that Kelly would be 'okay' with the fact that I've been sidetracked. I promised to work on the puzzle with her. She's looking forward to it. I really should go up."

"You know what I've been looking forward to today?" His smug, filthy stare was intolerable. The day had been such a breakthrough for her. She didn't want it ruined by this animal.

"I can't anymore, Clint." It was the first time she had the courage to confront him. If she were lucky, he'd figure she wasn't worth the effort of a struggle and would move on to someone else. If not, he could concoct some lies and throw her onto the streets ... with Kelly.

Instead of anger, she saw a glint of pleasure in his eyes. "Well, not in the mood tonight? Other plans? Plans to hunt down two beds in a city that's only got space for a sliver of the women out on the streets? Of course, your loving husband would probably run down here to pick up his blushing bride."

This was the first time Clint had ever threatened to divulge the location of her hiding place to her husband. As contemptible as he was, she never thought he'd do that. She stood motionless as he lifted her skirt and tore away her panties. He never touched her with his lips, never forced open her blouse. He sat down in his chair behind the desk and pulled her on top of him, pushing her legs apart. With a humiliating cruelty, he thrust himself inside of her, his piercing stare never leaving her eyes. It was a swift, chilling act, unlike the other times he had taken her. She fought to meet his stare, knowing that if she could be strong enough to avoid hiding behind the darkness of her eyelids, he would not have won. He would not have demeaned her. Her eyes would hold the reflection of his own wickedness. When he was through with her, she rose and silently left the office. One more month, she thought. She could live through one more month.

Tina slipped her phone into her purse as Elisa passed in front of her wearing a blank expression far different from the one displayed in the dining room only minutes ago. Her gaze followed Elisa as she walked slowly upstairs and directly into the bathroom. A minute later, she turned to see Clint Andrews step out of his office and head for the dining room to finish eating his cookies. His expression was pompous and self-satisfied. She had to force herself to keep from taking him down right there and then. It needed to be done right. It needed to stick. She would find a way to get Elisa to open up, she told herself. And as revolting as the thought was, she would buddy up to the monster munching contentedly on his dessert. Clint Andrews, she knew, loved his dessert.

CHAPTER 12

A stack of magazines littered the overstuffed peach sofa upon which Helene Rossi lounged, letting the fresh coat of nail polish dry on her perfectly pedicured toes. That morning, she had treated herself to a mani-pedi to break up her monotony, but she grew restless and slipped into her shoes about five minutes too soon, so some repair work was in order. It presented ample time to reflect upon her day.

Earlier, when the nail salon proved ineffective in calming her nerves, she turned her attention to the gym to embark upon the ninety-minute workout she completed at least four times a week. Perched upon the Lifecycle, she checked out the array of women who dominated the treadmills during the midday hours. Surely she could dig up a girlfriend or two from the assortment of ladies walking, jogging and running themselves ragged in pursuit of a better version of themselves.

Helene could not comprehend why it was so difficult for her to acquire friends—or at least female friends. Men did not hesitate to initiate conversation with her while in line at the market or while lingering over a latte at the mall. Women, on the other hand, were quite a different story. Her sister said it was because she was too pretty, that women were wary of being upstaged by her or reminded of their physical shortcomings. Most shied away from her like she was contagious and those who didn't traveled in circles of wealth beyond her means, confidence bolstered by skillful cosmetic surgeons and hefty bank accounts to cover the cost. What they lacked in looks they made up for with fabulous jewelry and exquisite couture. After striking up friendships with a variety of such women, Helene had managed to send her charge account balances soaring to an all-time high. Jake put his foot down and suggested she find a more appropriate group of besties, though he wasn't much help at suggesting how she go about doing so. The gym was his one viable recommendation, but it wasn't panning out well at all.

Back at home, after her workout, she tossed this month's *Cosmo* on the pile of magazines on the coffee table. *Vogue, Vanity Fair, People* ... they were mind candy with little relevance to the real world, and that's exactly what she craved. An insipid cooking show droned on in the background but Helene paid little attention. She had developed the benign habit of flipping on the TV when home alone, accepting the fact that an electronic voice was better company than no voice at all. Now it provided comforting background noise, even though she wasn't technically home alone.

Jake was sound asleep in the bedroom down the hall, where he had secluded himself in pursuit of a nap that would likely evolve into a nightlong sleep. The indulgence, Helene assumed, was preferable to the companionship of a wife who seemed to be constantly seeking an exucse to pick a fight. She couldn't deny, even to herself, that she was increasingly hard to please.

He'd been up at four that morning for an editing session that kicked off at five, and after several hours in the stuffy, dimly lit editing booth, he walked back through the front door at home with a weary face. As she smiled through his forced attempt to participate in a dialogue of daily events with her, it was obvious that he could barely keep his eyes open. She could hardly get angry when he asked if she'd be upset if he took a snooze.

But she was tired too. Tired of living this way. Something had gone off-kilter in this marriage. She'd known that for at least the past year. But she had given up a lot to commit to this marriage, and she wasn't inclined to throw in the towel. She loved her lifestyle, though she was increasingly less certain of her feelings toward her husband. The chemistry between them had changed, making her acutely aware of how little she and Jake had in common. Perhaps the same was true for him, she pondered. Sex was the one thing they had enjoyed with gusto. Yet the sex had changed. It had grown predictable and tame, by the Rossis' standards, providing the most definitive signal that her marriage was falling apart. Jake was so distant lately, less talkative, animated, or playful. She valued a solid union, but not one that required so much effort to keep intact that she'd be drained of her energy or enthusiasm for anything else. Life was too short.

She flicked off the TV, shoved the hefty pile of magazines into the chrome rack on the side of the sofa, and went to join her husband under the quilt. Hell, why not? If she was going to do nothing more productive than mull over the bleak state of her marriage, she might as well do so in the comfort of her own bed, with Jake's warm, hard body to lean against. Nowadays she felt closest to him while cuddling against the curves of his body under the covers when he was lost in sleep and didn't even know she was there.

She pulled off the T-shirt she'd been lying around in all evening and slipped out of her panties. Ever since their first night together, they both slept in the nude, enjoying the feel of each other's silky skin as they'd press up against one another periodically through the night. If this marriage did crumble, she thought as she eased herself against his back and slid her arm around his chest, she would miss sleeping with this man. Not just the sex, but sleeping with him. She never felt safer or more relaxed than lying in bed next to Jake. Too bad it wasn't enough.

As she moved even closer to the warmth of the body, she asked herself if she'd been wrong not to tell him that she'd spoken to the doctor today. It wasn't that she was keeping anything from him. He just didn't seem in the mood to hear it. His conversation was filled with stories about the documentary and the lousy management at the station and his favorite topic, Julianne Sloan. Helene had heard enough stories about Julianne Sloan to last a lifetime and wondered if

Jake realized how often he rambled on about her. She also wondered if he had feelings for her that he wouldn't admit to himself, much less his wife. She couldn't compete with the relationship he and Julianne shared, one built from a professional history, understanding and respect. She'd given up the notion of trying to compete long ago.

The doctor didn't have much to say anyway. Helene had always been regular with her periods, but for the past six months, that had not been the case. She used a diaphragm most of the time, but when she skipped a period for the first time, the thought did occur to her that she might be pregnant. She waited a couple of weeks, saying nothing to Jake. Then, after one more week, her period finally came. She had been consistently irregular since that time and finally, today, decided to call her doctor. Of course, Dr. Newman explained, there was the chance that she was pregnant, but judging by the pattern Helene described, the doctor was inclined to think that perhaps the condition was stress induced. More and more women were finding that stress was affecting their regularity as well as their frame of mind. She should come in for a pregnancy check—drugstore tests were unreliable—and if the results were negative, he'd write a prescription for hormones to induce menstruation, Dr. Newman instructed. It was hardly worth making an issue over, Helene decided, sitting up and supporting herself on one elbow as she stared at her peacefully dreaming husband.

Marty, one of her favorites at the office, handed Elisa a stack of messages when she returned from her lunchtime errands. Then he handed her a slip from the message pad he had obviously not wanted to get lost in the clutter. "Your lawyer called. He said it wasn't urgent but asked that you get back to him today." Elisa walked into the office kitchen nook and sat down to eat her chicken salad. She had finally saved enough money to hire a lawyer—a decent one too. She was Adrienne Phelps' cousin and Adrienne had arranged for her to take the case at a much reduced fee in order to help out an employee.

Adrienne had been the first person in a long time to make Elisa feel important and in this short time, Elisa had grown to feel close to her. With her self-esteem on the rise, she felt more comfortable sharing the details of her disintegrated marriage and the drama with her parents, who were thoroughly rattled at first but had grown used to her situation by now. This week she had made plans for a girls' night out with her old friends to fill in the gap of the past couple of months. She was succeeding in her new job and didn't want buried secrets to taint the pride she was finding in her own accomplishments.

Elisa's lawyer had been in periodic contact with Peter, who had been advised that his wife was filing for divorce. He had also arranged for Peter to have visitation rights with Kelly. Elisa was not yet ready to interact with Peter, and she made arrangements to take Kelly to Grandma and Grandpa's house on visitation days, where Peter could pick her up and drop her off. On the night before his first visit with his daughter, Elisa phoned him and, with some reservation, told him that she and Kelly had been staying at a family crisis center. She did this to spare Kelly from being put in the position of keeping secrets from her father and because now that legal proceedings were under way, she knew that his learning the precise location of his child's whereabouts was inevitable. She never revealed the name of the shelter, as that would have jeopardized the safety and privacy of everyone staying there.

When she shared the information of her temporary residence, Peter was flabbergasted. The thought that his wife and child preferred a shelter for the destitute over the lovely home he had killed himself to provide was more than he could bear, he told her. He rambled on about being mortified at the thought of his family living in a shelter, not only because of the desperation it represented, but also because of how it would look to his friends if ever they heard about it. He could barely compose himself enough to speak but ultimately fizzled out. The call was short and over with.

Now that the mystery of her whereabouts was not an issue, her parents begged her to come stay with them. Their reaction to Elisa's choice to seek refuge at Horizons rather than to seek the assistance of her family was even more emotional than she had anticipated. At first, there was pure shock—shock at the thought that their son-in-law had been brutalizing their precious daughter. Then there was embarrassment—embarrassment that word would spread to taint the Tate family as one of those ugly statistics that always seemed so removed from "nice" people. The embarrassment led to guilt that they had been such failures as parents that their daughter could not even turn to them in a time of crisis. The guilt endured long after they coped with the shock and embarrassment and in addition to managing her own set of confused feelings along with those of her daughter, Elisa attempted to assuage her parents' grief.

Yet agreeing to move into their guest room was not an option. Elisa feared that, well-meaning as they were, their prodding for details and penchant for doling out advice would set back the healing of which she was so proud. Worse yet was the possibility that they would see themselves as peacemakers and attempt to convince her to return to the husband, who would, no doubt, affirm that he was a reformed man committed to making things work. Instead, she chose to finish out the month at Horizons where she would lie in her bed at night thinking of ways to brighten up the new apartment and of new ways to master the tasks of her job. She did not think about Peter, and she did not think about Clint Andrews. Sometimes she thought about Tina Beyers.

Tina had been at the shelter for a few days now and seemed to take a real liking to Elisa. She was warm and caring and seemed to genuinely take pleasure in learning of Elisa's success with her job and in witnessing the rejuvenation of her spirit. Tonight, when Elisa finally announced to Marsha that the apartment was prepped for moving in, she was surprised to see that Tina was standing close behind her and had undoubtedly overheard. She immediately made Tina promise to keep the secret, as she feared that if Clint Andrews found out, he would force her to leave ahead of schedule. Tina vowed to keep silent, but on the way to the family room, she pulled Elisa aside and begged her to meet her for lunch the next day ... in order to celebrate, she explained.

No one was around when Julianne entered the manager's suite and deliberately shuffled some papers to announce that she was entering the area before she offered a curious, "Ted?"

When she received no response, she strolled into his office, expecting to find it empty. Instead, he sat perched on his green leather throne and, never looking away from his computer screen, muttered, "Just sit a while, Julianne. I'll be done with this in a minute." She sat in the chair across from his desk and once again found herself feeling like a little girl being called into the principal's office. With the lateness of the hour, she figured she must really be in hot water about something. She stared at him as he tackled the keyboard with commanding speed, working confidently and silently.

Finally, he swiveled his chair and looked up at her smiling. "You look lovely, Julianne. Have you done something different with your hair?"

She was startled. She and Ted had this unspoken shared realization that they did not care for one another, and they always avoided small talk and social conversation. They could tolerate each other professionally, period. This comment seemed grossly out of character for him. "It's probably just a mess by now. It's late. I'm surprised to find you here at eight o'clock. Is something wrong?" she asked, bringing the conversation back to work.

"Nothing's wrong at all. I just realized that with your boss out on leave, I probably should have been a little more attentive to your needs. I was thinking about it last night on my way home from an art opening at my neighbor's gallery. I saw an old friend of yours at the opening. I knew I recognized him, but I just couldn't place him. And then he came up to me and said he'd met me at one of our station's award dinners. Allen Miller."

Julianne had pushed the thought of Allen to a far corner of her mind, determined to rally from her moronic behavior. It wasn't so much the mention of his name that threw her for a loop. It was the way he said it. His tone carried an undercurrent of intimacy, an implication that his encounter with Allen Miller was more than just casual. His next comment proved that her instinct was on target.

"Allen said he was worried about you. He thought you needed to stop working so much, that you need some kind of outlet. He said you are a phenomenal woman. That was his exact word: *phenomenal.* You know, Julianne, we all need outlets. It's not healthy to let your work keep you all pent up inside. It can be frustrating for a strong, healthy woman like you."

She sat there speechless. As if she were staring at a movie screen, her mind created the image of Allen Miller and Ted Marshall gulping down glasses of champagne at a pretentious art opening and comparing notes on Julianne Sloan. Those notes, she knew by the manner of Ted's reference to the conversation, had little to do with her professional attributes. Most likely the two macho men fell comfortably into locker room lingo. She was livid. She was humiliated. She was at a complete loss for words.

He stepped around to the front of the desk, positioning himself directly in front of her and leaned back, supporting his weight on his outstretched arms behind him. As she sat sunken in her chair, he towered over her. She was forced to throw her head back and look up at him, for she would have been staring straight into his crotch otherwise. She realized even before she uttered her first word that her voice would come out strained and feeble, but she had to say something.

"I'm perfectly fine, Ted. Actually, great. I appreciate your concern. I'm sure you and Allen had a lot to talk about. You're really quite similar. I'd never thought of that before. And neither of you has to concern yourself with me. I have all the outlets I need." She added that last statement as an afterthought. She just couldn't let him think she was so naive.

"I don't know. It's eight fifteen. You're still at work. It's deserted around here and still here you are." The way he said 'deserted' had a menacing tone to it. He sat down on the arm of the chair next to her and leaned closer to speak, as though trying to comfort her. All she could think of was that he was right about one thing: the place was deserted. "I'll tell you what," he continued, "let's grab some dinner and just relax. We could both use it. If it makes you feel any better, you can mix in a little work and tell me how that women's special is moving along."

Here she was again on old familiar ground. The flirtations. The invitations. The references to her personal life and lingering glances where the eyes did not belong. And so it goes for women in business. Or not in business. Just for women in general. She was good and sick of it. She was tired and overwhelmed and nauseated by the pompous ass in his big fancy office.

For a minute, she succeeded in tuning him out and thinking back to the days of innocence, when she thought her career drive and carefully honed skills would give her access to any position she was willing to work hard enough to attain. The opportunities seemed boundless. Women were ready to explode onto the forefront of the business world as never before and the television industry was no exception. She just needed to be enterprising and at the top of her game. She knew she was good. Very good. And she knew she was determined. What she didn't know was how many cards were stacked against her from the start.

Her education with regard to differences between men and women at the workplace began with her first job as a desk assistant in the newsroom. Though she had worked at part-time jobs since she was sixteen, she had never given much thought to the gender lopsided management teams everywhere she worked, always more men at the top. By the time she nabbed the desk assistant job, however, her awareness was piqued because the stakes were so high. That job marked the beginning of her career. She was the new kid on the block and therefore was assigned the graveyard shift, holiday hours, and weekend schedules that any low man on the totem pole would expect. She readily accepted this fact and never uttered a word of complaint as she dug in to pay her dues.

That changed eight months later, when Zak Neuberg was hired as the department's newest desk assistant. She would finally enjoy the glory of having seniority over somebody, she smiled upon reading the hiring announcment. As it turned out, the laugh was on her—and it was quick in coming.

Each Wednesday the department posted a work schedule for the following week. Writers, desk assistants, and field producers were listed, along with the technical crews. With Zak's arrival, Julianne was chomping at the bit to see how her shift would be upgraded, freeing her up to live a more normal life, including dinner with friends, even an occasional movie! It seemed to good to be true. And it was.

The very first schedule to be posted after Zak Neuberg's arrival reflected the exact same rotten hours she'd been dealt for the past eight months. No change at all. Her finger scanned angrily up the sheet from Sloan to Neuberg, where she saw that Zak was given Sunday and Monday off and that he was on the 10:00 a.m.–6:00 p.m. shift, while she remained assigned the 2:00 p.m.—10:00 p.m. shift. Plus, she was down to work both Saturday and Sunday. Okay, she wasn't a complainer by nature, but anyone would have to agree that this situation really stunk, so she made an appointment to see Jack Conklin, news director at the time. Since desk assistants were so low in the pecking order, it was the first time she had the guts to ask for a one-on-one with him. But this scheduling thing really set her off.

In his office, after the six o'clock newscast that day, she stated the facts clearly, concisely, and calmly, hoping the schedule was attributable to an innocent oversight that would be rectified once brought to light. So much for expectations. What she got was her first lesson on being a woman in the workforce.

"I understand your position, Julianne. But let's be fair. Zak has a two-year-old son and a pregnant wife and has asked us if there is anything we could do to free him up for some time with his family," Jack explained in the fatherly tones saved for novices in the department. "It's not easy raising a family today. I'm sure you can understand that. Zak's under a lot of pressure, financially and personally."

Jack Conklin was an intimidating figure, but he really got her dander up and she was ready to take him on. "So I'm being punished because I don't have a baby. Parents are entitled to better schedules? Besides which, I'm under just as much stress and financial strain as Zak Neuberg. I have college loans to get off my back, a car to pay off, and I'd like to be able to pay my rent without counting my pennies each month."

"I wouldn't consider any job in this newsroom as punishment, Julianne. And I never would have pegged you for a whiner. I know you're disappointed and you're relatively new here, so I'm going to cut you some slack, but let me give you some advice. Don't worry about who gets what schedule around here and don't be jealous of Zak. Just do your work and do it well and you'll have a successful career ahead of you." He got up and circled around to the door, opening it to the bustling newsroom outside, thus signaling that her first meeting with the news director had concluded. *Welcome to equal rights,* she thought as she marched back to the assignment desk weighing the futility of bucking the system.

Now, years of career achievement later, she was in the station manager's office instead of the news director's office and the nameplate read Ted Marshall instead of Jack Conklin, but the simple truth was, as the saying goes, *the more things change, the more they stay the same.* She was still spending a disproportionate amount of careery energy maneuvering through gender challenges and while her technique had certainly become more refined as she inched her way up the ladder, she was no more tolerant of the sexism now than she was then.

"I have dinner plans, Ted," she said, rising from her chair.

"Can't they be changed?"

"No, Ted, they can't," she said, looking him straight in the eye. He eased down into his chair. Then he lowered his eyes, looking down at her thighs with a stare that pierced her clothing. She rose and as she did, he caught her by the back of her knee, brushing beneath her skirt and stroking her flesh with his thumb. She jumped back and swung into the chair where she had been seated, toppling it to the floor. An ugly smile came to his face.

"Your boyfriend said you had a hell of a lot of fire in you." He stood up and pinned her against the desk. He was rubbing up against her body, pressing his chest to her breasts as his hands caressed her buttocks. It all happened so quickly that she stood paralyzed. But only for a moment.

"If you rape me, if you touch me for one more second, I'll have your ass," she said firmly and calmly. She knew that panic would render her helpless and she saw him flinch slightly at the harshness of the word *rape*.

"I'm fiery enough to bring you up on charges and nasty enough to create a scandal—you're the married one, not me. There's a string of pricks just like you who've already been hung out to dry by the media, so take a number. Let's not overlook that I'm strong enough to dig my nails into your flesh and give your wife a lot of questions to ask when you come home tonight. If I were you, I'd cut my losses and get the hell away from me now."

With that, she mustered all her energy into one terrific shove that caught him off balance. She quickly moved past him and darted through the doorway. She wanted to leave him with a statement that would put him in his place, give her that upper hand, but she was too flustered. She shot out the doorway and never looked back.

At home that night, she wondered how long it would take Ted Marshall to get her fired. That he would do so was not in question. It was merely a matter of what story he would invent and how long and drawn out a process it would be. This was streaming through her mind when, just before midnight, the telephone shrieked through the silence. She answered it to hear Jake's voice.

He had been out of town for the past three days, shooting a story downstate. She had been aching for him but didn't realize how severely until she heard him say her name. It was late, and he sounded exhausted. She clung to the telephone, not wanting to waste this time talking about anything painful or distressing, just wanting to escape into the pleasure of his voice. Evening phone conversations were rare treats, mostly limited to evenings when his wife was partaking in a girls' night out. These talks were precious to them, perhaps because they were so forbidden and perhaps they were both so hungry for them.

When they spoke, it was only of trivial matters and playful, harmless innuendo. Everything deeper was understood between them and didn't have to be validated with words. "I wish you were lying here with your head on my lap," she said into the phone seductively.

"You do, huh? Well, we wouldn't be lying there like that for long."

"I don't know, Jake, you sound pretty tired. I think I would be too much for you tonight," she teased.

"I seem to recall handling you pretty well, Miss Sloan. I'll refresh your memory when I get back."

"Hurry back," she said with sudden seriousness as each hung up the phone.

Julianne didn't allow herself to think about Helene or Jake and Helene together. It was a reality. It was what it was. She saw no point in dwelling on it. She didn't think about the future either, except for every once in a while when she reminded herself that this love affair was destined to end in heartache for her. It was because she saw this outcome so clearly that she saw no reason in fighting it. If it was inevitable that she'd be heartsick, she may as well enjoy the pleasure for as long as possible. It wouldn't hurt any less if she deprived herself today instead of tomorrow. She was starving for affection, not sex but love. And Jake quelled that starvation. So, she decided quite coherently, she would experience this romance to its fullest potential and resign herself to paying the price later.

Jake's call had been a welcome escape from the trauma of the evening, and she relived the conversation and the sound of his voice over and over again until it lulled her to sleep.

Tina breathed a huge sigh of relief when she spotted Elisa rounding the corner and heading to the diner. She hadn't really expected her to show up. Somehow Elisa seemed to already be distancing herself from Horizons and all it represented. Now, with a job she apparently enjoyed and an apartment waiting for her, she exuded a new strength. Tina hoped that this strength could be channeled into helping to take down Clint Andrews, but she knew that winning over Elisa's cooperation was a long shot.

"I'm really happy for you, Elisa." Tina smiled as they nibbled on their breakfast. "Especially because there is such a pattern of returning to a hellish life and running away again and again and again. I give you a lot of credit."

"I'm sure you'll do the same thing. You don't seem as worn down as the rest of us.

It's probably not too late for you to get hold of your life."

"There's a reason I don't seem as worn down as everyone else." Tina went on to confess why she was at the shelter and what this angle to the story would mean to the documentary and to the system, a system that gave Clint Andrews the keys to corruption.

Elisa listened, expressionless at first. Then she recoiled, protecting herself from the betrayal of this woman who had invaded the privacy of so many lives. However noble the motive, she was a fraud, just like Clint. Twice she had been the victim of deceit in a place that was created to protect victims. It made her proud to have arrived at an emotional state in which she could take care of herself and her little girl—and survive a world in which no one else could be relied upon for help.

She slipped her jacket on and started to leave the table. As she turned toward the door, she saw Julianne Sloan entering, and she stood motionless as Julianne approached.

Julianne reached out and gently grasped Elisa's hand. "I know you must be angry with us. I don't blame you. But we're not doing this for a good story or for ratings or anything like that. We're doing it to try to fix something that's terribly wrong. Tina and I, as well as Jake and a lot of the people we work with, want to stop Clint and people like him. We'll never stop everyone. But that doesn't mean we shouldn't go after the bad guys we do have a chance to nail. We want to get some rules established. There's no reason for this ugly mess to fall between the cracks. That's a pattern just like the patterns of abuse at home. We've got to shred those patterns. We've got to try to stop the hurt, to stop being victims. Tina going undercover wasn't the perfect plan or the best plan, but it seemed like the quickest plan. Please don't give us away to the others at Horizons. Please. And won't you talk to us about Andrews? You'll be out of there; he won't have anything to hold over you. Just think about it."

"He won't have anything to hold over me? Do you think I want to keep dwelling on that low point of my life? Do you have any idea how pathetic it is to lose all regard for one's own self? For one's own body? To give your body away just because it's too hard to deal with any more fights? To actually convince yourself that your body isn't such a big deal anyway? Not a big deal. I believed that. And he is the only person who knows how pathetic it was, how pathetic I was. I have to put that behind me. I'm taking control of my life now. And I love it. This is the best I've felt in so long. I deserve to enjoy it. I'm not going to let Clint Andrews ruin *this* for me too."

Did she know what it was like to lose regard for one's self? One's body? To want to put the low points behind her? Elisa's questions thundered through Julianne's brain. She knew. God, she knew. Thanks in part to the same bastard who'd crippled Elisa's progress. Only that wasn't entirely true. Julianne was honest enough with herself to know that she was more a victim of her own choices and decisions, her own desperation and hunger, than she was of Clint's evil ways. He was just the catalyst to her nightmarish discovery that she was in emotional quicksand, feigning happiness by negating the voids in her life. Maybe it was a blessing. For had she not stopped suppressing her needs, they might have festered beneath her calm surface, undetected and spoiling the good parts of her life.

Perhaps striking back at Clint Andrews was the way for each of them to reclaim her dignity and prove to herself that she was back in control. How she longed to share these feelings with Elisa—to come clean to a woman whose private life was already an open book. But she couldn't bring herself to do it. Pride got in the way, along with humiliation. It was too much. *I'm sorry, Elisa.*

Elisa hesitated as she prepared to make her exit. "I won't say anything to the others at the shelter. But I think what you're doing is wrong. Those people don't deserve to be lied to. They've lied to themselves long enough. And I can tell you this: Clint will either come on to you or he won't. If he's not turned on by you now, forget it; he'll get somebody else to toy with. Keep your eyes open. Look for the timid one in the group. Or look to see if there's a light under his office door late at night. You want to do this. So do it. Don't expect us to do it for you. We just don't have the strength." She walked away from the table and, after taking a few steps, looked back at Tina. "Good luck. Nail that bastard."

Tina returned to her room at Horizons with new determination. It was going to be tougher to build a case against Andrews without Elisa's help. And he hadn't been coming on to her. Maybe she could change that, give him a little push. She changed into a simple skirt and sweater and softened her makeup. She tried to look more like Elisa, more like his type. She carried a coat and a couple of bags with her as if she were heading out to run some errands. Inside the dark green satchel, peeking through the opening in the front latch was a camera set to record. One of the engineers at the station had shown her how to rig the device, which was often used by investigative reporters. Tina had invented some reason for needing it and he had no cause to question her.

Now, switching the electronics into record mode, she wandered down to Andrews's office and knocked timidly on the door. He called for her to come in, and she approached shyly, smiling with vulnerability. "I wondered if maybe you knew of some jobs in the area," she whispered. "I really need the money. I thought that if you wouldn't mind, maybe you could help me, make a call or two for me. I'm not quite up to interviewing yet. I mean, I'm willing to go out on interviews. I just don't think I'd sell myself too well. I thought that if you knew of an opening somewhere and could vouch

for me, it would make a big difference. It would mean a lot to me."
Entrapment? No, she told herself. Just a little push.

He got up, came around to the front of the desk, and sat down
on the chair next to hers. "You did the right thing coming to me,"
he said softly. "I'd be happy to make some calls for you. You're very
sweet." He raised his hand and rested it on her cheek affectionately,
as if testing her to see if she'd pull away. She did not. Then he slowly
extended his fingers across her face and into her hair. It only lasted
a moment. "You come back down tonight, after dinner, and we'll
see if I have anything for you," he said. His words were innocent
enough. The glint in his eyes, however, alluded to something more
menacing than his words.

Tina sat up straight in her bed and stared out the window,
contemplating her plan for the dangerous encounter that was only a
few minutes away. She thought of calling Julianne but then realized
that there was little point in the two of them suffering through this
anxiety attack. This was a situation only she could control. Control.
That was key. If she maintained control, physically and mentally,
she'd be fine. As she stared out the window, the hours flowed by, and
at nine thirty-five, she changed into her clingy V-necked sweater,
brushed her hair, checked the video recorder, secured it carefully in
her satchel, and headed downstairs.

At first, there was no response when she knocked. She looked
down and saw a golden shaft of light escaping below Clint's door,
confirming that he was indeed inside. She knocked again, and he
called for her to come in. When she entered, he was speaking quietly
on the telephone, so she walked over to the wall where his credenza
stood and casually started looking at the magazines and books neatly
stacked on top. She rested her satchel on the corner of the credenza
with the lens pointed at the desk and guest chairs across from it. It
was an innocent enough move, freeing up her arms and hands to
browse through the assortment of publications.

When he finished his call, she approached the desk and lowered herself into a chair. He leaned forward and spoke in a tone of exaggerated compassion. "I'd really like to work with you, Tina, to find something that would make you happy. I've been making some calls and looking through the agencies' listings. The truth is, there's not much out there right now. There are a couple of possibilities, but so many people are interested in them that I'm not sure I can pull any strings."

Either he meant what he said—she just wasn't his type and he wasn't going to go out of his way for her—or he was baiting her. It was up to her to play the next card, but she had to be subtle ... and calm ... and careful. Now it was her turn to move forward in her chair. As she sat forward, she saw his eyes lower to follow the movement of her breasts. His hands were folded in front of him on the desk. She took her hands and placed them lightly over his. It was a gesture that could be dismissed as mere friendship, nothing more. In silence, in a moment that seemed to stand still, she watched his demeanor morph from ally to predator. She lowered her face, feigning helplessness, desperation. Finally, she spoke. "I know how hard you try to help us, and I'm really struggling to find a job right now."

He came around to sit beside her. She turned slightly, acutely conscious of the camera nestled in her bag only a few feet away. She made sure to position him properly. He gently placed his hand under her chin and raised her face to his. "I've always thought there was something special about you, Tina, a kind of spark that would really be something if you took a flame to it. A woman like you must really miss the closeness of a man in your life." His eyes moved from her stare to her lips. His hand still held her face turned up to his. His thumb moved slowly across her lower lip.

"I'm not ashamed to say how much your help would mean to me," she said.

He brought his hand down to her thigh and let his fingers fall between her knees, slowly creeping up her inner thighs. His gaze never left her lips. "The question is ... are you too shy to show it?"

Time seemed to freeze. They sat staring at each other. No speaking. No movement. No sound.

Then the silence was abruptly shattered by a mechanical thud that startled them both. It was a sound as familiar to Tina as the morning alarm clock and at this moment as threatening as an explosion. It was the recording system shutting down after three minutes of warning flashes to alert that a shutdown was imminent. With no one manning the equipment, the flashes went unnoticed. That was not the case with the thud. Tina's mind became jumbled with a flurry of thoughts. How would she talk her way out of this? How dangerous was this man? How much had been captured on video before the battery died? She had no time to sort through any of these questions. Clint was on his feet.

"What the hell was that?" he said, his eyes scanning the room urgently. The sound led him to the satchel. Tina moved quickly, snatching it up before he could fully comprehend what was happening. He spun around and grabbed her arm. "I said, what the hell was that?" By now, he understood that he was the victim of a trap. He was the victim. And he didn't like it one bit. His face, now hard and cold, began to turn dark red. His grasp tightened around her arm and she twisted violently to tear herself free. She put every bit of strength into one gigantic shove and darted immediately to the door, throwing it open to slide her bag across the hallway floor, gently enough so as not to damage the gear, but distant enough to reach safe space. If he wanted it, he'd have to venture out of the office to get it where someone might witness the tumult. He lunged toward her and flung her against the open door. He kept his voice low so that no one would hear, but he tightened his grip on her arms. "All right, goddamn you. What the hell is going on? What are you trying to do?"

She knew that as long as she kept her weight against the doorframe and kept the door ajar, he couldn't really hurt her. Someone would hear. She needed to keep him off balance and find the moment to escape down the hall. "I'm trying to show that you're an asshole who is preying upon these women. I'm trying to show that you're a criminal and a bastard."

The stunned expression on his face told her it was time to push him away. She flew down the hallway, in full sight of four women in the living room watching TV. He couldn't seem to move his feet more than the two steps outside his door, where he watched her lift her bag. She turned to look at him, emboldened by the distance between them and the presence of the others. "And this bag of tricks is a tool of the trade. The television trade. You've just made your television debut, Mr. Andrews. The lead role. I'm sure you'll get rave reviews, maybe even go viral." She turned and walked out the front door leaving everything behind but the satchel.

He stood there frozen for several minutes and then stepped back into his office, shut out the lights and stared vacantly out at the blackness of the sky.

CHAPTER 13

The ten o'clock news droned on softly in the background as Julianne lay on her back in bed, staring up at the smooth white ceiling, her mind conflicted ... painting an image of Jake's strong, beautiful face, then allowing that tender image to turn ugly. Uncontrollable conflict. They had planned to have dinner together at her apartment that night. She was going to make the ultimate sacrifice and actually cook! *Was going to ...*

She spent a full hour at the grocery store, contemplating her purchases. Her repository of recipes was limited to dishes that were relatively goof proof and quick to concoct. That meant pastas and salads or entrees that could be purchased fully prepared at the gourmet counter and then fussed with at home to add personal touches and pass for homemade. For some reason, this evening she was swept up in a whirlwind of culinary adventure and decided to shoot the works: her own antipasto, veal marsala, marble cheesecake from scratch. She was more than a little nervous as she embarked upon this challenge but armed with two cookbooks, sixty dollars' worth of groceries and the vision in her mind of Jake's sure to be shocked expression when she presented the gastronomical delight, she set about her tasks. She'd even left work an hour early in anticipation of the culinary challenge ahead.

First the cheesecake. This was actually the only item Julianne was confident in preparing. She'd mastered her mother's recipe when she was fourteen, and it was her signature contribution to friends' dinner parties. With the cake gently deposited in the oven to bake, she started unwrapping the veal only to have the task interrupted by the telephone and Jake's jittery voice.

He wouldn't be able to make dinner. That news was nothing compared to what followed. He was home with Helene who had just delivered the jolting news that she was pregnant. He was thoroughly rattled and barely conversant. He managed to sneak in this quick call while Helene started dinner, but there was no way he could leave the house tonight. He wasn't in any shape to talk further. He'd call later. The whole conversation lasted less than a minute.

The shock of the pregnancy and all it meant was slowly beginning to sink in and with it came a rousing anger. Though tempted to aim the anger at herself, where she knew it belonged of course, she opted to direct it instead at Jake, and she did so with a fierceness she'd never felt before. It was definitely better that he not come near her just now. She grabbed a trash bag and haphazardly stuffed in all the fresh groceries she had painstakingly selected only a couple of hours earlier. She marched down the hall and defiantly swung the bag into the garbage shoot. She stood, listening to the pathetic *thunk* it made following its decent. It was a childish and wasteful gesture but she had no intention of forcing herself to be rational, mature or supportive tonight.

She waited for the cheesecake to finish baking, and before it had even cooled, she set it down on a place mat in the center of her bed where she proceeded to pick at it with a fork and a bottomless cup of coffee—spiked with Kahlua. And so her evening rolled by until Tina's shaky voice jolted her out of her self-pity.

The instant Julianne answered the phone, Tina dove into the story of her confrontation with Clint Andrews. A roller coaster of emotions carried her from panic to rage to terror to triumph. She sounded utterly exhausted—keyed up one minute and barely lucid the next. They set a plan to meet at Julianne's apartment the next morning at eight to screen the video that still lay buried in Tina's satchel. She assured Julianne that she was safe in her apartment since no one at the shelter, including Clint, knew her real last name or address. The two of them encouraged each other to get some much-needed rest, but each knew the words were more of a gesture than a likelihood.

Julianne returned to mindless nibbling while alternating between imaginary portraits of Jake Rossi and Clint Andrews. Twice she heard her answering machine recording desperate, angry calls from Clint Andrews. She got up long enough to turn down the volume of the machine so that she wouldn't have to listen to his menacing messages.

It was more than likely that Clint would pay her a surprise visit during the night. She called down to her doorman to make sure that someone was on duty. She fabricated a story about receiving several obscene phone calls and wanted to be extra careful in case someone had gotten hold of her address. Vic, the doorman, promised to be on top of things at the security desk. Though only sightly reassured, she returned to the safety of her bedroom, where she lay restlessly through the remainder of the night.

When she rolled over to check the time and saw that it was after seven in the morning, Julianne jolted out of bed to put on a pot of coffee—dark French roast, the strongest blend in her cupboard—before stepping into the shower. This, she knew, would be a full day. After meeting with Tina, she'd be going over to Pam's house. She had already asked if she could stop by for a visit. Pam was the only one she could turn to following the confrontation with Ted. She still didn't know what her next step would be regarding Clint Andrews, but she was certain of one thing: he was bound to make himself seen that day, at her office or at her home.

Tina showed up shortly before eight. She was too anxious to wait any longer and was relieved to find Julianne also ready to get started ahead of schedule. Tina's edginess had transformed into a mood of quiet victory overnight. She was more determined than ever to see that her time and risk would result in taking down Clint and holding accountable the system that allowed him to reign supreme.

Tina still wasn't sure how much had been recorded before the battery kicked off but she knew that at least part of the ugly scene had been documented.

She and Julianne stood mesmerized as the video began to roll. It was there—dark, slightly fuzzy, a bit muffled. But it was there. The hand under her chin. The thumb across her lips. It was barely discernible but blowing up the video would be a piece of cake. Zooming in on his hand would expose his fingers between her legs. "Are you too shy to show it?" It was there. The video stopped abruptly after he uttered those words. But they were there.

Tina and Julianne sat down on the floor, resting against the couch, and shared a deep, warm smile. "You did it." Julianne beamed.

"You did it too." Tina breathed a long sigh of satisfaction. "First on my agenda is heading to the station to make copies and get into an edit bay. Our editors can enhance the video to look so much better than it does on my computer. I'll keep the master disc and a backup locked in the video library at work. What do you think, two more copies? One for me to keep hidden at home and one for you to keep locked in your desk. Or … do you have a safe deposit box?"

"I will have one by this afternoon," Julianne answered. "As soon as you're through making dubs and can get a copy to me for safe keeping." She paused. "You know, this is the first beat we've taken to think about where we go from here. If we don't handle this right, it'll get buried. Except for Jake, no one at work has any idea what we've done." She paused to think. "Let's each make sure our notes are in total order, documenting how all this started, the people we spoke to. We can't use names, even first names … not yet. We can call them Lady A, Lady B, you know. Later we can see if at least Elisa will come forward. We could still really use her help. Even with this video, some could say you came on to Clint and the poor guy was just doing what came naturally. Add as much detail as you can. I will too. Let's meet back here at six o'clock. I'm calling in sick today."

At eleven thirty on Friday morning, Julianne rang Pam's doorbell. For days, she'd been rehearsing how to ease into telling Pam about Ted's monstrous behavior. Now were the added complications of the Clint Andrews recording and plot to blow open the situation at Horizons. Her mind was spinning as Pam opened the door and greeted her with a warm hug and calming smile. Once inside, she felt as if she were in a different world. The woman she was used to seeing behind a corporate desk wearing nondescript business attire looked perfectly suited to her gray sweats and totally at ease with a delicate new baby cradled in her arms.

As Pam prepared an early lunch, Julianne sat at the table cuddling the napping infant, soothed by this departure from the stress of the last few days. There was a serenity that swept over her, making it easier to launch into the conversation that was the reason for this visit. She'd start with the Ted dilemma and cross the Clint Andrews bridge when she came to it.

"I need your advice on something, Pam. It's pretty awful, and I need you to hear me out before you say anything. I haven't shared this with anybody yet." Pam made it easier for her guest by continuing meal preparations at the kitchen counter, listening but not staring as the story unfolded. Julianne let the floodgate open, spewing details her about the incident in Ted Marshall's office earlier that week. Julianne fixed her gaze on the baby's perfect pink fingers. Pam chopped at her vegetables mercilessly.

"If I confront him, I know he'll fire me. He's probably gathering ammunition already. If I tell anyone in personnel, they'll tell Ted that I reported him. They can't even keep vacation records organized, much less handle a case of harassment. If I ignore it, he'll just keep on bothering me ... an easy target, a career-obsessed woman who'll eventually succumb to his advances. I actually believe he thinks he'd be doing me a favor, my 'needing an outlet' and all."

"No. If you ignore him, he won't keep bothering you. It's all in how you ignore him." She stated this in a quiet matter-of-fact tone. It was the voice of someone speaking from experience. She set the knife on the chopping board and walked to the table with a stack of plates and silverware. As she set the table, she looked into Julianne's eyes.

"When a man is like that, Julianne, it's never to just one woman. It's the way he is, the way men like that are. They put the hit on whoever they choose as often as they choose. But he only did it to me once. It was just before my wedding. He and I flew to New Orleans for the programmers' convention and walked back to the hotel together from one of those gaudy bashes. He'd started downing scotch early in the evening, and I figured that was why he kept brushing up against me as we were walking. Then, in the hotel lobby, he insisted we stop for a nightcap. He started creating a commotion when I didn't want to join him. I figured it was easier to go along with him than to stand there and cause a scene. You know how loud and crass he gets when he's been drinking. Anyway, I'm sitting there sipping my Chardonnay when he starts asking me about the wedding and if I'd thought about how boring it was going to be to spend the rest of my life making love to just one man. He said I'd never struck him as the boring type, at work or in the sack. Those were his words; I still remember them: 'in the sack.'

"I was dumbstruck. I just sat there. I'd had my share to drink that night, too, and it took a minute for his intentions to register. He laughed and patted my knee and said that the least I could do was treat myself to a final fling, especially in a wild city like New Orleans. I excused myself to go the ladies' room, but really I headed straight for the elevator and up to my room. I just left him sitting there. That night I wrote a note to him, saying that I knew he had too much to drink and probably wouldn't remember that he had said some inappropriate things to me. I didn't know what other word to use. *Inappropriate.* No kidding. I wrote it with a cold, professional tone—no emotion or anger. I didn't want him to know how he rattled me. I wrote that as far as I was concerned, that evening never happened. We would never acknowledge it again.

"I said that if he ever spoke that way to me in the future, I'd report him and if that wasn't enough, I'd have my future husband break his face. Do you believe it? I actually used the phrase 'break your face.' I was trying to be cool, but I was really steamed. I went on to say that I could afford to risk the job now that I was getting married to a successful man, and I guaranteed to hurt him physically if he even thought of hurting me emotionally. I wrote it very simply and had the hotel bellman slip it under his door.

"The next day, it was as if nothing had happened. He wasn't distant or defensive,

as I'd expected. It was if this was just typical for him. He'd tested the waters. I guess sometimes he wins and sometimes he loses. Just make sure he loses when it comes to you."

"You never said anything to anyone?" were the first words Julianne spoke after absorbing this rattling story.

"What for? I handled it. There's a lot more to being a successful businesswoman than excelling at your job. That's just the tip of the iceberg. You know that. We learn how to take care of ourselves. It's hard enough to get a job in this industry ... so damn competitive. You can't throw yours away so easily. Just forget it. Give him the cold shoulder and emotionally disengage. He'll back off." Pam returned to the salad bowl as if the discussion was closed. "How's the documentary coming? Good stuff?"

Julianne was really confused now. She'd been thinking up all kinds of options for dealing with Ted's behavior and the more she thought about it, the more outraged she became. Now here was her role model, the closest thing to a mentor she had, telling her that it's just part of the business—for a woman. No big deal. Just live with it and get used to it. That was an option that had never occurred to her. It wasn't the advice she expected to get from a strong, smart woman like Pam. Yes, she was smart. Maybe she was also right. Only deep down, Julianne really didn't think so and was uncomfortable with the realization that their values could be so dissimilar.

She wanted to tell Pam about Tina's undercover work and the Clint Andrews video, about the plan to expose him along with the system that supported him. But she decided to ease her way into that conversation without giving too much away. Now she wasn't sure how Pam would react and what support she'd get from her boss. She thought for a minute. "Great stuff. We're going to cover the whole problem. First spousal abuse, then system abuse. I know it sounds corny and cliché and all that, but I've been wanting to do a show that could actually make a difference for so long. This doc is it."

"Ted filled me in on your feelings about the shelter's administrative guy. He's adamant about ..."

"I'm doing the show the best way I know how: fully and accurately. That's what I'm doing, Pam. You'll be back at the station by the time it airs. You'll have to decide what you want to do when you see the rough cuts. I've already decided what I'm going to do. You can report me now if you want to. I'm not changing my mind." Okay. So now Pam knew the program wasn't going to be as ordered by management. She just didn't know the details. Julianne felt comfortable with that compromise but was still wary of Pam's support.

Pam filled their plates and then sat down, reaching over to maneuver the baby from Julianne's arms. Her face lit up as she looked down at the little face. "I think we should enjoy our lunch and I should show you Hailey's new outfits. They look like doll costumes. I lay them out sometimes and look at them just for fun. To tell you the truth, work seems a million miles away right now. I'd just as soon keep it that way. You've been with me for a couple of years, Julianne, and you must know that you're very important to me. I care about you personally and I trust you professionally. But I'm your boss, not your big sister. You'll figure out the best way to handle things; I know you will. I'm on maternity leave for only a few more days, and I'm not going to ruin it with problems at the station or even thoughts of work. There's time enough for that later. That may sound selfish, but that's what *I've* decided to do and I'm not changing *my* mind either.

Julianne hesitated as she exited the subway down the block from her office. She had so many reasons for opting to go to work instead of retreating to her apartment after lunch with Pam. The fact that she'd be showing up at the office in perfect health after calling in sick just a few hours earlier was of little concern. Of more relevance was the gut feeling that Clint Andrews would be tracking her both at home and at work. The TV station was the more logical place of refuge.

And then there was Jake. She wasn't ready to talk to him, to juggle that load of emotional turmoil on top of everything else. The sick part, she thought to herself, was that she was aching to see him as much as she was dreading it. She'd known that the Jake situation would explode eventually. Married men led to unhappy endings. Now she just wanted to get on with it, get past their first contact since *the call*. And she knew that the Clint Andrews story was destined to explode, too. After all, that's what this project was all about. It's just that she never figured on both scenarios exploding on the exact same day of her life. She hadn't prepared herself for either situation emotionally and now realized that it was sink or swim time for Julianne Sloan. Either she'd buckle under pressure or she'd kick butt ... and she wasn't the type to buckle.

She swung through the revolving door into the building's massive lobby. There, just as she suspected might be the case, sat Clint Andrews crouched on a long sofa in a corner of the reception area. He sat forward in the seat as if he were ready to spring into action at any given moment. That moment came when Julianne came into view. She met him eye-to-eye.

"I don't get what's going on here, Julianne."

"We're doing a documentary about domestic violence, Clint. About physical abuse, emotional abuse, system abuse targeted at women. That's what's going on. I'm not getting into it with you any deeper than that. I'm doing my job." She spoke calmly and coldly and turned to walk to the elevators that would carry her to the station, hopefully unscathed.

He reached out and yanked her arm, forcing her around to face him. "You've got to be kidding if you think you're going to walk away just like that. You haven't exactly been the pinnacle of professionalism."

She got the message. He was threatening to expose their affair, detail their exploits, and it make her skin crawl. Still, she stood tall, refusing to let him fluster her. His temper continued to flare. "I'll have my lawyers on your ass inside of an hour. I've been sitting here all day, Julianne, and I intend to find out what you were setting me up for and what that hell you intend to do with that piece of crap recording you took of me." This time his voice was threatening and cut through the usual commotion in the lobby. The security guard turned to check out the situation, and she and Julianne exchanged a look indicating the potential for trouble.

Julianne pulled her arm free and shoved Clint away from her. "First of all, step back and get your hands off me. That may work for you in your little kingdom. But it won't work here. Secondly, it's fine to call your lawyer. That's your right. You're smart enough to know that—and you're smart enough to have figured out the rest, Clint. I have nothing else to say to you right now."

As she spoke, Jake stepped out of the elevator, noticing first the security agent on her feet in careful observation of the couple in the corner and then turning his attention to that couple, Julianne and Clint Andrews. Jake had no knowledge of what had transpired with Tina the night before. At first he thought that Clint was putting the moves on Julianne much the way he had during their first meeting at Horizons. The expression on her face, however, signaled a very different dynamic. Jake approached them as they stared each other down in silence. Julianne spotted him and, in a still-icy tone, shifted her attention to him, saying, "I have everything under control, Jake." Clearly being dismissed, he stepped back to the elevator bank, where he continued to observe the situation.

Clint decided to try a different tack. His expression softened, and his voice became low and intimate. She could not believe that he was so arrogant as to think that he could charm his way out of this mess. "Look, Julianne, it's really hard to talk in here. You must have someone who can cover for you today … or I can wait. Let's have dinner and talk like two people who know each other. We know each other. And I know you don't want to hurt me. So let's just work our way through this misunderstanding."

"We don't know each other at all, although based on my research, I have to think I know you a lot better than you know me. But then, I've been *working* on knowing you. You affect a lot of lives, Clint. And if you knew me better, you'd know that I want to use my work to affect people's lives too, but in a good way. That's what this documentary is all about. I was a journalist before I earned a living covering fashion shows and movie junkets. I know what I'm doing and I know you have valid reasons for being upset. As I said, you're not stupid. Maybe you're just not as smart as you think you are."

She left him standing there, finally speechless, as she headed for her office. Jake was waiting a few yards away, near the elevator. "It's okay, Jake. I don't need some knight in shining armor coming to my rescue. Most women don't, you know. Men just like to think we do." She spoke with a chilly voice as she stepped into the elevator, Jake following. Her underlying anger was obvious.

"I know you're mad at me. I get it. Let's just talk about everything. This isn't exactly fun for me either, Julianne," he said as the elevator came to a halt and they stepped out.

She stopped dead in her tracks and looked directly into his eyes. "I'm sure it's not. And I'm equally sure you're not responsible for my stupid decisions, the dumb things I let myself in for, my shambles of a life. I blame myself for all that. I'm accountable for what I do. I get it. But, yeah, I'm still plenty mad at you. You are the married one. You are the one who can walk away from this straight and into the arms of somebody waiting for you at home. So don't even think of insulting my intelligence by turning to me for sympathy, okay? And you know what, Jake? I don't even have the time to deal with this whole mess right now. I have a different mess on my hands. At first, I was overwhelmed by everything hitting the fan at the exact same time. Now I think maybe it's a blessing. Putting your career on the line has a way of upstaging your love life."

She left him standing there dumbstruck as she marched down

the hall, an air of defiance in her step. An unexpected smile came to her lips. It was as if she were suddenly invigorated by it all, as if she were recharged and confident in the woman that she was, in the strength she now remembered she had. Funny, she hadn't realized she'd lost her edge until she found it again. Instead of heading up to Ted's office to update him on the doc and prepare him for the legal nightmare that would surely follow, she changed her course and her strategy and headed for the newsroom.

The four o'clock news was on the air, which meant that the preproduction chaos for this show was over but that everyone was in frantic preparation for the all-important six o'clock show. She had hoped to arrive earlier, but the process of opening the safe deposit box at the bank had seemed to drag on forever. As was the norm, the news director, Mick Hoffman, was leaning back in his ragged leather chair in the newsroom, engrossed in a wall of television screens that monitored the competition as well as their own newscast. She took a seat next to him silently. She knew better than to distract him during the show. The consumer reporter's story was just wrapping up, and she could see the displeased look on his face.

Now was a commercial break. While continuing to follow the action on the other monitors, he shouted a barrage of notes to the producer of the six o'clock show. "That was at least twenty seconds fat, Deb. Remind our reporters to worry more about how the package holds together and less about how many times they get their face into the story. I keep giving that note, but no one seems to give a damn. Tomorrow I want shorter packages, fewer needless reporter stand-ups and more meaty stories. This isn't a morning show. Forget the fluff. In fact, forget waiting till tomorrow. Make sure I see what I want on the ten o'clock show tonight." With that off his chest, he gave Julianne a casual glance, offering just a hint of a smile before turning his attention back to the video wall.

"What's up, Julianne? Bored back in programming? Need a news fix?" He was cocky but in a cool, almost endearing way. A lifelong news junkie, Mick's journalistic principles made him as much a pain in the ass to management as her creative drive and stubborness. Because of this, they shared a mutual respect and unspoken bond. Yet even after three years as associates, they barely knew one another. An unannounced visit like this was rare indeed—and a signal that she had something specific to discuss.

They both continued gazing at the screens as they spoke. "Today's been anything but boring, Mick. I need your advice on something. Can I talk to you after the show? Right after?"

"Programming coming to news for advice? Make my day!" He was only pretending to give her a hard time. To act any other way would take the fun out of their "friendly enemy", news versus programming, relationship. Actually, Mick was the only guy on the station's management team she genuinely liked. True, he was part of the boys' club, but more because his peers assumed he was one of them and not so much because he lobbied for that exclusive membership.

Still staring straight ahead he said, "Come back in fifteen minutes. I'll be in my office." With that, his attention was committed to the show, saying to no one in particular, "Let's remember to tell Tim how refreshing it would be to hear him deliver two sentences in a row without flubbing his lines."

She traipsed back to her department, where she found the offices deserted except for the cheerful gung-ho intern who sat manning the phones.

"Hi, Robin," Julianne muttered as she unlocked her office door. "Where are the troops?"

"Oh, Julianne, we didn't think you were coming in today. I'm glad you're feeling better. Louise is out doing her piece on the blues fest, Sam left about an hour ago because his edit session started today at five a.m., and Lianne is upstairs in the music library looking for some cuts Louise needs for her story. That leaves yours truly. Can I get you anything ... besides this stack of phone messages?"

"I don't even want them. That can all wait till tomorrow. I just ran in to pick up a couple of things."

"You might want to check this one thing out. There are six messages from a Clint Andrews. He said it was urgent. He even came by here midafternoon, but he said he didn't have an appointment. Oh, and Ted Marshall came down here looking for you a couple of hours ago. I'd never even seen him before; he must not come down here much. Anyway, Lianne was here then and she told him you were out sick today."

Julianne was immediately in her office, collecting her files on Horizons and research notes on domestic violence along with research on the proposed victims assistance plan that was up before Congress. The separate file on Clint Andrews was placed on top. She continued conversing with Robin through the open door of her office. "Do me a favor, Robin, and see if Ted is still in his office. If he is, say that's it's very important that I get in to see him in an hour, even though I know it's late. Don't say I'm here. Just say I called you and asked you to get in touch with him for me. If he's not there, don't leave a message; just hang up."

She listened through the door as Robin placed the call. "Yes, she realized that it might be inconvenient, being that it's getting so late. But she said it was very important." There was a pause. "I'm not sure where she called from. I think she's just planning to stop in to see you in an hour and hopes that you'll be there. Okay. Thanks, Mr. Marshall."

Robin stepped around the desk and peeked in to deliver the message. She figured some discretion was in order since she and Julianne had just lied to the big boss. "He'll be there."

"Thanks, Robin." Julianne stuffed her papers into her satchel, locked her office, and went to find Mick Hoffman.

Mick was waiting for her like a little boy anxious for arrival of the ice cream truck. For Julianne Sloan, queen of producers, to come to him for advice indicated that something important was happening or had already happened. She told him about the documentary and gave a detailed account of the whole Clint Andrews layer of content.

He listened patiently, intently. It was his kind of story; she had his undivided attention. When she told him about the touch spot she was in, consciously defying management, and said that she and Tina had actually managed to get video on the guy in action, her voice became noticeably jittery and he leaned in, assuming a friendlier supportive posture. When she finished, he sat back, stretched, sighed, and looked at her with one of his half smiles. "You know, Julianne, I spent two years fighting to get an investigative unit for this news team. Last year we got it--and we're damn good at this kind of stuff. If you would have shared the story, we could have helped you with this. You have a reputation for being stubborn, you know, and secretive about your work."

Yes, they loved giving each other a hard time just for the hell of it. After all, anyone in the business understood that news and programming were archrivals, vying for budgets, equipment, on-air promotion, and accolades. She shot back a smile at him. "Don't forget the part about my being a bitch. Stubborn, secretive bitch. That about sums it up. The perfect description of me according to the executive conference room crowd, I'm sure." She took a more serious tone. "The thing is, you should be glad you weren't a part of this or your butt would be on the line along with mine."

"The first thing to deal with is the security of the video. I'm sure you and Tina took care of making a copies and protecting their whereabouts. Now, the trick is to make sure our lawyers position the tape as part of a news gathering effort. That way it will be treated with a lot more leniency within the legal system. Everyone's afraid to get caught screwing with freedom of the press. Just position it as news. Position the whole show as news. It isn't logged that way now, is it?"

"No. So far it's classified as a public affairs special. It could be classified in the FCC programming log as news, I suppose. That would give us more freedom, fewer restrictions." She spoke slowly, thinking through his rationale. "You are absolutely right. If this video were shot as part of a news program, it would be legitimized. We'd avoid a ton of legal hassles. And there's no reason why this topic shouldn't be considered news material. It was just put under the public affairs umbrella because that's the department that had a budget to fund production ... and where I could work on my own ... without the involvement of the news director." She smiled at him again. "Thanks. Great advice. At the risk of pushing my luck, can I ask you something else?"

"Go for it."

"Any words of wisdom on how to handle Ted? Think I can salvage my job?"

"Probably, since the whole station knows he has the hots for you, if you'll pardon my being crass. But knowing you, you won't want to play that card. So try this. Tell him you ran it by the news department and everyone thought the station could kick some ass with this stuff. You do the special; we'll do a five-part series in our investigative report slot on the ten o'clock show. We'll time it out to air during sweeps. Tell him one of my strongest stories for sweeps just fell through—which is no lie, by the way—and that we could use a strong ratings hook. Prostitution rings, serial killers, and battered women always get good numbers, and we did the prostitutes and serial killers during the last ratings period."

His dry sense of humor was the perfect remedy for her jitters. "Of course, you will have to share the story and the video. And you should be prepared to take some heat from the newsies down here. They won't exactly be enamored with the notion that the programming department is going out on their own to do investigative reporting. I can't say I disagree. But I'm not going to blow a good story. Besides, I haven't saved someone's hide for a while, so it may as well be yours."

"You're the second man today I've asked to refrain from this damsel in distress mentality. Don't make this a male/female thing, okay? I know I don't have much leverage here. I need and appreciate your help. But let's refrain from the helpless female bit, please." She looked down, embarrassed by her own predicament.

"I just said that I haven't saved a hide. I didn't say a female hide. This is me you're talking to—not Ted Marshall or Don McBain or the rest of the boys upstairs. Get it?"

"Got it. Thank you. Even if he doesn't buy it, thank you." She started out the door, then looked back at him with a cocky grin of her own. "And if he does buy it, don't expect it to be a piece of cake working with me. Stubborn, secretive, and bitchy, you know." Without waiting for a reaction, she headed off to Ted Marshall's office.

Julianne was about due for a break, and she got it when she met with Ted Marshall. He had stayed at the office late to meet with her, as she had requested, but by the time she walked into his office, he was more aggitated and preoccupied than she had ever seen him. He had just been notified that the head of the New York station had been fired following six months of declining ratings and revenue shortfall for the fiscal year. The heir to the coveted position, running the station in country's top market, would be named within the week. Ted had been invited to throw his hat in the ring--no surprise since Chicago was the third largest market. He was assured that he had a leg up on the competition due to his station's ascent in ratings and revenues. The position was likely his if he wanted it. However, in keeping with protocol for all candidates, corporate headquarters required that he immediately provide documentation pertaining to his past two years of service: quarterly revenue reports, ratings tracks, annual profit margin, Emmy Awards. Ted had bigger things to worry about than a local public affairs special.

While he made sure Julianne understood how displeased he was with her bullheaded tactics and blatant disregard for his instructions to take the high road in presenting the shelter, he simply had bigger fish to fry. With Julianne at his side, he dialed business affiars for a brief conference call regarding the special, advising the lawyer and Julianne to communicate with one another directly until Pam returned from maternity leave, at which time Pam would take over for Julianne when it came to business affairs.

"Just make sure you keep us clear of a lawsuit," he barked at them both before ending the call. As she prepared to leave, he added, "If I were you, I'd make damn sure this was the best show of my career. You and I sure are bumping heads lately … and heads aren't exactly what I had in mind." She ignored the innuendo and cleared out of the office before he had a chance to give deeper thought to the situation.

By the time Julianne made it back to her apartment, Tina was in the lobby waiting, with a stack of files in one hand and a Giordano's Pizza box in the other, a deep-dish reward for their hard work! The two of them munched and worked in silence for hours. At about nine thirty, the doorman rang her bell to announce that she had a visitor, a Mr. Andrews. She explained that she was unavailable.

She and Tina grabbed their laptops and began mapping out the format for the special. They had great material from their silhouette interviews with the women. The hidden camera stuff was strong. Now it was time to structure the content, first building empathy and understanding for the victims to achieve maximum impact as they peeled away the layers of story, "peeling the onion," as producers described the storytelling process. Skill in peeling the onion was what separated good producers from great ones. They considered themselves to be among the greats and embraced the opportunity to put their talents to good use. The hidden camera video would serve a dual role, first a tease of what would unfold, then the climax to the doc.

Tina left just before eleven, but Julianne sat there on her couch staring at the computer screen. Something was missing. The show had all the elements a producer longed for: dramatic interviews, meaty content, shocking statistics, heart and soul and a villain. But it needed one more thing. It needed triumph. Spirit. Hope. Proof that things could be better, that women could empower themselves to make things better; that's what was missing. That was the void. There was one person who could fill that void. Her name was Elisa.

The next morning, Julianne juggled a record amount of items as she struggled to navigate the key into her office door at seven o'clock. She was eager to start screening video and construct an edit outline, but not so eager that she could skip her bagel and coffee. She sipped and chomped while she scanned the morning paper and station's news portal. Every now and then, her thoughts drifted off to Jake and her lousy luck with men. But she made up her mind to shove that mess aside for now. She was aware of her pattern for obsessing over relationship conflict, to torture herself with the same questions about how she could have been so simpleminded, to punish herself by reliving the joy of the good and the drama of the bad. Right now, she had a concrete distraction. If she could force herself to shove Jake into a separate corner of her mind, a corner that she would deal with later, the initial pain might diminish. Besides, she knew that production and all the chaos that came with it was her best medicine.

All of these thoughts were darting through her head when she heard a soft knock on the door and looked up to see Jake in the doorway. "It's been a while since I've seen you here so early. You okay?" he asked.

"Yeah, I'm okay. I asked Tina to fill you in on what was going on with the special, Clint, Ted and everything. Did you two have a chance to talk?"

"I'm up to speed on the show. I talked to engineering and convinced them to pull me off camera duty so I can edit what we shot for the doc myself. Other than you and Tina, I know this material better than anyone. So that's all under control. That's about all I can say, that it's under control, Julianne. You and I aren't going to be able to work our way through this if you won't talk to me."

"Work our way through this? I didn't think that was an option, Jake. Look, what's done is done. As far as I can see, you and I don't have anything to talk about anymore. Your wife is pregnant with your baby and that doesn't leave much room for me, does it? So at least give me the satisfaction of being the one to cut loose. I'd rather spare myself the ugliness of being dumped."

"Why the hell do you see yourself as being dumped? Helene's pregnant. I'm still not sure how I feel about fatherhood right now, but I'll have lots of time to get used to it. I know I don't want her to end the pregnancy. But I don't love Helene anymore. Her being pregnant doesn't mean that I've instantly fallen back in love with her. You're shutting me out so that I won't hurt you. I get that. But what I'm trying to say is that I'm not going to hurt you. I love you."

She looked at him, utterly confused. "Jake, I don't want you to make promises you can't live up to. And you're right. I want to spare myself as much pain as possible. I'm not going to say something trite like 'I knew this day would come' or 'It was fun while it lasted.' Honesty, I never really thought about forever. But I did think that maybe you'd finally get yourself to leave Helene; maybe we'd have a shot of taking things further. You don't know how many times I played out the scene in my head. You walking into my bedroom as I lay sleeping and then my eyes opening to see you standing above me with a huge bouquet of red roses in one hand and your suitcase in the other. You'd bend down to kiss me and the rest would be history. Nice dream, huh? I never thought I'd have the nerve to share it with you, but what the hell."

She turned away from him and stared out the window. "I'm tired of dreams and dreamers. I'll get over you like I got over a lot of other things in my life. I can't tell you how disgusted I am with myself. I don't know what came over me, how I lost track of who I am. I hate so much of what I've done lately, including falling for a married man, but I'm dealing with it. I'll get over it, and I'll get on with my life. You'll be a great daddy and probably fall back in love with your wife at some point. That's the real ending to our story. So let's just let it be. I want us to be able to work together. You've been my partner in production for years now, and you're the best shooter and editor I know. If you keep pushing the personal stuff, I won't be able to function with you professionally. Let's at least salvage that part of our relationship."

"I'm not going to push you, Julianne. And I'm not going to make any promises, because you're right. I don't know if I'll be able to keep them. I guess this is just our own version of a hiatus. Let's take some time to let things settle down. Let's make a kick-ass show together and have some fun doing it, like we used to. Maybe the rest will take care of itself. I know that sounds naive and ridiculous. I just feel like things will work themselves out." He paused and then extended his hand. "Come on down to the screening room with me. I have some great shots I want you to see."

She took his hand and smiled. It felt warm and strong and friendly. This was the Jake she trusted. She had to make their professional relationship work. It was too good, too rare. It would be insane to sacrifice it all because of the personal fiasco they had made. Julianne knew that once she put her mind to something, she would succeed. She was determined not to lose her friend and colleague, Jake Rossi.

"Only if you'll spring for another coffee on the way," she said.

CHAPTER 14

The door to the screening room flew open with a viciousness that stunned both Julianne and Jake. Ted Marshall stood there, filling the doorway with a cold, angry stance that was as menacing as it was out of character. Staring at Julianne, he directed his first words to Jake. "Leave the producer and me alone for a minute. We have some business to discuss."

Clearly Ted's tone was one of unchallenged authority. Jake's position at the station had afforded him little opportunity to interact with the general manager. He stepped around Ted respectfully but boldly. At the doorway, he looked back at Julianne. "I've got a couple of calls to make. I'll be right down the hall." His voice was quiet and reassuring. The door closed behind him. Ted stood solidly in place.

"You little bitch. Al Sanger just paid me a surprise visit." Al Sanger was the head of legal affairs at the company's corporate headquarters. His voice was a powerful one within the company, as thunderous as his personality. He would have a large say in which of the six general managers would ultimately receive the kick upstairs, the New York promotion. More often than not, a personal visit from Al Sanger was perceived as the kiss of death. "He couldn't believe I was stupid enough to throw stones at the biggest public service campaign our station had done in years, that I was a big enough fuckup to do an exposé on *ourselves*. It seems your Mr. Andrews' lawyers contacted corporate, filled Sanger in on all the lovely details and now my ass is grass. He was so pissed off he flew all the way down here to personally pull me out of the running for the New York job. Probably the only reason he didn't fire me altogether is that he wants me to squelch this whole fiasco from the inside. Quietly."

He walked toward her and cupped her face in his hands. His fingers trembled with anger, conveying a physical threat through his touch that left her paralyzed. He was proving his dominance, a supremacy that would be earned by his size and gender if not by his title. "Consider your show dead, Julianne, and you along with it." He released her face as if he were throwing away a toy he now found useless and boring. He left the room as fiercely as he had entered.

Seconds later Jake darted back through the doorway. The expression on Julianne's ashen face, one of total stillness and awe, stopped him in his tracks. She stared straight ahead into the flickering blank screen of the monitor. "Don't come in here," was all she said.

Five minutes later, when her hands had stopped shaking and Jake had given her time to collect herself, she filled him in on the details of Ted's little visit. She passively watched him respond with what she perceived to be protective anger on her behalf mixed with what she sensed was confusion over what could be done to mitigate the damage and squash the bully. She then proceeded to call Lianne, asking her to bring the coat and tote bag she had left in the office to the elevator. She headed for home and the dark sanctuary of her bedroom, where she stripped off her clothes and immersed herself between the comforting sheet and soft, plush covers.

It wasn't the complexity of her predicament or threat of losing her job that kindled Julianne's emotional overload. It was the restrained violence, the vile rage, the physical touch laced with controlled force that triggered a response in Julianne she had no choice but to confront. Maybe it was time. Maybe denial was not the way to put the experience of Allen Miller behind her once and for all. For when Ted Marshall stormed through that door displaying a fury targeted directly at her, when he cupped her face with a brutality kept in check by mandatory self-restraint, when he exercised his executive right to humiliate her at her place of business with her peers holding vigil outside the door, that's when the hidden memory of the most demeaning day of her life erupted to throw her into a shattered emotional state.

She stared at the blank bedroom wall is if it were a movie screen with the scene playing out before her very eyes. She and Allen Miller had the starring roles, and the set was this very room, only dressed in the colors and quilting she had so adored before he ruined it for her, resulting in immediate replacement when she at last threw him out.

It was a Sunday, and she had stayed home to screen tapes while he went to a Cubs doubleheader with his brother and one of the guys from work. Six and a half hours of fraternal togetherness was apparently not enough for them, so the trio embarked upon a beer drinker's tour of Rush Street, a tour on which each stop was punctuated by a shot of tequila. By the time the cab poured him on the doorstep and the doorman punched his floor in the elevator, Allen Miller had been transformed from a cheery fan to a bleary drunk. It was a sight that had become more and more familiar at home, and Julianne had just about had it.

She knew better than to provoke him with a verbal assault while he was in this pathetic state, so she opted to give him the cold shoulder, ignoring his slurred attempt to make conversation and relocating from living room to bedroom where her laptop sat idle on the bed, waiting for her to screen a rough cut. Alan stumbled to the kitchen with the goal of constructing a sandwich for himself. In a matter of seconds, he became outraged over his inability to find the jar of mustard, which was hidden at the back of the shelf behind fruits, vegetables, bottles, and jars she'd brought home from the grocery the day before. He screamed for her to get her butt into the kitchen and find the goddamn mustard. Determined to maintain her cool, she turned up the volume on her computer and continued screening the cut. In what seemed like an instant, Allen was at her bedside and, in a violent rush, reached for the laptop, yanking it from her grip.

She would have been mortified had she not been stunned. She sat frozen as, with one sweeping motion, he proceeded to send the laptop flying across the room, fracturing the glass door that led to a small balcony. While her horrified eyes followed its flight, Allen bolted toward her, cupping her face with his right hand as he tugged her off the bed with the left. He dragged her to the kitchen where he shoved her face into the chamber of the open refrigerator. While keeping a tight grip on her arm, his free hand forced her cheek against the top metal rack, its jagged silver edge piercing her tender skin.

"I told you to find that fucking mustard!" he yelled, grabbing the front of the rack and wrenching it out of the refrigerator as the contents were strewn in all directions, crashing on the linoleum, the counters, against the cabinet doors.

Julianne realized the futility of a struggle. His grip was that firm, and her senses were that numb. In a flash, he had her down on her back on the wet disheveled kitchen floor, and he sat straddled on top of her, turning her face to the side and pushing it into a pool of thick, chilly mustard that oozed from its fragmented jar. One jagged piece of glass cut into her cheek, and tiny drops of blood mingled with the thick yellow liquid as the mess trickled down toward her neck. "There's the fucking mustard, Julianne! Was that so hard?" he spat at her as he sprang to his feet and disappeared through the doorway. Seconds later, as she lay silent and still frozen on the floor, she heard the bedroom door slam shut.

When she managed to lift herself up from the clutter, she stood motionless, staring blankly at the mess. Not a whimper fell from her lips. Not a tear escaped from her eye. As if in a trance, she proceeded to gather up the broken bottles and torn cartons, mopping up the spills and collecting the berries and restoring the kitchen to its proper condition.

She stuffed the disarray into two trash bags and made her way down the corridor to the garbage chute, lowering the remnants of Allen's rage into the cavern as she turned to see the couple from down the hall staring at her filthy wet clothing, stained with all the colors of the rainbow. They said nothing. She brushed past them and back to her apartment and the safety of the bathroom, where she tore off her stained jeans and sweater and stepped into a fiercely hot shower. Only then, with streams of clean hot water engulfing her and washing away any physical evidence of the incident, did she submit to a savage sob that evolved into an intense cry. It was a cry that lasted the better part of an hour. And then it turned to fury. The fury was directed not at the monster who had overpowered her but at herself for her inability to manage her lover, to succeed in a relationship, to gauge the pressure of the moment and react accordingly.

When Allen was drunk or in a lousy mood, he had a short fuse. He had warned her about it. She knew it full well, yet she persisted in igniting his temper time and time again. What was wrong with her? Was she a fool? Was she hopeless? Was she well on her way to racking up yet another rotten relationship while her girlfriends and associates were moving on to their second and third babies? Why couldn't she get it right?

These were the questions she pondered as she sat atop the toilet, finally rising to dry her eyes, brush her hair, and smooth lotion over her skin. Quietly she inched open the bedroom door, where she saw Allen lying on his back sounding the heavy breathing of a drunken sleep. She crept into the room and under the covers beside him, lying on her side away from the face that reflected her failure. The slight stirring that marked her arrival prompted him to shift toward her, draping an arm over hers and nuzzling his nose into the crook of her neck. She breathed a sigh of relief. He still loved her. It would be okay. She would do better.

The next morning, he rose early and greeted her with a cup of coffee as she emerged from the shower stall. He handed it to her timidly and she realized that although he knew something had gone terribly wrong the night before—the shattered balcony door and raw cut on her left cheekbone provided haunting evidence of that—he had no recollection of the actual events that had transpired. And she had no intention of refreshing his memory, much preferring to let both the scars and the relationship heal.

It wasn't until later, after she had barely escaped the total destruction of her spirit following months of progressively frightening episodes, that she allowed herself to face the facts of the situation. It took far to long, but at last her anger and disgust were directed to where they truly belonged. Up until then, she rationalized that he hadn't actually punched her. He had never forced sex upon her. The cut from the mustard jar was just an accident. And so the words *abused* and *battered* and the meaning that went with them were shunned as part of a language that belonged soley to pitiful victims.

But down the road, when his burst of anger erupted during their final fight and he stung her with one swift crack in the face, it was as if he had inadvertently slapped her senses back into place. It was *him*. She was a survivor, and he was an asshole. And an animal. And a bully. And the enemy. She would survive by eliminating him from her existence. Yes, she finally threw him out and belatedly celebrated her strength and power.

Following "The Ted Incident," so enlightening an event that Julianne gave it a name, her emotional journey back to the Allen chapter and countless ill-fated relationships prior to that played out in her head as if in slow motion.

She had buried so much hurt for so long, eager to accept the blame rather than slay the bully, refusing to acknowledge that she had allowed herself to be brutalized, victimized. Now Ted Marshall's actions had penetrated her emotional hiding place. That reminiscent brutal grip as his hand cupped her face triggered what was, in fact, life-changing self-awareness. At last she was forced to confront her cowardince and compliance, to accept accountability for her victiization. At the same time, Horizons preyed upon mind, guilt weighing upon her for being so judgemental of the women there. She craved to vindicate herself *for herself.* In doing so, maybe she would help those like her. Maybe the doc on Horizons was destiny. Maybe Clint Andrews was the key to redemption.

Two dozen assorted doughnuts carefully arranged on a Lucite tray covered the top of the file cabinet next to Elisa's desk. It was her way of celebrating her two-month anniversary on the job. She sorted through the mail and glanced at her reflection in the large glass door that marked the entrance to the office suite. She wondered how many assistants before her had stared at their reflections day in and day out and realized that probably no one before her had used that sheet of glass to help transform her life.

It was that image she saw staring back at herself day after day that gave her the fortitude to keep pushing herself … to learn, to ask questions, to brush back her hair, brush on her makeup, and brush up on her social skills. Little by little, that reflection became a person Elisa actually liked. She watched her own transformation as if she were witnessing the ugly duckling transforming into the swan. She liked what she saw, and it gave her the motivation to become more daring, more dynamic than she ever imagined she could be. The craziest part of it all was that she felt absolutely comfortable with the woman she had become.

Perhaps that's why she had agreed to meet with Julianne after Marsha called to say that Julianne had come by the shelter, pleading with Marsha to get in touch with Elisa on her behalf. They planned the meeting for today after work at that same neighborhood deli down the street from Horizons and around the corner from the apartment she and Kelly now occupied. But she had a job to tend to first. She rushed to complete her paperwork so that she could close her computer for the day and meet Adrienne Phelps at the site of the company's newest building, an eighteen-story high-rise facing Oak Street Beach. It was under new ownership and had undergone renovation.

Adrienne had lobbied hard to win the management rights to the building. It was primarily an apartment complex, but the row of exclusive shops that lined the lobby set the building apart from most of the residential high-rises in the area. Adrienne had asked Elisa to do a walk-through of the building with her at four in the afternoon. She understood that she was being groomed to take on a building of her own one day and looked forward to shadowing her boss on-site.

At three thirty, Elisa phoned Kelly to make certain she was

starting her homework so that she could get it out of the way before her father picked her up for their Wednesday night outing. Since Elisa was planning to go directly from her job to the meeting at the deli, Jenna, the babysitter, agreed to stay late in the event that Peter was detained at work. After checking on Kelly and going over the phone messages with Marty, Elisa headed out to meet Adrienne. She gave herself an approving glance as she passed through the glass doors. The doughnuts were just part of her anniversary treat. She had also indulged in a bright blue silk blouse that hugged her figure and looked businesslike all at once. The flow of the fabric and cut of the neckline made her feel sexy, soft, and pretty. It had been a long while since she felt truly pretty.

She arrived at the building right on time. It was a wonderful structure, with apartments that were bright and lakefront views that were exquisite. Of the two-bedroom apartments, 90 percent were rented, and all the one-bedroom units were taken, mostly by professional singles willing to cough up the hefty rental fee in exchange for the luxuries the building had to offer. Adrienne was waiting in one of the smaller two-bedroom apartments on the first floor. She had been using this apartment as her home base while the manager's office in the lobby was being repainted.

After collecting her papers, coat, and purse, she handed Elisa two sets of keys. "Here you go. This is the master set of keys for the building. I've already made a backup set for me to keep downtown at the office. Keep your master set in a locked desk drawer. And these are yours for the apartment," Adrienne said with a forced nonchalant attitude that belied her inner excitement.

"What?" Elisa asked innocently. "Where do they go?"

"In your purse, I'd expect. Isn't that where you always keep your keys? Happy anniversary." She broke into a wide smile. "Now don't screw up."

Elisa's eyes were brimming with tears, and her voice was gleefully shaky. "Kelly will never believe this. I don't even believe this. Are you sure I'm ready?" she asked timidly.

"I'm sure you're *not* ready to take it on youself. But you won't have to. I'm going to be managing the building, and you'll be assistant manager. I can't reside on site -- you can. I own my town house and I have others buildings to handle. I was going to hire someone with a lot of experience to manage this place full time, but I'm afraid to delegate. These new owners are taking over properties all through Chicago and I want to be their go-to building management firm. So I want to be hands-on, only I need support. You, as things happen, need to learn the business and are leasing your place month to month. This unit will be ready for occupancy in two weeks, your occupancy. So, here we are. You tell me, Elisa--are you ready?" Adrienne spoke in a voice that was bold and professional, looking Elisa straight in the eye. "You tell me."

"I'm ready."

An hour later, Elisa entered the deli, and Julianne was noticeably startled to see the vibrant brunette with a never-before-seen bounce in her step.

"Wait a minute," she teased as Elisa made her way across the room. "I'm expecting someone named Elisa. You seem very nice, but I don't believe we've met. Do I know you?"

"Very funny," Elisa laughed. "Even I'm not sure I know me. But Kelly keeps insisting I'm her mom, so I guess I'm the lady you're expecting."

"Actually, you're nothing like the lady I was expecting and I'm not quite sure what to say. Can you fill me in, off the record if you like? I'm just so amazed. The changes are written all over you— your face, your walk, your dress, even your hair. Auburn highlights, right?"

"The do-it-yourself version. I'm still on a tight budget, although that should be opening up a little now. Congratulate me. I got a promotion today, complete with an apartment."

"Ah, working your way into the world of real estate, from what I gather. Marsha wouldn't give up much information, just a couple of clues. The important thing is that she agreed to call you for me." She paused to take in the details of the new Elisa. "Has Marsha seen you lately?"

"I stopped into Horizons last week. It's funny. I think I purposely moved into a place close by so that it wouldn't feel as scary as venturing out somewhere distant and, if I started second-guessing my decisions, I could run back for a reminder of what the last few months had been like for me. When I moved to the apartment and Peter started coming around to pick up Kelly, he was always on his best behavior. There were actually times—I can't even believe I'm saying this—when I almost buckled and thought I should give him another chance ... for Kelly's sake, mostly. That's when I'd take an evening stroll over to Horizons and remember how hard I had to work to get where I am. I feel strong now, but there's a part of me that will always be connected to that simple little room on the second floor."

The server came by and took their order. "I don't know about Marsha, though. She starting to talk about going back to Kent. This isn't the first time she left him, you know. I remember her telling you that when you shot her interview. She'll probably go back for the next round. She's just stuck in this stupid pattern. Anyway, she said you wanted to talk to me again, but I'm not sure why. My part of the story's over, I would think."

"It's just the opposite. You're the best part of the story." Julianne reached across the table and squeezed Elisa's hand. "You're the happy ending."

Elisa dropped her eyes and stared down into her cup. "It's scary for me to think that way. It's only been a couple of months that I've been on my feet. I don't know that I'll make it. I mean, I think I will. I guess I'm just afraid to count on it ... or to jinx it. Two months isn't much stacked against all those years of my lousy marriage."

"It's enough to inspire a lot of women who are in trouble. Hell, you're impressing the hell out of me. I look at you and I don't see a victim anymore. I see a woman in control of her life, her happiness. You're our happy ending, Elisa. Enjoy it."

They both laughed softly. "I want to talk something else over with you," Julianne continued as the waitress delivered their salads, treading softly and gauging Elisa's reaction. "I want to tell you a story about Clint Andrews—about me and Clint Andrews and my producer, Tina. I'm just asking for you to hear me out. That's all for now. Will you just hear me out?"

"I'm listening."

Julianne went on to recount the scheme to catch Clint Andrews's obscene behavior on a video recording, the battles with her boss, the hold on the show.

"And you're fired?" was Elisa's first comment.

"You know something? I'm not even sure. 'Dead' is what he said. I guess that means fired, but since I'm all for holding on to my job, I think I'll wait for a more literal dismissal. It's been weeks now. He's probably just waiting for the right excuse to lower the ax, something that won't stir up HR issues, but I'm not going to let that ax over my head ruin my life. If it comes, it comes. Life happens. In the meantime, I plan on using my position at the station to pave the way for some meetings with battered women's organizations. They can work with us to lobby Congress. Two of the specials I worked on before I came to Chicago were so well received they made it to special screenings on Capitol Hill. My station may be too timid to back me on this issue, but it's not the only place in town. If they keep the doc in limbo, where it is now, I still have the video discs and flash drives safe and sound. The show can move forward somewhere else...and so can I. That's priority one for me right now, keeping the materials safe. Want to take a guess at priority two?"

"I couldn't begin to guess."

"Priority two is somehow convincing you to come forward and be the final nail in Clint Andrews's coffin. Tina's video is great. But she's a television producer, a plant. She had to initiate things; you know how that can be twisted around to imply entrapment. And nothing actually transpired between them. It won't have the same impact as the story of a woman who actually had to tolerate and survive him."

Elisa thought for a minute and then looked up at Julianne. "A lot of women—not to mention men—would say I didn't have to tolerate it. They'd say I chose to. That I made the choice willingly. They can't understand that it's a matter of control. I didn't have control, and I didn't have the strength to fight for it. It's so complicated."

"They're the ones we have to work so hard to reach." They sat in silence. Julianne knew it was unfair to push too hard, but with Elisa wavering, now was the time for closing arguments. "Look, I know it isn't easy. I can't say I know what it's been like for you. I haven't lived through it and I won't insult you by pretending I know what you're feeling. But I do know that so many gaps in the system just lie there, getting bigger and bigger, hurting more and more people, all because something fell through the cracks somewhere and no one took the time to do anything about it even when it was noticed. I'm sure no one set out to give heartless bastards license to abuse women seeking refuge from abuse at home. No one would intentionally do that. But it's happening. We found a gap. You, and who knows how many others, fell between those cracks. Not all of them will gain back the strength to take control. Maybe they need us to take it back for them."

"I don't know if I can live through all those bad memories again."

"Two months ago, you didn't know you'd be holding down a job, moving into a new home with your daughter." She paused and lightened up the conversation. "And looking like you belong on the cover of *Vogue*. If you did that, you can certainly do this." She decided to make one last plea. "Maybe you can make the pain count for something."

"I'm just not sure that I'm ready. I feel like Humpty Dumpty and I've just started putting all the pieces back together again. I can't give you an answer so fast, not today. But I'll think about it. Honestly, I'll try. And one more thing, Julianne. I know you're a producer and you're looking for a new angle on a story—and this is a good one. But this is just one little part of a great big problem. All the Clint Andrews in the world don't add to all the husbands and boyfriends who treat their women like garbage. You and I know it's a matter of control. But it's control of our own lives, our own happiness. Don't let this one little part mask all the other parts. It's up to us to empower ourselves. That's the point I'll make. It may not be the point you're interested in."

"I'm interested."

Julianne waited outside Ted's office until he instructed his secretary to let her in and closed the door behind her. She was cool and reserved when she approached his desk. He continued writing, never looking up to acknowledge her presence. She plunked her bag down on the chair beside her and sat waiting for him to break the silence.

"I thought you'd have moved on by now," he finally said, still not looking up.

"Well, I thought it would be a good idea to get clarification on what exactly my being 'dead' means."

He sat back in his chair and looked at her, actually smiling. Then he got up and began circling around to the front of the desk. "You are one ballsy woman, Julianne. And I mean ballsy. First I try to be friendly with you—offer you a little extra attention—and you blow out of here like a bat out of hell. Then I tell you not to rock the boat with this pet crusade of yours and you have to play the hero and involve the station anyway. And now you top it off by having the guts to come in here and ask me if you're actually on deck to be fired. Unbelievable." He crossed his arms and wedged himself between her chair and the front of his desk, leaving her little room to move.

She spoke with little emotion and carefully delivered words. "You gave me the go-ahead to do my job and produce a show about domestic violence. And that's what I did. If our research uncovered an important aspect of the problem, I was certain that you, as a community leader and head of this station, would want to do the right thing, even if it meant eating a little crow and admitting that we made an error in judgment when we backed that shelter without vetting it properly. It was--*is*--certainly a mistake we could own up to in light of the corruption of power we uncovered. As for your idea of friendly, it seemed more than a little threatening at the time. I wasn't sure if you were propositioning me or were about to rape me."

He smiled smugly. "It started with the former and ended with the latter."

She pushed her chair back, freeing up her legs, and stood up, grabbing her bag and walking toward the door, which she had left opened.

"What, no goodbye?" he asked caustically.

"Oh, I'm not going anywhere, Ted. Of course, you might be." She swung her bag over her shoulder. "You should spend a little more time down with the news folks, Ted. You'd love the great little gadgets they use for their undercover work these days. Take this little camera." She held up her purse and aimed it at him as if she were focusing a camera. "You'd never even know it was on. Neither did Clint Andrews."

She turned and walked past the secretary stationed at her desk a few feet away, invigorated and simultaneously enraged. While she was pleased with her own ability to catch the rat in action, she was fed up with the system that continued to turn a blind eye to such behavior. By the time she arrived back at her office, Lianne was extending the telephone. "Pam's on the line."

Julianne was pleased with Pam's sense of timing. Now back on the job, Pam was on the opposite end of the long, stately corridor. Julianne had planned to stop by Pam's office on her way out for a coffee run. She needed to share the story of what had just transpired.

"Are you crazy, Julianne?" were Pam's first words. "What are you doing to yourself?" Her voice was cold with anger. Julianne handed the receiver back to Lianne. "I'd better take this in my office."

"I haven't been out of Ted's office for two minutes, Pam. I can't believe he called you already. And I certainly can't believe your reaction. Are you sure we're talking about the same thing?"

"We're talking about the same incident, but I don't think we're talking about the same thing at all. You're talking about some feat of female heroism, some act of martyrdom, some triumph. And I'm talking about a naïveté that I thought you were well beyond. You're not going to destroy his career. You're going to destroy your own. He's not Clint Andrews, some juicy story that's loaded with sex and sleaze and the makings of a promotable television show. You've got the power of the press and the power of viewers' appetite for titillating TV on your side when it comes to Andrews. You've got no one, not anyone, on your side when it comes to taking down your boss. Who's going to punish him, all the others who've been doing exactly what he was caught doing from the time they stepped into their first jobs? If a decision were reached to make an example of Ted Marshall ... to take a stand against that kind of behavior ... all of corporate America would take the fall. No one will back you and no one will believe you. There are smarter ways to play the game, Julianne. You should know that. Just about anything would have been smarter than that prank of yours."

"Do you believe me, Pam? I mean, I have it on camera in case you don't. I'm just wondering. Do you believe me?"

"I believed that you were politically savvy. I was wrong. I'm telling you now to drop this whole thing."

"What whole thing? Clint Andrews? Ted Marshall? What?"

"I'm telling you to drop it, Julianne."

"Officially? Are you telling me officially?" The phone went silent. "I don't get it, Pam. How can you condone this?"

"It's not a matter of what I condone. It's just the way it is. You have to know which battles are worth fighting and which are unbeatable As a woman in this business or any business, you have to identify the pitfalls, plan your strategies and stay ahead of the game in order to stay in the game. Otherwise, you won't make it."

Again the line fell silent. "Ted wants that video brought to his office now. Now, before you have time to make copies. There won't be any shining promotions in your future for a while but at least you'll still have your job."

"I won't still have my job, Pam. Get real. I'm not that naive. Only I won't have the video either ... or my integrity ... or my self esteem. And I don't think I'd like that. Tell me, how does it feel?"

Pam let that comment pass, not diverting her focus from the issue at hand. "You're being very shortsighted, Julianne—and pigheaded. Just send up the recorder. You've made your point."

"Tell Ted that I'm holding onto that video and I intend to hold on to my job as well. Just tell him to cool his jets; I'm not going public with it. I'm hanging on to it for safekeeping, to give him an incentive to back off. To tell you the truth, Pam, you've thrown me for a loop. I expected so much more from you. It's really too bad."

With that, she returned the receiver to its hook, grabbed her jacket off its hook and scanned her desk in search of any papers or office work in need of her attention that night. Suddenly, a wave of pure exhaustion swept over her and she slumped back down in her chair and swung around to stare out the window.

Several minutes must have passed as she sat gazing out into space until she was startled by a sharp, deep voice behind her. "So this is what you programming people do all day while we news hounds are out serving society." She turned to see Mick Hoffman looming in the doorway. "You look tired, Julianne. Tough day taking on the tyrants?" His smile and typical sarcasm could not have been better timed.

"What do you think, Mick? They deserve a good kick in the butt, don't you think?" She gathered her purse and papers. "Come on. Be my personal escort to the elevator."

"I just wanted you to know that I looked screened the rough cut of the show. You guys did one hell of a job—not quite up to news standards, you understand," he added, knowing he couldn't risk being accused of being complimentary to a programming person. "We'd like to go with the story as a three-parter the second week of sweeps, which means that if you want to take advantage of the on-air promotion and cap off the week with your documentary, it's going to need to be wrapped in the next three weeks. I know it means you guys are really going to have to get cranking on your final edit. Is three weeks realistic?"

"Easy, no. Realistic, yes. The rough cut was pretty strong. Three weeks will work. I'll have Lianne run the plan by Pam for approval in the morning. It can't sit in limbo forever. No one's got a problem with the scheduling of the show, just what's in it. And I think I've just taken care of that."

At the elevator she pulled him aside from the others waiting. "Thank you for working with me on this. I know you didn't have to and it'll probably mean you're on the outs with the boys' club for a while. I just want you to know how much I appreciate it. And that goes for Tina and the rest of the crew too."

"No big deal. It's a good story." He started to walk away and then turned to her. "You're a damn good producer, Julianne. If they don't see that upstairs, do yourself a favor and go where you can do your best stuff. I'll vouch for you any day." He walked back to the newsroom as she waited for the elevator and a much-desired escape from the office.

She thought it was an apparition at first. Helene Rossi sat calmly on the taut leather sofa in the lobby of her apartment building, a magazine casually draped over her lap. She looked up at Julianne with a benign stare that gave way to a vague smile. "Guess who's coming for dinner," she said in acknowledgment of Julianne's confounded expression.

"Come on upstairs," Julianne finally offered, thinking how the last, absolutely last, thing she needed today was to even think about Jake Rossi, Helene Rossi, and the soon-to-be baby Rossi. She suddenly remembered that Lianne said Jake had been hunting her down all afternoon. He'd left three messages. Obvously his urgency was tied to his wife's unprecedented visit.

"I'll make coffee ... unless you'd rather have wine. Oh, you're not supposed to have wine, right? Or coffee. I have chamomile tea."

"Chamomile it is. Let's splurge."

Entering the kitchen, Helene leaned against the counter as Julianne reached for the tea kettle. "Jake and I talked about everything today...the baby, our marriage and finally about the two of you. I didn't know it was you, Julianne, but I sure as hell knew it was somebody. A women can tell when her husband's fallen out of love with her. She may choose to ignore it, but she's aware of it just the same. To tell you the truth, I almost laughed when he told me it was you. It was too obvious and you just don't seem his type. All those nights and weekends you were working together, I was almost relieved. You'd keep him so busy he wouldn't have time for other women. I had dismissed you as competition years ago. By the looks of things, maybe neither of us is his type."

"On the other hand, maybe all women are," Julianne countered, regretting the comment before she had even completed it. "No, that's not fair to Jake."

Helene found that remark laughable. "Fair? You're still worried about what's fair to Jake? My, my, you are special. He did find a real gem in you. I give him that."

"I'll tell you what," Julianne interrupted. "Before this conversation deteriorates into something far less civil than the way it began, why don't you just tell me what you came here to say. Give me hell, Helene. I'd do the exact same thing if I were in your shoes."

"Well, that gives further credence to what I thought. You and I are nothing alike. You'd give the other woman hell, but that's not what I intend to do at all. I intend to give you my husband."

She pushed away the still unfilled cup and walked to the windows, gazing out into the night as she continued to speak. "I fall into that socially hip category of liberated women--enlightened, informed, oozing with self-esteem. I've watched enough daytime talk shows to know that a baby isn't a cure for a bad marriage. It's a temporary distraction, a crutch. You of all people must know that ... and Jake. The two of you worked months on that divorce special last year and I remember you covered the hell out of the 'staying together for the sake of the kids never works' angle."

She turned to make eye contact with Julianne. "You know what? I'm actually a proponent of that theory, from firsthand experience. I lived through my parents' lousy marriage and their decision to tough it out was sure no great favor to me. When they weren't screaming at each other, they were cold as ice and one was always bitching about the other to me. Not only was I the go-between, but I was also shouldering the guilt of knowing they were sacrifcing their happiness for me. I don't intend to bring up my baby that same way. The way I see it, Jake's not in love with me. He is in love with you--and no baby in the world is going to change that. So you might as well have each other. I don't want him anymore." She began collecting her things to leave.

"You may as well know that my generosity ends there. I intend to get one hefty alimony settlement and break the bank for child support. That's what I think is *fair*. I want this baby and we'll be fine. I had a job long before I got married and I haven't forgotten how to take care of myself. Jake and I will smooth things out enough so he can be the good daddy. And I will get on with my life. Lots of men have fallen in love with me before and I have every belief that someone will again. I deserve the real thing."

She lifted the empty cup and extended it to make a fake toast. "So here's to the future." She directed herself to the front door, turning to leave her host with one final thought. "Just remember that old saying, Julianne: Any man *you* can take can be taken *from* you." With that, she was gone.

Julianne poured the boiling water over the tea bag in her cup, lowered herself to the floor, and leaned back against the cupboard, cradling her cup between both hands. What a day this had been. And the evening was far from over.

It was nearly nine o'clock when a brilliant streak of lightning cut through the sky and brought Julianne back to reality. She had been lounging on the thick pile carpet in front of the tall living room windows to stare out into the vastness of the evening for well over an hour. She had achieved her goal of losing herself in that vastness for a few brief while, escaping from her anguish, anxiety, and insecurities. Life had grown entirely too complicated in an all too short of a period of time and now, allowing herself to wallow in her distress for the first time in ages, she felt incredibly overwhelmed.

The best thing she could do, she supposed, was to treat herself to an evening of doing absolutely nothing. Nothing. No work, no exercise, no phone calls, not even a book. She would sit by the window staring aimlessly into space until that too lost its luster and then she'd retreat to the bedroom and the safety of her pillows and quilt. The lightning bolt seemed to signal the conclusion of part one of that plan, as rain soon streamed across the glass, blurring the view. Julianne set about turning off the lights and checking the door lock, prepared to call it a day.

She had just stepped into the bedroom to undress when the doorman's buzzer startled her. A woman was there to see her, he announced. The guest said she was not expected but that she was sure Ms. Sloan would want her to come up. Her name was Elisa Tate. Tate. That was the first time Julianne had heard mention of Elisa's last name, and she was taken aback that she hadn't thought to ask what it was before. At the shelter, the women were not expected to divulge that information to the producer, and later she had never even thought to inquire. Hearing that Elisa was confident in sharing her last name gave Julianne hope that the Elisa who appeared strong on the *outside* at the coffee shop was actually strong on the *inside* too.

Any doubt was put to rest when her unexpected guest entered the apartment. Julianne welcomed an Elisa with an aura entirely different woman from the one displayed only months ago in that modest room on the second floor of Horizons.

"I know it's really not right for me to pop in so late like this. But it was important that I talk to you tonight while I'm feeling so full of energy. I was thinking about that promotion I got. Work is going really great and my divorce is moving ahead and Kelly seems to be handling everything okay. Tonight I even got myself to go out on a date. Do you believe it? I met a man, David, who owns a store across the street from the building where I'll be working. He took me out to dinner tonight. And now I'm rambling on like I'm sixteen. Anyway, he made me remember what it's like to be in the company of a truly nice man. I'd forgotten. I'd been thinking all day about what you said to me ... about how we could take down Clint Andrews. Tonight I realized that it would be wrong for me to do nothing just because it would be easier. I'd regret it later in life. The last thing I need is more regrets. I think ..."

"You'll go public?" Julianne finally interrupted, as Elisa's energy had filled her home, leaving little room for response.

"I'll testify if he's brought up on charges. As for your show, if it's not too late, I'm willing to discuss what happened, but I'd like my face to be in shadow like it was before."

"When can we shoot, Elisa?" Julianne asked, wanting to get a concrete commitment before Elisa had time to change her mind.

"Tomorrow would be the best. You and I are probably both thinking that I'm likely to get cold feet if I have too much time to think about this. So tomorrow. After six. That's when I get off work and Kelly has a slumber party at a friend's house. You name the place. I'll be there."

"We can set up right in my office at the television station. It will be private and we can get right to screening and editing the material when you're done. Six thirty all right? And bundle up those feet so there's no risk of letting them get cold. You're doing the right thing, Elisa."

"Yeah. I know." She turned to leave but then stopped and looked at Julianne. "You know, it really has nothing to do with this man I had dinner with. I mean, he's very nice, or at least seems to be. It was just our first dinner after all. It was more that he made me see that I'd become bitter and ugly when it came to men. I don't want to grow old being a bitter, frigid man hater. And I certainly don't want to influence Kelly that way. I guess I just wanted you to know that it's my decision to do this. In case things don't go so well, I don't want you to think you pushed me into it."

She smiled at Julianne with the warmth and intimacy of a friend. She had turned out to be quite a remarkable women, inspiring at a time when Julianne needed a little inspiration. Elisa stood before her as a woman who had taken control of her life. That control gave her a confidence and strength that was electrifying.

When she left, Julianne gave up all thoughts of going to bed and instead grabbed her laptop and began writing new script material to set up the story of the woman who would tell of her experience with Clint Andrews and a side of the system that would finally be brought to light. As promised to Elisa, she would also write her happy ending.

The next morning Julianne strode straight to the editing room instead of making the routine stop at her office. She knew that Jake would be in there before daylight, as the programming staff had to start early in order to clear out of the edit rooms in time for news personnel to take over by midafternoon. Sure enough, he was cutting together an interview when Julianne popped her head in. "Can you stay late today? We need to shoot a last-minute interview in my office. Elisa's going to talk."

"I don't believe it. You actually persuaded her." He sat back and smiled at Julianne in genuine appreciation. "Of course, I shouldn't be surprised. I know how persuasive you can be."

That look on his face took her back to a time when she enjoyed simply sitting back and staring at the sharp lines of his face and the soft strands of hair that insisted on blocking his eyes. She was still crazy about Jake. She wanted to tell him so and forget all the problems for a while. Instead she said, "It was her idea, actually. Wait until you see her, Jake. She's so different. She's putting her life together. And she's ready to speak out."

"Maybe *we* should try it. Speaking. Maybe the putting our lives together part will follow. We need to talk at least. After the interview."

Julianne never looked away from his eyes. "After the interview. Six thirty in my office. Can you arrange for the crew?"

"I'll take care of it. I'll take care of everything, Julianne." She knew he was talking about a lot more than a camera and microphone. She left him to finish his work and followed the long hallway down to her office. After all the commotion with Ted and the confrontation with Pam, she expected to feel as if she were entering a war zone.

Yet she didn't feel that way at all. When she flicked on the lights and stared at a desktop nearly lost under a massive pile of papers, a calming wave of normalcy swept over her.

She sat down and began sorting through the stacks of messages, memo's and edit notes. Soon Lianne arrived and took a seat across from her, filling her in on the day's schedule. Sam and Louise had been handling the *Chicago Sizzle* chores like champions and Julianne realized how much she had neglected them during the course of producing the documentary. Now Tina was back on *CS* part time, focusing on the doc in the early hours of the day with Jake, then changing hats to cover the celebrity scene at night. It was quite the three-ring circus.

For the first time in ages, Julianne sat back to appreciate how well run a circus it actually was and how lucky she was to have such talented people around her. She even allowed herself to realize that it wasn't all luck. Part of it was her. She knew what she was doing. She was good at her job. And at sizing up people. And at handling tough situations. Okay, she'd gotten temporarily thrown off course. She'd made mistakes with men. Lots of mistakes. She had been flustered and scared and was shooting from the hip. She'd lost control. But it was at this very moment, with mounds of paperwork work before her, three lines lit up on the phone, and a room full of frenetic staffers outside the door that her instincts, talents and true character pushed their way to the surface. In an instant, she once again felt good about who she was. Things would be okay. She'd make them that way. That's all there was to it.

Neither Pam nor Ted made their presence felt all day. It was if an unspoken cooling off period was in progress. She knew that Pam was at work on the opposite end of the hall, but both women let that fact go by unacknowledged. At six o'clock, when everyone except Tina and Julianne had left for the day, Jake arrived with the crew and began setting up in Julianne's office. Jake had managed to assemble the same crew that had make the trek to Horizons. Half an hour later, Elisa sat in her comforting pool of darkness and calmly told the story of a man who had robbed her of her last shred of dignity, faith, and sense of self.

The interview lasted just over twenty minutes. At times, Elisa's voice cracked with emotion and trembled with anger as she recounted the particulars of her experience. She fought to explain that it wasn't the act itself that was so repugnant. It was the fact that this man preyed upon her when she was in no condition to protect herself. This point was critical to her. She had to make it clear. That was the ugliest part of what had happened—what was bound to happen again and again unless those with the power to do so came up with a better way to manage their system.

By the time she left, there were no more tears. They were replaced by feelings of strength, cleansing and empowerment. A contagious pride swept through the room. For now, the interview was enough. When the story went public, there would be many more interviews ahead and they would be less kind and less polite. Elisa would surely be the target of attack as Clint Andrews and his supporters fought to clear his name and deflect the larger issue. Julianne prepared Elisa for this as she escorted her to the elevator. Elisa said she was ready, and Julianne had only to look into her eyes to know that it was so.

CHAPTER 15

ight months later ...

Elisa nudged Kelly and offered a teasing smile as her daughter agonized over whether to order French toast or pancakes. It seemed a monumental decision to her. Elisa realized how wonderful it was to have this as Kelly's greatest dilemma of the day. It was a wonder to see her daughter growing into a young woman. Now that things had transitioned into a smooth, calm routine at home, Kelly seemed to be a happy preteen, enjoying her life with renewed vigor.

She would even talk to Elisa about her dad now. Elisa assumed that it had been painful for Kelly to discuss one parent with the other, as if her refusal to acknowledge the divorce proceedings would alter their inevitability. But now that her mom was dating and her dad appearned to be resigned to the dismantling of the marriage, Kelly semed freed from the pressures of nurturing her parents or manipulating them toward a reunion. Instead, she turned her attention to more pressing matters, such as taking shopping trips to the mall, sharpening her flirtation skills in preparation for her first school dance and deciding whether or not to order a side order of bacon to accompany her pancakes, her ultimate breakfast selection.

As Julianne was about to enter the diner, she stopped to observe Elisa and Kelly through the glass wall of windows. A wave of pleasure washed over her. How at ease and exuberant they looked. By the time she reached the table, her face glowed with an ear-to-ear smile. "It's a good thing you're on time. Kelly was about to start gnawing on the menu," Elisa said.

"It's the producer in me. Always on time. Time is money and all that jazz." They placed their orders and sat chatting and sharing updates on their lives. The idea to congregate for breakfast was Elisa's, as was the choice of location--the same diner located down the street from Horizons, the one where she and Julianne had shared their dark conversations only months ago. For so long, this had been Elisa's place of refuge, the spot where she could find solitude and linger over a cup of coffee, for hours if necessary, until she could muster up enough fortitude to go out into the world again and get on with her life.

Well, she had forged ahead with her life, and this little breakfast reunion was her way of celebrating that fact and tearing away the veils of sadness that marred this place, this street, this neighborhood in her mind. After this, the three of them would walk past Horizons, and after dropping Kelly off at school, Elisa would accompany Julianne to work for an advance screening of the kickoff news story that would hit the airwaves the following week, leading up to the premiere of the special.

Elisa had already heard radio ads for the story over the weekend. Jolts of anxiety had shaken her as she listened to the announcer's gripping voice invite viewers to take a chilling journey into the world of women suffering violence at the hands of the men they loved and torn apart by a system put in place to help them. It had been her world. And it was indeed chilling. And it wasn't over yet. There was so much healing to be done. She knew it and she was getting help.

Adrienne agreed to let her take Thursday afternoons off in exchange for working half a day on Saturday so that she and Kelly could begin family counseling. Peter still refused to address the subject of therapy for himself, but she could tell from Kelly's good spirits after returning from her weekly visits with her dad that he was not mistreating his daughter, so she decided that his refusal to seek help was his own problem. She was learning to let go of situations that were out of her control and concentrate on making the best out of situations that were.

A biting wind pushed at their backs as Julianne, Elisa, and Kelly strolled past Horizons, propelling them past the fortress filled with memories so fresh that each felt a mild pang of apprehension. The small front yard was now enclosed by a short wooden fence painted pale yellow. The grass was littered with children's toys strewn about haphazardly. A teenage boy kept a protective eye on two little girls tossing a Frisbee. Not one smile could be found among any of these children's young faces. They were playing but having none of the free-spirited fun deserved by kids their age. Even Kelly seemed to understand that something was so wrong and so sad about this sight. She swung her arm around her mom's waist, drawing her close as they paused for a moment and silently gazed at the sprawling house.

Elisa peered at the second floor, finding the window that marked the room where she had hidden from her husband and her own emotions for so many weeks. "I was right when I said I thought Marsha was going to go back to her husband. She went, and she's already back here. This is one of the few houses in town that will take a woman back, but I think even Horizons will make this a last time for Marsha. Too many other women are looking for that first hand to grab on to, you know."

Elisa's voice was little more than a whisper, almost as if she were talking to herself. "I heard she talked to her husband, Kent, a couple of weeks ago and he insisted she was out of her mind—that he never touched the kids. Never, he insisted. So she convinced herself that she had misread the whole nasty situation and went back home last week. She wasn't ready to bring the girls back from Milwaukee—and it's a good thing too. He had a few beers and decided to punish her for 'those filthy lies'. That's what he called them, she said. Filthy lies. He cut her lip with the beer can and fractured her nose with his fist... and here she is back at Horizons.

"I was so sure I'd be able to get through to Marsha, but I'm not so certain anymore. She needs to want to get real help. She got so mad at me the last time I tried to tell her to stash away some money and get the hell away from him. I'm giving her a week to calm down before I start pestering her again to see my lawyer. I already set an appointment for her but she doesn't know it. I've got to try to get her there, but there's only so much anyone can do."

"It's probably hard for her to see how far you've come in such a comparatively short time. It must make her even more aware of how caught in the mire she is."

"She needs to want to get out. And she's not at that point yet. I think she'll get there, though. I just hope it's before he breaks more than her nose."

Then Julianne caught a pair of eyes piercing through the living room curtains. Clint's eyes. She couldn't make out the rest of his face. But those angry gray eyes cut into her and sent a chill through her body. She didn't think Elisa saw him standing there as she gradually inched away with her daughter and Julianne was glad that those two had been spared that moment. Hopefully Clint's face was no longer haunting Elisa's dreams as it was Julianne's. Soon that face would be full screen on the ten o'clock news.

Yes, the story was alleged. Yes, he would refute each and every allegation. Yes, he was innocent until proven guilty and, yes, the board of Horizons would most likely keep him in place for a short while in an effort to avert appearing guilty of wrongdoing. However, ultimately the heat from the exposure and public reaction would grow too intense and he'd be out. Julianne and Mick would be sure to keep the heat turned up high. Yes, his word would stand up at least as well as his accuser's. At least initially. At least until the follow-up story featuring two other women Elisa had coaxed into coming forward. Yes, a lengthy, and sure to be ugly, battle would ensue in the press and perhaps the court, enough to substantiate the need for policies to be in place to govern institutions like Horizons, whether publicly or privately funded. And yes, Clint Andrews was surely finished being entrenched in this or any other shelter. Clint Andrews. One man in a system plagued by problems. But it was a start.

Julianne hailed a taxi she spotted rounding the corner and the three of them piled in. Kelly was off to school, and Julianne and Elisa were off to a private screening.

A pleasant calm filled the newsroom, not unusual for ten o'clock on a Thursday morning. Pandemonium never really set in until midafternoon, when decisions had to me made for the five and six o'clock shows. While this temporary state of tranquility was a blessing to the news staffers, Julianne wished that things could have been just a touch more chaotic in order to give Elisa a taste of the flash and dash of the operation when it was running at full speed. For first-time visitors to a TV station, the activity of a newsroom made for a memorable experience.

Instead, she and Elisa were greeted by an exaggerated gesture to enter the news department's domain by its reigning king, Mick Hoffman, who sat slumped back in one of the assistant's rollaway chairs with a lazy smile on his face and his size thirteen loafers gracing the desk of his assignment editor. To look at him at this moment, one would never assume the intensity that would characterize his actions only a few hours ahead.

Mick rose to greet them, having given a greenlight to the visit and private screening the day before. Even though he had viewed the documentary footage and his news pieces that had been created from that footage over and over again, he had never actually seen the face of the woman who had become the centerpiece of the story. Jake had done an expert job of shooting her in silhouette and protecting her identity. Mick knew that when she spoke, he wouldn't recognize her voice, either. It had been filtered to alter the tone even before being edited onto the master recordings.

Julianne witnessed a rush of pleasure consume Mick as he finally met the woman he had heard about for so long and with such passion from Jake, Tina and herself. When he extended his arm for a handshake as he approached Elisa, she sensed that he was startled by the delicacy of the hand that was nearly enveloped by his sturdy palm.

Could it be that the nature of the woman's slight frame shook him into imagining what it must have been like to be dominated by men whose brutal force, or sheer size, most assuredly overpowered her?

"You may want to screen the news pieces before the doc. The first one airs Monday. We're saving it for the ten o'clock show. And following the story each night, we're going to run a promo for the documentary in the commercial break. By Saturday, when the doc airs, we'll have built a great audience," Mick said, visibly exhilarated by his work, while Julianne shared Elisa's mounting anxiety as they approached the edit room where Elisa would screen this most public display of her most private torment.

Julianne eased Elisa into a chair directly facing the monitor, where she could focus solely on the material and avoid the eyes of those seated beside her in the darkness. After hitting the PLAY button on the edit console, Julianne stepped to the back of the room, where she stood beside Mick as all three watched the series of five three-minute stories. Piece by piece, they unraveled the anguish and desperation of women lost in a system that seemed oblivious to their needs. And they saw the dramatic takedown of one man who represented the perils of that system. The news editor had done a brilliant job of running with the ball, giving the miniseries the hard-edged investigative flavor that made it an excellent complement to the documentary's more humanistic approach.

With each night's story, the findings became clearer, the man's credentials were scrutinized more closely, the specifics of his portrait were painted with greater repugnant detail. This wasn't the show Elisa had expected to see. That would come later, in Elisa's documentary. This was a ratings getter. An attention grabber. A peek at violence and sex and immorality in a way that Julianne could see shocked Elisa as she realized it was constructed around her own experiences. She was shaken. She was not upset. She was vindicated.

Each piece had rolled with only a few seconds in between, avoiding the need for polite chatter. When the final piece faded to black, the story dealing with the evil that lurked within the walls of a place called a safe house and the unexpected price of refuge, Mick walked to the console and shut down the machines. Julianne faded up the lights slowly, transitioning them back into the here and now at a pace that would not be jarring. She pulled a chair up next to Elisa, who was staring at the blank monitor, and clasped her hand with genuine affection. Mick remained at the back of the room, listening unobtrusively.

After a few moments, Elisa looked straight into Julianne's eyes. Her face was somber. Her voice was strong. "It's good." She paused before adding, "Thank you." She turned and looked at Mick. Slowly a slight smile brightened her face. She was gaining some distance from the intensity of the material. "Thank you," she repeated, this time to him.

Tina walked in with a cardboard tray holding four white paper cups of coffee and a couple of doughnuts that had obviously seen better days. "I heard our guest of honor was here, so only the best," she teased, offering the sorry excuse for refreshments. "I thought that if it's okay with Elisa, I'd screen the doc for her myself. I was on the five a.m. editing shift today and I have an hour to kill for lunch at ten thirty in the morning, when lunch is the last thing on my mind. What do you say?"

"I'd be honored," Elisa was quick to respond. "It'll give me a chance to fill you in on my new main squeeze. I think the last time Julianne and I sat down and talked about him, we had just gone out on our first date." The two women exited the room, and as Julianne was about to follow, Mick reached for her arm and gently held her back, letting the door close to ensure privacy.

"I didn't want to get into this while our guest was here," Mick started, staring calmly into Julianne's tired eyes, "but you and I have a busy day ahead of us. I got a call from our lawyers about an hour ago and they're insisting on going over the story again with a fine-tooth comb before they'll let it air on Monday. It seems our local attorneys were so gun-shy at the prospect of targeting Andrews and shining the light on those rich contributors to the shelter, including our own parent company, and I was reminded, that they're running chicken. Not to mention the fact that we don't exactly make the state's system sound so terrific and we're bound to ruffle some political feathers. Anyway, the upshot is that they've called in the corporate bulldog lawyers. Saving their asses, I guess, in case the shit hits the fan. There's a conference call scheduled in two hours with the New York legal department, our Chicago business affairs team, Ted, Pam ... Hey, I wouldn't be surprised if the janitor shows up. It's to address the news stories, but you know they're going to want to cover the same issues for the doc in a couple of days, so you may as well get it out of the way at the same time, if you want to sit in."

"As if I have a choice." She smiled. "Just let me go get my notes together."

She started to walk out the door, but a nagging feeling made her turn back to him. "You're worried, aren't you? You think they're going to give us a hard time ... pull the stories."

"All I know is lawyers are chickenshit. It's easier to play it safe, just in case. My reporters go nuts every time we have to deal with those guys. And with all the finger pointing in these stories, they have a lot to be chickenshit about. It's not going to be easy. But I'll tell you this--I've never changed one frame of one story because I was challenged by one of our New York suits. And I don't intend to start now."

With Mick gazing down into the cracks in the worn tile floor, Julianne slid out of the room and down the twisted hallway to her office and mountain of production notes.

"Really gripping," the first raspy voice offered as his overall commentary via the large speakerphone that sat prominently placed in the center of the pretentious walnut conference table that took up most of the sterile room.

"Very compelling," his anonymous associate chimed in. Gripping. Compelling. The two most obvious descriptives called into service by lamebrain New York executives in their high-priced suits who couldn't tell quality television or upstanding journalism from primetime reality show trash. Mick and Julianne shot each other knowing smiles but quickly returned to their appropriately serious expressions, as they knew they were under careful scrutiny by their bosses. Everyone was eager for the slightest excuse to tone down the material. Everyone was poised for input and edit notes. Everyone except Julianne and Mick.

For two and a half hours, the legal eagles pecked away at the research. Each fact could be substantiated. Each allegation was clearly identified as such. The pieces were clean. Julianne and Mick sat back, satisfied with their presentation and comfortable with the clarity of the situation. They had covered all their bases. And their butts. That's why the next comment to erupt from the speakerphone caught them so off guard.

"Just one critical change," the gravelly one said with matter-of-fact delivery. "The administrator ... that Andrews person ... You'll have to edit out his name and do one of those blurry video effects to cover up his face. We can't just expose him that way. His lawsuit will be filed before the sun comes up." The room fell silent. So did the phone line before he added, "The good news is that it won't take a thing away from the story. It will be just as powerful without the unnecessary risk. It's probably not even that big of a technical hassle."

Ted Marshall and Pam Avery stared down at the table, fearful of making eye contact with the producers, as did Don McBain, who had been asked to sit in on the meeting as head of the sales department to make sure the content of the pieces would present no problems on the revenue side of things. *It's too bad the janitor isn't here to lend his opinion,* Julianne thought. *It most certainly would be preferable.*

"There won't be technical hassle at all, because there won't be any editing. The stories are solid. They're accurate and will hold up in court one hundred percent if it comes to that," Mick said firmly.

"It won't come to that—it can't come to that—because we simply don't have the money or the manpower to start dicking around in court over a nonissue. The story is just as good without showing the man's face or divulging his name. In fact, it'll even add drama and mystery to the piece."

"Thanks for the creative input, but I don't want drama and mystery in the news. I want to deliver the story. It's thoroughly vetted and completely credible. If we're afraid of taking risks, we shouldn't be in the news business."

"Or producing documentaries." This time it was Julianne chiming in. "You can't sell your shows short. You'll lose the respect of your viewers, not to mention your colleagues, your peers, and your staff. This material must not be altered. It was selected and produced to have impact. It's clean work."

"It's got to be fixed." The tone of the gravelly speaker conveyed that the discussion was being brought to a close. His word was law. "And don't take it so seriously, you two. No one is criticizing your work." Oh, great. To add insult to injury, they were being patronized. "Good luck with the ratings." He hung up, and one by one, Ted, Pam, and Doug marched out of the room without saying a word. Julianne and Mick stared at each other, speechless.

Julianne finally broke the silence. "Come on. I have a call to make and you may as well share that experience with me. I'll be glad to have had a witness if and when I need it.

They walked down to her office. Lianne bombarded her with a pile of at least twenty phone messages and Sam and Louise pounced on her to settle a dispute over the length of Louise's story on the casting call for the new male lead of daytime's hottest soap. Sam was determined to trim it to three minutes to allow more time for his piece on the charity chili cook-off featuring everybody who was anybody in town donning an apron for a good cause. Louise was determined to milk her story for at least one additional minute. All those hunks were sure to translate to better ratings, and this was a sweeps period. "Cooking competition, two minutes. Soap star, two and a half," Julianne barked, practically slamming the door in their faces. She hadn't lost her perspective on what hunks meant to her viewers. "And hold those damn messages for later. No, wait. You call them all back, Lianne, and say I'll get back to them tomorrow."

She pushed away two piles of mail on her desk and sat down with Mick at the guest chair across from her. "I refuse to alter the story."

She said it with the calm matter-of-fact tone that revealed a naïveté typically foreign to her.

"It really doesn't matter if you refuse, does it?"

"What do mean, 'it doesn't matter'? I'm saying that the show remains intact and, if you stick with your convictions, so will the news pieces."

Mick leaned forward and rested his elbows on the desk, staring warmly into her eyes. She sensed he was thinking that she'd become too close to it all, too emotionally entangled. The businesswoman had evolved into the warrior. She realized he saw that, as did she. Now her goal was to make him see that the trick was to turn the warrior into the businesswoman.

"It doesn't matter that you agree or disagree to alter the story," he began, "because the liability issue has already been exposed. It's gone to a higher corporate level. It doesn't make an iota of difference what Julianne Sloan and Mick Hoffman will or will not consent to do. The powers that be will simply pull the plug on the whole damn thing. Your documentary and my news pieces—the whole sequence of stories, certainly the Andrews piece—will sit dead on the shelf in the video morgue. Your power has its limits, Julianne. Your authority is superseded by every person who sat patronizing you in that room just now. And so is mine. Willingness to go to war is all well and good but it doesn't mean much without weapons. Right now the arsenal consists of the corporate guns, the lawyers, who just made their chickenshit stance pretty damn clear."

She rested her head in her hands and closed her eyes. Was he right? Was she was thinking with her heart and not her head? No, she knew herself better that that. Managing her personal life so ineptly was one thing. But when it came to her job, she was a pro and a survivor. She never rolled over and played dead. That was for those more cowardly and lazy. Too many people had invested too much of themselves to buckle now. It wasn't a question of whether or not she could take on the hotshots and win. It was a matter of how.

She raised her head from her palms just enough to reveal her eyes, and when she did, they had quite a glint to them, a spark of excitement and mischief. The entire energy of the room shifted into high gear from those two sparkling eyes. Mick sat up straight in his chair, apparently ready to spring into action alongside his compatriot.

"Umm. They just think they have all the weapons. There's one they don't have in their war chest at all. One they don't even know exists."

She dialed New York. When the switchboard picked up, she asked for the executive vice president of legal and business affairs, Edmund Horvath. Julianne didn't have Mr. Horvath's direct extension. She had never spoken to the man. She had never dreamed of calling him. Now his line was ringing.

A half-eaten turkey and swiss on rye sat on the plain white porcelain plate that seemed lost on the massive antique cherrywood desk. Edmund Horvath seldom went out for business lunches. If people wanted to meet with him, they could do it from across the desk. Wasting two hours over rich meals seemed a frivolous way to conduct business, and at this stage of his career, Edmund Horvath could do things his way. He'd served as CEO of the media conglomerate for the past five years, after being ensconced as head of the legal division for twenty years prior, managing FCC compliance, triumphing over retransmission disputes, and navigating the nuances of new media liability. His impeccable executive profile was marred by a single extremely high profile case--the network's sole female sportscaster who sued, claiming gender discrimination, and won.

In the wake of the bitter defeat, much of his energy the past year had been devoted to restoration of his Goliath-like aura. Buoyed by the keen legal minds and shrewd financial brains on his staff, he was direct, intense, ever so cool. There was much chatter within the ranks when Edmund Horvath broke into a sweat, just once, at a press conference following the sportscaster verdict. Irritated at the exposed chink in his armor, he was determined to never damage his image again. To that end, a cunning media spin doctor had been retained and had successfully squashed bad press for the compnay and its CEO since the sportscaster debacle.

Every month Horvath would hop aboard the company's private yet to pay an unannounced daylong visit to one of the major market stations under his command. He realized it was vital that his presence be felt among the executive rank and file and that his management style permeate the local legal teams. His visit to the Chicago station was coming up next month, nearly a year after he had last stepped foot inside the establishment or wasted his time discussing business with Ted Marshall. Marshall was the least favorite of his general managers and would not have been promoted to GM at all had it not been for the fact that Horvath was out of commission for three months treating his prostate cancer a couple of years ago and his second-in-command had seized the opportunity to fill the Chicago spot with his old drinking buddy, Ted Marshall. It was a bad choice, an act of arrogant nepotism which Horvath saw as the final nail in the coffin of his former right-hand man, who was coerced into taking an early retirement shortly after Horvath's return from sick leave.

Other than the fact that he couldn't stand Marshall on a personal level—he was slick and disingenuous, your typical corporate kiss ass—he did seem to run a smooth ship, driving revenue growth, averting legal headaches, and winning accolades for community outreach, so Horvath never went to the trouble of firing the man. Plus, his station's award achievements consistently generated positive press. If there was one thing that Edmund Horvath craved more than ever, it was positive press, a proven contributor to an increase in stock value.

He was hunched over a pile of correspondence regarding an FCC complaint filed when some idiot rock star uttered a string of profanities during a live concert special--dumbass engineer was asleep at the wheel and missed the seven-second delay that was the safety net for live telecasts. His secretary interrupted his train of thought to announce that Julianne Sloan from the Chicago station was holding on line one. It was an odd occurrence. Other than the general managers, no one from the local stations made direct contact with Edmund Horvath. He slipped off his glasses, rubbed his tired eyes and picked up the receiver.

After her awkward introduction, he managed to place Julianne Sloan as the producer of that magazine series that had won its time period for the last two years and garnered impressive reviews in the press. Yes, Julianne Sloan was rumored to be one sharp little cookie—not too hard on the eyes either, he had heard from his minions.

He sensed her discomfort at making this call, shoring up a good deal of effort to portray herself as confident and cool. Hoping she would get right to the point, he listened attentively as she explained that she was calling because, along with some talented and passionate colleagues, she had put a lot on the line these past several months to produce a kick-ass special that had, thanks to the good sense of the station's news director, also turned out to be a kick-ass series of news special reports.

He was on the brink of losing interest when she proceeded to divulge her motive for placing the unprecedented call. It seemed, she explained, that Horvath's risk-averse army of attorneys had opted to take the easy route by sacrificing the meat and potatoes of the content rather than exercise due diligence and vet any potential legal liability. In other words, they were too lazy to do their jobs so that she and her colleagues could do theirs. Since a lot of people had, she continued, lived and breathed and even risked their own well-being to deliver a show with some guts to it and some potential to nudge the lawmakers into positive action, she had chosen to push the issue rather than play dead. Hence the phone call.

Horvath notice a change in her tone as she plowed forward with a plan to, as she put it, negotiate. Julianne Sloan, he marveled, was so brazen as to suggest a negotiation with him, Edmund Horvath! She had an offer, she told him, that she hoped would inspire him to call off the dogs.

Seven hundred eighty miles west of Edmund Horvath's corporate suite, nestled in an office a quarter the size of his, Julianne Sloan mustered up every fiber of fierceness within her to put her offer on the table. She had a video recording in her possession, she revealed, that was safely tucked away and would absolutely bury the Chicago station manager on a sexual harassment charge. The impact would be felt company-wide. Competitive press outlets would see to that. If he wanted specifics of the recording, she defiantly remarked, he could go right ahead and discuss the matter with Ted Marshall. However, if he'd rather wait a day and screen it for himself, she'd be more than delighted to air express it to him—no e-mail link that could be hacked. The point, she emphasized, was that seeing how the gender discrimination verdict rocked the company, she was inclined to believe Edmund Horvath would prefer to avoid an encore lawsuit. Plus, surely he must realize how cases like this trigger deep investigations that embolden additional victims to come forward. Who knows how many secretaries and producers and such might be inspired to speak out. There would be ongoing stories for the press and discontent among the stockholders to whom the CEO was accountable.

Maybe, Julianne propsed, the wise thing to do would be to squelch the hullabaloo and placate her, a downtrodden victim of sexual harassment, by supporting the special that she'd worked so hard to produce. Maybe the lawyers could be convinced that any marginal risk associated with airing the special was nothing compared to imminent risks in tampering with it. Would Mr. Horvath be comfortable suggesting to his staff that they get off their butts and earn their keep by putting some effort into clearing legal roadblocks instead of putting the kibosh on anything that hinted at a problem? Maybe he'd be so inclined just as she'd be inclined to keep that video buried in its nice safe place and forget their telephone conversation ever took place. Just an idea. Would he mind thinking it over? she inquired. But not for long. The first news story was set to air on Monday night. With all due respect, she concluded, it truly seemed like a matter worthy of consideration.

On the other end of the line, Edmund Horvath was immobilized by this gutsy broad who apparently had him by the balls. She was quite the negotiator, affording him time to think about what the hell was going on. She had grit. Horvath liked grit. She had evidence; he didn't doubt that one iota. She held the threat of a nasty court case. More bad press.

He never interrupted her. He never questioned her. When she had finished, he simply responded with an emotionless, "You'll hear from me, Miss Sloan. Soon. Thank you for your dialing me into the situation."

He hung up the phone with his left hand and with his right pressed the intercom to his secretary. "Get Ted Marshall on the phone."

Mick asked Julianne if he could buy her a beer after the six o'clock show, even offering to spring for a cheeseburger for the lady who had more moxie than he'd seen since he left New York. They enjoyed an evening of sparring over the state of their industry, politics and the Chicago school system. In the back of her mind, though, she was probing the more personal side of Mick Hoffman--so smart, strong features that were quite pleasing and a heart that apparently remained intact despite years in the news business. Why still single? she pondered. She was quietly examining their relationship while he was busy examining the gargantuan mound of toppings on his burger. It was a professional relationship, pure and simple. There had never been sparks, flirtations or pizzazz. He was a great guy ... but not for her. She thought of Jake. And she thought of how life was brimming with riddles and tricks and setups for disaster. Two guys, two choices for the mind, but only one for the heart. She was just crazy about Jake.

After a couple of hours, Mick realized he needed to return to the newsroom for the ten o'clock show. He had an army of soldiers under him whose job, in part, was to make sure that the news director didn't feel he had to work eighteen-hour days. But this was a ratings period and he wanted to be there. He apologized as he paid the tab.

After walking the two short blocks back to the station, Julianne decided to quickly stop by her office to check for messages in the event that Horvath had tried to contact her. No such luck.

She flicked off the lights, yanked the office door closed and swung around while balancing a stack of files, collection of magazines and her trench coat, which proceeded to topple to the floor. She was staring down, calculating the least problematic way to retrieve all of it without losing her grip on what remained in her hands, when a knight in shining armor caught sight of her dilemma and came to her rescue. Jake Rossi.

"What's this? Practicing your juggling act? I heard the circus is in town and holding auditions. Actually, I think we're covering them." He decided to toy with her a bit and made no immediate gesture to collect the items or relieve her of the hodgepodge of belongings to which she clung.

She shot him a coy smile, enjoying this long-missed moment of play. "You're just going to stand there and watch me suffer, aren't you macho man?"

"I'll watch you any way I can," he answered with an underlying message in his voice more than in his words. "Of course I'm tempted to help you out here, but I'm not exactly sure what's in it for me, and you're the one who's always telling me I have to think of myself first."

"With everyone *but* me, and don't you forget it," she teased back. "Besides, I wouldn't be so sure there's nothing in it for you. It just so happens there's a bottle of Chardonnay, half a wedge of brie, and a semi-stale loaf of sourdough bread in my kitchen … all with your name on it." She wasn't sure she was doing the right thing. Far from it. It was ridiculous to believe that things would work themselves out with such simplicity. On the other hand, what was the virtue of simplicity? Maybe what was of greatest value was something one had to fight for. The lines of right and wrong had become so blurred the past weeks that the only thing Julianne knew for sure was that the rules of right and wrong often changed just as people often changed. Punishing herself—or Jake—for not being perfect and for falling short of a useless set of expectations would serve no purpose. Maybe she'd be miserable with him. Who knew? She just knew that right now she'd be miserable without him.

He looked genuinely surprised at this invitation. Though obviously enjoying the verbal banter, it was apparent to her that he did not wish to be perceived as a pushover. "I don't know. Chardonnay. There's no telling what will come over me with a bottle of Chardonnay in me. I might lose control."

"I'm counting on it. Anyway, it's just a half bottle for you. You believe in sharing, don't you?"

"Yeah. And in talking. Let's make a beeline for the bread." He swooped down to grab her coat, placed it over her shoulders, reached to take the load from her arms. She gladly handed it over and tucked her hand through his arm as they left the building and headed home.

Once inside, they were like two teenagers seeing each other for the first time after a summer separation. They chatted incessantly about their day, what they ate for lunch, who was on *Kimmel* the night before. They chatted about everything except anything that mattered. That would come later. There would be plenty of time. For now, they just needed to get back on track with one another, hear each other's laughs, see each other's eyes, feel each other's hands as they roamed their bodies with a warmth, depth, and deliberate leisure they had not experienced since their first night together. They slept well that night, nestled against one another. Semi-stale bread had never tasted so good.

At two minutes past nine on Monday morning, her office phone rang. Lianne wasn't in yet, but Julianne had already indulged in two cups of coffee and one and a half bagels. She was really hungry this morning. She picked up the receiver to hear Ted Marshall's cold, hostile voice deliver a set of carefully plotted instructions.

"Organize your notes, files, transcripts, research, anything relevant to the special and lay it out in the executive conference room. Patrick Garland and Jeffrey Jackson are flying in from New York to personally evaluate the materials and assess our legal liability for the doc and news segments. The mountain's coming to Mohammed. There's no time for them to assess the situation from across the country. We're right up against our own air date. I can't say I'm thrilled about having all these corporate honchos breathing down my neck, but I don't expect that my comfort level is of any interest to you." She offered no response and knew that he didn't really expect one. "Just for the record, I've come clean to Horvath on the whole ridiculous episode with you and that piece of shit video recording, so you don't have that to hold over me anymore. You've played that card, Julianne, and I don't ever want to hear mention of it again."

She laughed to herself. He was still fooling himself into thinking he was in command of the situation, superior to her. What an ass. "Everything will be assembled in the conference room and prepared for inspection," she said. "But I'm sure you'll agree that it would be better to use the *Chicago Sizzle* production conference room, where we can lock the doors and monitor who goes in and out." She decided to let him think she was deferring to him on this. If his male ego needed to be fed, no big deal at this point.

"Fine. They caught the first flight out of JFK this morning, so they'll be here shortly. Be on standby." He hung up.

Things were going to work out. She just knew it. She reached for the phone and dialed Edmund Horvath's number for the second, and what she realized would be the last, time of her career.

"Tell Mr. Horvath I appreciate the immediate attention he's given to this matter," she told his secretary, realizing that disturbing him again would characterize her as a nuisance. "And tell him he won't regret it. Our research is impeccable. We can win any claim brought against us. I think that's already understood by the parties in question. I don't think they'll be stupid enough or wasteful enough of their time and money to challenge us. We'll earn viewers, awards and some respect with this special, and we won't lose any legal battles either."

He may have only come through for her because of his disdain for bad press, because it was the prudent thing to do given his options, because it was his job to protect the company image and stock price above all else, or simply because the good old boys had to stick together. But he did come through. And for that she was grateful.

It was a typical Saturday morning in so many ways, yet not in others. The alarm clock shook her awake at seven so she'd make it to her eight o'clock aerobics class. Only this time when she rolled over to turn it off, Jake latched onto her arm as soon as she'd silenced the damn thing. He rested her arm beneath his as he snuggled deeper under the covers for more sleep. She pressed her body against his back and brushed a kiss across his shoulder. She wasn't going anywhere.

This time it was the ringing of the phone that jarred them awake. When she turned to check the time, she was startled to see that it was already a quarter past ten. Funny how easy it was to sleep late when she felt at peace.

Pam's voice greeted her when she finally lifted the receiver. Pam used to call on Saturdays to see if Julianne wanted to go to brunch or take a spin class with her. But since the latter part of her pregnancy, those little outings had pretty much ceased. And since the ordeal at the office, Julianne doubted they would ever resume. This was why she was so surprised to receive a weekend call.

"I didn't think I'd be waking you," Pam started out. "I know you like to get an early start on Saturdays."

"No problem. I've been up for a while. I was just wondering if I should make a second pot of coffee," she lied.

"I knew that you'd be sitting on pins and needles, so I'm calling to let you know that I just heard from the head of the legal department. They've cleared the news pieces and the doc for air. Well done."

They've cleared the news pieces and the doc for air. It was the one sentence she'd been yearning to hear all night. She'd won. She'd identified the game and then figured out how to play it—and she'd won.

A surge of emotion ran through her, mostly from acknowledgment that the body of work would make it to air, that the mission was not aborted. They had come so close to losing a battle that so many victims were counting on them to win. Julianne needed this reminder that she had the power of her own resources to attain success, to pull herself from a quagmire and seize control of a situation, personal or professional. She had been so beaten down from disappointment and from confronting her own shortcomings. She had relinquished her self-esteem because she was exhausted. This triumph, a triumph achieved from her own determination and intelligence, was what she needed more than anything else in order to rally her spirit. She had proven her ability to herself … not her father or boyfriend or lover or boss. To herself.

She nearly forgot that Pam was rambling on with more details. "The guys from New York worked through the night so they could get home for the weekend. They said they're comfortable with your research and corroborating material. They called Mick and me, as head of programming, before heading back East. Congratulations. You pulled off quite a coup. And I don't think I've told you yet, but the show looks terrific. Better make a space on your mantel for another Emmy."

Julianne sat in silence, taking it all in. She couldn't have gotten a word in edgewise if she had tried. Pam was on a roll.

"And there's something else. I just wanted you to hear it from me. I know that by the end of the day, the rumor mills will be running at full speed. I had dinner with Ted Marshall last night and I resigned. Three years as program manager is enough. I'm ready for a change. I'm not too pleased with some of the decisions I've made over the past few months, Julianne. I'm sure you know some of the ones I'm thinking of. But I am pleased with this decision. I've taken a position with the mayor's office of special events, starting next month. It's part time, and that will give me more time to be at home and to work on my writing. I don't think I've told you that I've started writing again; I have a stringer's assignment in place with the Sunday magazine section of the *Tribune*. It's time to get back to doing the things I love.

It will take me a few weeks to wrap up my projects at the station, so I'll still be around for a while. I just wanted to tell you myself."

"I'll bet Ted was flabbergasted. He probably thought he had you in his camp for good ... or as long as he'd want you there."

"I don't know or even care what he was thinking. That's the third thing I wanted to tell you. Brace yourself. I scheduled my meeting with Ted yesterday at five thirty so I could hand him my resignation at the end of the day. Anyway, just when I was wrapping up with him, he got a long-distance call from Edmund Horvath and asked me to wait in the outer office while he took it. It couldn't have lasted more than three minutes. When I went back inside, Ted told me that he'd just been fired. Asked to resign—that's how it will read in the papers. He was in shock, really. He thought Ed Horvath was one of his staunch supporters. He even thought that mess with the hidden video last week—Ted told me about that, by the way—was water under the bridge. He thought Horvath bought into his 'I did what any red-blooded man would do, only I got caught' theory. Even I knew from seeing them at two company dinners together that Ted made Horvath's skin crawl. Anyway, Ted's out."

"Too bad you didn't hold off on the resignation," Julianne said. "You could have thrown your hat in the ring for the general manager's job."

"Get real, Julianne. It's at least five years until another woman will be welcomed into that exclusive circle. There are two women GMs in the mix now, two out of thirty-two. That will suffice for at least ten years," she chuckled. "You, on the other hand, will be just hitting your stride in the decade ahead. Think about it."

"I'm thinking about all of this. My head is spinning, to tell you the truth. Can I take you out to lunch Monday to celebrate? I'd really like to, Pam." Julianne felt an unexpected rush of affection toward her former mentor. Before all the ugliness of the past few months, they had been productive allies as well as friends. She realized that the good shouldn't be forgotten because of the bad. Life wasn't black and white, roses and thorns.

"Monday. Lunch. You've got it. And I have the rest of the weekend to pick out someplace good and expensive, so get ready."

"I'll bring my gold card. Thanks for calling me yourself. You made my day, and it isn't even noon yet." She hung up the phone and turned to unload the information on Jake. He had been silently attempting to piece the story together by listening to her half of the conversation. "You won't believe it," she teased. "But first, coffee."

It was just before six on Monday evening, and Elisa couldn't find Kelly's red pumps anywhere. She'd bought them especially for this night. Kelly was joining Elisa and her boyfriend, the store owner from across the street, for dinner. It would be the first time the three of them were going out someplace special together—weekend jaunts to the park or pizza in the kitchen didn't really count—and Elisa wanted Kelly to look and feel special. Where were those shoes?

"Look what I found," Kelly teased as she waved the shoe box that had been buried deep in her closet, beneath the mess so typical for a girl her age. Kelly looked tremendously pleased with herself at her fine detective work and plopped herself in the middle of the bed to schmooze with her mom.

"Come clean! Where did you find those shoes? I've been looking for them for the past half hour," Elisa laughed, lovingly swatting her daughter's behind with a rolled up *Glamour* magazine.

"It only stands to reason that you would put a shoe box—any shoe box—in *your* own closet out of habit, dear clotheshorse mother of mine. Or shall I say shoe horse? You probably couldn't even help yourself. Your brain just went on autopilot."

"Very cute, darling daughter," she called over her shoulder as she rushed to blow-dry her hair. "Of course, now I don't know how I'm going to be ready for our date when he gets here. He's due at six thirty. You'd better make sure you're finished dressing so that you can entertain him if I'm not finished, okay?"

"Okay, but if he starts teaching me poker again, I don't know if you'll ever get us out of here."

Elisa would get him out of there all right. All three of them. And well before seven o'clock. That was the time the documentary was scheduled to premiere. For some reason, it was critical to Elisa that they not be at home glued to the tube when it aired. She needed to be out doing something good. Feeling good. It was symbolic to her. It would mean she had dealt with the past, was busy with the present, and was preparing for the future. She and her daughter would not be at home witnessing their past pain on the screen with the rest of Chicago. Kelly, perhaps, would never see it.

Elisa knew that it was important for Kelly to understand the program and her mom's participation in it, yet not be further traumatized by what had transpired during their time of transition at Horizons. Children were children; that was not to be forgotten. Therefore, earlier that week, she'd asked Julianne to send her some clips, nothing sexually explicit or horrific, so that she could view them with Kelly in the warm safety of their living room.

After dinner last Thursday night, they sat together on the living room floor watching the stories unfold, hearing the tales of abuse and frustration from the friends at Horizons and listening to Elisa describe how a man who was supposed to help her did anything but help. The meaning came through, but in a way that was manageable for her young daughter. Every few minutes, Elisa would stop the video so that she and Kelly could talk about what was being said. She encouraged Kelly to ask questions and express her anger and fears. She stopped the video before any portions of the interview dealing with Clint Andrews. She took her time and shared with Kelly what had happened—in vague, protective terms.

After each pause, she asked Kelly if she was sure she wanted to see more. Kelly nodded, so they watched together and let the tears roll down their cheeks together. When it was over, they hugged. And then they moved to the sofa where they sat silently for the next hour, with only the softness of the hallway light illuminating the room. Elisa stroked Kelly's hair. Kelly tucked her head under her mom's chin and wrapped an arm around her waist. There was nothing more to say at the time. They would talk later, once Kelly had time to process it all.

The talk came the following afternoon, when they took their six-block walk to the grocery store and stopped for a snack. A long, honest discussion ensued as they prepared to move past the impact of the television clips and proceed with a night on the town with a great new friend. In new red shoes. The healing wouldn't be finished in a day or a month or even a year. But they would heal.

Elisa's thoughts turned to her new love. The first time he reached out to her privately, tenderly touching her cheek, it was difficult for her to respond. In part, she was afraid to be vulnerable and in part, it was a result of having turned off her senses when it came to dealing with men. Emotions couldn't be turned on and off like a light switch. She'd invested so much energy in protecting herself by going numb that it was tough to let her guard down and allow herself to feel. Yet this wonderful man had come along just in time. Maybe he'd be around for only a short while. Maybe he'd just help her through this transition. Maybe he'd be with her forever. It was too soon to tell. But he had, thankfully, entered her life before she had turned into the frigid woman who seemed to loom in her future. She had the wherewithal to heal.

The phone sat ringing away on the kitchen counter while Jake, Julianne assumed, stood staring at it. Though Julianne had given him permission to answer her phone, she understood that he wasn't entirely comfortable doing so just yet. Without fail, that phone rang when she was in the shower. Usually the machine wound up taking a message. This time, since she was nearly dry, she dashed for the receiver. As she did, wrapped in her old terrycloth robe and shaking her hair loose from the confines of a shower cap, she caught Jake's admiring glance.

The caller was Mick Hoffman, and she assumed he was calling

to wish her luck with the special. It was early Saturday evening, and the special would be airing in less than an hour. Wrong. That wasn't his reason for calling.

"You'll never believe this, Julianne. Guess who called me about an hour ago? Forget it. You'll never guess. I'll bet you'd recognize his voice, though. None other than your personal good buddy, Edmund Horvath. You'd better sit down for this one. He offered me the general manager's job. Ted's job. Me. A news director. They have never promoted a news director to the GM spot at any station in the company. Hell, it's not done at any company I know. Well, he offered it to me. I didn't even know how to respond; it came so out of the blue. He's flying me to New York on Monday to talk about it." The phone went silent. "Are you still there?" he asked a few seconds later.

"I'm in total shock. A news director taking the GM spot? And you? You're so anti-corporate. I cannot believe it. I guess it's true; anything *can* happen. Management *is* capable of recognizing talent and great leadership. Just when I was beginning to doubt that it was possible."

"Oh, fine. Now you tell me that you think I'm talented. And it only took years for you to share that tidbit with me. I'm flattered. Truly," he teased in mock sarcasm.

She followed up in a tone that was at once serious and exhilarated. "Go for it, Mick. Kick some butt. Take the uphill ride on this career adventure of ours."

"I want you to take it with me. I want you to be my program manager. I'm nervous enough about this without having to worry about filling the most critical job at the station ... next to news, sales, finance, and my own spot, of course," he laughed.

"You think Horvath would ever put me in there? Come on. I'm just surprised he hasn't fired me yet. A promotion isn't even conceivable."

"I think you're wrong. You know how New Yorkers respect moxie. I think he likes guts and dedication and fearlessness. You've shown him that you've got them all. He just needs you on his side and I can assure him that you will be. If I take the job, I'm going to offer you the program manager's job, so get ready ... because I think I'm taking the job." The line fell silent again. "I'll call you from New York on Monday to fill you in, but get your head around it. Oh yeah, and break a leg with the documentary. May your ratings be as high as your aspirations."

She lowered the receiver and lowered herself on the chair, too stunned to think about the wet robe or dripping feet or much of anything. Jake sat on the floor propped up against the side of the sofa, once again waiting for details. This had been quite a day for phone calls.

Closing credits crawled onto the screen as the title graphic for the documentary *A Dangerous Proposition* dominated the picture. It was dramatic. It was intense. Just as intended. Julianne sat on the floor. The only light in the room was the bluish-gray glow of the television screen. The music swelled as a montage of women's action shots, faces blurred beyond distinction, filled the screen, accompanied by their comments as they looked toward to a brighter future. Yes, it ended with a spirit of hope. That had been a primary goal. Now, in her living room and not the edit room, here like any other person sitting at home watching TV, she knew she had done her job, planted the seed of hope.

She was equally successful in battling the legal department. The lawyers verified that she'd done her homework, provided solid evidence and could back up every fact. She'd placed the spotlight on one rotten apple by the name of Clint Andrews, and now the search would be on to seek out the other rotten apples before more lives were spoiled. It was a start.

The show had made her sad. And it had made her happy and angry and afraid and determined and jubilant. It had evoked all those emotions. Not because of her accomplishment in delivering a fine piece of work—nothing to do with her producer role at all. But as a viewer. Elisa, Clint Andrews, Marsha and all those others at Horizons had been part of a story that took Julianne and the vast Chicagoland audience on an emotional roller coaster ride. Maybe it would make a tiny difference in a gigantic world.

The program faded to black, and she clicked off the set and leaned back against Jake, pulling his arms tightly around her. This was life, she thought. One long, tumultuous, exciting roller coaster ride. And for her, the ride had only just begun.

60060258R00175

Made in the USA
San Bernardino, CA
08 December 2017